I Spy, I Saw her die

A gripping, page-turning crime murder mystery conspiracy crime thriller.

IAN C.P. IRVINE

Copyright © 2015 IAN C.P. IRVINE

All rights reserved. Without limiting the rights under copyright observed above, no part of this publication may be reproduced, stored in or introduced into a retrieval system, or transmitted in any form or by any means without the prior written consent of the copyright owner.

This is a work of fiction. Names, characters, businesses, places, events, technology and incidents are either the products of the author's imagination or used in a fictitious manner. Any resemblance to actual persons, living or dead, or actual events is purely coincidental.

ISBN-10:

1537298925

ISBN-13:

978-1537298924

Cover Design by Ray Luck

raymondoluck@hotmail.com

DEDICATION

Dedicated to Margarete Sauter, my wife and children.

And to my parents with thanks for all they have ever done for me.

Other Books by Ian C.P. Irvine

Haunted From Within

Haunted From Without

Time Ship

The Orlando File

The Messiah Conspiracy

London 2012 : What If?

The Sleeping Truth

Alexis Meets Wiziwam the Wizard

Chapter 1

London

One year from now

October 8th

12.30 p.m.

For most of us, death comes when we least expect it. For Eva Baczkowski it would be no different.

Eva liked England. The people, the weather, the jobs. And the men. Everything about England was better than where she came from. She would never go back to Poland. Her home was here now.

A new life, so full of hope. So full of promise.

Eva laughed aloud in the car. She hadn't been as happy as this for years.

It was only her third month in England, but just over thirty minutes ago she had been offered the job of her dreams: a saleswoman in Selfridges in the perfume department.

Every day she would be surrounded by beautiful people. Beautiful smells. And beautiful women.

Eva also liked women.

In Poland, people said she was strange. Different. Not a good Catholic. But here in England she was free.

Free to live, love and do anything she wanted.

With whoever she wanted.

The traffic lights in front turned to red and Eva slowed down, came to a halt and began to daydream.

She would soon be able to afford a good car. Not one full of holes with a steering wheel on the wrong side.

Her small car had driven her all the way from Krakow in Poland, with all her worldly possessions stuffed tightly inside, but Eva knew it wouldn't pass an English MOT. Nor could she afford to have all the things fixed that were wrong with it.

Perhaps she would meet a rich, young, handsome man in Selfridges who would whisk her off her feet. They would get married, maybe... and then she could afford a good, English car.

Eva looked up.

An aeroplane was flying overhead. She followed it as it flew directly above her car and then disappeared across the top of the tall building on her left.

The sky was blue today. Bright blue. There were no clouds.

At first the black object that seemed to separate from the building above her had no real form. It was just black. Initially small, but quickly growing larger.

As she stared at the object, time seemed to slow down, and her mind fought rapidly to make sense of the anomaly with which it was presented.

Different shapes and comparisons swept through her head, but none of them made sense.

Until, with a shock, one memory registered in her mind, and struck a chord.

She suddenly remembered an image from a television programme she'd seen a few weeks ago, from a documentary on the BBC recounting the terrorist attack on the World Trade Center in New York.

The image was of what the English documentary called 'the falling man'.

When she had seen it for the first time on the television it had fascinated her and now as she looked up, directly above her through the windscreen, her mind connected the two images together and told her they were similar.

In fact, they were the same.

Eva's eyes widened.

Adrenaline shot into her veins and she gripped the steering wheel in panic.

She didn't have time to scream.

The person accelerating to Earth above her, heading straight towards her, arms and legs flailing the surrounding air, hit her car at over fifty miles an hour.

A head and a torso punched through the roof and the windscreen, smashing into Eva with the force of a falling baby elephant.

The body of the falling person merged violently with Eva's, crushing her head and pulverising her rib cage and internal organs, which exploded and splattered like a squashed tomato all over the inside of the car.

The traffic light in front turned to green.

The sky was blue today. Bright blue. There were no clouds.

Outside the car, some pedestrians began to scream.

Chapter 2

London

Saturday

September 28th

9.30 a.m.

Ten Days Earlier

Ray Luck stirred, reached out with his fingers and caressed Emma's hair. Soft, golden, beautiful.
As was the rest of Emma.
He turned towards her, cuddled up closer and whispered in her ear.
Emma opened her eyes briefly, smiled, and then fell back into a deep sleep.

Sunlight streamed into the room, confirming the forecast from the night before: a late Indian summer was on its way. This weekend would herald the start of three well above average weeks, warm days of sunshine and balmy nights, each an average of five degrees hotter than normal for this time of year.
Global warming.
Yet another indictment of what mankind was doing to the world, but which was certain to be dismissed and diminished by everyone who thought more of the dollar than the planet.
Ray hated politics. But he loved life.
Life was great.
Especially with Emma.

Deciding to nip down to the deli to get freshly brewed coffee and some croissants for Emma, he slipped out of bed, showered quickly and let himself quietly out of his expensive two bedroom flat on the top floor of their shared building.
Walking down the road, he breathed in the fresh morning air and as he always did every single time he walked down the street, he admired the beautiful, elegant Georgian facades of the white, terraced houses in the square in which he lived, all of which faced onto communal private gardens in its centre.

The rent in this part of South Kensington was exorbitant but the first instant Ray had seen the flat, he knew that if he was going to live in London, this had to be the place.

As a cyber consultant for one of London's top security firms, Ray could afford it. He was lucky and he knew it. People were prepared to pay highly for the skills he had to offer and Ray was happy to take their money, for as long as they were prepared to pay it.

Thanks to the growing threat that cyber crime posed to almost every business in the world, people like Ray were in short supply. Unlike his friends who had been hit hard by the recession, Ray had not been out of work for a single day since he graduated from university.

It was the law of supply and demand.

For every cyber specialist like Ray, there were at least ten jobs.

Supply was short, demand was high.

It was only a short walk to the corner deli, run by an Italian who'd moved here twenty years ago and still had his thick accent, almost singing each word as he spoke. On a Saturday morning the deli was full of the same faces out walking the dog and collecting the papers. Ray smiled and nodded at a few of those he knew, and chatted to an old lady with silver hair and the biggest diamond ring he had ever seen.

The community was one of many things that made this area special, and although probably one of the poorest people in the square, Ray didn't feel out of place. People were friendly.

Collecting his coffees and the croissants he left the shop and stopped by the newsagent on the way back.

Scanning the headlines, he saw that the war on ISIS in Egypt had taken another turn for the worse: they had consolidated their position in Cairo, and now it looked certain that the only way to make any progress was to commit another task force on the scale of Desert Storm, when Britain and its allies had gone to war with Iraq.

Tucking a copy of the Times under his arm he started back towards his flat: he didn't want the warm croissants or coffee to go cold.

As he turned back into the square, he thought of Emma and last night.

She had been quite cold towards him. It worried him a little.

A few weeks ago they had started going through a bad patch, but then things had improved for a while, and Ray had been looking forward to this weekend.

For lots of reasons.

Tonight was going to be a big night.

After seven years of being together, Ray was planning to pop the question.

The question.

The one that he knew he had been avoiding for a while now, and which was probably the reason behind Emma's strange comments as of late.

Ray knew that something was bothering her. After he had cooked her dinner he had tried to talk about it with her last night, but she had avoided proper conversation.

A headache, that time of the month, and a hard week at work had all been reasons for her to go to bed early without any real discussion between them.

But tonight Ray would make everything right.

It was all planned.

Tonight was going to be special.

A woman with a cat on a lead was coming towards him on the pavement. Seeing it, Ray quickly covered his mouth with his free hand and crossed the road: the last thing he needed now was to breathe in a mouthful of cat scent and for his cat allergy to flare up.

Darting between two cars - a Porsche and a Land Rover - he skipped onto the pavement and carried on up the square on the other side of the street.

It was then that he saw the envelope lying on the ground a few feet in front of him.

A sixth sense told him to bend down and pick it up, so he did.

The envelope was sealed, and turning it over, he found no address on the front. It was quite heavy, about two centimetres thick. The envelope bent in his hand and whatever was inside felt like paper. Looking around him there was no one else who could have dropped it. Crossing the road back towards the entrance to his building, he stuffed the envelope inside the folded newspaper as he fished out his keys and opened the door to the stairwell.

Upstairs, when he let himself into his flat and walked in, Emma was sitting in his dressing gown on the sofa, eating a piece of toast.

She looked up, her expression rather serious.

"Where have you been?" she asked. "I woke up and you were gone..."

"Your favourite coffee, and some fresh croissants," Ray replied, holding them up. "I wanted to treat you."

He walked towards her, putting the coffee on a side table and bending forward to kiss her.

Her eyes searched his, and for a moment Ray thought she was going to say something, but then she closed her eyes and returned the kiss gently.

Ray hesitated, then volunteered to go and get some plates, whilst handing over the bag of croissants and the papers.

"What's this?" Emma called after him as he left the room.

"What?"

"The envelope in the papers?"

"Envelope?" Ray enquired, thinking for a second. "Oh, that. I just found it on the street outside. There's no address on it... Why don't you open it up and see what's inside?"

He returned to the room, two plates in his hands.

Emma was looking up at him, her head shaking in disbelief and a quizzical look in her eyes.

"You found this outside?" she asked, waving the contents of the envelope at him with her right hand.

It was a wad of crisp, new £50 notes.

Ray stared at the money.

"How much is there...?" he asked.

Emma shook her head again.

"I don't know... thousands... tens of thousands... There's got to be. They're all £50 notes... There's a fortune here!"

Ray hurried across and sat beside her, reaching out and gently taking them from her hand.

"Bloody hell..." he whistled.

"Ray... you just found these? Outside?"

"Yes. Just now. On the other side of the road, near the railings."

Ray started to count the money, putting them into piles, each containing a thousand pounds.

"Fourteen... fifteen..." he said aloud, finishing at "Twenty thousand pounds, exactly."

"Twenty thousand pounds?" Emma parroted back.

"Exactly." Ray reiterated.

"Bloody hell," she replied.

"I just said that..." he said, looking back up at her, their faces expressionless.

For a moment they stared at each other, then Emma looked back at the money, and Ray laughed. Nervously.

"So, who does it belong to?" she asked.

"I've no idea... it was just lying on the ground, in the envelope."

Ray reached across to take the envelope that Emma was still holding firmly in her left hand. She let go of it and Ray looked inside. He lifted the envelope to his nose, and sniffed it.

"Nothing. It's empty."

"So... What are you going to do with the money?" she asked, her eyes searching his questioningly.

"What do you think I should do with it?" Ray replied.

"You can't keep it. It's twenty thousand pounds. You have to hand it in."

"To whom? The police?"

"Of course... you've got to take it to the police station."

"Are you joking?" Ray asked. "You want me to take this in and just give it to the police?"

"Of course! That's the right thing to do!" Emma said, standing up.

Ray reached across the table and picked up his coffee, taking a few large sips.

"It's going cold," he said, pointing at Emma's.

"Forget the coffee, Ray. Tell me what you're going to do with the money!"

"I don't know. Keep it, I suppose."

"Brilliant. This is just typical of you. Just *typical*." She said, turning her back and walking towards the bedroom door, before stopping and coming back.

"What do you mean, 'typical'? " Ray asked, standing up from the sofa.

"I mean, you never do the right thing. Never. The right thing to do is to hand it over to the police, but no, *oh no*, Ray Luck isn't going to do that, *is he*?"

Ray stared at Emma, sensing from the tone of her voice and the way the conversation was so suddenly changing focus, that this was not just about the money.

"What do you mean?" Ray said, dropping the money on the sofa. "Of course I'll do the right thing. I always try to do the right thing!"

"You mean, like watching other women take their clothes off on that stupid program you use to spy on people in their own homes through their TV or computer cameras?"

"I don't do that anymore. I promised you I'd stopped that. You watched me delete the program. I erased it. You saw me write over it so that I could never use it again! Why are you bringing that up? It's got nothing to do with this!"

"But you used to watch it, didn't you? You even wrote the program so you could get your rocks off whenever I wasn't around."

"Emma, I promised you. I deleted the program. Anyway, you watch Big Brother. It's just the same. I just like to watch people living their real lives..."

"No, it's not the same, Ray, and you know it."

She stopped and took a deep breath.

"So are you going to take the money to the police or not?"

"No. Taking the money to the police is probably, actually, completely the wrong thing to do!"

"The wrong thing? How on earth can being honest, doing the *right* thing, suddenly be the *wrong* thing?" Emma asked, storming back over to the sofa and sitting down.

Ray sat down beside her, picked up her coffee and handed it to her.

She pushed his hand aside.

"I don't *want* the bloody coffee. I want you to tell me what the hell you mean!"

"I mean, look at it... it's twenty thousand pounds in new fifty pound notes. In a brown, unmarked envelope. No name. No identification. Nothing. If you or I had that much money and were carrying it around outside, there's no way I'd just stuff it all in an envelope, without a business card, or an address. I'd have it in a wallet, or better still, a briefcase padlocked to my wrist. The fact it's just stuffed in an envelope and sealed like that means it's got to be dodgy. It's most likely stolen, or drug money or something..."

"*Stolen? Drug money? How did you work that one out?* Someone could have just got the money out of a bank, or was given it as a present. Maybe for the deposit on a flat, or something?"

"Possibly. Maybe... but the more I think about it, the more it feels like it's drug money. And the last thing I'm going to do is take a pile of drug money down to the police. I'm telling you, the worst thing you can do is to get your name and address associated with anything to do with drugs. I'm not getting involved with anything like that again."

"People can't think like that... If, and it's a big 'if' Ray, a *HUGE* if, if this *is* drug money, then it's down to people like you and me to do the right thing. Handing it over to the police *is* the right thing to do."

"Emma, it's drug money. I promise you. I can almost taste it, and after what happened to my brother, you know I won't have anything to do with anything that has any connection to drugs. I repeat, I'm not getting involved again. And I'm not taking it to the police, and I'm not talking to anyone else about it." Ray paused, the memory of his young brother's death caused by an accidental drug overdose in the school playground choking him up. He swallowed hard. "I'll give it to charity," Ray announced, resolutely. "I'll give it *all* to charity. But I'm not taking it to the police."

"Take it the police first, and if no one claims it, then give it to charity..."

"Emma, if no one claims it, they'll just keep it and we'll never see it again."

"They won't, Ray. They'll hand it back..."

"You honestly think so? I love just how naive you are Emma. I love it."

"You just called me naive? I'm *naive*?"

Ray stared back at her. Her face was beginning to turn red.

"No..."

"*Naive*? I can tell you this much, Ray Luck... This might be your 'lucky' day, finding twenty thousand pounds. But you just lost me. I'm not so naive any longer to think that this relationship is going to last. We're just too different."

Tears were beginning to stream down her face.

Ray jumped up and went towards her, wanting to wrap her in his arms and pull her close.

She stepped backwards.

"*We're just too different, Ray*. I can see that now. In fact, I've been seeing it for quite a while."

"Please, Emma, calm down... Can we just sit down and talk about this?" he said, waving gently at the sofa.

"No, I'm sorry, Ray. It's over."

"*Over*? Why? I just said, I'm going to give the money to charity. All of it. I promise. Any charity you want. You wait and see, I'll do it today. This morning. I'll do the right thing, okay?"

"The right thing? It's been seven years Ray. You're selfish. You only ever think about yourself. And as for the 'right thing' to do, you wouldn't know what that was if it hit you right between the eyes!"

Five minutes later Emma was gone, pulling the front door closed behind her.

Ray stared after her, tears welling up inside.

What was that all about?

What had just happened?

Should he run after her and beg her to come back?

The woman he loved, the woman he had planned to propose to that very evening, had just walked out of the door.

What should he do now?

Her last words rang in his ears, "*...and as for the right thing to do,.... you wouldn't know what that was if it hit you right between the eyes!*"

"Shit!" he shouted aloud.

Emma was right.

The truth was, Ray didn't know what to do next.

Chapter 3

London

September 28th

8.00 p.m.

Ray Luck was getting drunk. Slowly, but surely.

He had spent the day wandering along the banks of the Thames, sitting on different benches beside the water and staring at the river as it flowed past.

The water was calming. It helped him to concentrate. To plan. To think of what he should do next.

With each period of time spent sitting on a different bench, he was able to think back upon his relationship with Emma, figure out a reason why she must be so upset with him, and then compose a text message on his iPhone, apologising to her for whatever it was that he must have done.

By the time he had walked from Waterloo train station to Tower Bridge along the South Bank, he had sent twenty text messages, and left ten voice messages.

As he crossed over the river to the Tower of London, a single solitary beep signified the arrival of a text message.

From Emma.

"Ray, Please stop. It's over. Believe me. No matter how many times you text me, I won't change my mind. Even now, you don't know that the right thing to do is to just leave me alone! I did love you Ray. I did. But not anymore. I'm sorry. Emma."

Not having eaten all day, the first beer had an immediate effect.

By the time the second was finished, he was feeling quite tipsy.

There would have been a third too, and a fourth and a fifth, except for the fact that Ray had not brought enough money with him.

Sadly, he had left the twenty thousand pounds at home.

After Emma had gone, he had sat alone in the flat for an hour, staring at the money.

He knew that it wasn't the cause of their break-up, that the reasons were already there before he had found the envelope, but he couldn't help but wish that he had never set eyes upon it.

For a moment he had considered burning it all.

But then he remembered that he had promised... *sort of*... that he would give it all to charity.

Before he had left, he had hidden the money and collected the diamond ring from his hiding place underneath the loose floorboard in the bathroom.

He had stared at the ring, sitting crossed legged on the bathroom floor, imagining in his mind how it could have been... how the evening *should* have played out.

Ray was not a stoic, but he hardly ever cried. So when he felt the tears beginning to flow, he fought back, picking himself up, having a shower and then leaving the flat.

He didn't know where he was going. Or what he was doing.

He just knew that he had to walk. To think. To escape the confines of the house.

He had no set plan.

But just in case, he had taken the ring with him.

They had met when he was nineteen years old. In a club in Oxford.

She was a beautiful second year student at Christ Church College, reading History, and he was a fresher from Hertford studying Computer Science: tall, slim, athletic, apparently very good looking.

Within a week they were dating, and ever since they had been together.

Seven, fantastic, years.

Bloody wonderful years.

Standing in the middle of the pedestrian bridge halfway across the Thames between St Paul's Cathedral and the Tate Modern, he looked down into the river and watched it flow past underneath.

A thought crossed his mind.

Throw the diamond ring into the water.

As he pulled it out of his pocket, he looked at it, imagining once again the moment he was to have slipped it onto her finger.

The receipt in the box declared that the ring had cost him one-and-a-half thousand pounds. When he had seen it in the shop, he had instantly known that this was the ring for her. He knew she would love it. When he walked into the shop to buy it, he would have taken it, even if it had cost ten times as much.

It was beautiful: a single, one carat stone set in a platinum ring.

Preparing to toss it over the edge into the water below, he pulled his hand back, mentally primed and just about to throw it,... when he felt the phone vibrate against his leg.

A message had arrived.

The best present any parent can give a son, is a sister.

Claire was younger than Ray, smarter and the 'best Luck' he had ever known.

"Did she say yes?" she had enquired in her text message.

She was the only person he had told about tonight, about what was meant to have happened.

Now, returning the ring into the box, and putting it back into his pocket, he called Claire and told her the painful truth.

"Are you okay? Shall I come down and see you?" Claire had asked.

"No. I'll be okay. I think I just want to be by myself."

"Don't call her again, Ray." She had warned. "I know you love her, but you have to let her come back to you. Either she will, or she won't, but if you contact her anymore, you'll just push her further away."

"You're probably right."

"I know I am. I'm a woman."

She paused.

"What are you going to do now?"

"I'm going home."

"Call me if you need to talk, okay?"

"I promise."

Thirty minutes later, Ray walked up the steps to the front of the grand building he lived in, took out his key and opened the main door.

He was so wrapped up in his own thoughts, that he didn't see the three men in black suits on the other side of the road, walking up and down the street, searching the pavement.

He also didn't notice when one of them looked across and watched him enter his building.

The flat felt empty. As soon as he walked in the door, he could smell Emma's perfume. Hanging up his coat and taking off his shoes at the door - a habit he had learned while living in Japan with Emma one summer - he walked through to the bedroom and sat on the bed.

The bedclothes were still rumpled from the night before. Lying down, closing his eyes and sniffing the pillow, Ray tried to imagine Emma being there again.

It wasn't easy.

She had always breathed life into any room she had entered. But now she wasn't there, the effect was the same, but in reverse.

That essence of life had gone.

For the first time in years, Ray felt alone.

Taking his clothes off, he walked through to the bathroom and stepped into the shower.

Sitting on the floor, he wrapped his arms around his knees and pulled them into his chest, and let the warm water rain down upon him.

He began to cry.

The tears flowed and he sobbed heavily. Wave after wave of hurt, confusion, longing and pain boiled up from within, overflowed and were washed away. After five minutes they dried up and stopped.

He sat there for another ten minutes until the water began to run cold.

By the time he stood up, reached for the towel and started to dry himself, a calmness had descended upon him, and he was feeling slightly better.

It was then that he noticed that Emma had left quite a few of her personal possessions in the flat: perfume and toiletries in the bathroom, jewellery, a hair-dryer, clothes and shoes in their bedroom. A nice coat in the cupboard, a pile of her favourite CDs and DVDs in the lounge, and her Kindle on the bedside table.

Seeing these, Ray knew that there was a possibility of him seeing Emma again. She would have to come back to collect them... or he could take them over to her.

For a second, hope flickered, but was quickly extinguished when he realised that equally, she could come round and get everything when he was at work or out: the most likely scenario.

Ray walked to the fridge and pulled out a four-pack of cold beer.

Ray had a plan to make the pain go away.

He was going to vanish into his virtual world. Get drunk. And have some fun.

The second bedroom in his flat was the place where Ray went to disappear. During the day it doubled up as an office, from where he often worked from home and performed his duties for his company. For the past four years, he had been working as a Cyber Analyst and a Penetration tester, alternating between the two roles on a three-monthly basis. For twelve weeks he would be paid to try to find a way to hack into the computer networks of paying clients, trying to discover vulnerabilities or backdoors into their security architectures and software. When he did find them, as he always did - it was just a matter of how quickly he could do it and how many he would find - he would explore the company's networks, see how deep he could go and investigate what damage he could potentially do. Once he had identified all the ways he could break into a network, steal corporate data, and disable their systems, he would write up a comprehensive report and then present it to the client. He always loved the look of surprise and horror on a client's face as he showed them just what he could have accomplished, had his intentions been malicious.

Sometimes he felt slightly guilty when employees within the client who were responsible for their IT security were subsequently fired. It didn't happen often, but either way, after his report was delivered, quite often his company was immediately given a contract to manage the security services on behalf of the client. He felt bad for those who had to go home and tell their wives that they no longer had a job, but in general he knew that he was performing an essential role: if he had not done his thing and broken into their network, purely with a positive intention to help, it could alternatively so easily be a Russian, Chinese or Eastern European hacker who was out to steal the company's Intellectual Property Rights, to disable their systems, or steal their money. And if that happened, the company could go broke, and end up having to get rid of many more staff. The truth was he was saving people's jobs, not threatening them.

After three months aggressively hacking into the networks of clients, he would then switch to working within the Security Operation Centre at his company, Castle Security Defence, or 'CSD' as the brand logo simplified it. Once back in the SOC, he would spend the next twelve-week shift analysing the data traffic that they monitored on the networks of companies who paid them to protect their businesses. He would look for strange events or patterns in the data that told his experienced mind that the company was being hacked, or had already been hacked. He would find out what the hackers were doing, and how they were doing it. And then he would blow the whistle, stop it all happening, make recommendations on how to prevent it in the future, and give guidance to other colleagues in CSD as to what damage had been done and how it should be fixed. Although the information they provided to their clients was often enough to help identify who the hackers were, they left the rest up to the client. Sometimes the client called in the police, and arrests were made, but often there was nothing that could be done anyway, because the hackers lived in another country or were supported and shielded by a foreign government.

Ray wasn't so interested in what happened afterwards. His interest, his fascination and his passion were in finding patterns and trails in the 'big data' every company generated these days, and discovering hidden cyber attacks that other analysts could not.

Ray was one of the best.

If he had been a criminal, he would be very rich indeed.

That was not to say that he was squeaky clean.

There had been a time, once, long ago, during which Ray Luck had learnt his trade, when he had played the game and made some money.

Not a lot.

But enough.

Before he was caught and offered a job by the company that had caught him.

CSD.

Thanks to CSD his life had diverted down a new track, back onto the straight and narrow. The best part was that he was still doing all the things he had done before, but this time getting paid for it. Legally.

Ray loved his job. He relished what he did.

When he entered his 'den', switched off the lights, and sat in his black leather swivel chair surrounded by banks of flat-screens and glowing panels, blinking lights and computer terminals, Ray was in his element.

Once inside, surrounded by the comforting hum of his servers and their cooling systems, he would forget the life he lived in the 'real' world, and become immersed in the digital underworld, the dark web, digital crime, cyber hacktivists, malware and bitcoins. In microseconds he would jump from one continent to another, from one network to the others it linked to, from a host to all the servers it connected with. He would follow packets of data as they swept through networks across the world, surfing digital waves and boring through firewalls with ease. Once he had logged on to the internet, he could be anyone he wanted, go anywhere he fancied, and do anything he wished. No one would notice him, and if they did, Ray had gone to extraordinary lengths to ensure that anyone else who had the same skills as he had, would never be able to find him.

To everyone else, Ray was invisible.

And yet, from this room, Ray could see everything that happened in the world.

Almost literally.

That was the story of Ray Luck. The professional cyber expert employed by CSD.

The story of SolarWind, the name of the alter ego Ray Luck now assumed in cyber space, was slightly different.

Ray had adopted the name, because in his mind it conjured up the feeling of an unstoppable, high energy force that could sweep across the galaxy at lightning speed. Likewise, his cyber world 'avatar' was unstoppable. No firewall, no DMZ, no defence-in-depth security strategy from any company, had ever stopped him. True, sometimes it might take him a little longer than normal to hack through the well organised security defences that some companies would put up, but in general, if SolarWind was motivated, had the time, resource and determination, he would always succeed. Seldom did he give up.

That said, the lessons Ray Luck had learned in the real world when he had been caught by CSD had taught him a lesson he had never forgotten.

Ray was always in control. As 'SolarWind' he never stole anything in the cyber world that would be considered as breaking a law. He never hacked into government or official sites, where some government agencies might take offence, particularly the NSA, FBI, CIA or any other US affiliated government bodies. He knew that if he was caught, a deportation order and a one-way flight to the US was a realistic consequence. Secondly, he was extremely cautious to ensure that if he did penetrate a business or large company that he would always leave immediately and not touch anything should he discover that the company ran industrial processes or was part of the Critical National Infrastructure. Thanks to the experiences he had learned during his paid career, he understood that a significant proportion of the infrastructure upon which most countries depended for the provision and distribution of gas, oil, water, electricity and food was built upon old networks using 'Operation Technology', which unlike modern 'IT' networks, had little or no ability to defend themselves against cyber attack. A mistake made when hacking into the network of an oil plant, or a chemical factory, could have disastrous consequences, not to mention what might happen if he accidentally shut down or opened up the wrong valve in a nuclear power plant.

SolarWind just wanted to have fun. He wanted to play in cyberspace. To explore and get kudos for doing what few others could. He certainly did not want to harm anyone, get caught, go to prison or steal anything.

It wasn't that he was a coward. He just wasn't a fool.

In the past five years, he had watched too many of his peers, cyber colleagues and even some personal cyber-world friends all go that little bit too far and get caught.

Three were in prison. One was dead - from dubious circumstances that had never been explained - and another was now working for the government.

Ray cracked open his first beer, switched the Play button on the old Denon hi-fi system that he had inherited from his dad, and settled back to the latest Coldplay album.

It would take SolarWind ten minutes to log on through the various levels of security defence he had built around his own virtual world, moving down through the multiple network security levels he had established until after having passed through two of his outer layered demilitarised zones - DMZs for short - he was authenticated by the central operating system and admitted to his own private network.

From within the cocoon of his multilayered set of DMZs, through which no other cyber entity would ever be able to pass without the data-processing power of the NSA -and even then it would take them months, if not years to break the encryption and find the right passwords - SolarWind could operate at will, virtually doing anything he wanted to.

Luckily for society, SolarWind was a good citizen, a good person, and had a conscience.

Sadly, SolarWind knew others like him who were almost as talented, some even more so, who were angry citizens, who bore grudges against the world, and revelled in their ability to wreak havoc and cause as much disruption as possible.

For the most part, SolarWind did not associate with such people as much now as he used to. From time to time, he would come across them at hacker conventions, or he would bump into them on the dark web, or on the normal internet. Occasionally he might even cross their path when playing around inside someone's network, having penetrated a company's network defences.

However, SolarWind was still, and probably would always remain, a participating member of several of the largest online hacker clubs, and although the membership came from a wide spectrum of society, they all shared a common, unwritten social code: you never ratted on a cyber-bruv, a fellow member of that club. No matter what.

As Ray Luck, the Dr Jekyll of the partnership, sometimes Ray would suspect a known cyber-bruv as being the perpetrator of an attack he might be investigating. Whenever that happened, it caused a few deep-seated personal conflicts of interest. Typically, he would end up warning the other hacker, firing a ping in their direction, and giving them a cyber heads-up that they were under surveillance and would soon be caught. So far it had always worked: the other hacker would give up, retreat, and leave Ray as the victor, without forcing him to choose between his job and dobbing in the cyber-bruv to the authorities or the company who had commissioned him to test their network defences.

So far.

Ray knew that one day his luck would run out and he would have to make a choice.

Little did he know, as he cracked open his second beer and settled down for the first fun of the evening, that such a day was going to come sooner rather than later.

Outside on the street, the four man team of mysterious men dressed in black climbed back into their two black sedans and drove off.

They had found nothing. The twenty thousand pounds was still missing. The good news was that someone had given them a tip off.

Someone, when asked, had actually remembered seeing a good looking, tall, athletic, young man walking down the street about the same time the money must have gone missing.

It wasn't much. But in their capable and highly experienced hands, such information was invaluable.

The man was young, white and probably a local.

He had been carrying a brown bag and a newspaper.

And a coffee.

Chapter 4

London

September 28th

10.35 p.m.

Ray Luck was no longer getting drunk. He was drunk.

Finishing the fourth can of beer he went to the kitchen and came back with a bottle of red wine: cabernet shiraz. His favourite.

After the third beer Ray had stopped trying to randomly hack into the companies he found online. His personal rule of never hack when you had drunk too much was one he never broke.

It was like driving when under the influence.

You could make mistakes. Crash and burn.

Damage something, or leave a trace as to who you were.

He wasn't scared that someone might follow his cyber tracks back to his flat...no one would ever be able to break through all his defences and identify who he was, or where he lived. At most they could perhaps guess what country he was in, but beyond that on the internet he was anonymous and untouchable.

No, what worried Ray was that as SolarWind, he had a reputation as one of the world's top hackers, and the last thing he wanted was to do something stupid, and accidently leave a glass slipper behind that someone would eventually trace to SolarWind.

Ray had spent years establishing a reputation in cyber space, and he didn't want to give any cyber-bruv a cause to doubt him, dis him or pull him down.

So, whenever it came time to stop knocking on firewall doors, Ray would stop hacking and look for other forms of entertainment.

He would log on to a hacker chat-room and, using one of many of his aliases, would swing by from one room to another, chat with peers, and find out what was happening in the dark web.

There was always something interesting to find out. Always.

Or occasionally, if he was really bored, he might switch his large computer screen to what he liked to call "Big Brother Mode", run a small computer programme he had developed to help him survey networks for CSD called '1984' and start to watch the world around him.

1984 was one of the simplest, but finest, computer programmes he had written. Four years ago, it had only taken him a few nights of coding, but it had kept him entertained and given him hours of endless fun ever since.

It was based on a similar idea to the 'Big Brother' television program but was far better: written to see what information he could gather from the cameras customers installed and ignored in their company networks, Ray had discovered that 1984 also gave him the ability to reach into homes all over the world and watch people living their normal, everyday lives.

It worked as follows.

The program scanned the web looking for cameras that were switched on and connected to the internet. Once identified, his program would identify them and categorise them as belonging to one of several main groups, classing the majority of them as either CCTV cameras, live-video feeds for television stations, security cameras, video-conferencing cameras, laptop or computer connected cameras, or cameras that were embedded in or connected to flat-screen televisions in people homes. To avoid any problems with data protection laws, and to keep 1984 on the good side of any laws governing privacy, when viewing public CCTV cameras the programme automatically stripped out the IP addresses from the information presented on screen, thus ensuring that anyone who used the program - i.e. Ray - would never be able to identify the country or people picked up in the videos. Of course, it would be a simple matter to 'change' the program so that this information was made available, but Ray had never felt the urge or need to do so. The commercial version of the program that they used when looking at specific companies however was more targeted. You chose the IP address range you wanted that related to a specific company, and then went fishing.

When running the public, internet searching version, of all the groups that 1984 broke the video feeds down into, Ray found the last four groups the most fascinating.

When using 1984 to look at companies, he couldn't believe that businesses would buy video conferencing equipment, install it in their boardrooms where they discussed their most sensitive corporate secrets, and then forget and be totally oblivious to the fact that a video-conferencing camera and audio equipment were pointing at them and listening to every word that was being said during their highly sensitive board meetings.

The same went for home computers with cameras attached to them for Skype and messaging, and likewise for the new internet connected television screens with embedded cameras built in and permanently switched on.

His program 1984 took advantage of a simple fact that very few people seemed to have learned: when a camera was embedded in or attached to a computer which was connected to the internet, just because the owners were not using Skype, or a video-conferencing or video-messaging app to look at and see someone else, it didn't mean that someone else couldn't see them.

In fact, the opposite was mostly true - if a camera was connected to the internet, and his program could find it, 1984 would switch it on, and establish a direct video feed from the camera to the big screen in Ray's second bedroom.

1984 divided his viewing screen into rows of smaller images: Ray could choose how many rows he wanted, and how many video images he could view in each column.

Normally he would set it to watch twenty one remote cameras at a time, the images from each camera appearing in a little window in one of three rows and seven columns.

Using his mouse, Ray could pick any window he liked and it would automatically appear full screen on a second large flat screen in his room.

Ray found it fascinating.

Sometimes it made him feel what it must be like to be God, being able to see directly into people's homes, and observe them doing anything and everything you could possibly imagine.

The majority of the time he couldn't understand what people were saying because most of the images he found most interesting and drew his attention came from countries where Ray could not understand one word of the mother language.

However, Ray soon discovered that although people might wear different clothes, eat different food, and speak different languages, the things they did were mostly very similar.

They would sleep, laugh, cry, drink, eat, read, listen to music, read, work, iron, dance, argue, fight, get naked, masturbate to the pornography they were watching on their screens, or have sex.

On a scale of one to ten, watching people reading was the worst, and continually scored zero. At the other end of the scale, occasionally, he would discover a very attractive woman taking her clothes off. Sometimes, he would watch couples have sex, although it had surprised Ray when he had started watching the output from 1984 how quickly watching other people having sex became quite boring. The most interesting thing he found from 1984 was the ability to watch other people argue. He loved to observe their behaviour, to listen to the to's and fro's of the arguments. He found their confrontations fascinating.

Emma had hated 1984. When she had first discovered Ray watching it, she was shocked.

She had accused him of being a pervert. A sick voyeur.

He had promised that we wouldn't watch it anymore and had gone through the motions of deleting it. In fact, he had told her that he had deleted it. Which was a lie. But not a bad, terrible lie, because in truth, he had really cut back, and he had hardly watched it all in the last few years.

Only occasionally. When Emma wasn't around and he was lonely.

Or drunk.

The truth was that 1984 fascinated him.

It wasn't just about finding naked women and watching them, although, obviously Ray wasn't going to *not* watch one if he saw one... But it was much more than that.

If he had been an author, he would have been inspired by the ability to see real-life stories unfold before him so that he could then turn them into chapters of a book which would fascinate others.

One of Ray's favourite episodes from 1984 was when he watched a man in Brazil bring a woman home to his apartment, make love to her on his bed, only to hear his wife coming into the house.

He had hidden the other woman under the bed, and when his wife had come in he had feigned sleep.

His wife stripped off, climbed in beside him, and the man and wife started to make love.

After a few minutes, the woman under the bed had tried to crawl away and sneak out of the room.

From his vantage point of the camera embedded in the TV in the bedroom, Ray had watched as the wife had turned round and seen the naked mistress sneaking out.

All hell had broken loose.

But that was not the end of it.

After twenty minutes shouting at each other the wife had reached out to the mistress, who then climbed into bed between the man and the woman.

What followed next was every heterosexual man's fantasy, and Ray was no different.

It had been a one off. Ray had never seen anything quite like that again.

Thankfully, in the past few years, Ray's life had been so full of Emma that he had not felt the need to indulge so much in a life of voyeurism.

Tonight though was different.

Ray was alone. And he hated the feeling that accompanied it.

So, instead, he was determined to lose himself in the lives of others, and the rest of the bottle of wine.

In recent months 1984 had become a distant friend, but tonight they were going to be fully reacquainted. Emma was gone, and now there was no reason not to watch it.

Tonight, 1984 was the only friend he had.

Ray poured his glass, watched as the little boxes on his screen started to fill up with video streams from around the world, and began to browse the lives of others.

It had probably been about six months since the last time Ray had run 1984. What immediately impressed Ray was that the average standard of images that he was now viewing was remarkably better than those he had seen last time he had logged on.

Although it was a surprise, Ray quickly realised why.

In the past year there had been a dramatic uptake of HD TV's, most of which now had good quality cameras embedded in them. For those that didn't, the resolution and quality of the cameras that you could now buy from any computer store to attach to your TV was much better than ever before. Cheaper, but better. The wonderful advantage of economies of scale.

The second reason was that the average speed of broadband piped directly into people's homes was much greater. Fibre optic cables were being laid everywhere, and the price of affordable bandwidth had plummeted. Nowadays, lots of people were watching TV online, catching up on programmes they had missed or watching movies in real time from subscription services.

The amount of detail that could be transported across network links had risen dramatically.

Thanks to all these advances Ray Luck was now able to watch Mrs Jones at Number 36 strip off her clothes in High Definition, while some man in Japan was getting drunk drinking Saki and dancing round his living room. A family probably in South America seemed to be playing some sort of game, and a couple speaking French were fighting, literally - they were kick-boxing each other. About five women on different screens were all naked and lying on beds, touching themselves, which Ray quickly realised was a sign of the times and one of the latest developments in on-line porn: they were paid sex-workers providing on-line chat room services where subscribers could contact them and in response the women would do whatever they were asked to do for three minutes at a time...or something like that. Ray had never subscribed and did not know the intimate details.

In the bottom left of his screen a teenage girl was crying her eyes out. The sadness was palpable. Ray was drawn to her, and he directed his mouse towards the screen image, clicked on the picture, and watched it go full-screen on the other display.

The girl was reading a letter and sobbing her heart out.

Almost as if with a sixth sense, Ray immediately understood what was going on. The girl had just been dumped. He watched her crying and wished more than anything that he could reach out and comfort her... but he couldn't.

The sadness was infectious. After two minutes of viewing, his own sadness began to surface, and he felt a sudden pang in his chest. An emptiness. A longing. A loss.

He closed the window down and returned to viewing the main screen.

People were reading, knitting, sitting on sofas staring at the cameras, cooking, ironing. Almost every aspect of modern life was being captured for his entertainment.

Top right, a screen window that until now was showing a bedroom but no occupants suddenly became interesting.

A beautiful woman walked into the room. She came over to where the camera was and bent over towards him.

She was wearing a red, figure hugging dress. Her breasts were large and full, and a wonderful, exposed cleavage caught Ray's immediate attention. Ray clicked on the image.

The light flickered on the other display, and the image went full screen.

As she bent forward, Ray got a full view of her cleavage, and in spite of the beer and wine, he felt an immediate physical response.

The woman was gorgeous.

She was obviously fiddling with something underneath the camera, or close to it.

Suddenly it went dark.

She had switched the light off in the room.

"Shit..." Ray swore, thinking that was that, and all the fun was over before it had begun.

Luckily, a few seconds later, before Ray had managed to switch channels, the camera in the woman's room started showing an image again.

This time the room was much darker. Another light had been switched on somewhere in the background.

"*Yes!*" Ray said aloud, as the woman standing in front of the camera came into full view.

The woman was stripping off.

Ray watched her remove her dress, unveiling black-stocking clad thighs, and a wonderful body.

She half-turned, looking across the room and said something to someone off screen.

Ray quickly lent forward and turned the volume up, switching off the CD playing on his hi-fi.

She was speaking a language he didn't recognise. Not English, or European. If Ray were to guess, it was probably Arabic.

A man's arms encircled her body, and he watched a hand unclip her bra strap.

Her breasts fell free. Heavy and beautiful.

The man - Ray couldn't see his face - was kneeling in front of the woman, kissing her stomach. His head moved down, exploring between her legs.

The woman moaned and grasped the man's hair with both hands.

She rotated slightly away from the camera, and the man shuffled across round in front of her.

Ray could only see the back of the woman, who was leaning forward, but from the sounds he heard, he could tell that the man was kneeling up, and fondling and kissing the woman's breasts.

"Shit!"....Ray swore again, realising that he had forgotten to hit the 'record' button.

Reaching forward, he switched on the external hard drive and started to capture every second for his own personal future entertainment.

The man stood up in front of the woman, and they started to kiss.

With still no clear view of his face, the man lifted the woman up and walked backwards away from the camera carrying her in his arms. For a second or two they disappeared from view. Then the unmistakable sounds of a woman making love filled the room. The woman was moaning.

Incredibly, and at this point Ray laughed aloud and reaffirmed his love for modern technology, the camera in the TV in the distant room picked up the sound of the lovers coming from a bed, swivelled round to find them and zoomed in.

A second later the image of a woman straddling a man filled the screen.

Although there was less light further away from the camera, Ray could still easily make out that the woman was bucking back and forward on top of the man, who was lying across the bed, sideways on to Ray.

Ray took a large sip of his wine and smiled as he watched the woman's large breasts bounce up and down. They were incredible.

Much larger than Emma's.

Emma's breasts were beautiful - Ray had never really thought twice about their size - but this woman's breasts were undeniably special!

"You are one lucky bastard!" Ray chuckled, glancing at the man, whose face was still in shadow.

Just then, the phone rang.

For a second, in Ray's drunken state, he thought it was the phone on the TV, but then after a few rings, he realised that it was his own landline.

Looking back at the screen and the action that was going on, he was about to ignore the phone, when a thought occurred to him.

It might be Emma.

Turning towards the door, Ray dropped the remote control onto his chair, and stumbled out the room.

The hands-free phone had been left on the table in the kitchen. Interestingly Ray hadn't noticed that before. Had Emma called someone that morning after she had woken up?

He made it just in time.

It was his sister.

"Are you okay? I haven't heard from you again... I was just wondering if you were okay. We're just going to bed..."

"I thought you might be Emma..."

"Sorry, it's just me. How are you?"

"Drunk."

"Understandable, and not surprising. Just make sure you don't drink too much."

"Don't worry, sis. I'm a big boy now."

"I know you are... you are okay though?"

"Yes...I'm just...Listen...I'm okay...I don't feel like talking now... Can I call you tomorrow?"

"Sure. When your hangover has got better. Don't forget to turn everything off..."

"Night night, sis..."

The was a moment's pause, his sister thought about saying something else, but didn't.

"Night."

And she hung up.

The moment Ray walked back into his den and looked at the screen he could tell that something had changed.

The woman was standing in front of the camera. The man was standing near the doorway on the other side of the room, in darkness and not visible, and the woman once again close to the camera, her right side visible with a clear view of her curvaceous breasts. Her head was not in view, and standing closer to the camera she blocked Ray's view of the man's head and face.

She was shouting aggressively at the man in her native tongue and waving her arms in the air.

The man was listening to her, and shouting back at her when the woman paused to take a breath.

How the situation could have deteriorated so rapidly was incredible, but this was exactly the sort of thing which made watching 1984 so addictive.

Ray settled down in his chair again, and picked up his wine.

The man walked away from the woman, and was gone, disappearing into another room.

The woman turned around, looking at the wall where the camera was, scanning for something.

She came closer and then disappeared off camera for a few moments.

Ray could hear her doing something but could not see what it was. There was the sound of rustling.

The man shouted something from the bathroom. It sounded like it was in English, but Ray could not be sure. He certainly did not understand it.

The woman shouted something back, and a moment later reappeared in front of the camera, dressed in her clothes, a long coat, and carrying a bag.

It looked like the evening's entertainment was almost over.

Ray knew this part very well...the woman was about to storm out of the house, or flat, or apartment or wherever it was.

She was standing with her back to the camera when to Ray's great surprise, she called out aloud in English, "Please, come back here!" to the man.

A second later, the man reappeared in the doorway, his face still shrouded in semi-darkness, although this time Ray could make out the silhouette of his face, head and shoulders.

"Where are you going?" Ray heard him ask. "You can't leave. Not now."

"I go!" she shouted back at him. "You bastard. I leave now."

The man was walking towards her. Ray could hear the footsteps and his voice getting louder, but his head and face were once again, frustratingly, not in view, the woman's torso again blocking his line of sight.

"Don't go. There's something else I have for you." The man said, his voice gentler.

The woman hesitated.

"Perhaps," she said. Sounding calmer. "Come here..."

The man came closer, now standing in front of the woman.

It appeared as if he slipped his hands inside her coat and around her back, knocking the bag that was hanging from the woman's right shoulder so that it seemed to slip forward towards the front of the woman.

There was the sound of kissing.

The woman moaned, seemingly getting aroused.

What happened next, happened very fast.

The woman moved back from the man, the man shouted something, the woman screamed...

There was a struggle...it only lasted a few seconds, the woman screaming again, and the man shouting once more.

Suddenly, the woman stepped back, turned towards the camera with her hands against her chest, holding something, and fell forwards towards what was presumably the TV with the camera in it. She banged heavily against the lens and the TV, the camera wobbled, and then the image went haywire for a second, different confused images flashing across the screen.

When the image settled down, the camera was looking along the floor, pointing at a strange angle towards the woman, who was also lying on the floor.

Ray stared in disbelief at what he saw.

The woman's hands had slid to the side, revealing what was unmistakably a long knife handle sticking out of her chest.

Her face was staring at the camera, her eyes wide open and unblinking.

The image on the camera began to flicker.

Sitting bolt upright Ray bent towards the screen, studying the woman's face.

A man's torso appeared, kneeling over the body, a hand reaching to her throat to feel her pulse.

The man bent down, turning his ear to the mouth of the woman, listening for a breath, his face turned away from the camera.

The image on the screen flickered again a couple of times, then disappeared.

The screen went black, and the room was silent.

Ray Luck breathed in deeply, trying to keep calm.

He couldn't believe what he'd just witnessed.

It was not an act, a film, or a play. This was not Big Brother, or any reality TV show. This was real.

He had just seen something that he would never forget for the rest of his life. In the time that he had left on this earth, he would replay the past few seconds in his mind over and over again.

Without a shadow of a doubt, Ray Luck knew he'd just watched an innocent woman being murdered.

Chapter 5

SOHO, London

September 28th

11.35 p.m.

Adam Grant sat in the chair by the window, looking out at the dark river Thames flowing a few hundred metres below his penthouse flat.

He was not a happy man.

In fact, he didn't mind admitting, "I am FUCKING pissed off!"

The man standing behind him in the dark suit, his head slightly bowed, his hands clasped in front of him, did not say anything.

Two tall, muscular men, also wearing dark black suits, stood by the man they were guarding, one beside and behind each shoulder.

Adam Grant swivelled round in his chair and looked up at the man in front of him.

The lighting in the room was subdued, allowing the London city lights to flood into the apartment and for those inside to be surrounded by the vibrancy of the city.

"Well?" Adam asked.

The man Adam was looking at said nothing. His name was Ben, and this was the part Ben hated. He knew exactly how it went. Normally he was one of the two men standing behind whoever it was that was being 'talked' to by Mr Grant.

And normally it was his job to take that man outside afterwards, anywhere, so long as it was somewhere very far from here, and then either beat the man to a pulp, cut off one of his fingers, or kill him. Which punishment was meted out always depended upon how angry Mr Grant was, or how much the person deserved to be punished.

The fact that Mr Grant was 'fucking pissed off' did not bode well for Ben.

"Well, Ben. What the fuck do you have to say, then?"

"I'm sorry, Mr Grant?"

"Is that a fucking question or a statement?"

"A statement."

"You're telling me it's a fucking statement. I'd be truly sorry if I had to tell one of these two bullies to take you outside and ...well, you know the story only too well, don't you Ben? And that's why I would be fucking sorry. You're a good man. I'd hate to lose you. How long have we been working together now?"

"Five years, Mr Grant."

"Five years? Doesn't seem so long. We must have been having fun. Time flies, as they say."

"Yes, Mr Grant."

"Except, I haven't been having any fun recently, have I Ben?"

"No, sir, Mr Grant."

Adam stood up, and walked across to Ben, standing directly in front of him and looking up into his eyes.

"What the fuck do you think you were playing at when you lost my envelope? And where the fuck is it now? Why haven't you found it yet?"

"I'm sorry, Mr Grant. I've already told you, it was an accident. I must have dropped it. I'll make up the twenty thousand. I can give it back to you tonight if you would like. I accept it was my fault."

"Twenty grand? Do you think it's the money I'm upset about? The money? Bloody hell, Ben, twenty grand is nothing to me. You know that. It ain't the money, Ben. It's the fucking envelope!"

Ben looked up, for the first time looking at Mr Grant. He didn't understand.

"The envelope...?" he began to ask.

"Yes, the bloody envelope. It's covered in my DNA. I was the one who put the money in the envelope, licked the bloody flap, and stuck it down. That's my bloody saliva. If someone fucking finds that envelope with the money in it, and hands it into the police, they'll trace the notes to the Bond Street robbery, match my DNA on the envelope and have a concrete case against me. Fuck, Ben, I might as well walk right into the police station now and dob myself in. If someone hands that money in, Ben, I'll do time."

"I'm sorry, Mr Grant..."

Mr Grant stepped a little closer, his hot, garlicky breath blowing up Ben's nostrils.

"Ben, you're a good lad. But you know the score. I've got to punish you. I really should. Except, I'm also one who respects loyalty, and good service. And I like you, Ben, you know I do, right?"

Adam paused.

"You KNOW I like you, right, Ben?"

"Yes, sir, Mr Grant. I know you like me."

"Good. That's good." He replied. "And because I like you, I'm going to give you another last chance. I'm going to give you another chance to find that fucking envelope. And I'm going to be reasonable too. I'm going to give you some more time. You've got a week. Seven days. One hundred and sixty eight fucking hours to find and bring that envelope to me." Adam Grant paused, walked away, sat down in his chair, and looked out of the window at the Thames again. "I think you know the rest,... what will happen if you don't find it? That's what's meant by the reference 'last', isn't it? As in, your last chance. Dead people don't have any more chances, do they? You'd better go now. I think you need all the time you can get. You fucked up Ben. Big time. Now you'd better unfuck it up."

Emma lay in her bed, shaking. The tears had long since dried up. And so had the texts and phone messages from Ray.

It seemed that he had given up on her.

She felt empty. Weak.

Ray had been the love of her life.

It had been so difficult to make this decision, but she knew that it had been the right thing to do.

They had become different people.

There was a dark side to Ray that, truth be told, had attracted her to him in the early days, but which now scared her a little.

At the same time, she was attracted to his strength: his physical, muscular strength and also his character.

But he frustrated the hell out of her.

She had made it painfully obvious over a year ago, that she was ready to move on to a new stage in her life, but Ray had just not been able to see it.

Nine months ago she had been offered the dream job of her life. In Canada.

She had not even told Ray about the offer. After thinking long and hard about it for a month, she had turned the job down, hoping...*hoping* that Ray would grow up, become an adult...and pop the question.

She had waited. And waited. And then waited some more.

And yet, there was still no ring. No talk of living together. No real talk of a future they would share.

She had tried talking about it with him, but each time she brought it up, he seemed to change the subject.

Her best friends had told her, that if it didn't come naturally from him, she should not chase it.

The last time she had mentioned it...she had taken him to Brighton for the day. They had ambled up and down the little narrow streets full of antique jewellery shops, and Emma had stood outside, cooing and saying "wow" and "look, that one's beautiful..." while pointing at rings. Engagement rings.

Ray had been nervous.

Later that afternoon, he had made an excuse, and disappeared for thirty minutes, somewhere. Then that night, over dinner in a nice restaurant near the pier, he had given her a ring.

A 'friendship' ring.

Silver. Worth about thirty pounds.

He was beaming. So proud of himself.

She was shattered. When they got back to London that night, she developed a headache, came home to her own flat by herself, and cried.

She couldn't have made it more obvious if she had tried.

Emma had come to terms with the fact that Ray was a lost cause. Commitment was obviously not his thing. He wasn't growing up, but she was.

So last week, when the company in Canada had called her up again, saying that the person they had hired had not worked out, and would she reconsider, she told them she would.

Opportunity only knocks once.

Or so they say.

For her, against all the odds, it had knocked twice.

She would not make the same mistake twice.

Emma *was* heartbroken.

She loved Ray..."No, I DID love Ray", she corrected herself verbally.

But she knew now that that was not enough.

This time next month she would be in Canada.

A new job. A new country. A new life.

The future had never looked brighter.

With that thought in mind, Emma buried her face in her wet pillow and started to cry again.

Ray Luck blinked several times and steadied his breathing.

The external hard drive?

Quickly looking at the flashing white light on the front of the box, everything seemed fine and he was reassured that he had just recorded it all.

Scanning through the little images on the other main screen, just to be sure, he checked that there was nothing more to see.

His guess was that as the woman had fallen, she had smashed against the camera which was probably embedded in a TV, or given what happened next, actually probably just attached to the TV and sitting on top of it.

The camera would have fallen, got knocked off the top of the TV... the TV probably fell over too, the power was lost, and the camera switched off.

But not before revealing the dead woman on the floor of the room with the knife sticking out of her chest.

Ray ran through the sequence of events in his mind again.

Had he made a mistake? Had it all really just happened? Maybe it was not real...was it some sort of weird reality show that he had inadvertently jumped into?

He quickly dismissed the thoughts, turned to his computer, and stopped 1984 from running.

Going to the Start panel, he found the external hard-drive, and located the file he had just recorded.

His adrenaline still pumping through his system, he got himself a hot, strong coffee from the kitchen and came back, and started to run back through the images he had captured on the big screen again.

The screen flickered, the video started and Ray relived the experience once more.

The room in the video appeared quite dark. The man was standing up in front of the woman. It was then that Ray remembered that he had initially forgotten to switch on the hard-drive and that he'd missed the opening sequence, the woman coming into the room with a red dress, the view of her breasts, her stripping, the man coming into the room, some foreplay starting.

Ray halted the video, grabbed a notebook and quickly wrote down what he could remember of the part that he had seen but not recorded. He didn't want to forget something later, especially since he was quite drunk and would find it very difficult to remember details in a few hours.

Noting items of interest and recording thoughts and observations as they occurred came naturally to Ray: it was part of the discipline of his job as a cyber analyst.

If he saw something that could be important, he noted it down. It was the little things that often came together and signified something far more important.

Starting the video again, he watched it through several times, pausing it at different points, making notes, absorbing as much of the detail as possible.

Time and time again, he studied the moment when the man murdered the woman, seeing her fall, waiting for the camera to follow her, steady its image on the floor, before capturing her blank, death stare and the knife buried deeply in her chest, seconds before the camera feed then died.

The woman was - had been - beautiful. Her body amazing. If it was not for the way it all ended, Ray would probably have got quite aroused when watching it.

On the contrary, there was nothing erotic about death.

Fetching a new cup of coffee, Ray came back to his chair, and sat and stared at the image he had frozen on the screen: the picture of the woman lying on the floor on her back, the knife handle emerging from her chest.

He drank the coffee, staring at the dead woman.

Thinking.

Going over it all in his mind.

Over and over again.

One question kept coming back to him.

What should he do now?

Call the police?

How would that conversation go...?

"Hi, This is Ray Luck here... I'm a cyber security consultant. I work for one of the largest Cyber Security companies in the world... trusted by governments and industries everywhere... In my spare time I hack into people's homes and spy on them. Totally illegal I know. Breaking the law, yes? Probably lose my job now and go to prison? Okay. No problem. By the way, I just saw someone being murdered."

It didn't sound so good, did it?

There were a few other small problems.

Ray did not know which police to call. Which country was the woman murdered in? Where was she murdered? In someone's house? A hotel room?

And who had been murdered? By whom?

Ray wound the video back to the beginning again, searching for answers to some of the questions.

The thing that was bugging him most was that nowhere did he seem to get a clear shot of the man's face. He was a mystery, an enigma.

But something else was nagging at him too...something...

When the woman had got dressed and shouted at the man in English, threatening to leave, the man had reappeared in a doorway, coming back into the room.

For a few seconds he had been facing the camera, and his body and head seemed as if they were in clear view and not obscured by the woman's body. Focussing on the few seconds of this part of the video, Ray found that although the outline of the man's body was visible, there was no obvious detail. He was too far away and where he was standing was shaded from the source of light in the room, mostly in darkness.

When he started walking towards the woman, the man had moved over slightly into the room, and the woman then came between Ray and the man. His face was totally hidden.

Watching that part over and over, Ray noted a few more points: the man seemed to have put some clothes on. Like the woman, he was not naked anymore.

Pyjamas? A dressing gown? Trousers and a shirt? Ray could not make out any details.

Moving through the rest of the video, Ray confirmed that there was not a single point when the man's face was visible. Apart from those few seconds in the door, he had magically been out of view the whole time.

"Shit!" Ray swore, speaking aloud to himself, a habit he often had when sitting for hours on end by himself, trying to hack into a network. "The man's invisible! I can't see him."

Slumping back in his chair, he glanced at the clock.

It was 3 a.m. He had lost track of time.

Sleep would be impossible now...Ray was wired.

Having watched the video a million times now, what else did he know?

Ray decided to go through the outstanding questions, one at a time.

Question One: where was it filmed - in a hotel room or a bedroom? In someone's house?

He thought he might know the answer to that one.

When the woman was stabbed, she fell forward against the camera, knocking it from whatever holder it was being held on, and causing it to fall.

In Ray's experience, most fancy TV's in hotel chains now either had a camera embedded in it, or no camera at all. It was highly unlikely that a hotel would buy cameras as extras and stick them on top of the TVs. What for? Perhaps in a business suite, but not in a hotel room. The fact that the camera was attached to the top of what was most likely a TV, meant that it was almost definitely a private bedroom in someone's house.

Also, unless it was a palatial suite, the room was too large for a hotel. It seemed to have several private rooms going straight off the main room, which were probably a bathroom and maybe a large walk-in wardrobe. Which made sense, thinking about it, because the man walked through the door, and seemed to come back dressed in something. Pyjamas perhaps?

If it was a house, it seemed to be a BIG house. The owner had to be well off. Who else could afford such a big bedroom with an en suite and other rooms coming off a bedroom?

Also, few people had large TVs in their bedrooms.

Whoever had such a large, well-equipped bedroom was most likely loaded.

But where was it? What country?

That was not so obvious.

Once again, Ray went through the whole video sequence again from the start.

This time around, he was not looking at the people, but focussing on the background. He was looking for books, newspapers, pictures on the wall...anything small, or large, that he hadn't noticed yet, but which could give a clue as to the country where the murder had taken place.

He found nothing.

What about the woman's clothing?

Was it indicative of anything?

Unfortunately, Ray was not a fashion expert. It didn't help him at all.

He thought momentarily about Emma...she might know, but as soon as he thought of her, he felt a pang in his chest, and he forced himself to refocus his mind on the video, blocking further thoughts of her.

The woman was foreign. It had sounded like some Arabic language, guttural, quite harsh and very expressive, but he wasn't sure. If he could identify the language, he might be able to locate the country.

The man seemed to be English. Or he could be American, or... actually, all Ray could really tell was that he spoke English with a good English accent. It didn't mean he *was* English.

On the other hand, it seemed that the woman had been intent on leaving. If she was going, the room belonged to the man. Which meant that if he could identify the accent with which he spoke, he would get a clue as to where the man's house may be...Was she a foreign woman leaving an Englishman's house? In England?

It was a long shot, he knew. But he made a note of the thought anyway.

He ran the video a few more times, but nothing new surfaced.

Ray was not making any progress. He had reached the point of diminishing returns.

The coffee was beginning to wear off. His eyes were hurting.

He yawned.

Ray looked at his watch.

The little hand was pointing to the seven, the big hand at two.

Bloody hell.

He'd been up all night.

For a moment he considered showering and making some breakfast, but it was only a passing thought.

Ten minutes later he was lying in his bed.

Asleep.

Chapter 6

St Cecilia's Square, London

South Kensington

Sunday

September 29th

08.40 a.m.

Ben stood on the corner of the beautiful St Cecilia's Square, watching the rich bastards who came out of the white Edwardian terraced buildings and either started to jog, cross the road to the private park in its centre to meet up with their personal trainers, jump into their Porsches, or amble slowly down to the corner shops and the delicatessen.

They were looking for a young white man, who might soon buy croissants and a newspaper. Just like he was reported to have done yesterday.

There was however a small problem.

They were all fucking white. Every single last bastard amongst them.

Ben was black. He wasn't a racist. Never had been. But he did recognise the class divide. In this part of town, most of the billionaires and lesser class of millionaires were all white.

Ben loved this square.

Not only because quite a few of his very rich customers were here, and he earned an awful lot of commission from them on the items he supplied to them, but because he genuinely loved the architecture and the 'ambience' the whole place oozed.

One day, when he had done enough deals, or pulled a few successful raids, this was one of the places he would like to live.

For now though, the art of continued living was something that he was more determined to focus on.

Purchasing a house in this area would be quite difficult if this time next week Ben was dead.

What made Ben slightly angry, actually *very* angry, was that he had himself not been the person who had lost the envelope. That honour went to one of his team, Petrov. Not the brightest of this crew. Not the bravest. But certainly the most loyal and hard working. Petrov would do anything for Ben.

Which had made it quite difficult for Ben to decide how he should be punished, for his incredible, stupid, bloody ineptitude.

How could the fool have dropped an envelope with twenty thousand pounds in it?

For now, though, punishment had been postponed.

Ben had taken the rap, a typical action which the men who worked for him respected and admired him for, and it was Ben who would take the bullet if things did not go well in the next seven days.

On top of that, Ben needed as many eyes and ears on the streets as possible, and Petrov would work twice as hard as anybody else to recover what he had lost. Ben knew that.

This morning the plan was simple.

Watch out for any young man who went to the deli, bought croissants, a newspaper or a coffee.

If any did, someone from his team was to approach them, make some polite enquiries, point out that an envelope had been lost, and make known that there was a sizeable reward for any information that led to its safe return.

For now, no one was to apply any pressure.

There would be no violence.

Just a few polite questions, a mention of the reward, and a telephone number where they could be contacted.

Of course, if in a few days they were no further forward, violence would be the next step.

Ben was a clever man. He had survived in this game almost intact all of these years by living off his gut instinct.

So far, it had never failed him.

And right now it was telling him that this was the place. The missing money was here somewhere. In one of these houses. Being looked after by one of the bastards living in luxury while he lived in a tiny two bed in Brixton.

As far as the possibility of the envelope having been handed into the police, Ben was not so concerned.

The envelope had contained twenty thousand pounds. Good money. Money which even these people would not ignore.

Ben knew he could count on whoever had found the money to keep it. It would be a different story if it had been dropped on the pavement in a poorer area of town - it would have been handed in to the Klink within hours. Poorer people had more to gain from keeping the cash, but they also had a greater sense of what was right and wrong. Invariably, the majority of them would always do what they considered to be the right thing. They would hand it over to the police.

Here in St. Cecilia's Square the people were different. These people had all become rich by stealing from the poor people beneath them. They had been stealing for generations, and were experts at looking after themselves first, and thinking of others ...practically never.

Although it was the envelope that was the most important thing, Ben did wonder about the twenty thousand pounds.

He would not be surprised if it had already been spent. It had only been twenty-four hours, but the chances were that some rich bastard had quickly blown the money, Mr Grant's money, on cocaine and prostitutes.

Which, ironically, probably meant that it been indirectly returned to Mr Grant already.

Just then, one of his crew across the road waved and pointed to a man who had just walked past him.

A young man, tall, brown hair, and an expensive jogging suit and trainers on.

The funny thing was, in spite of the fact that he had all the gear, the man was not jogging. He was walking.

Right into the corner deli.

Ben crossed the road and followed him in.

Ray stirred in his bed, the sunlight streaming in through the window making him wince and reach for the pillow and the duvet to cover his head.

Buried beneath the soft eiderdown, his brain was given a few seconds of respite before the memories of the day before began to hit him.

Saturday had been a day that had started with so much promise.

He had intended to end it with a proposal, a 'yes', and a bottle of champagne.

Instead he had spent it alone, with 1984, and it had ended in a hangover and a murder.

And he was the key witness. The *only* witness.

"Shit..." Ray muttered and buried his head deeper in the mattress.

"What am I going to do?" he asked himself.

For a second he thought about calling Emma to tell her what he had seen and ask for her advice, but as soon as he thought of her, he felt that thrusting pang in his chest again, as if someone had just stuck a blade into his heart and twisted it.

At the thought of the knife, a mental image of the dead woman lying on the floor filled his mind.

"Shit!!!" Ray swore again.

Pulling back the cover, he glanced across his bed to where Emma had been lying only just yesterday morning.

Naked. Beside him. Underneath the covers.

He reached across and pulled her pillow over and sniffed it.

He could smell her.

For a while Ray's mind filled with thoughts of Emma. Memories of places they had been together. The sensation of holding her close to him. Of making love to her. Her soft lips.

His thoughts started to go round and round in circles, trying to figure out what he had done wrong.

Had they *really* split up?

Would she call him again and give him a second chance?

He lay there for an hour, thinking, analysing everything.

But after an hour, nothing had changed.

He was still single. Emma had gone. And the world looked like a very dark place.

And yet, he was still alive. Unlike the woman whom he had watched being murdered.

Shit! What was he going to do about that?

He thought again about calling the police, and quickly discounted it once more.

Climbing from his bed, he wandered through to the kitchen, made a coffee and dragged himself through to his den.

A few minutes later, he had got the recorded video running and was watching the murder again, replaying it over and over.

It began to drive him mad that he couldn't see the face of the murderer.

There were those few seconds when the man was standing in the doorway, in otherwise clear view and not obscured in any way. But he was in darkness and it was impossible to make out any features.

If only there had been more light!

Ray sat there staring at the screen.

If ONLY he could see that man's face.

And then it dawned on him.

The answer to his problem.

RobinHood.

It was time to call RobinHood.

Although most people didn't know it, Ray had a dark past.

After the death of his brother, who was killed by a drug overdose when he was barely a teenager, he had begun to rebel against authority. It had started with arguments with his dad, which he seldom won.

As he got bigger, and the arguments more heated, Ray had taken to the streets, and for a while had joined a gang and hung out with like-minded youths, all struggling to find an identity, independence...and some respect from others.

Incredibly, thanks to his high IQ and the ability to learn everything almost without trying, he had done very well at his exams and was offered places at several universities, eventually choosing Oxford.

At Oxford he had fallen in with a bunch of other students that he had met at one of the university debates. Like him, they all rebelled against authority, although this was mostly done in an intellectual way, with very little real action.

Within months, finding his studies too easy leaving too much time on his hands, Ray had sought out another, more aggressive club: The Oxford Anarchists.

The members came from all walks of life, and met every Thursday in the Trout, a popular pub on the outskirts of Oxford.

Ray had become fascinated by the rhetoric and passion expressed during their meetings, and very soon he volunteered to start joining in some of the anti-establishment demonstrations that were being planned.

During his first very heated demonstration opposite the House of Commons in London, Ray got carried away, and threw a bottle at a policeman.

He was arrested, spent a day in the cells, and was bailed out by his father.

Instead of fighting with Ray and showing anger, rather surprisingly his father had cried.

Driving Ray back up to his college in Oxford, his father hadn't said much at all, an uncomfortable silence filling the space between them.

Ray knew better than to say something before his father broke the ice, so he remained quiet during the journey.

Only when the car pulled up in front of his digs, did his father say anything.

As tears ran down his cheek, he said: "Ray, I'm not angry. I was young once too. I did my fair share of things which my dad frowned upon and which could have got me into some really serious trouble. If I hadn't ended up in the navy, and got some real discipline rammed down my throat, I can't tell you what would have happened to me. I'm not upset with you son, I'm just worried. Please think carefully about the choices you make. You're an adult now, son. If you want to carry on being an anarchist, it's your choice. But, please, think about your future. Think about the opportunity you have here at the university. Don't mess it up son. I know what it's like to get involved...if you don't break free from this group you've joined, you probably never will. Do it now, son. Break free. Find your kicks elsewhere. You've got a good future ahead of you. Don't ruin it for yourself."

His father had reached out, asking for a hug.

For the first time in years, Ray had agreed.

His father had pulled him close, held him tightly in his arms and cried.

After what seemed like ages, he had pulled back, wiped away some tears, smiled at his son, and said, "You're a good man, Ray. Your brother would be proud of you. Just like we are."

He smiled, almost managing to mask the hurt Ray saw in his eyes at the mention of his brother. "I love you, Ray. Since James died, I never told you often enough. I should have, and I'm sorry. I love you, I always have. Promise me you'll remember that, okay?"

Ray nodded. His dad was acting a little weirdly.

His dad smiled again, nodded, and then turned around and got back in his car and drove off.

Ray never saw his father again.

He died of lung cancer three weeks later.

What got Ray was that his father must have known he was dying when they last talked, but he had not said anything.

The memory he was left with, from that day till now, was of a father who truly did love him. A strong man. A man of principles. And a good father, whose last advice had changed his life.

After the funeral, Ray never went back to the Oxford Anarchists.

Instead of funnelling his latent anger at the UK government, he began to direct it increasingly online, into the developing world of cyber-space.

He was soon joining in and regularly contributing to online forums of fellow hackers, all keen to explore the art of hacking, develop their skills and boast about them to others.

Ray had become a regular and well respected member of the cyber underworld.

Here, in a world that no one could touch or see, he found the respect he had always craved.

For a number of years he had explored his wild side, developing an online personality and set of cyber skills that few could match.

Within the cyber community he had made many acquaintances and some good friends. Except for three people, he had never actually met any of the people he hung out with online in real life.

RobinHood was one of the exceptions.

After exchanging conversations in hacker chat rooms for several months, Ray had discovered that like himself, RobinHood had a shared interest in anarchy and had been a card carrying anarchist for several years -

Ray realising in hindsight that the name should really have given the game away sooner.

Over the past eight years, SolarWind and RobinHood had met several times in pubs in London. They hadn't seen each other for four years now, but Ray knew he could call him if he needed help. As he did now.

Last time they had met, RobinHood worked for a well known film production company.

He was a special effects expert and using CGI could make anything appear to happen that he wanted, being paid to create his own fantasy worlds into which he could then disappear.

If anyone knew how to take the film that Ray had recorded, find the face of the man standing in the doorway, and use computer enhancement tools to play with the imagery and extract and construct the face of the murderer, RobinHood would.

Ray and RobinHood had never been to each other's houses before, but Ray knew that RobinHood used to live in London.

If he was still here, then it should be easy to track him down, and find him.

In fact, it didn't take him long at all.

He simply looked up the last email he'd got from him and replied to it.
"We need to meet up. Face to face. Need your help! Urgent."

An hour later, an email alert Ray had set on his computer pinged, and he jumped up from watching some boring Sunday morning TV, ran through and read it.

"Long time no hear, SolarWind. I'd be glad to help, cyber-bruv! I'll send you a separate email in two minutes with instructions where to meet. Tonight!"

Chapter 7

Jamboree Night Club

Limehouse

London

September 29th

9.30 p.m.

Ray didn't know RobinHood's real name and had never asked it. Likewise RobinHood had never asked his.

As Ray paid the entrance fee to the Jamboree night club and swept aside the heavy, crimson velvet curtain that separated the real world from the inside, he smiled to himself.

The Jamboree was just typical of RobinHood. Whenever they met it was always in some bizarre location that Ray had never been to before.

This place was no different.

The bar was hidden away at the back corner of an industrial building in an area of Limehouse that Ray had never been to in his life before.

To get in, you had to ring a bell at the front of the building and tell the night guard that you were going to the bar. He then buzzed a set of heavy, iron, electronic gates that opened and let you into a large courtyard.

The only way to find the bar was to follow the music. There were no signs, no advertisements. It reminded Ray of a secret bar in Moscow that he had once visited.

A man sat at a desk, half hidden in a doorway. Ray stepped into the door, the man smiled, asked for six pounds, and Ray was in. That part was easy.

Inside the light was dim. On his left there was a drinks bar on one side of a large, square room, some stools dotted around the edges. The walls were bare concrete, with large rectangular grey ventilation ducts and thick electrical cables running along the ceiling.

Large canvases covered the walls, which on quick inspection seemed to depict people who were members of an audience dancing to music.

Turning to his right to identify the source of the music, he saw that a makeshift stage dominated the other end of the room opposite the bar.

Heavy red curtains hung from the ceiling on either side of the stage, imitating the curtains at a theatre. A piano, stage left, was being played by a man dressed in Victorian clothes and wearing make up to make him seem as if he was dead. Large black circles surrounded his eyes, and his skin was painted grey. The effect was quite spooky.

A woman in a red, French-style dress with red bows tied around two childlike pigtails was playing a violin and making strange faces at the audience.

A bald drummer, and a bass-guitarist with a bright yellow top hat and large red eye glasses, coloured shirt, strange boots and yellow trousers stood behind her, playing away.

They seemed to be playing some sort of weird, bohemian music from a French cabaret.

Some young students were dancing on the floor in front of the stage, obviously getting quite drunk, but enjoying the bizarre ambience of the place. Judging by the way one of them was swaying to the music and staring into space, alcohol was not the only drug he had taken tonight.

Apart from the lighting on the stage, the room was dark, and it took a while for Ray's eyes to adjust.

There were about twenty people in the bar already, which for a Sunday evening was quite good going, especially in a place hidden so far away. Those not dancing were clustered in little groups around tables at the edges of the room, with a few people at the end of the bar: they seemed to be watching a man in the corner, an artist, who was painting a large canvas, probably the same man who had painted all the canvases on the wall.

Turning round completely, Ray looked at the people immediately behind him, and found RobinHood.

He was sitting at a small table just behind the curtain covering the entrance, looking straight at Ray.

The table was empty and Ray took a seat beside him.

"Long time no see, SolarWind," he said, offering Ray his hand.

"Too long." Ray replied, accepting the hand and shaking it.

In the years since they had last seen each other, RobinHood had changed a lot. He'd put on a lot of weight, grown a black beard, and started to go bald. But he still had the same piercing dark eyes, which were now fixed on Ray and examining him.

"What do you think of the band?" he asked.

"Weird. The man gives me the creeps."

"Me too. But that's the idea, isn't it? You don't like the music?"

"I didn't say that," Ray said, shuffling a little closer so that they could speak without anyone hearing them shout at each other above the music. "The music's weird, but it's interesting. I quite like it."

"So do I. So what've you been up to? What do you need some help with?"

Ray looked around the room.

The table beside them on the right was empty, the heavy curtain hung down on his left, blocking the entrance to the bar.

The music from the band was loud, and Ray was assured that no one would be able to hear them. He shuffled closer with his chair towards RobinHood.

"I was surfing the cameras... you know, seeing what was happening in people's houses and hotel rooms... and I saw something." Ray started to explain.

RobinHood looked across at him, his eyebrows raised.

"Saw what?"

"Something bad..."

"Bloody hell, am I meant to bloody guess what you saw, or are you going to tell me. Spit it out, man, spit it out."

"I saw a man kill a woman."

RobinHood sat up straight, looked around quickly, and then leant forward.

"No shit!"

"I'm telling you the truth. I saw a man kill a woman. Stab her in the chest with a big knife..."

"Fuck me..."

"Actually, he'd just fucked *her*...Afterwards they'd had an argument. She started shouting at him. She'd got dressed, was just about to leave, and then she shouted at him again. He came across the room to her, they started to reconcile, kiss and make up, then next thing you know she was shouting at him and he was shouting back. They fought briefly, she screamed and fell to the ground. She knocked the camera off the TV as she fell and it fell to the ground beside her. The last thing I saw before the camera died and the transmission stopped was a whacking, great knife stuck right into her chest, and her eyes all glazed over. As dead as dead can be."

"Fuck me..." RobinHood said again.

"I'd rather not." Ray said, whimsically, trying to make light of it all. RobinHood didn't laugh. He was thinking.

"Any idea where it was? Any way to track down who it was?"

"I've been through it all a million times in my head and examined the footage over and over again..."

RobinHood reached across and grabbed hold of Ray's wrist tightly.

"What do you mean? Did you RECORD it?"

Ray nodded and then looked around the room again before continuing.

"Yes, I did. As if you wouldn't! The moment she got naked and started showing off her incredible breasts, I recorded the whole thing!"

"You actually recorded the man murdering her?"

"I said so, didn't I. I've got it all."

"Bloody hell..." RobinHood said, whistling aloud and settling back in his chair.

He picked up his bottle, drank the rest of it, and waved it at Ray.

"I need another drink, and a few seconds to think. You want anything?"

Ray nodded.

"A bottle of cider."

RobinHood got up, pushed the table forward as he eased himself around it, and walked across the room to the bar.

Ray looked back at the band, staring at them without really seeing. The music - weird but wonderful - washed over him. He stared at the lead singer, the sweat now running down his face and smearing the black mascara around his eyes like a crying woman.

This whole thing - the music, the bar, the conversation, meeting RobinHood again the night after Emma had left - it was all so bloody bizarre! He was just thinking about getting up and walking out, when a bottle landed on the table in front of him, and RobinHood edged back into his seat and sat down.

"So, you've got this all recorded?"

"I told you. I have."

"And what do you need me for? Where do I come into this?"

"It's simple. I've got a problem and I think you're the one person I know who can help me solve it."

"Which is?"

"I can see the woman who got murdered really clearly. She's in view a lot, especially when she's lying on the floor and facing the camera. I can't forget her face. I see it all the time when I close my eyes... I can't get rid of the image of her staring straight into the camera... at me... with those dead eyes of her. If she walked into the bar right now, I'd spot her immediately. I'll never forget her face!"

"I wouldn't worry about that, mate. From what you say, the last thing she's going to do is to walk into this place. Or any place."

"Funny ha-ha. But you know what I mean. The woman's dead, I know that. But it's the man that worries me. Nowhere on the recordings the man's face easily visible. There's only one part, for a few seconds when he is standing in a doorway on the other side of the room, that the view of him is not obscured by the woman. You can make out his body - I think - but he's in shadow, and his face is so dark you can't see it properly."

"Aha... I think I get you now...," RobinHood smiled. "You want me to work my magic on the man and pull his face out of obscurity. Clean up the images and play with them until you can see what this guy looks like?"

Ray nodded.

"Actually, I don't work for the film production company anymore," RobinHood explained, "... but don't worry, I've still got everything I need."

"I want to see this bastard's face. I need to know what he looks like."

"Why? What will you do when you know? Are you going to the police?"

Ray was silent. He picked up the bottle and drank a few gulps down. When he was finished, he wiped his mouth, and turned to RobinHood.

"I don't know. I don't know what I'm going to do. The murder could have been anywhere in the world, and I know that if I go to the police I could get arrested..."

"The right thing to do would probably be to tell someone about this..., you know..." RobinHood said.

Suddenly a voice echoed in Ray's head: Emma's voice - *"... the 'right thing' to do, you wouldn't know what that was if it hit you right between the eyes!"*

"...but then again." RobinHood continued. "What would be the right thing for *other* people to do, is not always what would be the right thing for *us* to do."

RobinHood stared at Ray for a moment, then slowly turned his face to the band, picked up his drink and took several long swigs from his bottle.

Ray stared at RobinHood, studying him, thinking ahead.

He'd come here tonight to meet RobinHood for one specific reason. He'd been thinking about it all day, and he knew there was no other way.

But could he trust him?

The music suddenly changed pace and the man started singing in French, some sort of strange French cabaret song. Ray could feel the hairs on the back of his neck rising. It was eerie music.

"So," Ray heard RobinHood ask, bringing his thoughts back to the here and now. RobinHood was looking directly at him. He leaned forward towards Ray.

"Have you got it? Did you bring it with you?"

Ray didn't reply. Instead, he looked about him, surveying the other people in the room.

Thankfully, nobody else in the room seemed in the slightest bit interested in them, and even if they were, it was too dark in their corner for anyone to see them properly.

Ray grabbed hold of his bottle. He downed the rest of it and stood up.

He felt a hand on his wrist.

"Did you bring it with you, SolarWind? If you want me to help, I will, but obviously, I need the video."

"You promise you won't copy it and put it on YouTube?"

RobinHood laughed.

"What? So that SolarWind, one of the most respected hackers in Europe can tell everyone else in the community what I've done, and stop anyone from ever trusting me again?"

"*You promise?*"

"I do, SolarWind. I do. I'm annoyed you asked. You should know you don't have to."

"In that case, I'll say goodbye." Ray replied.

For the briefest second, Ray saw some confusion in RobinHood's eyes. Ray reached out to shake RobinHood's hand goodbye.

RobinHood grasped it, felt something hard in the palm of Ray's hand, and smiled.

"I'll get right on to it, SolarWind. I'll ping you as soon as I have anything."

"This is between you and me, you swear? Just us two!" Ray emphasised again.

RobinHood nodded, clasping his hand around the USB stick, retracting it slowly and putting it in his pocket underneath the table, out of view from anyone in the room.

Ray looked down at RobinHood. Yes, he thought, he had put on weight. A lot.

SolarWind turned, pulled back the curtain, and stepped into the empty courtyard outside.

As he walked towards the DLR to catch a train to Canary Wharf, it began to rain.

Heavily.

10.45 p.m.

David Anderson sat in the corner of his bathroom, rocking himself back and forwards, his arms clasped around his knees.

His girlfriend, Chloe, was knocking on the door, crying and slowly becoming hysterical.

"Let me in, David. Let me in! What's the matter? You have to tell me!"

She began to knock again, this time more loudly than before.

"You've been in there all evening. If you don't come out now and tell me who did that to you, I'm going to call the police..."

David heard her speaking, but didn't move.

The trouble was, he didn't know who had done this to him.

Three men had grabbed him from behind, bundled him into the back of a van and driven off.

They had immediately put a bag over the top of his head, and two of the men had sat on him.

After ten minutes driving, the van had stopped.

The men had not removed the hood, but they sat him up, and pushed him back against the side of the van.

They then hit him once, in the solar plexus, knocking all the air out of him and forcing him to double up and fall back onto the cold floor of the van.

As he gasped for breath a man spoke.

A deep voice, a slight accent that David couldn't place.

"Where is the envelope?" the voice had asked.

At first, David didn't hear him, his mind and focus being elsewhere: on just trying to breathe.

The man spoke again.

"This is how this works, David. Every time I ask you a question, you answer me. If you don't, we hit you again, but twice as many times as we hit you the time before. So, since you haven't answered my question yet, now we hit you twice more."

Two heavy blows rained down upon David, one to the lower back, and another in quick succession to his stomach.

David screamed aloud with the pain.

"Ready for my next question?" the man said. "...And by the way, the answer to that question is yes or no. If you don't answer... it's eight blows this time..."

"I'M READY! DON'T hit me... please..." David coughed and said as loudly as he could. "What do you want to know?"

"I want to know where the envelope is!"

"What envelope? I don't know what you are talking about..."

"We think you do, David."

"I DON'T. I don't know what you are talking about!"

"I'll repeat. We think you do. We've been making enquiries. We followed you. We know who you are and where you live. We know you went for a run yesterday morning. Bought papers, food from the corner-deli. Walked your girlfriend's dog, like you do every Saturday morning, before you go home and fuck her. What's her name? Chloe? Lovely name. Lovely girl. We took some photos of her, so we know what she looks like. You're a lucky man, David. Very lucky. So tell us what we want to know, otherwise..."

"I don't KNOW what you are talking about!" David pleaded.

At this point, although David couldn't see them, the two men who had been hitting him looked searchingly at their boss, doubt beginning to show in their eyes.

Ignoring them, Ben stepped forward, bent down and put his lips to the side of David's head.

"The thing is David, and I'm going to be very honest with you here,... I'm going to trust you, and by the way, if you break that trust, I'm going to kill you... you see, the thing is that we lost something, an envelope, on the pavement beside the park where Chloe lives. We know that you went for a walk about the same time, and that you must have passed where we dropped the envelope. We know that someone picked the envelope up. And kept it. And we think it was you."

"Why? Why do you think it was me? It could have been anyone!"

It was a good question. A question that Ben didn't have a good answer for.

So he slapped David across the side of the head as hard as he could.

"I ask the questions, you give the answers. Do you understand?"

David quickly nodded. And then quickly added a verbal '*Yes*' just to be sure.

"I'm going to ask you one last time, David, and you had better tell me the truth now, because if you don't, I think we will kill you. I must admit, I haven't decided yet completely. Perhaps we will cut off your fingers first, but then we will kill you. Do you understand?"

David nodded.

"Good. So where is the envelope David?"

David had started to shake.

"I DON'T KNOW. I HONESTLY DON'T KNOW. You HAVE TO BELIEVE ME!" the man shouted back, curling into a ball on the floor and tightening, obviously expecting the blows to rain down upon him.

There was a sudden pungent smell, and one of the men quickly stepped back as David's urine began to flow across the floor of the van.

Ben swore to himself. Fuck! This was not going the way he had expected. Or hoped.

The two men in the van with him were staring at him, shaking their heads gently.

It was obvious that the man did not know the answer to the question he was being asked.

Ben looked at his Rolex and realised it was getting late. They had been parked in the mews for too long now. They could be drawing attention if anyone heard them.

Squatting beside the man on the floor, he whispered.

"Messy. Very messy, David. A bit childlike if you ask me. Are you a little boy, David? Will you go home crying to mummy? Will you tell her what happened here today? If we let you live?"

"No! I won't. I promise. I won't tell anyone. Just don't kill me! Please!"

Ben put one of his gloved hands on the man's shoulder.

"Okay, David, I've decided to let you go. I believe you when you say that you don't know where the envelope is. Which for me, quite honestly, is a bit of a problem. I was sure you were the one who had taken it. So, this is what we are going to do. I am going to release you. And you will help us find the envelope, okay?"

"Yes! If you release me, I'll help you find it. I promise! I will!"

"That's good. And I believe you will, because if you don't, I think that perhaps instead of killing you, we will probably just kill Chloe instead. Do you want that?"

"Yes.., I mean NO! I mean, Yes I want to be set free, and yes I want to help you find the envelope, but NO..."

"But no, you don't want us to kill Chloe? Is that it? You love her? You don't want her to die?"

David was starting to sob now.

"Please, just let me go. And don't hurt Chloe. I'll do anything you want. Honestly I will. Honestly..."

They had driven for another ten minutes, the van had stopped, the doors had opened, and he had been pushed out of the back door, hitting the ground hard.

David fell flat onto the road, smashing his face against the ground, and instantly tasting the blood from his burst lips.

For a few seconds he lay still, listening to the engine of the van moving away from him, stunned and aching all over.

After a few moments, there was no more sound, no kicks to his ribs, or punches to the body. He seemed to be alone. And alive.

Pushing himself up into a sitting position, he groaned in pain as he slowly reached up and pulled up the hood over his head.

It came off easily and looking around, he found himself in the middle of a quiet cobbled courtyard surrounded by industrial buildings.

It took several minutes before his head began to clear, his breathing calmed down and he was able to take in his surroundings.

Mentally he flipped into survival mode. He didn't know where he was. He was injured, shaken and bleeding.

Home. He had to get home.

Not recognising anything, he slowly got up and started walking.

As he hobbled towards the entrance of the courtyard, he heard traffic and was relieved to see a big red bus pass by in the street beyond.

It was just beginning to get dark and looking at his watch he realised that it was almost seven o'clock.

What should he do? How would he get home?

His trousers were soaked in his own pee, blood was pouring down his nose, he was covered in bruises, and he looked a complete mess.

Public transport was probably out.

Feeling into his pocket, he was relieved to find his wallet.

A taxi it was then.

Standing at the side of the main road that he had come out onto, looking for a taxi, he started to think about the last words they had said to him:

"Tell the police, tell anyone, and we will come for Chloe. She's a beautiful girl. Maybe we won't kill her. We'll just slash her face a few times, so that every time she looks into the mirror she will see what you did to her. We'll cut off a few fingers on each hand, and we'll beat the living daylights out of her. And then, just when she's started to get better and cope with her injuries, if she ever does, we'll come back and complete the job, cutting the rest of her fingers off."

They had hit him in the small of the back then, and he had almost blacked out with the pain. They'd waited for him to start moving again before continuing to map out exactly what they now expected from him.

"The thing is David," the leader had explained. "I obviously made a mistake. Got the wrong guy. But I know how you can help me fix things. You see, you can HELP me to find the man I should be looking for. While we were making our enquiries, shall we say, we were told that someone had seen a young man walking down the side of the road just about the time my envelope was lying on the pavement. I don't know who it was, obviously not you, but you're going to help me find him. You're going to make enquiries for me. Find out who that young man could have been. And you're going to start making polite enquiries if anyone found the envelope *you* dropped. Do you understand?"

For a second David didn't realise that he was expected to answer, then panicked and rushed to shout back 'Yes' before they hit him again.

"Good," the man continued. "In fact, this will work out quite nicely. You can even go round all the houses in your street, knocking on the doors for us, until you find the right man."

"But I don't live there... I just visit Chloe..."

"Not my problem, mate. Just knock on the fucking doors, ask people. Put up a notice in the local shops. I don't fucking care HOW you do it. Just do it, okay?"

David nodded, then quickly followed with a loud 'yes' just in case they hadn't heard him.

"We'll call you. Every night. You can tell us how you are doing and if you have found it."

"But you don't know my number?" he replied, stupidly.

"Of course we will, 'cos you're going to tell us it right now. Aren't you?"

"Yes, I am." He replied quickly, complying immediately and giving them the information they needed.

"What was in the envelope?" David asked. "I'll need to know, if I'm going to tell people it was mine, and they've found it."

Ben thought about that one for a moment. It was a good point. If he himself had lost something and then located the person who had found it, the other person would surely ask him to describe the contents of the envelope before returning it to him.

"Twenty thousand pounds."

David nodded.

"What colour was the envelope and how big was it?" David asked.

"Bloody hell, you ask a lot of questions!" Ben replied, slapping the hooded man roughly over the head. "But since you ask, I'll tell you. It was brown. And I want the envelope back with the money. If I get the money back without the envelope, we'll come for Chloe. Do you understand?"

David nodded.

For a moment there had been hope. Hope that if he forked out twenty thousand pounds of his own money, that the thugs would leave him alone. David was a derivatives trader in the City, and raising the money wouldn't be difficult for him. But could he just stick it in any old brown envelope and get away with it? He knew he couldn't. There was obviously something special about the envelope.

"Is there anything written on the envelope? Anything particular that might help me identify it?"

The man slapped him again.

"You ask too many questions. I've helped you enough. Now you just go and do your bloody job. We'll call you tomorrow night. Every bloody night until Saturday. If you haven't got lucky by then, Chloe gets it. DO YOU UN-DER-STAND?"

"Yes," David had answered.

A second later, the van ground to a halt, spun round and David was thrown to the floor.

He felt two sets of powerful hands grab him by the arms and shoulders and hoist him up. The van doors opened and he felt them propel him out through the doors into the courtyard beyond.

It was twenty minutes before a taxi agreed to stop for him. Several had started to slow down, got close, and then sped off again.

The one that did finally stop demanded an extra forty pounds up front for the fare, to cover the cost of cleaning the seat afterwards.

"What happened to you mate?" the driver asked, after David stumbled inside, and slammed the door closed behind him.

David was just about to reply when he thought of Chloe.

"I fell," he replied. "Down some steps... Can you take me home now please?"

He was still shaking when he rang the doorbell to Chloe's third floor flat, crashed past her when she opened up, and barricaded himself into her toilet.

He'd been there ever since.

Chapter 8

London

Monday

September 30th

7.15 a.m.

Ray woke, stirred, and went back to sleep. There was another hour and forty-five minutes before he had to go through, log on and start his day.

He worked from home on most Mondays, trying to extend the weekend as long as he could. He found that if he knew he didn't physically have to go into work the next morning, that he could avoid the Sunday night blues, and spend every single spare second he had with Emma.

Emma.

Shit.

He hugged her pillow tighter, and sniffed it again, worried that the perfume was already beginning to wear off.

Every time he thought of her, he felt that sharp pain in his chest. He'd never experienced anything like it before. It was difficult to describe it exactly...like a feeling of dread, loss, excitement and fear all bound up together. As soon as he thought of her and felt the pain, adrenaline would pump into his body and he'd immediately start to feel sad, the reaction to her name being accompanied by a pressing feeling of loss and emptiness.

He tossed and turned in his bed, trying to fight the world around him, but it wouldn't go away.

Eventually, he reached out behind him, grabbed the corner of his own pillow and threw it against the door in frustration.

Putting her pillow back beside him on the mattress, he climbed out of bed, and went to grab a towel from the cupboard.

Just then the phone rang.

"How are you?" the soft voice of his sister asked.
"Great. Never better."
"Have you heard from her?"
"Nope."
A moment's silence.
"What are you doing today?" she asked.
"Working."
"Good. It'll take your mind off things."

"I know."

"You don't want to talk, do you?"

"Nope."

"Ray, you haven't called her again, have you? You know, I don't think that that's the best..."

"No Alice, I haven't. I'm never going to call her again. Ever. That's it. We're over. Done. Her choice. She made it abundantly fucking clear that she never wants to see me again. And you know what, I'm better off without her!"

Another silence.

Ray wasn't convincing anyone, let alone himself.

"I'll call you later, Ray...tonight, when I get back from work?"

Ray swallowed, fighting back a few tears.

"Yes," he coughed, then spoke more softly. "Please."

Fifty press-ups, a hundred squats and sit-ups later, showered, breakfasted and

dressed, Ray poured himself a fresh coffee and wandered through to his den.

Whereas one half of the large second bedroom was dominated by the world of SolarWind, the other was occupied by his home-office: two large screens, a couple of laptops, a desk-tower, two servers, firewalls, several external hard-drives, a landline, and a VoIP phone connected to one of the laptops.

Ray powered up the screens and laptops, switched on the hi-fi and took a sip of his coffee.

Although he had some of the best technology in the world at his fingertips, it never failed to amaze him that it still took an age for the computers to load everything up and be ready.

Choosing a new CD from the tower beside the hi-fi, he replaced the CD in the tray with some Kaiser Chiefs, and turned up the volume.

A few minutes later, Ray logged onto the CSD network, and when asked for his pin and SecurID token, he copied the six digits from the display on the small RSA key fob, and waited for the VPN to log him onto the corporate network.

Scanning Outlook, Ray caught up with new email since last Friday - mercifully only twenty that needed responding to - and then settled down to the job in hand: hacking into the accounts department of the new bank that they had signed up last month.

Within minutes he was lost in a different world, playing the game that he loved, and still finding it difficult to believe that he was actually being paid for doing it.

Without doubt, Ray had the best job in the world.

He loved the challenge. The detective work. The chase.

He had long since become addicted to the adrenaline that flowed through his blood as the excitement built, and Ray began to map a client's defences in his mind. Ray never rushed. He always took his time. Methodically learning as much as he could about the structure of a client's network, the defences they had in place and the systems that they used.

He took copious notes, which he would rely on later to help him build his report for the client. When he felt that he was ready to slip past a client's defences and step inside their network, he would always take a break. Go for a walk. Do some more sit-ups. And think.

Had he missed something?

Was there a better way?

Was he walking into a trap?

When it came to his job, Ray was a perfectionist.

Getting into a network was mostly quite easy. Getting in *undetected* - that was the trick! And it was a skill that Ray had developed and honed over the years, learning from both his failures and successes, until he had got to where he was today.

This morning, Ray was impressed. The new client was clever. Had impressive security defences, and had obviously spent a lot of money selecting and implementing the most advanced products and software.

Their systems and software were up to date, and Ray was struggling to find any vulnerabilities that he could exploit. Over the years, Ray had built up a wealth of experience along with a suite of software tools that helped him automate the basic hacking processes. Normally it would be quite easy to scan all the ports he could find in a network, identify hardware and software and establish a list of vulnerabilities in their business applications or operating systems that would allow him to manipulate their systems so that he would be given access and admin rights to a client's network.

But today it was harder than normal, and as he played, his respect for his adversary grew.

And he began to understand why they were paying Castle Security Defence so much money.

It seemed as if they had recently built a new layer of defence across their systems and were keen to test it out.

CSD had some of the best penetration testers in London, with a reputation second to none.

If their new security defences could stop the 'good guys' in CSD from getting in, then chances were, they would be highly effective in stopping the bad guys too.

If.

It was six hours before Ray discovered the answer to that question.

And in this case the 'if' did not apply. Once again, it had simply been a case of 'when'.

Ray had done it again.

Incredibly, Ray found that one of the pages on the bank's website allowed him to inject some SQL code directly into a window that then allowed him, through a series of additional steps and procedures, to get onto a web server, penetrate a firewall, elevate his admin privileges, and hop from one part of the network to another, until eventually, bingo, he was granted access to the main server from which their latest banking applications and accountancy software was run.

Job done.

Normally, when Ray had completed the job he had been asked to do, he would start to prepare his report with the evidence he had gathered, explaining the steps he had taken to penetrate the network defences, gain full access and put himself in a position where he could have committed specific additional cyber crimes - had he wanted to do so.

Having cracked the passwords, given himself the correct admin statuses and gained access to servers, business applications and any systems he was interested in, Ray had enormous power to do damage to his client's businesses.

At the touch of a button he could delete a customer database, erase essential business programs, or wipe out account information. In the case of this bank, he could easily commit financial fraud by creating a string of new fictitious accounts loaded with cash, or transferring money from one account to another.

Throughout the world, cyber crime was rocketing. Criminal hackers with the right experience and significant resources were peering together and forming organised crime syndicates that were developing ever more sophisticated attack vectors against high value financial targets.

Cyber attacks were being conceived and launched that took many months or even years before they were successful. Where targets had put in place significant cyber defences, hackers planned for the long haul, conducting organised, military style manoeuvres. Months were spent scanning networks, probing their servers, firewalls and gateways, gathering information and looking for weaknesses in their infrastructures, and vulnerabilities in the software code or operating systems which they could exploit to launch an attack against their target. Where the targets had deployed additional security measures that could only be overcome with specific knowledge, the hackers turned to social media, email phishing schemes, and old-fashioned detective work to identify key individuals in an organisation, and then obtain their passwords and details from them.

In spite of all the security precautions put in place, Ray always found it amazing how easy it was to get hold of vital passwords from so-called responsible people in key posts in target organisations.

Sometimes it was just as simple as calling a receptionist, asking for the person responsible for 'X' or 'Y', getting transferred, and then pretending to be someone from the IT department, who was trying to fix a problem or make some authorised changes to the systems. By having a little knowledge of the company - which you could easily find from websites or groups on LinkedIn, Facebook or Twitter - what the company did, its structure, a few of the bosses's names - you could drop a name or a line, and get almost any information you needed. Sometimes, the best way to get a password was simply to ask for it. The practice had become so common, and so many people fell for it, that nowadays it had even got its own name - 'Social Engineering'. Another way to get important details and passwords was to send specially crafted emails direct to the employees of companies. If the first one didn't work you would send a series of emails, linked and related to each other, each one referring to senior people in an organisation, and attaching made-up emails from those individuals. The people who received the emails saw the attached fake emails from their bosses, instructing the IT department, for example, to make changes to the systems, and to get the passwords from employees directly... People reading the email chains they received were convinced by the authority and authenticity of the emails, which contained so many details about the organisation that they just *had* to be real. Most of them would end up clicking on included links and then supplying all the information requested by the very official looking forms on the website to which they were directed.

Of course, in reality the link took them to websites which were created by the hackers, and the details and passwords which they typed into the forms they were presented with, went straight into the hacker's database.

Over days, weeks, or months, the knowledge gained by hackers in these so called 'Advanced Persistent Threats' or 'APTs' for short, eventually gave the hackers all the information they needed to access a company's network and achieve anything they wanted to do.

Advanced - because the technologies and tools and methods being used by hackers to break into networks were more sophisticated than ever before. Cyber security companies like CSD were struggling to keep up!

Persistent - because the hackers would not give up until they got what they wanted. If the payload was worth it, hackers kept right at it until they struck gold. Sometimes they really had to work for their money, but when an attack succeeded and the walls of Jericho came tumbling down, the cyber criminals could all become multi-millionaires in minutes.

Threat - because such attacks had got everyone scared. If a business was hit by a successful APT, it could be the end of the company.

Which was why Ray and hundreds of others like him around the world were employed to try to help businesses stay one step ahead of the attackers.

To protect them.

To keep them secure.

To keep them safe.

Ray looked at his watch. Incredibly it was already almost 4.30 pm and he had forgotten to take lunch, so caught up was he in the excitement and chase of finding the chink in his client's armour that would allow him to wound them to the core.

Sitting back in his chair, he was surprised to realise that he actually felt quite sad. There was not the usual high that always accompanied his successes. Instead, now that his attention had been drawn back from his screens, he was overcome with a feeling of sadness and loss.

Emma.

Thoughts of her invaded his mind and brought him down.

Ray swore, shook his head and tried to block her out of his thoughts.

He stared at the screens, seeking escape.

Having made it all the way to the centre of the bank's financial systems, he was sitting now facing the entry screen to the bank's core financial application.

The flashing prompt on the screen challenged him to enter a password and his ID.

"Login", one of the words on the screen commanded him.

Ray smiled.

It was if he was being instructed, compelled to action by a force greater than he could resist.

Yet Ray knew that he must resist. Sitting at the entrance to the bank's crown jewels, he was Ray Luck. Not SolarWind. He was being paid as a member of CSD. Now was not the time to play around with the bank.

"Login", the screen challenged him again.

Ray didn't have a user-id or a password to login with.

So he couldn't comply.

Yet.

The truth was that he knew that if he wanted to challenge himself to do it, he could find a user-id and a password. He *could*, if he *wanted* to.

"Login!"

Ray thought about his life.

Things were not going great. Were they?

He'd behaved himself, tried his best... and look how he'd been rewarded.

Alone. Single. Without Emma...
Getting a few passwords and user ids wouldn't be difficult.
How long would it take him?
He looked at the clock on his wall. Almost fifteen minutes to five.
Could he get them by six o'clock?
Ray laughed to himself.
How about five thirty?

Moving across the room to his other desk, he picked up the phone and called the receptionist at the bank. From there he asked to be transferred from one department to another, writing down names, taking notes, copying phone numbers and extensions. A couple of times he had to hang up and call back. Once someone hung up the phone on him. But within five minutes he had the names of three people who worked in the department he needed to target, along with their email addresses, all of whom were definitely at work that afternoon. Turning to another screen, he searched LinkedIn and Facebook until he found them, made some more notes about their likes and dislikes, their hobbies, interests and some of the achievements that they had claimed to have made on LinkedIn. Hacking into the company HR server, he downloaded some org charts, found the names of the people he was now interested in, and noted down details of the people to whom they reported.

Then he prepared to send them each an email.

A typical spear-phishing email which contained an email chain. The email at the bottom of the chain was made to appear as if it came from one of the VPs of the bank, the next one from their immediate boss, and then another one from the same boss asking why they hadn't responded to the first email.

Urging them to respond. *Telling* them to respond.

Instructing them to fill in the survey from the IT department and make sure his team was not the one that would hold up the installation of the new SAP system.

"Make sure that you do it before you go home tonight, please," the email urged.

It was now almost twenty five minutes past.

If he caught them now, just before they went home, they'd feel under pressure, and their normal judgement might go out the window.

That was the plan.

He waited three minutes, adding a further calculated delay which would increase the time pressure, then picked up the phone, dialling the first of the names on his list.

"Hi, Bianca? It's James here, from IT. I was wondering if you got the email this afternoon?"

"James? What email?"

"You didn't get it?"

"No."

"Not another one. That's why I'm calling you... half of the people still on my list haven't responded because they didn't get it... and they didn't get it because their system is needing to be patched... which is the whole point of the email.. I'm sorry... just let me check something... I think I can go into your Inbox on Exchange and increase your limit so the email will come through... yep, I can see it now... it's not spooled to your server yet... There you go... that's fixed it, the email should pop into your Inbox any second now..."

At his end Ray hit the send button on the email, sending it from a fake account he had created on the Exchange server for their corporate Outlook.

"By the way, how's the hill walking coming along? Did you do that West Highland Way Challenge that you mentioned the last time we spoke?" Ray bluffed, reading from his notes of the achievements that Bianca had boasted about on Facebook.

There was a pause at the other end of the line as Bianca tried to figure out how Ray knew about it. She'd forgotten completely that she'd ever spoken to this guy James in IT before...

"Has it arrived yet?" James asked, distracting her thoughts.

"Yes," Bianca replied, staring at the screen. "It just did..."

She opened it up and started to scan the contents.

"Good," James replied. "Whatever you do, fill in the form before you go home, otherwise Michael will go spare. It's only you and Debbie Wales that haven't filled it in yet..." Ray said. Debbie Wales was the next person he was going to call.

"What form?"

"Scroll down in Michael's email... see that blue linked URL underneath the paragraph about the new SAP installation? Good... click on it, and just fill in the details... It'll only take a few minutes... "

"Will it take long... I have to pick up my son in thirty minutes..."

"It won't if you do it now... Anyway, I'd better go... I have to catch Debbie too, before she goes as well. Good luck with your half-marathon next week..."

Disappointingly, Debbie Wales had already gone home by the time Ray called her, but another colleague, Janice, was ever so helpful and cheerful. She was really touched that James had remembered her birthday next week, even though, for the life of her, Janice couldn't ever remember telling James about it in the canteen.

Under pressure, wanting to leave at the end of the day, and convinced by the internal knowledge that James from IT had, especially since it was being pushed on them from above by their own boss, both Janice and Bianca visited the webpage that Ray had created several months ago and had used to trick some employees from another bank during a legitimate, paid exercise. All Ray had had to do was change the name, logo, the addresses, and bingo, it was good to go.

By the time Janice and Bianca had left to go home, Ray had their email addresses, their passwords, and their SecurID PIN numbers, which he had immediately recorded in real time as they authenticated themselves to his webpage as requested, and which he then instantly reused to log on to the real application server before the token had expired.

Two out of three. Not bad.

And it was only five forty-eight.

Okay, so, he hadn't done it by five thirty, but that was an unrealistic target and Ray had known it.

The good news was that Ray was now logged onto the bank's main systems under the identities of two of the banks trusted, authorised employees. Who had both now gone home and had no inkling of what Ray was just about to do.

Chapter 9

London

September 30th

7.15 p.m.

David stared at the front door, willing himself to open it up and step outside. Chloe would be home soon and he knew he had to go before she got back. The problem was that he'd been staring at the door for the past hour, too scared to step forward, turn the handle and leave.

Scared for two reasons.

First, because he was sure they were waiting for him outside. Ready to grab him, drag him back into the van and kill him.

Secondly, because his plan to run away was not proving to be as simple as he had hoped. It turned out that he actually did love Chloe. He couldn't just leave her. If he did get away, they knew where she lived. They'd come for her. Slash her. Take her beauty away from her. Destroy her.

And David would be to blame.

In spite of himself, he couldn't let that happen to her.

It had been a long, long night, followed by an even longer day.

He'd spent the evening locked in the bathroom, refusing to come out. When Chloe had begged to be allowed in to use the toilet, he'd passed her out the bucket she often used to hand wash her clothes in.

Before he'd finally fallen asleep on the bathroom floor he'd cried and shaken with both fear and anger.

Though mostly it was fear.

They were going to kill him. He knew it.

But WHO were they?

Why had they grabbed him?

How on earth had they had mistaken him for someone else? And who on earth had they mistaken him for?

David was too young to die. He'd too much to live for.

For a start... after all the years of struggling through university and working every hour God gave him in the bank, he'd finally made it onto the derivatives desk. Last year his first bonus had been five hundred thousand pounds. *FIVE HUNDRED THOUSAND POUNDS!*

And he was only twenty-seven.

This year he would earn more. Seven hundred and fifty thousand, maybe one million. It was a dead cert.

If only he'd be alive long enough to collect it.

Secondly, he was too good looking to die.

Perhaps it was a stupid reason for someone to be granted life whilst others may be killed, but David didn't see it that way.

He was good looking. Women loved him, and he loved women. He adored them.

Sometimes two, maybe even three at the same time.

Money, good looks, and sometimes a little of the white stuff helped, but together it was a magic combination. A brilliant combination.

A combination that so few people had. So few...

He was one of the lucky.

Until now.

He'd run through it all a million times already, trying to remember every single second, striving to make sense of it.

Who did they think he was?

When he'd woken in the morning, Chloe had gone, and his mind felt much clearer. He began to think more rationally.

What exactly did they know about him, whoever they were?

They knew his name, where Chloe lived - *where CHLOE lived!* - and his phone number because he had given it to them... but apart from that they really had nothing on him.

He could walk away. *Go.* Leave Chloe... and they would never find him.

Yes. That was the simple solution.

He could just leave and this would all be over.

The plan seemed so simple.

He'd showered, got dressed, taken some paracetamol to dull the incredible pain that wracked his body, and swigged a glass of whisky. That seemed to do the trick.

He had been about to pack his night bag and go when his phone had rung.

Terror had surfaced within him from out of nowhere, a blinding panic coursing through his veins at lightning speed.

Dropping his phone and running to the bathroom he'd bolted the door and cowered on the floor.

They said they'd call him, and now they had.

The phone stopped, rang again, and then went silent.

It was half an hour before David opened the door, crept across the carpet and picked up the phone. Checking the display, he discovered it was his office calling him, probably because he'd not turned up at the desk or called in sick. His position would be open, he'd let the team down... a black mark against his name.

Fuck!
Looking down at his trousers he realised that he'd wet himself.
Pissed his own pants again.
Twice in two days.

Popping his jeans in Chloe's washing machine, he stepped back into the shower and let the water run down over his face, calming him.
He thought about Chloe.
A vision of her beautiful smile popped into his mind. She was gorgeous.
A second later, he imagined a knife slashing her cheeks open and blood pouring out...
He hit the side of the shower with his fist, cutting the skin across his knuckles.
Fuck!
Fuck!
Shit!
David just couldn't walk out of the door and leave Chloe.
He couldn't let them do that to her.
Did that mean that he loved her?
Was David finally, actually, in love?
Shit!
He swore again.

He'd been in love before. Once. With the woman who worked in the supermarket. She was twenty eight. He'd been fifteen. She'd taught him how to kiss, how to touch her, how to make love. He'd fallen for her, slept with her, adored her, and then she'd dumped him.
"You're just a kid!" she'd said, brushing his attentions away with a red face. "Now leave me alone, or I'll tell your dad. Buzz off!"
David had been getting his revenge on women ever since, enjoying their heavenly bodies without ever getting close to them.
Until now.
Until Chloe.
So when she opened the door twenty minutes later and walked into her flat, he was waiting for her.
"We need to talk," he said.
She looked at his bruised face, screamed and started to cry.
"Come in, sit down," David continued. "... There's something I have to tell you..."

11.00 p.m.

At 6.15 p.m. Ray had shut down his laptops, powered down his servers, and crossed to the other side of his den. Switching on and booting up the ultra-secure private network of SolarWind, Ray had become a different person.

Almost literally.

By 7 p.m. he was pacing up and down his flat, trying to make up his mind and wrestling with his conscience.

For someone with half of his skills, making a lot of money would never be hard. Legally, or illegally. Illegally was far easier, but perhaps a lot more fun.

For someone with all of his skills, making a vast amount of money, illegally, was actually not that hard at all.

The only downside was the threat of being caught.

It wouldn't be so bad if the victim of the crime was a UK or European-based bank, but nowadays, anything involving American clients would almost certainly incur the wrath of the American administration, leading to an arrest warrant and a deportation order.

The UK government just loved to comply with their Yankee cousins. There would be no fight.

Within months SolarWind would be in prison, locked up in Guantanamo Bay, or dead.

The problem for now was that the client Ray had been working on *was* a US based bank.

Ray had already drunk several cups of coffee, and the carpet was probably wearing out, due to the heavy pacing back and forth he had been doing in the past hour.

He knew what to do.

He knew how to do it.

In fact, he'd already done some of the preliminary work.

Also, others had done it before him... most recently a bank in the middle east had been hit for over forty-five million dollars and those responsible had almost got away with it.

SolarWind had studied their cyber crime, and was amazed how close they had come to getting away with it scot-free. But they had made a few fundamental mistakes - mistakes that SolarWind would never make - and those who had masterminded the crime had been caught. SolarWind however, would not have been caught. If he had done it. Or repeated it.

Which he now could. But only if he could make up his mind...

When the unlucky bank had been hit, the cyber criminals had hacked their way into the central computer systems of the bank - as Ray Luck had already done today with a different bank. With the usernames and passwords that they had somehow obtained - probably in a way similar to how Ray had obtained his - they had logged into several accounts and using the authority of those who employees whose identities they had assumed, they had started to create a large number of new, fictitious accounts. They had then removed the upper limit which capped the amount of money that any of these account users could normally withdraw and issued new debit cards to these account users. The new cards had been sent to a series of addresses, at which members of the cyber crime gangs were waiting. At the same time the new cards arrived, the bank automatically issued new PIN numbers for those cards, and also sent them to the same addresses. Of course, the cyber criminals were still there, waiting for the pin numbers. And once they had them, they abandoned the addresses where they had been waiting for the cards and pins, all of which had been rented under false names and paid for with stolen cards anyway, and then they had disappeared into the night.

The cards, along with the pin numbers, had then been cloned, and large numbers of the cloned cards had been sent to other members of the gang across the globe.

These team members - the money mules and cashers - had taken the cloned cards to ATMs across their countries and withdrawn huge amounts of cash.

It was a while before the bank began to suspect that something funny was going on, and by the time they did, it was too late.

The cyber gang had become very rich indeed.

Ray, aka SolarWind, knew exactly how they had done it.

He knew he could do it too.

It would take a bit of organisation, but... now, what with Emma not being around, what else should he do with his time?

Emma.

He stopped in mid-pace.

His eyes welled up. He swallowed hard, turned around, and walked back into the den.

Angry. Confused. Alone.

He had made up his mind.

He knew exactly what he was going to do next.

11.15 p.m.

Chloe's Flat

When the phone eventually rang, David was lying in bed with Chloe, holding her tightly in his arms, her slow, deep breaths soothing him as she slept.

He had told her about the mugging, that there had been a case of mistaken identity, and that there was still some danger to him.

He had mentioned nothing about the threats to her.

Which is why, after they had made love, she had fallen asleep, his strong arms making her feel safe, loved and wanted.

David had left the phone in the dining room, and as he slipped out of bed and hurried towards it, he hoped that Chloe would not wake up.

"You took your time, David," the voice at the other end said. "I don't like to be kept waiting. From now on, you keep the phone with you at all times, do you understand?"

It was a question.

David replied as quick as he could.

"*Yes!*"

"Have you got it?"

David began to shake.

"No." He replied, his voice quivering with fear. "...No, I haven't."

"Do you know who *has*?" The man asked.

Another question.

"No."

"Then, David, I suggest you better find out soon. And just in case you need a reminder of the reason you should bother to pull your bloody finger out and do something, I recommend you go to the front door and see what just came through your lovely girlfriend's letterbox. I'll call you tomorrow. You'd better have some good news for me by then. Sleep *well*."

The line went dead.

David pulled the phone away from his ear, staring at it as if it was something he'd never seen before, his hand shaking, his mind numb. Then he remembered what the man had said, and letting the phone slip out of his hand and drop to the floor, he hurried to the front door of the flat.

A brown envelope lay on the carpet, just below the letterbox.

Kneeling down, he picked it up, turned it over and examined it.

There was no writing on the outside, and it was not sealed.

Gently, he slipped a finger inside and pulled up the flap.

There was a single photograph inside.

A photograph of Chloe getting into her car outside their building.
It was daylight.
David noticed that she was wearing the same dress that she had on when she'd got home from work.
Which meant they had taken the photograph that morning.

And that they were outside.
Watching him.
And waiting.
David rushed to the toilet and threw up.

Chapter 10

Castle Security Defence Headquarters
Central London
Tuesday
October 1st

9 a.m.

Ray smiled at the receptionist, swiped his card at the electronic gate, touched the screen with his thumb, and waited for the waist high glass door to swing open.
"Good morning, Ray!" the text on the LED screen on the wall in front of him announced, and the gate swung quickly open.
Ray stepped through, walked across the hall and called the elevator. When he heard the soft, gentle 'ping' and the doors finally opened, he stepped inside and rode it to the eleventh floor of the Central London offices of Castle Security Devices.
CSD operations were split between two locations, the office on the south bank of the Thames, and another office in a cheaper and more isolated business park in southwest London.

From his desk in the corner office, Ray had what he thought was one of the best views in London. From where he sat, he looked over the plaza below to the River Thames only a hundred metres away, directly opposite the Tower of London on the other side of Europe's greatest river.
The two tall towers of 'Tower Bridge' stood impressively on his right, and diagonally below him was the dome of City Hall, the futuristic offices of the Mayor of London.
Since Boris Johnson had left, and become an MP angling for control of the Conservative Party and hoping to become Prime Minister at the next election, Ray hardly ever gave the building a second glance.
He didn't like Boris, and he didn't like his successor, but at least Boris had had some charisma.
And for an anarchist to admit that, it was certainly saying something.
A woman's voice caught him by surprise as he stared at the two sides of Tower Bridge, watching them start to rise to let a three-masted tall ship pass underneath.
"So?" was all that the woman, his boss, asked. "I wasn't expecting to see you so soon. Have you cracked it already?"
Ray turned and looked straight up into her light blue eyes.

She was an attractive woman, but Ray no longer looked at her in that way. He now just saw the one thing that he really didn't like.

Authority.

She used to be one of his colleagues but when their boss left to join one of the new government agencies that had sprung up to help protect the nation from the growing cyber threat, she had been promoted, and he hadn't.

"No." Ray said simply.

"No what?" she asked. "'No' as in, 'I'm losing my touch, and I couldn't hack my way in yet?', or 'No' as in, 'I'm not going to tell you how, but I've done it again. I made those walls of Jericho fall down one more time, and 'hallelujah!' I'm in and all over them!'", she exaggerated, waving both hands in the air and looking skyward.

Ray smiled.

"Sadly," he replied, shrugging his shoulders slightly. "Sadly, it's the former. Their defences are good. I couldn't get in...At least not yet...They are good. Very good."

"So what are you doing in the office, then? Why aren't you still at home, trying to find a way in?" she asked, seeming a little annoyed.

This was a big client. Worth a lot of money to CSD.

It was a good question.

One to which Ray didn't have an answer which he could give to her yet. He hadn't been expecting to see her this morning.

"I've been trying since Friday. I worked over the weekend," he lied. "And I needed a break. A little inspiration."

"Do you want any help?" she asked, her voice a little more friendly.

"No. Not for now... I just need to think and get some fresh air."

"Fine. Okay... but how long do you think it'll take you to get in?"

Ray shrugged again.

"I don't know. Hopefully a few days. There's always a way in. Always."

She looked down at him, her lips quivering as if she was going to say something, but then thinking better of it.

"Fine... but you'll let me know as soon as you get in, right? As soon as you do?"

Ray nodded.

"As soon as I do, you'll be the *first* to know."

She smiled, turned, and walked away.

11:45 a.m.

For most of the morning, Ray sat at his desk, just staring out of the window. Numb. Thinking. About Emma. About last night. About how he had possibly just made the biggest mistake of his life.

And he thought of Saturday night.

Incredibly, yesterday he had been able to forget about it almost completely.

How was that possible?

On Saturday evening he had watched a woman being murdered, and he'd simply forgotten about it?

Mind you, it had been rather an eventful weekend.

On Saturday morning, he had found twenty thousand pounds.

On Saturday afternoon his girlfriend had walked out on him hours before he was going to propose to her.

In the evening he had watched a snuff movie. A *real* one, although perhaps not a deliberate, premeditated murder. A bloody murder, nevertheless.

Then he had met up with one of the world's most notorious hackers.

Followed by Monday where he had successfully hacked into one of the most secure banks in the world.

And then started to execute the perfect cyber crime. Although he didn't exactly need the money did he? He'd already got twenty thousand pounds.

All this, followed by lying to his boss, and threatening continued employment in the best job in the world.

In short, a few interesting things had happened.

Deciding that he needed some fresh air, he left his desk and wandered down to the plaza, ambling over to the bank of the River Thames and sitting down on the concrete wall.

In spite of it being October, the sun was shining, and it was surprisingly warm. Almost hot enough to take off his jacket and walk around in his shirt and tie, the mandated office attire: the smartest hackers in town.

He stared down into the water, his own mind a river of thoughts.

Thinking back on Saturday he felt destroyed. Disgusted. And scared.

Thinking back on yesterday, he felt elation.

Surely that was wrong.

In fact, he knew it was wrong.

It *was* wrong.

SolarWind had committed the cardinal sin. He'd broken the law.

It was almost with surprise that Ray finally felt his stomach rumble and realised that he was hungry.

Wandering along the side of the river, he eventually found himself in a pub, ordered some pub-grub - steak and kidney pie, chips, gravy and peas - and found a corner where he could disappear for a while.

Just about to sit down at the table, he reached out to a paper that someone had left behind, and turned it around to look at the headlines.

Seeing the photograph on the front cover, Ray dropped his plate of food onto the floor, the plate smashing and his lunch spilling everywhere.

The world around him suddenly began to spin, and he grabbed the edge of the table to steady himself, taking deep breaths and trying to calm his nerves.

Sitting down, staring at the paper, the unmistakable eyes of the woman who was murdered on Saturday night glared straight back at him.

The title above the photograph announced quite stoically, "*Israeli Model Found Murdered In North London.*"

As he hurried out of the pub, rushing out for fresh air and sunshine after having scanned the article, three phrases stuck in his mind, "Israeli", "mugged" and "stabbed to death."

Ray made it to the side of the Thames in time to vomit into the murky waters flowing past only feet below.

"Mugged and stabbed to death on the streets of North London?..." he muttered to himself, wiping his mouth clean. "Like hell she was!"

As he turned and hurried quickly towards London Bridge tube station, he felt that the eyes of everyone around him were following him. Staring at him. Boring into the back of his skull.

Ray knew he had to escape. He had to get home.

Quickly.

He needed to think.

1:00 p.m.

For the second day in a row, David sat in Chloe's flat, too scared to go out of the door. But feeling a little excited.

Excited because he had made his mind up that he was not leaving, and the reason he was not leaving was because he was in love.

Being in love, actually being emotionally attached to a woman, was an experience he had not allowed himself to feel since the shop-assistant.

"Wham, bam, thank you ma'am." Had been his motto ever since he had been emotionally abused by his first love.

The incredible thing was that David did not want or choose to be in love with Chloe. He just was.

Which, in his mind, meant that it had to be the real deal.

The icing on the cake, of course, was that Chloe genuinely seemed to love him back.

Last night he had held her close in his arms as he told her how he had been mugged.

He had told her everything except about the danger to her.

Chloe had wanted to take the day off work and stay with David to help him plan how they would go about finding the twenty thousand pounds and the envelope, but David had finally persuaded her to leave him alone.

He was always able to think better by himself.

The other reason he didn't want Chloe to stick around too long was because although he had managed to pretend that he was not as scared as he truly was, he knew he couldn't keep it up too long.

His own personal nervous breakdown was just around the corner, and it was best if Chloe wasn't around to witness it when it happened.

Not now that she was so special to him.

So, when she left, David sat on the sofa, cried twice, thought of Chloe, stared at her photograph, and did precious little else.

A few times he got up, walked to the window, pulled back the curtains and stared out at the street to see if he could see anything. Or anybody.

The third time he did it, his phone rang.

"David," a voice said. "You can't see us, but we can see you. Don't worry. We're here. Waiting. Outside. To protect you."

"Protect me from what?"

"From anybody who tries to mug you when you find that £20k, and the envelope. You are trying aren't you? You are sitting inside your flat, making a plan for how you're going to recover my money, aren't you? AREN'T YOU?"

A question.

"Yes. I am. I am. Honestly."

"Good, because from out here, it looks very much to me as if you are just shitting your pants and are too scared to come outside... Oh, listen... what was that?"

There was a loud bang on the door. And then another.

"Two knocks, David? Can't be opportunity, can it, because we all know opportunity only knocks once. No. It's someone else. In fact, I can tell you who it is. Do you want to know?"

Question.

"Yes, I do."

"Well, it just so happens I was going to tell you anyway. It's my friend Petrov. He's a good lad. You might remember him? He was the one that broke your nose. Or at least tried to. Of course, if it isn't broken, he could try again. Would you like that?"

"No. No. Please don't."

"Then get your bloody ass out of that fucking flat and find my money. If you haven't done something about it by tomorrow, I think me and that lovely lady of yours are going to get nicely acquainted. Do you understand?"
Question.
"Yes. Yes, I do."

An interesting thing happened after the call.
David started shaking.
Not from fear.
But from anger. The call had been strangely positive, galvanising him into action.
Now that he realised that he loved Chloe, things had changed. For the first time in his life, he had something serious that he could lose.
He looked at the photograph again.
The thought of someone harming her made him angry.
An inner voice spoke to him, urging him to channel the anger and use it, shape it, turn it into something positive.

David knew that time was running out.
If he didn't do something soon, Chloe was going to get hurt, and it would be his fault.
Standing up, he walked through to Chloe's office, turned on her printer and her computer and started typing.
An hour later he left the flat.
He had a plan.

2.30 p.m.

From outside in the black-windowed car, Ben watched as David slipped out of the front door, and started going from door to door on the street. He watched him stick several pieces of paper to the lamp posts along the road and disappear around the corner.
Nodding to Petrov and his boys, they all jumped out onto the street, and Petrov followed after David.
Ben walked up to the lamp post, looked at the A4 piece of paper that David had stuck on, and smiled.
"At last, some bloody progress!" Ben muttered to himself, then turned back to the car, got in and drove off.
It was time to start making a Plan B. All the other routes Ben had been down had turned up a big fat zero.
It seemed now that David was his last hope, and if at the end of the week he'd come up with nothing, it was looking more and more likely that Ben would not see the start of the next.

With Petrov following David, and the others still searching all the other streets and parks nearby, Ben was finally able to slip away and start to make a few arrangements of his own.

He needed a new passport, and he needed it fast, and he knew just the woman who could get it for him.

2.40 p.m.

Ray finally made it back to his flat just before 3 p.m. He hurried up the stairs, opened the door and hurried inside, stepping over the post and papers on the floor behind the letterbox.

Ten minutes later SolarWind's network was powered up, he'd gone through the three layers of authentication and authorisation, and he had logged onto his secure email, which thanks to the TOR Project allowed him to send emails securely to other hackers in the dark web with no risk of his location or identity ever being discovered.

His email to RobinHood was short but sweet.

"We need to meet. Tonight! SolarWind."

Of course, there was no guarantee that RobinHood would notice his email until later that day. Ray was just banking on the fact that like other hackers, they checked their TOR email religiously: read, reply, delete.

At three thirty, Ray sent another email. This one slightly more urgent.

"Have you seen our friend? Urgent I know what he looks like. SolarWind."

There was no reply.
An hour later, still no reply.
While he waited, Ray watched the video. Over and over again. Almost obsessively. Who was the murderer?

On the way home he'd bought all the newspapers, and from each he had ripped the photographs that went with the various articles about the dead woman who had been murdered in North London by a drug addict who was later found dead in an alley-way with her handbag, mobile phone and wallet, having overdosed on heroin.

As he waited for RobinHood to respond, Ray compared all the photographs with the woman in the video, her face so clear and visible in the final scene, frozen in the act of death, her eyes looking out at him from the screen and staring straight through him into eternity.

There was no doubt.
It was her.

Chapter 11

London

October 1st

5.55 p.m.

Ray lay back on his sofa, staring at the ceiling in his lounge.

Occasionally his thoughts drifted back to Emma, but each time it did, he felt that pang of pain in his chest that he had begun to loathe and hate, and he instantly changed his thoughts to something else.

To the video.

And to the newspaper articles.

Ray was worried.

Instinctively he knew that there was something going on here that was far more sinister that it seemed.

This was no ordinary death. No ordinary murder.

As soon as he read that the woman had been mugged and stabbed to death in North London by a desperate drug addict whose body was later found with conclusive evidence linking him to her death, Ray knew that he had stumbled upon something far more concerning than he could have imagined when he had first watched the murder happen.

This was the stuff that conspiracy fanatics would thrive upon.

Fact One: According to the newspaper articles, the coroner's report cited a time of death of around 7 p.m. on the Sunday evening. Ray knew that the woman had been murdered on the Saturday evening, not the Sunday. Any impartial coroner would be able to spot the difference between death occurring on Saturday night or Sunday night.

Fact Two: The dead drug addict had been found with evidence which linked him to the mugging and murder of the woman, including DNA underneath his fingernails which belonged to the murdered woman. DNA and some dried blood from her body were also found on his clothing.

Question One: Where had the body of the drug addict come from? Had he been conveniently murdered to help create a concrete cover up story for her death?

Question Two: The inquest had already been held, late on the Monday afternoon, with judgement passed on her death. All the details of the murder by the drug addict were reported at the inquest and made available to the press who quickly printed them. Had that not all happened far faster than it normally would? A lot of information had been made public and printed. Was that normal? Or was someone working hard to divert public attention away from the truth? The answer to that question was obvious!

Question Three: Were the police part of the cover up? Or had somebody arranged it all to make it look like as it was reported? But how could they do that without the coroner lying? And the police were not fools... any experienced police officer could tell the difference between a body one day old or two days old.

That was three questions so far. Big questions. Ray knew there would be more. Unfortunately, so far there were no answers.

For the briefest moment, Ray wondered if there could be any way that someone would ever manage to detect that he had seen the murder take place. Obviously whoever found the body, or committed the murder, had serious connections. The sort of connections that could have the resources to...

"Shit!" Ray swore to himself. He was losing the plot. Ray KNEW that there was no way that they would ever know he had hacked into the camera, and that even if they did discover that someone had, they would never, ever, be able to trace it back to him.

SolarWind operated behind three ultra secure layered network perimeters, each with the best security in the world. All data packets leaving his network were further anonymised by a chain of servers around the globe, making it impossible to track down where the packets came from: a similar principle used by those who established the TOR project, but now enacted in a solution that was far, far better, and had been improved by the top cyber minds in the world who worked outside of military and government clutches...

When SolarWind communicated with others from his secure, core network, all traffic leaving and entering his network went through hundreds of proxy agents located randomly all over the globe. Someone might possibly be able to read an email he sent, but could never track down the location it was sent from, so long as he always sent his email through the system he and his peer hackers had nicknamed "Ghost". For obvious reasons.

Shaking his head, to clear his brain, and suppressing another random thought about Emma, he got up from the sofa and walked through to his den.

It was time to check if RobinHood had got his message.

He had.
His reply was short but sweet.
"Meet at the same place as before, outside, at 7.30 p.m."

Ray looked at his watch. He had one hour.

He showered quickly, dressed and hurried to grab his jacket, a black hat to help cover his face - just in case - and his wallet.

Almost without thinking, he bent down and grabbed the mail from the floor beside the door on the way out.

Scanning through the envelopes quickly he found nothing of interest or importance.

The last thing he looked at was an A4 piece of paper, folded in half.

He opened it up.

In big black letters, it read:

"Have you found £20,000 in a brown envelope? If you have, please call me. This was my savings to pay my way through university. Lost on Saturday morning, I will pay a £500 reward if you please give it back to me. My future depends on this money. If you have any information that can help me get it back, please help!"

There was a telephone number and an address. It was another flat in his street.

Ray shook his head in disbelief.

A momentary image of his dead brother's face appeared before his eyes, and a spark of anger flared within him.

Long ago he had realised that the only way to deal with the drugs aspect of his brother's death was to shut any and all reactions and feelings to drugs out of his mind. If he didn't, his anger and stress levels went through the roof.

For his own sanity and health, he had trained himself not to get involved in the debate. To stay well clear.

And this letter?

His immediate gut reaction was that it was a ruse. A lie.

The drug gang clearly just wanted their money back.

Hurrying out the flat, he screwed the paper up into a ball and stuffed it into his pocket, taking the stairs two at a time.

A minute later he was running down the street.

The man in the car saw someone run past, but because of the black hat, didn't get a look at his face. By the time he turned around to take a photograph, the runner was gone.

7.40 p.m.

When Ray finally made it to Limehouse, the gate to the courtyard where the Jamboree pub was hidden was still locked up.

Searching for the night-watchman who manned the cubicle in the nearby building, Ray eventually conceded that it looked like there was no one on duty.

Scanning the announcements board in the far corner, he discovered the reason: the Jamboree was closed tonight.

Blast!

Ray looked around him at the street.

It was an old cobbled street. Down one side ran several large, old, industrial warehouses. On the other side was a long series of arches, the arches now all filled in and turned into storage. A long time ago, a railway probably ran along the top of the arches.

A few cars were parked up and down the road.

The rest was empty, the street dimly lit, and reminding him of a scene from the 1920s, before the world went crazy.

Scanning up and down the road, there was no one to be seen.

He checked his watch.

It was now 7.45 p.m.

Had RobinHood come and gone? Had he missed him?

Across the other side of the street, something moved in one of the dark shadows underneath an archway.

Almost out of nowhere, a figure emerged and started towards Ray.

For a fleeting second Ray felt a tremor of fear... what if it was not RobinHood? Had someone been following him?

Without thinking about it, he reached up and pulled down his hat across his face, stepping back towards the gate.

The figure came closer.

"You're late!" the man said. "Follow me!"

Ray hesitated.

The figure turned.

"SolarWind, are you coming or what?"

Ray felt a surge of relief, and he swore at himself underneath his breath for being so stupid and edgy.

"RobinHood?"

"Who else were you expecting? The bloody police? The Sheriff of Nottingham, perhaps?"

"Sorry...," Ray replied, stepping up closer to RobinHood. "But after what's happened, I've just got a little jumpy, that's all."

RobinHood turned, "What's happened?"

Ray looked at him, "Did you not see the newspapers this morning?"

"No, should I have?"

Ray glanced up and down the street. They were still alone.

"Where are we going?" he asked RobinHood.

"That depends...," RobinHood, "On what you next tell me. What happened this morning, and why are you so jumpy?"

"I'll tell you, but walk with me as I do. Where do you want to go?"

"Like I said, it depends on what you tell me!... How about the DLR station?"

Ray nodded.

"Take a look at this," Ray said, handing over a copy of the Metro newspaper he'd picked up on the tube. "On the second page."

RobinHood opened up the paper, stopping and staring at the photograph under a street light. He scanned the article.

"It's her." Ray steady, looking over his shoulder. "It's the woman from the video."

RobinHood opened up his mouth to say something, but thought better of it.

"Exactly." Ray replied.

"Brilliant. This is all we need."

"So, have you managed..."

"... to clear up the video and see who the man is that murdered her?" RobinHood finished his sentence.

The two men were now standing facing each other under the lamp, alone in the street.

Just then a car swept around the corner and rattled past on the cobblestones, the sound echoing off the warehouse walls against the old railway arches.

"Not yet." RobinHood replied. "I'm running a programme that automatically refines any grainy images on videos and enhances and extracts them from their surroundings. It's similar to the ones the police and MI5 use. It's slow...it takes ages to run, going through billions of mathematical computations, but slowly, very, bloody slowly, it can find and clean up any image you need, almost regardless of the background it's in. It's amazing. Incredible. But very, very slow. I got straight down to it the moment I got home the other night, and it's due to finish..." RobinHood looked at his watch, "in about an hour."

Ray lifted his eyebrows, questioning RobinHood.

"Where? Is it on your laptop? Have you got it here?"

RobinHood laughed.

"Here? On a laptop? You're joking, right? This programme sucks up power. I've had to build a parallel array of about eight servers at home, just to get this thing to work."

"At home?"

"Yes. Let's go there. Given that we know that someone is covering this up, I think the sooner we find out who's behind it all, the better. And besides, it's probably best if we don't hang out in public together, especially if Mossad is following you!"

Ray stared at RobinHood, his jaw hanging open.

RobinHood laughed.

"I'm joking!" he said, and punched Ray on the arm.

But there was something in the way that he said it that gave away the fact that far from joking, RobinHood was being totally serious.

"Stay here for a moment, SolarWind." RobinHood said, lowering his voice. "Let me walk ahead a hundred metres, before you start following me. But don't lose sight of me."

Twenty minutes later, having stalked RobinHood all the way from Limehouse to Stratford, Ray followed RobinHood down a series of dark roads, across a large park, and then into a cul-de-sac about a mile away from the 2012 Olympic Park.

As he followed him, Ray noticed that RobinHood was walking a little strangely, almost as if he was in some sort of pain. Or perhaps it was just the way he walked? After all, Ray didn't really know him all that well.

RobinHood was about thirty metres in front, standing outside the door to a small, old church. As Ray came close to catching up with him, RobinHood opened up the gate beside the road, walked up the path, put a key in the main church door, opened it up and stepped inside.

Stopping at the bottom of the path, for the hundredth time that night Ray looked around him to make sure that he was not being followed, and then followed RobinHood into the church yard.

Nervously.

The last time Ray had been inside a church was at his best friend's funeral: dead at the age of twenty five, killed by a drunken idiot in a pub fight.

The heavy wooden door at the front of the old Victorian church was ajar. Ray pushed the door open.

Immediately inside there was another door, also open. Ray walked through, and couldn't help gasping with surprise.

On the outside, the building looked old, and run down. A Victorian church that looked like it hadn't seen much love for years.

On the inside it was a completely different story.

He was standing inside a modern, luxurious house, the interior of the church having been transformed into an amazing, spacious living space.

RobinHood appeared on his right, as if out of nowhere...

"Coat?" he asked, quickly closing and locking the doors behind Ray.
Ray looked at him, not understanding.
"Do you want to give me your coat?"
"Yes, yes...sorry..." he replied. "Do you live here?"
"Absolutely."
"But it's a church. I thought you were an atheist?"
"I am. And this isn't a church. It's a house. My house. Obviously, the God business hasn't been doing so well recently. People prefer to watch TV than pray for their souls."
"Did you do all this? It's amazing."
"I'll take that as a compliment. I did most of it. When I bought it, it was a wreck. The roof had fallen in. The locals wanted to knock it down, but it's a listed building. I got it in an auction and then got funding from the EU to do it up. They practically paid me to do it. Personally, I think it's crazy, but that's the government for you, isn't it? A bunch of idiots who don't know what they're doing. I saw it as my moral duty to take as much money from them as possible. I still do. Anyway, I know we both think the same on that one!"
"It's great. You've done a fantastic job!"
"I know. But as they say, you ain't seen nothing yet. Follow me."
They walked down a corridor that was probably once the aisle. When they got to the back of the church, on the left of where the altar probably used to be, but which was now a sumptuous living room with the most incredible stained glass windows, RobinHood opened a secret door which was cleverly embedded into a book case, and stepped down a spiral staircase into the vaults. Going through another few doors, they found themselves in the bowels of the building.
They came to another door. Locked, with a digital keypad on the wall on the right. RobinHood produced a key, turned it in the lock and returned it to his pocket.
He then turned to Ray and looked him in the eyes.
"The Inner Sanctum. I'll take you inside, so long as you make me one solemn promise."
"Which is?"
"Anything you see in here, you never repeat to anyone else, do you understand?"
Ray understood exactly what he meant. In fact, he couldn't believe that RobinHood was offering to take him inside to his den, but he recognised it for exactly what it was: a mark of respect from RobinHood to SolarWind.
"I promise. And I'm honoured."
"Don't be. Just don't bloody tell anyone about this."

For a second there was an embarrassed silence, then Ray apologised and looked away, allowing RobinHood to place a finger on the digital scanner and then tap his pincode onto the digital wall panel.

There was a small electronic buzz, and RobinHood pushed on the door.

"Come, take a seat." RobinHood said, inviting him in.

Ray stepped into the room beyond.

As soon as he was inside, RobinHood pushed the door closed behind him.

It closed tightly shut, with a loud, electronic beep. Locking them both in. Whether Ray liked it or not.

As they stepped through the doors, movement sensors detected them and automatically illuminated the room.

The space inside was large. With no natural light, and no way for anyone outside to see what took place within.

Three desks were arranged around the room, each covered with laptops, and multiple flat screens. There was the familiar constant hum of the servers which were arranged in several towers, as well as a few being placed underneath the desks. Cabling, neatly arranged and tagged, ran around the edges of the floor. Several speakers were attached to the walls, and Ray guessed that they were connected to the flashy sound system that sat on a small table between two of the desks.

Several large maps of the City of London and the River Thames dominated one wall, a large white board covered another, and a cork board hung from the third, onto which RobinHood had hung hundreds of newspaper and magazine clippings.

Knowing it would be rude to pay them too much attention, Ray scanned them quickly with his eyes, taking a mental note that most of them seemed to have a common theme: the banking system and public anger over the bankers' large bonuses

RobinHood pointed to one of the two black swivel chairs in the room. "Take a seat."

Ray sat down.

"Beer?" RobinHood asked, sitting down and rolling his chair towards a small, glass-doored, well stacked fridge that was just behind the entrance they had come in through.

Ray nodded and smiled.

"Nice touch!" he laughed, noting that this was one improvement that he could make to his own den, which was otherwise quite similar.

RobinHood took two beers from the fridge, prised the lids off with a bottle opener that hung from a string attached to the door handle, and handed one over to Ray.

"Cheers. Now let's see what we've got here then, shall we?"

RobinHood pushed his chair across the floor to the desk against the middle of the far wall, pushed the buttons on the side of two screens and after looking over at Ray, who then politely looked away so that he could not see, typed in several passwords onto the keyboard on the desk.

The two screens jumped into life.

Whatever the programme was that RobinHood was running, the job it was doing was obviously not yet complete. A dashboard filled the screen, full of numbers and figures, most of which Ray did not understand, except for one part: a box with a red surround contained a clock, counting down till completion - '98% complete. Minutes left: 3.'

RobinHood smiled.

"We're in luck. Good timing!"

He swivelled round and leant back in his chair, his eyes coming to rest on Ray.

"I can't believe you're here... in my lair. You're the first cyber-bruv to see this."

"I'm honoured. And I have to say, it's really cool. And probably the last location in the world you'd expect to find a place like this!"

"Exactly. Anyway, we never really got a chance to speak the other day. So how's things nowadays? Still working at CSD?"

"Yep. Pays the wages, and keeps me on my toes."

"Still being a good boy, then?"

Ray thought briefly back to last night and then lied.

"Yep."

"Incredible... If I had your talents, SolarWind, I'd be the richest person on the planet."

Ray swallowed hard.

"Flattery will get you everywhere, but you've always been just as good as me. How come you're not rich then?"

RobinHood laughed.

"Who says I'm not? Or perhaps I was, or will be again? You know the rule, if you've got it, don't flaunt it, right? Don't draw attention to your real self. *Ever.*"

Ray nodded.

He understood exactly.

The lessons learned by their flash cyber-bruvs who had paid the price for boasting of their successes were lessons well learned by the others who were still free, and apparently poor.

A screen behind RobinHood began to flash.

"Here we go..." he said, spinning round in his chair, and pulling himself closer to the desk.

Ray pushed himself across the floor to join him.

The dashboard had been replaced with a box with a red triangle in it.

"Are you ready for this?"

Ray nodded.

"I want to see the face of the bastard who murdered that woman. If we can identify him, then maybe we can..."

"We can what?" RobinHood hastily interrupted. "Tell the police? Help the authorities? Are you joking? You know I'd never do anything like that! I hate the bloody authorities..."

"I'm not saying I will... but..."

"But what?"

"Come on, a woman's been murdered. And someone's covering it up. We need to know what's going on!"

"Why?"

"Because..."

"WHY?"

"Because, I'm the only person who knows what really happened, and..."

A look of concern crossed RobinHood's brow.

"You've *changed* SolarWind. You're different. I can't believe you're saying these things. It's that good woman of yours that's done this to you, isn't it?" RobinHood said, then laughed.

Ray felt that pang of pain in his chest, and a wave of sadness crossed his heart, followed by an incredible feeling of loss.

"Just play the thing. We can argue about this later." Ray said firmly, redirecting his thoughts swiftly away from Emma. "If you don't want to watch it, then leave the room, or just give me the flash stick and I'll leave. Otherwise just hit play. I want to see this bastard's face now."

RobinHood said nothing, just looking at Ray and appraising him.

For a moment or two, Ray wondered what RobinHood would do next, but then he eventually spoke.

"Sure thing. I was just playing with you. Let's watch this," and with that he spun around again to the screen and clicked the 'Play' symbol with his mouse.

Coloured video immediately filled the screen. It was the opening sequence of the video. It looked just the same, nothing different from what Ray had seen before.

"It hasn't worked...this is just the same..." he started to say.

"Patience..." RobinHood cautioned. "You'll see in a second...we'll fast forward to the bit you want in the doorway where the man was standing..."

RobinHood looked down at some notes he had scribbled on a notepad on this desk, then moved the mouse along the play bar that appeared below the bottom of the video. A little window appeared at the bottom of the video and inside it they could see the scene that would play if they released the mouse at that step of the video.

RobinHood dragged the pointer along until the moment the video showed the man just about to appear in the doorway, and he then released the pointer with his mouse.

The image on the full screen changed, and they were at the point where they could see the dark contour of the man's body in the far doorway of the room.

"Ready? Watch this..." RobinHood said.

Pressing one of the Function buttons on the keyboard, the dashboard they'd seen previously reappeared to the left of the video on the screen, and RobinHood moved the mouse and adjusted some of the parameters within the dashboard, moving a red sliding bar in one of the graphics slowly up from zero towards the maximum of ten.

The images in the video immediately improved.

Almost incredibly a clear image started to appear in the doorway, and as the slide-bar advanced towards the ten, the image of the man became more and more defined.

At 'five' out of 'ten', RobinHood moved the mouse over the image of the man, clicked a few more buttons on the keyboard, and a dotted box appeared above the image. RobinHood grabbed hold of the edge of the box and dragged it around over the head and shoulders of the man. Rotating the wheel on the mouse, the man's head and shoulder grew bigger, the program zooming into that part of the image.

Advancing the slide-bar up again, the face of the man began to emerge clearly from the darkness.

As the slide-bar came to 'ten' out of 'ten', RobinHood played with the wireframe around his head once more, zoomed into the image again, and suddenly the face of the man, now clearly visible, filled the screen.

As with one voice, both RobinHood and Ray stared at the image before them, and then uttered the same, two words.

"Oh shit..."

Ray and RobinHood had both instantly recognised the man.

It was the face of Randolph Best, the Foreign Minister of Great Britain, one of the most famous and powerful men in Europe.

Chapter 12

London

October 1st

10.15 p.m.

When the phone rang, David picked it up immediately.
He'd been waiting for it to ring for the past hour.
Earlier on, when he had been out and about, knocking on people's doors, he'd left the mobile at home.
Stupidly, he'd forgotten to take it with him.
When he'd got home, he found that he already had one missed call.
There was no number associated with it.
But he knew who it had been from.

Today David wasn't scared.
He was angry.
Angry that whoever it was that was doing this, was playing him. Manipulating him. Toying with him.
He knew he should be scared, but for some reason today he wasn't.
His face and body ached, and the bruises were so bad that as people walked past him in the street outside, they stopped and stared at him. He could see people visibly recoil when he approached them.
David was also angry with himself. Why was he doing nothing about this? Why was he just complying and not fighting back?
He knew the answer to that question though. It was simple.
Chloe.
David was worried about Chloe.

"Hello?"
"David. Is your girlfriend with you? We know she's in the flat with you...we watched her go in. But is she with you *now*?"
"No. She's asleep..."
"Good. Open the front door."
"Downstairs?"
"No. The door to your flat."
"Why?"
"Open the bloody door. Now!"
David stared at the front door.
"*Now!*" the voice shouted one more time.

The bravery that David had felt earlier was rapidly disappearing.

Gingerly, he edged towards the door, keeping the phone pressed to his ear.

He flipped the chain off, slid the bolt and opened the door with his left hand.

There was no one there.

He looked down.

There was a black canvas bag on the floor.

"Put the bag over your head."

A tingle of fear pulsed through David's body.

"Why?"

"PUT the bag OVER your HEAD!" the voice said again, calmly. This time more quietly than before, the effect being to make David focus on his words and comply with them as directed.

"Turn around and face the door. Close the door behind you. And wait..."

"What for?"

"Do NOT speak again. Remain quiet. Just tell me when your door is closed."

Slowly David bent down and picked up the bag.

Every ounce of his being was telling him not to do this. Was this really happening? It was like some nightmarish scene from a horror film, and he was just going along with it.

The calm and bravado that he had felt before was gone now. In its place was a mounting terror that threatened to engulf him and drive him over the edge of reason.

He wanted to scream, to cry, to run... far, far, away... but he knew he couldn't. They would find him, catch him, kill him. He knew they would.

With trembling hands, he lifted the black bag up and pulled it over his head.

"Pull the cord tight..." the phone urged him, "... and tell me when the door is closed."

David stepped outside of the door and turned around.

"This is madness..." he said to himself in his head, too scared to say it aloud. "Madness..."

Reaching out with his hand, he found the edge of the door and pulled it towards himself.

It was pitch black inside the bag, his hot breath quickly heating the inside up. For a second, David wondered if he would be able to breathe, but then he realised the bag was porous and made out of cotton.

Breathing would not be a problem.

Slipping his fingers inside the edge of the letter box, he closed the door tightly, listening with dread as he heard the lock click home.

"The door is closed. What now?" he said to the voice on the phone.

"Now you wait. And I am going to come back upstairs to your flat and punish you. I need to hit you several times, hard, because you did not answer my questions fast enough. And I also have to cut off one of your fingers, so that in future you will try harder to find my money."

"My finger..?" David almost screamed aloud, reaching for the door, and giving it a push... but it was locked tightly shut.

"Shit..." he heard himself say loudly, his rapid pulse pounding in his ears and his body beginning to sweat. Down below, he could hear the heavy sound of footsteps rising up the stairwell as whoever the footsteps belonged to, came up the stairs two at a time.

"Fuck..." David said loudly.

"Don't go anywhere, David. Stay where you are. If you go inside the flat, we'll come inside and punish Chloe too. Do you understand? Wait where you are. Take your punishment like a man!"

On the edge of tears, David finally lost control of himself and for the third time in a week, he wet himself.

He felt the growing damp patch on his legs and smelt the urine, and for a few moments - all it took for one of the thugs to make it back up the stairs - he was distracted.

He felt a rough hand suddenly grab him from behind and propel him sideways against the wall so hard the air was forcibly expelled from his chest.

Two hands on his shoulders were pushing him down to a kneeling position on the floor.

"Put out your hand!" the voice commanded.

David's hands tightened into two firm balls.

"Question. Did you hear me?"

"Yes!" he shouted back quickly, and then slowly extended his left hand.

He felt someone grasp his fingers and screamed out of shock.

"NO!" he screamed. "Please... don't do it! I promise you, I'll find it tomorrow. Honestly, I will!"

"It's too late for that, David. I'm very disappointed with you. You've been very lazy. And I'm running out of time."

David felt the man tugging on his clenched fist, forcibly trying to extract the fingers.

"I'll give another twenty thousand pounds back... with the original twenty thousand. I'll give you twice as much... just please leave me alone. Don't kill me!" he pleaded.

"But we're not going to kill you David. We already told you that. We're just wanting a finger as a mark of good faith from you. Is that alright?" Question.

"No... *NO!*... Please..."

"Can I have the finger?"

"NO..."

"This is the last time I'm going to ask nicely, David. Extend your fingers and let me take a finger. No... actually, you must now ASK me to take a finger. Or I'll force you to ask me and I will then cut off two! Do you hear me?"

Question.

"Yes... I hear you... but please, NOT two fingers... One... just take one."

"Like I said, say 'please'?"

David hesitated, considering for a few fleeting seconds that he should stand up and simply jump over the banister onto the cold concrete below. It would be almost certain death. Instantaneous.

A word began to formulate itself at the back of David's throat. It tried to come out by itself several times, but David ended up choking and coughing.

"What was that? What did you say?" the voice asked.

"Please... Please FUCKING *please*... I said, *please* take my finger!"

"Thank you David. I thought you would never ask. It's certainly very nice of you to offer... and I think it would be simply rude to turn you down... so..."

David had never ever felt pain like it before. It started with a rough, pushing sensation on his left pinkie, a building up of pressure that lasted what could only have been a second.

Then there was the sound of a metallic click, accompanied seconds later by a stab of pain that went straight through him, on and on...

He screamed, felt himself falling, and felt a dull thud against his forehead as his head collided with the concrete floor.

After that the world went silent.

10.30 p.m.

Several doors away, just a bit up the street, Emma bundled the last of her stuff into her car, stepped inside and closed the door behind her.

Tears were running down her face, and she felt empty.

She had been dreading coming over to collect the rest of her belongings.

Part of her had been scared of seeing Ray again. She didn't know how she would react when she saw him. She missed him. More than she had expected to. There were questions in her mind that needed answers, and she had hoped that maybe, when she saw Ray, he would have helped her to find some of those answers.

She had deliberately left it until the evening to come over, hoping that Ray would be there. All day long she had been arguing with herself that the easiest thing to do would be to wait until he was definitely out and at work, and let herself into the flat then: no Ray, no confrontation, no conflicting emotions.

Absolutely no chance of him smiling at her, and her falling into his arms.

No possibility of a hug, a kiss, and all her resolve being swept away. But she had lost the argument.

The other part of her was much stronger.

Canada was beckoning. She had spent most of the day at the Passport Office getting a new passport, then sorting out some paperwork at the Canadian Embassy.

Everything was falling neatly into place.

Yesterday she had spoken with her new employer on the phone. They had called her. They wanted her.

In Canada, she had a bright future.

Yet, in London, she had Ray. Or used to.

He had stopped texting. He wasn't home. She hadn't heard a word from him in days.

Had he moved on?

She had begun to replay the last few months over and over again in her mind. Of course, she knew she was still right to have ended the relationship with him.

It was, at the time, the right thing to do.

But was it right now?

Words had been said. Actions had been taken. New emotions and realisations and thoughts and feelings had all surfaced since Saturday afternoon.

A year of feelings concentrated down into a few days.

There was so much that she could talk to Ray about...except she couldn't, could she?

The truth was, she missed him. It felt like her right arm had been cut off. Part of her was missing.

Of course, she knew she would grow used to being without him again. She had existed fine without him before, and she would exist just fine without him in the future.

Canada would take all thoughts of him away.

The finality of it all, however, was beginning to scare her.

Splitting up, moving to Canada... there would never be any chance for reconciliation.

On top of that, she felt guilty. Ray knew nothing about her plans.

If he still had any feelings for her, he would be devastated when he found out what she was about to do.

When she had arrived at the flat at 7 p.m., that part of her which she had allowed to confuse her into coming here tonight was actually excited. Excited about seeing Ray again.

Discovering that he was not there had been an incredible anti-climax.

After gathering her things together, she had tried to find reasons why she should hang around, waiting for him.

She had made coffee. Read a magazine. Tidied the kitchen. Watched some television.

The longer she waited, the more nervous she got.

Where was he?

At 10.24 p.m. she began to get scared that he would walk through the door with another woman on his arm. Laughing. Happy.

She imagined the shock on his face...the disappointment as he saw her.

That had been too much.

Wiping the tears from her eyes, she had looked around the flat one more time, switched off the lights, and closed the door.

Slowly she had walked down the stairs.

As she walked across to her car from the steps to the grand frontage of their - *Ray's* - building, a tall man in black clothing had rushed past her, not seeing her and banging into her.

For a second their eyes had met, and she had felt a tingle travel down her spine.

It had been a little weird.

The man never apologised, but hurried past her, jumping into a white van further down the road and speeding off.

For those brief few seconds her thoughts had been distracted.

She looked at her watch.

10.30 p.m. and still no sign of Ray.

Climbing into the car, she wound the window down and looked back up at the third floor of the building.

Once, she had thought, Ray's flat could have become her home.

Things could have been so different.

The problem was, Ray had never asked her. Obviously she and he had always had different plans.

And where was he now?

Out drinking? Celebrating? Forgetting her already?

Emma turned the key in the ignition, signalled, looked over her shoulder and drove off.

In just over a week, she would be on the other side of the world.

Leading a new life.

The future was so bright she would have to buy a pair of sunglasses.

In spite of that, just as her car turned the corner out of the road, she couldn't help but look back down the street - hoping - checking, that Ray hadn't just come home and it was not too late to see him...

Chapter 13

London

October 1st

10.45 p.m.

Ray paid the taxi driver, climbed out of the cab, and hurried up the steps, unlocking the door to the communal stairwell, and hurrying inside.

He rushed up the stairs, wanting to get into his flat and lock the door safely behind him as soon as possible.

His mind was awash with thoughts and emotions.

Today had started off weird and got progressively worse.

Within the space of twenty-four hours he had found himself the key witness in a murder that had such profound implications it scared him just to think about it.

But think about it he must, and would.

In fact, practically nothing could stop him from doing so.

The events of the evening at RobinHood's were like a piece of film that went round and round in his head.

After they had seen the image materialise on the computer, as the programme had finished cleaning and rebuilding all the pixels, it had rendered an almost crystal clear photograph of one of the most famous and powerful men in the world.

Randolph Best, the Foreign Minister of Great Britain, was unlike most other politicians. He commanded respect from all quarters, and all parties. Even anarchists like Ray had been forced to offer the man respect. He was the public face of his party and was an internationally respected politician and statesman, who travelled the world fighting for '*good and justice and defending the British way of life*,' as he was famously known for saying.

He was no coward.

As a young man it was reported that he had been a commander in the British SAS, and had won several citations for bravery for actions taken in Afghanistan.

There was no doubt that he stood up for his principles and fought hard for what he believed.

It was Randolph Best who had persuaded the British people to send troops to start defending the Egyptians from the onslaught of ISIS troops, after they had taken over most of Iraq and Syria and destabilised the Middle East.

The British - all cultures, religions, and walks of life - loved Randolph Best.

In recent months he had become increasingly involved in trying to find a way to bring peace to the Middle East and was personally championing several peace plans.

He was a good man.

Or so the rest of the public had reason to believe until tonight.

Over the past few years, Ray had become less and less of an anarchist, and more and more of a normal working man, thanks in part to the example that dear old Randolph Best had portrayed.

Not all politicians were bad.

And justice in Britain, so it seemed, had once again begun to return. On the streets of the UK, there had been fewer anti-police riots. The corruption that had seen the last government swept out of power had been dealt with, and Randolph was seemingly the herald of a new brand of statesman.

A statesman that even anarchists could trust.

"SHIT!" Ray had shouted aloud, a few moments after the shock had begun to wear off.

For a few minutes both Ray and RobinHood had simply sat in silence, staring at the screen in disbelief.

Both knew the implications of what they had seen.

"That bastard is just the same as all the rest. He's a liar, just like the others!"

RobinHood stood up and started to pace the room.

"I never liked the man. Never trusted him. Never did. They're all the same. All politicians are the same. They're all criminals. Every last man... and woman of them!"

"Shit!" Ray shouted again. "No wonder there's been a cover up. No fucking wonder!"

"Well, what do you expect?" RobinHood said loudly, standing behind his chair and facing Ray, gesticulating wildly into the air. "He's just another bloody Oxford boy, one of the fucking elite few that has always had everything handed to them on a silver platter, and who now spends every day screwing the great British public as if it's his God given right!"

"You know what happened, don't you?" Ray said, pointing at the face of Randolph Best on the screen. "He murdered that woman, called his Security Service in and they arranged the whole thing. They covered it all up. Made it look like a street murder by a druggie, fixed the coroner's report, and no doubt made sure that Mr Fucking Best has an alibi on the other side of the world somewhere."

"I hate the bastards. It's one law for them, and another law for the rest of us." RobinHood declared. "Always has been, and always will be. Unless we do something about it. Which we are going to... soon... and then we'll start to get our own back. You know, it's not too late, SolarWind. You should take this as a warning, a reality check, and come back and get active with us again. Once an anarchist, always an anarchist. We need you SolarWind. And we could do with your help pretty soon... We've got big plans!"

Ray looked at RobinHood. What was he talking about? What was he planning?

"SHIT!" RobinHood suddenly said, "If the spooks who work for the government have covered up the murder of the woman, then that means that Randolph has the backing of the Security Service or some other government agency..."

"Obviously... it's what you would expect... I just said that. He's the bloody Foreign Minister. Of course, he's going to have the MI5 and MI6 behind him. Protecting him."

"So how sure are you that no one knows that you were watching him? When the clean-up team walk into the room to recover the body, they'll see the TV and the camera lying on the floor, and given all this shit recently in the press about Russian hackers taking over our CCTV cameras, they'll be checking to see if anyone had hacked..."

"Calm down...think rationally. All the sessions on the servers would have been cleared long before anyone would have looked at any network connections, and I was surfing using the Ghost browser. It's secure...even if they could find any servers that might still have had records of any packets going back and forward from my broadband modem, Ghost would prevent them from ever discovering that I was at the other end of any of the sessions. And even if they did, they would never be able to get through my layered defences and find out it was me. There's no way. And you know that. So stop worrying!"

RobinHood nodded.

"And you definitely used Ghost, right? You weren't drunk and forgot to use the Ghost browser?"

Ray laughed.

"I NEVER do that. Don't be stupid. It's my 'First Protocol': don't drink and hack! Do you think I want to get arrested and deported?"

"Fine. Because we're both in this now..."

"No we're not. I'm in it, whatever this is... but you're not. It's only me. You're in the clear. This..." Ray said, waving his hand around the room, and at RobinHood, "never happened. You've got nothing to do with me."

RobinHood looked at Ray, not saying anything for a moment. Ray knew that he was thinking. Finally, he nodded.

"Okay. Good. If that's what you want, that's fine. You're on your own. Thanks."

Ray nodded and sat down again.

"Have you got another drink? Something harder?"

RobinHood nodded. "Whisky? I know I could do with one."

"Make it a double..."

"Come with me then... we'll go upstairs."

They left the room, and after RobinHood locked the door and the electronic lock audibly reset, Ray followed him upstairs.

They ended up in a large room lined with bookcases filled with thousands of books, reclining on two large leather sofas.

RobinHood picked up a remote, pressed a few buttons, and a gas fire embedded in one of the walls roared into life.

"Ice?" RobinHood asked, before nipping out of the room for a few moments and returning with two glasses of whisky.

"It's thirty-seven year old Glen Doig. You'd better love it." he said, handing a whisky tumbler to Ray. "It's probably the best whisky you'll ever drink... and also the most expensive."

Ray stared at the glass and the amber liquid within, not really paying attention to RobinHood's words.

"What do I do?" he asked, quietly.

"What do you mean?"

"I mean, what the fuck do I do now?"

"What do you *want* to do?" RobinHood asked.

"I don't know. Not yet. But I know I can't just let the bastard get away with it. Just because he's a politician... NO, I mean, BECAUSE he's a politician, he has to be held accountable. The government and everyone who's covered this up have to be held accountable. This is a cover up on a massive scale. It could bring the government down. No, actually, it *should* bring the government down. And since only I know the truth, I've got to do something."

RobinHood settled back on the sofa and laughed gently.

"That's more like it. But *what* are you going to do?"

"I don't know. What can I do?"

RobinHood laughed louder.

"You're SolarWind." he replied. "*You* can do *anything*!"

At the top of the stairs, Ray fumbled with his key, still nervous and thinking about the conspiracy he had uncovered.

Turning the key in the lock and opening the door to his flat, the smell of Emma's perfume wafted out of the hall and hit him immediately.

Randolph Best was quickly forgotten and adrenaline surged into Ray's veins.

"Emma?" Ray shouted, stepping through the doorway and hastily closing it behind him. "Are you here?"

Silence.

Kicking off his shoes, he hurried into the lounge, hoping to see her curled up on the sofa. Had she come back to him? Were things going to be okay after all?

For the past few days Ray had consciously tried to bury each and every thought that he'd had of her. To think of her was to hurt, to feel an emptiness and pain the like of which he had never felt before and which he couldn't endure. Perhaps now he wouldn't have to endure it anymore.

If she had come back to him, he would never do anything stupid again... From now on, he would be a changed man! The *perfect* man! He would tell her how much he loved her, how he couldn't live without her, how the past few days had been like hell...

The sofa was empty.

Her perfume was even stronger now though. She must still be here.

Hurrying through to the bedroom, he found it empty. As was the kitchen, the bathroom, and his den.

She was gone.

She *had* been here though, definitely. But she was not there now.

Collapsing on the sofa, Ray noticed the note on the coffee table: a sticky from his telephone pad. Reaching across and picking it up, his heart sunk.

"Ray, I came to pick up my things. I've left my key in the kitchen drawer. I'm sorry for everything. Emma."

Ray swallowed hard, his heart pounding in his chest, a feeling of despair engulfing him and threatening to suffocate him.

At first the tears came one at a time, but quite quickly they became a torrent that flowed and flowed.

Ray never tried to stop them.

He knew now that Emma wasn't coming home.

It was really over.

Chapter 14

London

October 1st

10.46 p.m.

David started to scream, even before he opened his eyes. The pain was like nothing that he had ever experienced before, a degree of pain that he could not have imagined was possible, even in his wildest and darkest imaginings.

Sitting up and fumbling with his right hand, he pulled violently at the hood that covered his head.

Still screaming, the pain more than he could bear, he began to panic. The hood was not coming free, the cord pulled tightly around his throat and was not loosing itself as he tugged at the bag.

Suddenly he felt two hands upon him again, and instantly he tensed. The man had come back for more of his fingers.

"No, NO!" he shouted loudly. "Leave me alone... Please!"

"David," Chloe's voice answered..."It's me..." and almost simultaneously he felt her fingers loosen the cord around his neck and the bag was pulled off.

The moment he emerged from the blackness, he started to gasp for breath and blink in the brightness of the stair lights. As he gulped the cool air in the stairwell, his senses came alive again, and another wave of pain washed over him.

"Help me!" David screamed, "Quick... get a bandage, or something..." he shouted, lifting his hand up in front of his face and seeing for the first time the space where his little finger used to be.

Simultaneously Chloe saw it for the first time and screamed aloud too, drawing in a sharp intake of breath and raising both her hands to cover her mouth.

"What... What HAPPENED?" she asked in disbelief. "Where's your finger? Who did this to you?"

David tried to stand up but slipped on the pool of blood on the concrete step and fell forward, stumbling against the wall. Slipping back down the wall to the floor, he tried to catch some breath. To calm down. He was feeling light headed.

Chloe was crying now, standing in the doorway and staring at his hand. As he looked up at her, he saw the fear in her eyes.

David breathed in deeply and forcibly tried to get a grip of himself.

Turning his attention back to his hand, he saw more objectively this time that his finger had been sliced off just above the knuckle. The blood was congealing now, and a plug was forming around the wound.

For a moment he stared at it, trying to control his thoughts and his breathing.

He felt Chloe's hot breath on the side of his cheeks. She was kneeling down beside him.

"Who did this to you David? *Who?*" she asked gently, between her tears. "The same people that beat you up?"

David took another deep breath. He had to get a grip.

"Chloe... please, do as I say... get a tea towel and some ice or frozen peas. Please..."

Chloe nodded, resting her hand gently on his shoulder. Sobbing, she stood up and took a step backwards towards her open door.

"... and your car keys! Don't forget your car keys!" he shouted after her as she backed through the door to their flat. "And put some clothes on... I need you to take me to hospital."

In spite of the pain, slowly David found himself beginning to think. Pulling his eyes away from his wounded hand, he started to scan the floor around him.

"My finger..." he said aloud to himself. "Where is my finger?"

It was nowhere to be seen.

Holding his elbow with his right arm and supporting his arm, keeping it high in the air with his hand pointing upwards, David stepped gingerly down the top flight of stairs scanning the steps below for his finger.

Nothing.

Peering over the banister down the stairwell, he looked to see if it had fallen down to the ground floor, but he couldn't see anything down there apart from the dark tiled flooring.

Turning around he stepped gingerly back up to his flat.

The blood had spilled down the steps, forming dark red pools which were slowly drying up and forming sticky, solid masses.

The blood on the floor outside his door was now almost all congealed, and the soles of his feet were sticky with his own blood.

Each time he took a small step upwards, he could feel it sticking him down, sucking gently at his feet, and making a squelching sound as he moved.

Glancing around him at the blood covering the ground, he felt suddenly weak and nauseous.

Stepping quickly to the banister, he vomited noisily down into the void of the stairwell.

Chloe sat beside David in the ambulance, holding his arm and resting her head against his shoulder.

She had run into their apartment, grabbed some peas and ice and then taken them back to David, wrapping them in a thin tea-towel and surrounding his hand with it.

Then she had hurried back inside, called an ambulance and got dressed.

She was in no fit state to drive, and she was worried about how much blood David had already lost.

"What the hell is going on?" she had screamed aloud in the lounge, away from David. Taking some deep breaths, she had grabbed some spare clothes for David and his pyjamas, and then hurried back to be with her man.

The ambulance had arrived a few minutes later. She buzzed them in and the paramedics rushed up the stairs, taking over and asserting order where there had been none.

They had immediately hooked David up to a saline drip, done some checks and given him an injection, and then rushed them both downstairs.

With the siren blaring and the lights flashing, they had hurried through the streets of London.

"What happened? Who did this?" Chloe asked one more time, softly, gently.

David did not reply.

11.00 p.m.

Ray picked up the bottle of whisky and examined the golden liquid at the bottom. He had drunk almost a quarter of a bottle. Not enough to make him drunk but certainly enough to make him feel a little better.

Emma was gone. Gone. Gone. Bloody GONE!

She wasn't coming back, and he certainly was not going to call her again.

What sort of coward was she that she had to sneak round when he was out, to collect the rest of her stuff? Could she not face him?

Why not?

It dawned on him then. Something new that until that point he had not considered.

She was seeing someone new.

She'd met someone else.

The reason Emma had split up with him, after all this time, was because she was fucking someone else.

It hurt like hell to think those thoughts, but deep down, it all made sense.

Ray was an idiot.
All that time he had been planning to spend the rest of his life with her, she had been planning to spend it with another man!

There were a few more beers in the fridge that Ray had brought home with him. Time to fetch one.
Or two.

There was nothing on the television tonight, at least nothing new that he hadn't seen before. He thought briefly about playing a game on his Xbox, then decided not to.
He was too angry to concentrate.
Fuck.
He thought of Emma again and how she had made a fool of him, and his temper flared.
He cursed himself.
He'd become weak. Fallen in love. Let someone else take over his mind and control his thoughts.
Ray hated giving up control. He hated being weak. He loathed anyone having authority over him.
Bastards.
If it wasn't women... it was the fucking government.
Telling people what to do... making laws... forcing people to do things they didn't want to.
Controlling them.
Herding them like cattle.
Taking away their rights.

Bastards.
Fucking, fucking bastards.

His mind turned towards Randolph Best. Another bastard in whom he'd begun to put his trust. In whom LOTS of people had put their trust.
A man who had spat in the face of the great British public... those who had supported him and believed in him.
RobinHood was right.
It was time to bring the fuckers down.
To show those bastards that they couldn't screw people over whenever they wanted to.

Ray stood up, reaching momentarily for support from the side of the sofa, but after steadying himself, moving slowly but surely through to his den, carrying another two beers and his almost empty bottle.

Like some people who can actually drive better after a few beers, Ray could surf the net and hack faster when he was drunk, than when he was sober.

If he wanted to.

If he chose to break the cardinal rule.

"*Don't drink and hack*!"

But as he sat down at his terminal, switched everything on and logged on to his secure networks, he thought once more about the beautiful woman that Randolph *Fucking* Best had murdered in cold blood and he knew exactly what he was going to do.

He'd got a plan.

And it was cool, because he wasn't going to hack.

He wasn't going to break the cardinal rule.

He was just going to have a little fun.

First things first though.

He needed an email address.

He needed the personal email address of Randolph F. Best.

Actually, for someone like Ray, finding something like that wasn't particularly hard.

Several years ago Ray has scripted a few lines of code that searched the net and found any records of a name associated with an email address. At the time he'd written it, he'd just wanted to track down an old school friend to get back in touch, but since then it had proved immensely useful.

He'd actually thought about selling it and letting the rest of the world use it, but then he'd realised that it was one of several tools which he had that made him stand out from others, cyber tools which made other hackers look up to him, and wonder what special weapons he had in his cyber kit bag: 'How the hell did he do *that*?'

The script dug deep into the public records, social media, and media files that anyone could find out there in the web, if you cared to look and had the inkling to do so. Most people couldn't write code like he could, though, so it would take them ages, but his program - *Hound* - would run in the background while he did something else, automatically searching the web and sniffing for what it could find.

The great thing was that Hound always found something.

And bloody quickly too.

With GHOST and Hound running together, Ray typed in the name of Randolph Best, pressed RETURN and then opened a new beer.

While he waited for a little picture of a dog to appear on his screen and start to wag and then point his tail - one of the worst animations he'd ever done - he sat back and watched the video of the murder on the other screen for the millionth time.

His anger flared again.

BASTARD.

Feeling a wave of alcohol hit his head, he blinked several times, and scrunched up his eyes to clear his vision.

Ray laughed.

"Shit... I'm getting drunk!" he said aloud.

Just then a hound appeared on his other screen and began to bark.

Ray turned away from the murder video and clicked on the hound's head.

Another screen appeared, and a list of emails, telephone numbers, addresses and contact details began to populate the screen, along with snippets of text which provided the context of where they had been found.

Ray started to scan them.

One by one.

The twenty-third entry on the list jumped right out at him.

It was a record from the Junior Common Room at Hertford College at Oxford. It had something to do with a 'Gaudy' that Randolph Best had attended... going back to his old college for a free meal and to give a speech and encourage other students on the path to greatness...

Something for the wealthy. A way of bonding and teaching other people in the rich and privileged club the secrets of how to keep the poor down and under the foot.

Bastards.

According to the snippet which had been recorded and then digitised later and stored in the college records, Randolph Best had invited the other students to email him with any questions or thoughts.

To all intents and purposes it looked like a personal email address, given out about two years before he'd got his first senior Cabinet position.

Bingo.

It was exactly what Ray had been looking for.

Ray knew that the chances were that the email address was still valid. Still real. Still an email address that Randolph F. Best would use to communicate with his inner sanctum: his friends, relatives and close colleagues.

Downing the rest of the beer, the adrenaline pumping through his veins, Ray blinked a few more times to clear the alcohol from his now fuzzy brain.

Smiling to himself, Ray used GHOST to open up a new fictitious Brazilian Outlook account. It took a few minutes to get it up and running, but once he had done it, he sat back and thought very briefly about what he was going to do.

Ray smiled.

After typing in the email address of Randolph F. Best, he focussed on the message he was going to send to the bastard.

Blinking, then taking another swig of his beer, he focussed his eyes on the screen.

The words were blurring a little, but his anger wasn't.

"Fucker. Bastard... *MURDERER!*" Ray swore aloud, putting the bottle of beer back onto the table too forcibly and watching as it bounced, fell over and then rolled off the table onto the carpet.

"Fuck..." Ray swore again. "I'm fucking drunk..."

The cursor on the screen blinked at him. Beckoning at him. Egging him on.

Ray's fingers crawled along the keyboard, typing in a message into the field where you put the title of the email.

He wrote two words:

"I spy..."

And then in the space where the message body went, he wrote.

"... I *SAW* her cry."

Ray smiled to himself. It was a simple message, but one that would get the point across.

"I spy, I *SAW* her cry."

He laughed, hit SEND, and then immediately began to feel a lot better.

He was going to show that fucker you couldn't play with people like him.

Ray had a plan.

He was going to make Randolph F. Best pay for what he'd done. But first he was going to play with him. He was going to make him sweat...

Chapter 15

London

October 1st

11.38 p.m.

RobinHood stood in front of the mirror and surveyed the pathetic individual that he had become.

Slowly, as each day passed, and as the grams turned to kilograms and the fat continued to accumulate on top of his 'one-pack', RobinHood loathed himself more and more.

He detested the way he looked.

He had never been a handsome man, and now things were just going from bad to worse.

As a child he had looked a little odd. Not terrible, but enough for the other kids to bully him for several years. Until one day he'd had enough and discovered that he could hit the other kids harder than they could hit him.

For the rest of his school days, he'd been one of the popular boys. Extremely clever, the teachers had been frustrated that he was wasting his talents and had tried to rein him in. They had encouraged him as best they could to make the best of himself and not to hang around with the other losers in the school. Their attention had two effects: first, he had rebelled and started to develop a hatred of others trying to impose authority on top of him. What right did they have to tell him what to do? Secondly, he had become angry.

Subconsciously though, he must have heard their voices and understood what they had tried to say to him, because in the last few years of school his anger had taken the form of deliberately trying to frustrate them even further by ignoring their teaching in school, but learning everything he could at home, studying hard and passing every exam with straight 'A's: "*See what I can do? By myself! I don't need you telling me what to do!*"

His favourite subjects were Maths, Physics and IT. IT especially.

One day he realised that he knew more than his teachers did about computers, and the feeling that he was better and cleverer than the authorities above him spurred him on to even greater heights.

About that time he also realised that computers were beginning to take over the world. They were everywhere you looked. Doing everything. Ruling everything.

For once the underdog had an opportunity to be free!

He had begun to really enjoy playing with them, writing code, developing his own software programs and exploring the power which mastery of IT and understanding computer networks could give him.

But being able to surf the web, explore virtual worlds and have fun was slowly being destroyed by the cancer of 'passwords' and 'logons' which attempted to limit you and prevent you from going places you wanted to.

RobinHood reacted by going all out to stay one step ahead of anyone who would attempt to try to throw up barriers and fences and hem him in.

Absorbing any book or magazine he could get his hands on and joining one computer club after another, RobinHood quickly learned everything there was to learn about computing, networking and IT security. And how to get around it.

He wasn't the best hacker in the world, but it wasn't until his second year at university studying computer science that he started to meet others who were better than him.

The internet gave him access not only to an vast number of networks to hack into and play with, but also to an incredible community of fellow hackers who also loved to break into networks, do a little damage just to show that they had been there, and then leave without getting caught.

The world of hacking expanded his horizons not just virtually, but also in real life: he began to travel the world, attending 'Black Hat' and cyber hacking conferences and meeting other like minded people who like him, could think of no other better way of sticking a finger up at authority than by hacking into their network and screwing it up.

RobinHood became a respected member of the hacking community, and he loved the way others looked up to him and held him in such high regard. It became a vicious circle to which he became addicted.

Being good at hacking made himself feel good and earned him respect, so he studied harder at it, got better, got more respect and enjoyed it even more. So he studied it harder...and got better...

It was at university that he had met SolarWind, one of the best hackers in the world. Soon they became friends, or at least RobinHood hoped that's what they were. They didn't see much of each other, but RobinHood had taken it as a good sign when it was him that SolarWind had turned to in his time of need.

In his third year at university, RobinHood had joined the 'Three-Ists Club', whose members all shared three main beliefs: they were all atheists, anarchists and hedonists. For years RobinHood had lived by the mantra:

'Live for today, don't worry about tomorrow, and don't think that there is any reason for your existence apart from one: to have as much fun as possible!'

Sadly, for RobinHood that mantra had now become slightly ironic, or perhaps even more meaningful, and the word 'tomorrow' was becoming more dubious and poignant as every day slipped by.

Hacking and anarchy had become a way of life for RobinHood. Thanks to his blatant disregard for all forms of authority, he felt no concerns whatsoever about hacking into networks and seeing what damage he could do. As far as he was concerned, all networks were fair game. If the IT managers were stupid enough not to have decent security in place, then it was his moral duty to teach them a lesson they would not forget.

It was also during his third year at university that he had earned the nickname RobinHood. It happened just after he had learned one of his greatest lessons in life.

Hacking wasn't just fun, it could be extremely lucrative.

RobinHood had just spent the previous summer working in a bank, trying to earn some extra cash to help put him through the next year.
He'd learned how to create accounts, transfer money, withdraw money...all the basic stuff that normal bank tellers would do.
Whilst there he had taken a particular interest in the systems and applications that the bank used in its everyday operations.
He had made notes.
Studied how everything worked. Learned the processes and workflows.

A few months later, several months into the academic year, and money running out fast, RobinHood had decided that things had to change.
He couldn't stand being poor any longer.
He couldn't stand sharing a flat with other poor people - his friends and fellow members of the Three-Ists club.

RobinHood also felt anger that the banks had so much money, and was enraged when he learned how much money they were paying their top employees in terms of bonuses.
Bastards!
The banks were part of the system, part of everything that was wrong about society. It was his moral duty to do something about it.

So, one Monday morning, about the time that banking activity would be at its peak for the day, RobinHood hacked into the headquarters of the bank he had been working in the year before, created a few new fictitious accounts for himself and all his friends and flatmates, and filled them up with money. He knew exactly what to do, and he did it.

He also knew that the risk of him being caught was minimal. Using his expert knowledge, he'd done everything according to the book. Committed the perfect cyber crime.

A few days later bank cards and pin numbers arrived at his friends' houses, and following strict instructions they had gone out and withdrawn all the money from friendly ATMs. The next day RobinHood filled their accounts up again, and later that day they had emptied their accounts again.

They'd done the same thing every day for a week.

At the end of that time, RobinHood had hacked back into the bank and deleted all records of the accounts.

Along with any records that the accounts had existed in the first place.

And any audit trail that could possibly exist.

In a single week RobinHood had stolen over £15,000 from the rich bank and redistributed it to the poor and very needy.

Hence his nickname which had been so aptly given and so well deserved.

Of course, RobinHood was no fool. Cyber enabled bank robbery was not something that could or should be repeated too often, lest it be accidentally detected. So, being smart, he restricted and controlled his crimes, only taking what he and his friends needed, and when they needed it, which roughly equated to the beginning of each university term. Careful only to transfer small amounts in and out of their accounts at any one time, and never anything over £2,500, by the time university was finished, their bank loans had been paid off - with the bank's own money - and they could each afford to take a long, well earned gap year off.

All financed and paid for by RobinHood.

Of course, being out of the country for a year had probably been a prudent thing to do, but when he came back nothing had changed, and there were no police waiting to arrest him.

So ever since, RobinHood had continued with his altruistic views, creating wealth and redistributing it to himself and his friends as needed.

For a while he had been a very popular man indeed.

Eventually though, as network security became tighter, hacking had become tougher and the risk of getting caught greater.

So RobinHood had stopped supplying his friends with cash on demand.

That wasn't to say that he had stopped lining his own bank accounts though.

On the contrary, like any drug, he was addicted to the adrenaline and buzz of getting away with it, and for many years the amount of money he had stolen had increased from month to month.

The more he had got away with it, the more he had taken.

It was incredible.
No one seemed capable of spotting what he was doing.
The bank was like his very own private bank account, a bottomless pit of money that was at his own personal disposal whenever he wanted it.
So RobinHood took more and more.
And more.
And then some more too.

Eventually he had so much that it had begun to lose its meaning, and the buzz had gone away.
So he stopped.
Curiously, the fact that he had actually got away with it made him even more angry at the banks than he was before.
Now he positively hated them.
How could they be so careless with other people's money?

Anger management had never been something that RobinHood had been particularly good at.
The only way that he managed to calm down was by cycling. Getting out on his bike and cycling for hours on end. Ever since he was sixteen he'd been crazy about cycling. He'd loved it.
It kept him fit, helped compensate for the hours he spent on his computer, and regularly got him out of the house.
Thanks to his cycling he could eat and drink whatever he wanted and he never really put on weight.

Two years ago, though, his world had changed, for the first time.
On a wet, rainy day, he had taken a corner too fast and his bicycle had lost traction on some wet leaves...

After coming off his bike at speed, sliding across the road, and banging into the wall against his back, he'd spent a week in hospital, only managing to leave with two walking sticks to support him.
It was weeks before he could walk properly again. But he got better one step at a time. Literally.
For months his back would go into spasm, almost at will. Wave after wave of the most intense pain would wash over him, pain the like of which you could never imagine and which RobinHood would not even wish upon his worst enemy, authorities or even bankers.
At night time he would wake up, desperate to go to the toilet, but knowing that as soon as he tried to move, as soon as he tried to rise from the bed, his back would go into one spasm after another.
And the pain...

The worst thing of all was that the doctors could do nothing for him. Nothing.

"There's nothing we can do for you!" they parroted. One after another.

"Just take painkillers, and hopefully it will go away."

Luckily it did.

For weeks though the only comfort he got was from sitting at his computer filling up newly created bank accounts, an old habit which had resurfaced.

For every muscle spasm, he rewarded himself with £1,000.

By the time the spasms had finally subsided he had another £75,000 in various accounts, just waiting for him to go out and empty them.

His life during that time was full of anger, an anger that got worse day by day.

Why had this happened to him?

Anger at the doctors for not being able to help him get better.

Fury at the government who had taken funding away from the NHS.

Rage at the bankers. For no apparent new reason, but because with so much anger, he had to be angry at someone.

For months his house had become his only world, his office and his computers where he spent most hours of his day: it took him so long to hobble down the steps to get to his den in the basement that once there he didn't leave unless he had to.

The floors of the church slowly became littered with debris: pieces of rubbish, scraps of food, letters, papers... and anything else that fell on the floor and which he could no longer bend down to pick up; the floor and anything beneath his waist had become another world. If something went there, he couldn't go after it. For months he had lived surrounded by the off spill from his life. It sickened him. Quite literally.

The other main comfort he enjoyed was food.

Lots of it.

For months on end he couldn't cook because the pots and pans were too heavy to carry or lift up, so instead he ordered food in. Junk food. Every day. Masses of it. Tons of it.

Food which quickly began to accumulate on his stomach. Growing. Expanding. Burying his waist and the remnants of any youthful figure that he had managed to keep.

With no exercise, the weight piled on.

RobinHood got angrier.

And angrier.

Someone had to pay.

Someone would pay.

But who?
The answer wasn't long in coming.
Two words.
The bankers.

And then, just when his back was returning to normal, and when he started to make plans to improve his life, a regular check-up with the doctor one Tuesday afternoon turned his life upside down. Forever.

How could this be?
Why him?
Surely the doctor was wrong!

But the doctor wasn't wrong, and RobinHood knew it.
The word cancer swum around and around in his brain, and RobinHood began to drown in fear, and anger.

Life didn't seem fair.
And it wasn't.
Life had never been fair to RobinHood.
Never.

Now living in a world of his own, RobinHood's anger at life morphed to fury, and then to incandescent rage. It boiled away within him, growing, expanding, getting ready to erupt. Then one day RobinHood woke up and decided that enough was enough. If he wasn't going to be allowed to live, then why should anyone else?

His plans changed. Now it wasn't just the bankers who were going to suffer, it was going to be everyone else in London too!

Chapter 16

London

Wednesday

October 2nd

06.10 a.m.

Chloe's head was buried underneath her pillow, trying to quieten her sobs so as not to wake David up.

They hadn't got back from the hospital until five a.m.

The whole time she had not been able get a word out of him.

The doctors had treated his hand, stitching it up and giving him several more injections before sending him home.

Perhaps if he had managed to find and bring the other part of his finger with him they could have sewn it back on.

David knew that the doctors didn't believe his excuse that he had cut his finger off accidentally with a knife in his garage.

If he had, where was the finger?

They had wanted to call the police, suspecting there was something more to it, but David had sworn there was not, eventually managing to talk them out of it.

"Go home and rest," the doctor had finally agreed, "... and take the full course of these antibiotics."

Chloe was no fool. There was something deeply wrong. Something terribly wrong. Yet, she knew there was no point in pushing him if he didn't want to speak. Instead, she hugged him, kissed him, cuddled him. Held his hand. Helped him get home.

Got him into bed and cuddled into him until he had fallen asleep.

Then she had turned over and started to cry.

Chloe had never been more scared in all her life.

When the alarm clock went off at 6.55 a.m. she stopped crying. She dried her tears on the edge of her pillow and was just about to sneak out of the bed when David spoke.

"Pack a bag. A small one, just a few clothes... and a different coat. Enough to change into when you get to work. And take one of your party wigs. The one with the long black extensions."

"Why?" Chloe asked, turning around and looking deep into his eyes.

"I want you to go to work as normal," he started, his voice monotone and matter of fact. "Take the bag with you... hide it under your coat... and then at about eleven o'clock slip into the bathroom, change and then leave the building. Just walk out of the front door."

"Why?" she asked again, softly.

"Walk to the tube station, get on a tube, change at the next station and then go to Paddington. Catch a train to Bristol and go stay with your cousin for a few days. At the end of the week go up to Edinburgh and stay with Cathy until I tell you to come home."

"Leave? Just like that? Why, David, why?"

"Please, Chloe. Just do it. For me. Please?"

For a few minutes Chloe stared into David's soul, searching for an answer. She saw none, finding only pain and hurt. And fear.

She inched forwards, folding herself into his chest and hugging him tight.

Thirty minutes later she left the flat. Her flat. Carrying a small bag of clothes under her coat.

9.05 a.m.

David had a plan.

An enforced plan.

One he knew he had to fulfil, or face the possibility that next time around they might cut off his hand, kill him or go after Chloe.

Over the past twenty-four hours he had been round the street sticking up posters asking people if they had found the twenty thousand pounds: he'd knocked on some doors - although only a few - and had pushed some flyers through half the doors in the street.

Today he was going to take it to the next level.

By the end of the day he was personally going to knock on the door of every flat or house in the square, starting with all the houses in his street. If no one answered he would leave the flyer. And he was going to double the reward.

Before he did anything though, he would make sure the bastards who took his finger knew what he was going to do.

He dialled the number he had been given.

The phone rang, but there was no reply.

He dialled it again.

The phone rang, but no one picked up.

"Shit!" David swore.

How could he contact them if they wouldn't answer the bloody phone?

Just then, the phone in his hand rang, startling the hell out of him.

"Hello?"

"David, hi. Have you got the money?"

"I just tried calling you..."

"I was busy. How's your finger? Do you miss it?"

There was a silence. A rush of fear and anger coursed through him at the same time.

"That was a question..."

David responded immediately.

"Yes. Yes, I miss it!"

"Do you want it back?"

"What... what do you mean?"

"I mean, just as a little reminder... if you want, we could put it in the post and send it back to you. If you want?"

"You've got my finger?"

"Yes. I thought it might make a good souvenir... but to be quite honest, it's beginning to smell a little... and every time I look at it, it points at me. It keeps reminding me that if you don't get me the money back by tomorrow, then I will come back and get another finger. From your right hand this time. Now, answer the question... shall I send it back?"

A wave of nausea and fear washed over him, and David retched onto the floor.

"I heard that, David. I'll take that as a 'no' then."

There was a pause, and David wiped his mouth and steadied himself against the bookcase in his lounge.

"Fine. No problem. I'll put it back in my fridge again then. Until later maybe. Perhaps we can send it to Chloe's mother in Oxford as a present."

"Her mum? How do you know she lives there...?" David replied, shaking. He couldn't believe what he was hearing.

"I've made it my business to learn everything about you and Chloe, David. *Everything.*"

"Why... Why are you doing this to me?" David asked, his voice shaking. "Why don't you come and find the bloody money yourself?"

There was a moment's silence, then the man's voice which came back was quieter, deeper and slightly more menacing than before.

"I ask the questions not you. Don't ever question me again, do you understand me David?"

"Yes."

"Good. But for your information, I'll tell you that we *are* looking David. We are. But I think you realise that if we go round your rich neighbours, asking, pushing for information, it might look a tad suspicious? You're ideal! You live there. You're one of them. They know you. They'll listen to you... let you into their houses even. You're our mole, David. Our undercover spy. And if you can't find out what happened to my money, no one will."

Another pause.

"David, tomorrow night. By tomorrow night, you will get me my money back. With the envelope. Tomorrow night, or I'll come and take both your hands. Then Chloe's eyes."

David's knees gave way underneath him, and he collapsed to the floor. His left hand was throbbing, and he felt dizzy and weak.

"Why me?" he began to cry.

"Wrong place, wrong time, my friend. I guess it was just bad luck."

David closed his eyes and swallowed, breathing deeply and bringing his emotions and his fear under his control.

"Listen, please... whoever you are. I called you to tell you just what I am going to do today to get your money back. I promise you, I will spend every moment I have trying to find your money. I'll do everything I can. I won't stop trying... But if I can't find it, it won't be my fault... you have to understand that!"

David waited for a reply, holding his breath, hoping, praying that the man at the other end would understand.

"We're watching you David. You have until tomorrow night. After that you won't need your skiing gloves anymore."

The phone went dead.

11.05 a.m.

The doorbell woke Ray up, its persistent, shrill, ringing drilling into his skull and boring into his fucked up brain.

"What?" he shouted hoarsely, pulling the covers back and holding his head with his hand, one eye opening slightly.

The doorbell rang again.

Ray coughed and cleared his throat.

"Wait... wait, I'm coming," he said, opening both eyes and rolling out of the bed.

He was still dressed from the night before.

Stumbling towards the front door out of his bedroom, he quickly tried to adjust his clothes and smoothed down his hair, but then gave up.

At the doorway, he peeked through the security hole to see who was there.

A young man he didn't recognise.

The doorbell rang again.

"Bloody hell! I'm coming!" he shouted back, this time managing some volume.

Flipping off the catch, he turned the handle and opened the door.

"What? What do you want so badly that you have to ring my bell a million times? And who are you anyway? How did you get through the front door and up the stairs?"

"I'm David. I'm a neighbour. I live at No. 33. Flat 4. With my girlfriend Chloe. I followed one of the other residents in."

"Great security. What time's it mate? And what do you want?" Ray asked, coughing, and blinking, then deciding it was better if he screwed his eyes up half closed. The light was very bright.

David turned his left hand to look at his watch. His arm was in the sling given to him by the hospital, his hand bandaged all over to stop the air getting to his wound, and protect it from further injury and the stitches being pulled on.

"It's just gone eleven."

"Wow. What happened there, mate?" Ray asked, noticing the bandages. "Lost a finger or two?"

The man nodded.

Ray opened his eyes and looked the man over. His face was bruised and haggard. He looked like he'd recently received a big kicking.

"What happened to you? Car accident?"

The man nodded again.

"Did you get my note?"

"What note?" Ray asked, suddenly feeling very rough. His head was throbbing.

"The one I left yesterday about my money? I lost £20,000. All my grant money."

"Ahhh..." Ray replied, the light beginning to dawn. He looked the man up and down again. "Bit old for a student aren't you?"

The man hesitated.

"I'm a mature student. Didn't get in at first. Had to retake some exams. Took a while to get a place."

"What are you studying...?"

"... Economics..." David replied after another slight hesitation.

"Where?"

"King's College?"

"Are you asking me or telling me?"

"What do you mean?"

"I mean, it sounded like you didn't know at first. As if you were making it up?"

David took a step backwards, his face flushing red.

"What do you mean, making it up? I lost all my money, and I'm desperate to get it back. There's a reward. £1,000 if you find it and give it back to me."

"I thought it was £500?"

"It was... I doubled it."

Ray was starting to get angry. The man was obviously somehow in trouble with a drug gang. What the problem was Ray didn't know, and didn't care. He had sworn to himself that he would not get involved with anything, *ANYTHING*, to do with drugs and that was never going to change. Ever.

Plus his head was throbbing. He was beginning to realise just how rough he was actually feeling.

He hadn't had a hangover like this for years.

Since before he had met Emma.

At the thought of Emma, a wave of anger engulfed Ray.

"Listen mate, I don't have your money. But I do feel like shit... and I need to get some strong black coffee before my head explodes. So, if you don't mind..." Ray said, motioning with his eyes that he was going to shut the door.

"Please..." the man before him said, an audible edge of desperation in his voice, "If you hear anything, or meet a neighbour who has found my money, please, call me on this number?"

Ray was just about to close the door when something in him made him pause. All of a sudden he could hear Emma's voice uttering the words *'do the right thing'* in his mind.

Ray paused.

He looked at him, staring straight into his eyes.

One desperate man looking into the eyes of another.

For a second there was a slight connection, a moment of mutual recognition.

"Is everything,..." Ray stuttered. "Is everything... okay, mate?"

David looked back at Ray, the connection lasting a few palpable seconds longer.

Then David looked away, towards the front of the building.

"Yes...," he replied, stepping away, edging towards the stairs. "Yes, everything's fine. I just need the money back. And soon. If... if you hear anything, please... call me?"

Then he turned and started walking down the stairs, his right arm cradling his left in the sling as he went.

"Do the right thing..." he heard Emma's voice prompt him again, followed by a vision of his dead brother's face.

"But what was the right thing?" Ray asked himself, watching the man go.

For a second he looked after him, wondering, then he stepped back inside and closed the door.

Ray wasn't stupid. The story about the money was made up. All of it. There was no way that the guy had lost the money. He was so obviously lying about the whole thing, Ray would have to be an idiot to fall for it.

What was more obvious was that someone had just kicked the shit out of him, and probably broken his fingers or broken his hand.

Someone was putting pressure on that man to find the money.

Why? Ray didn't know.

But right now that was someone else's problem.

Ray's gut reaction was, and always had been, that the money was drug money. And the last thing Ray wanted to do just now was to get involved in a drug war.

"*Do the right thing!*" he heard Emma's voice say again.

"Shit!" Ray swore aloud. Another wave of anger rolled over Ray, and he was suddenly furious that even now she was gone, she was still telling him what to do.

"Leave me alone!" he said, shaking his head to clear all thoughts of her from it. And succeeding.

Thoughts of Emma were immediately replaced with pain from the worsening headache and a string of memories from the night before as he suddenly remembered what had happened: coming home to discover the note, the whisky, and beer, and wine, sitting at his desk, watching the murder video, and...

"OH SHIT!" he shouted aloud, suddenly remembering the email he'd sent.

In a flash it all came back to him in blinding clarity.

"SHIT!" he swore again loudly. "What the *fuck* have I done?"

11.15 a.m.

David stood outside in the street, looking back up at the front window of the last flat he had visited. He had knocked on the doors of everyone on the stair and spoken to the residents in all but one. The last one was the man with the hangover who had stunk to high heaven of alcohol when he had opened the door.

David was excited. A siren was blaring at the back of his mind, a deep seated instinct telling him that the man - David didn't know his name yet - knew something.

For the few seconds that their eyes had met there had been a strange, weird connection. It had been quite uncomfortable, and so intense that David had been forced to look away.

The man in the flat had seen straight through his story and knew that David had been lying, that he had made up the whole story about the grant money. It was almost as if the man had taken a particular interest in what David had been saying and was probing him for the truth.

But why?

Why did it matter to the man what David was saying... and whether or not the details were true?

Why did he take the time to question him?

In total, David had now spoken to the owners of about twenty different flats, and whereas some had expressed concern and shown kindness, and promised to let him know the moment they heard anything, the man with the hangover was the only one to really probe and show an interest in the story behind the story.

To David, the reason why was obvious: the man with the hangover knew where the money was!

11.25 a.m.

Sipping a strong black coffee, Ray sat at his desk in his den and navigated his way impatiently through the different layers of his security.

Eventually he succeeded in using Ghost to log on to the fictitious Outlook account he had used to send the email the night before: an email account pretending to be based somewhere in Brazil.

"*Never drink and hack!*" he chanted to himself over and over again as he waited to see if anyone had responded to the email he had sent last night. "What the hell was I playing at?" he chided himself.

The Outlook screen opened up, and as it did so, Ray dreaded what he would find.

He had just sent an email to one of the most powerful people in the world, mocking him for murdering someone. Thankfully he had not gone as far as admitting that he had seen the woman actually being murdered, but given that the man had just murdered someone, if he saw and read the email, he might think it pretty strange and guess what David had been alluding to.

Would Randolph Best have seen the email?

Would he have read it?

How would he respond to it?

As the Outlook screen appeared Ray immediately saw that whereas yesterday he had no emails in his Inbox, now he had two.

Ray's heart leapt a beat.

He quickly scanned the titles.

One was from Outlook: an email welcoming him to the account and giving him Outlook blurb.

The other was from a name he did not recognise with a title that said, in bold, "READ THIS!"

Shit!

Ray clicked on the email and opened it up.

A wave of relief swept over him as he read the contents. It was an email from a man in Africa who had six million pounds to share with any idiot who fell for the phishing scam and would agree to help transfer it out of Nigeria.

Ray sat back in the chair and breathed in deeply.

Glancing quickly at the junk folder he confirmed that there were no other emails.

Except for one in his SENT file.

Ray clicked on it.

"*I spy, I SAW her cry.*"

"Fuck! Shit!" he shouted, punching the desk with his fist.
"What the fucking hell was I thinking?"

Ray stared at the email.

How could he have been such an incredible idiot?

Did he have a death wish?

"Yeah, right, just email one of the most powerful people in the world and tell them you think you know they killed someone!" he shouted at himself.

Ray read and re-read the email about twenty times.

Each time he read it, he got more scared.

Questions began to flow through his mind.

Doubts.

Fears.

Had Randolph Best read it?

If not, why not?

Was the email account still active?

How often did Randolph check that account and read his emails?

Had Ray's email gone through to the junk box?

Did Randolph scan it and then decide that it was rubbish sent by a mad man, and then just delete it? - Or was that being too hopeful?

If he had read it, would he understand what Ray was referring to?

Ray studied his email again...

He tried to imagine what someone else might think when they got the email and read it. How would the words be understood?

"*You saw her cry? Who? Who was crying? What the hell are you talking about?*"

Maybe Randolph would read it, think it was a phishing mail or some sort of scam and then delete it.

Perhaps, which was also possible, he got so many emails that he didn't read them all. And he never would.

Was Ray worrying about nothing?

Ray began to relax.

It could be that he had got away with it.

"Yeah, come on, I'm just being bloody paranoid!" he promised himself. "It's not like I said that I saw him actually killing her, did I!"

He laughed a little. A half-hearted chuckle designed to convince himself that he was being an idiot. That everything was going to be okay.

Standing up from his seat, he refreshed the Inbox one more time, just checking that no new emails had arrived, then laughed again.

"Chill Ray, chill!"

Finishing off his coffee, he frog-marched himself through to the shower, turned the temperature up and stepped in.

He stood there for a full twenty minutes until the water began to run cold.

As soon as he stepped out, he grabbed a towel and walked back through to the den.

Clicking on the Inbox, he bit his lip as he waited to see if anything new had arrived.

There was... nothing.

Chapter 17

London

October 2nd

1.30 p.m.

RobinHood checked his email for the tenth time that day. He hadn't heard a word from SolarWind in the past twenty-four hours and was really curious to know what was happening.

About an hour ago he had pinged him another email, but there was no reply.

He considered calling him but decided against it. Establishing a phone record that connected them both together was not something that seemed like a good idea.

Instead, he sat in his underground den and went through his plans for the millionth time.

He wanted to make sure that there was no room for a mistake; no way that once the cyber attack was launched that they would ever be able to trace it back to him.

He'd been planning this for almost a year now and was confident that it would work.

However, RobinHood knew that confidence bred complacency and complacency bred mistakes.

When SolarWind had been round the other day, RobinHood had come very, very close to telling him all about the project.

In the old days, he would have understood. Might even have wanted to come on board and be a part of it.

Truth be told, RobinHood would prefer it if someone of SolarWind's calibre was working with him on this: not only could the impact be much greater, but with each of them auditing the other's work, the chances of them making a mistake would be significantly reduced.

The problem was that SolarWind was no longer the passionate anarchist that he used to be. Gone were the days when they had sat together and planned the overthrow of the whole system.

Instead, SolarWind had got a beautiful girlfriend, and he...RobinHood... had got fat and got cancer.

It was a shame SolarWind wasn't on board, but there was a plus side.

Being forced to go it alone meant that only one person would claim the glory.

This cyber attack would leave the others trailing in the dust behind him.

By launching one of the most devastating cyber attacks of all time, RobinHood's name would become famous the world over, and in the eyes of all his cyber-bruvs and fellow anarchists he would be a hero. Forever.

In a few short days time, RobinHood was going to establish cyber history.

Time was short.

There was so much still to check.

And only a few days to go.

11.25 a.m.

Emma was almost packed.

Her two suitcases were full of the clothes and belongings that she had decided to take with her to Canada.

Her passport and visa were all in order, and the plane tickets were booked.

In a few days time she would be leaving for a new life.

The 'New World'.

And she would be closing a door behind her in a way that increasingly she had begun to worry about. Had she done the wrong thing...?

In fact, was she just about to do an even worse 'wrong thing'?

She missed Ray.

It was as if her right arm had been cut off.

She felt incomplete without him. She was missing something that at first she couldn't pinpoint, but over the past twenty-four hours she had realised exactly what it was.

What she missed was a tall, stupid, ignorant, lovable, funny, clever and obstinate, independent fool called Ray.

Why hadn't he contacted her?

Why hadn't he come chasing after her, demanding that she get back together with him?

Where was he the other night?

When he got home... assuming that he had gone home that night... maybe he had moved in already with some other woman... or gone on holiday... no, *assuming* that he had gone home that night, why hadn't he got angry with her or upset or heartbroken and sent her a text message.

Why hadn't he got angry with her?

Another thought hit her, one which really worried her. She remembered seeing the dirty dishes and the empty beer bottles in his flat. Obviously he had been drinking quite a lot in the past few days.

Had he got drunk, gone out driving and had an accident?
Should she call the hospitals? To check?
Should she call him?

The rational side of her knew that she was panicking. Being unrealistic. The truth was obviously that there was nothing wrong with Ray.

She had broken up with him.
He'd accepted it.
Then he'd moved on.

They were over.
Finished.

Canada was calling and going there would be the best thing she would ever do.

2.00 p.m.

David had continued on his way round the square, knocking on doors, talking to residents, passing out flyers, begging for information on the missing £20,000.

About half an hour ago, he'd even decided to increase the reward to £2,000.

He was getting desperate.

Yet, with every door that he knocked on he became more and more certain that he'd already found the person who knew where his money was.

His gut instinct was screaming at him.

In fact, it was screaming so loud that after he'd returned to Chloe's flat and grabbed something to eat, he decided that he would go back and knock on the man's door again.

Try again.
Push a bit harder.

He was even considering telling him the truth. Explaining exactly what had happened to him and praying that the man would take pity on him and just hand the cash back.

With any luck the nightmare could be over within a few hours.

Just then his phone began to ring...

David stared at the number trying to figure out if he knew it or not.

Was it them again? On yet another different SIM card with a new number?

The phone stopped ringing. David breathed a sigh of relief, but a few minutes later it started ringing again.

If he didn't answer it, he knew he'd worry who it was.

If it was them, maybe he should tell them about his gut instinct and the man in the top floor flat at number 23?

He picked up the phone and pressed the answer button.

"Hi..."

"David," Chloe's voice immediately shouted back. "Are you okay? I was so worried about you!"

Chloe.

Shit, he'd forgotten all about her! He was meant to call her!

"Hi! It's me... I'm fine... are *you* okay? Don't tell me where you are... just if you are okay!"

"I'm fine. Everything is okay."

"You remembered what I said?"

"Yes. I'm there. Now. Everything is fine. Don't worry about me."

A wave of relief swept over David.

"Fantastic! That's the best news I've heard in months."

Chloe laughed gently at the other end of the phone. David's heart went out to her, and in that moment he realised again how much he loved her.

"Chloe," he started, about to tell her. Then he remembered the latest threat to them both, and a vision of her with no eyes popped into his mind.

A combination of revulsion, fear and anger passed through him.

"Yes...?" Chloe answered.

"I just wanted to say I love you. That's all. You have to look after yourself for me, you know that, don't you?"

"I promise. But David, please, please look after yourself too. And call me as soon as this is all over! Promise?"

David hesitated, about to say one thing more, but thought better of it.

"We'll speak tomorrow. Don't worry. This will all be over soon."

They hung up.

At the other end of the phone connection, Chloe began to cry.

"What?" she said aloud to herself, now safe in her sister's spare bedroom. "What will be over? I don't understand what's going on!"

Although she was now safe, Chloe was more petrified than before.

All the way on the train from London, a single thought had been going round and round in her head.

"Would she ever see David alive again?"

3.00 p.m.

Ben was concerned.
He'd enjoyed working for Mr Grant.
They respected each other.
He understood why, if he didn't come up with the goods in the next few days, Mr Grant would have to punish him severely.
Possibly kill him.
If he was Mr Grant he would do the same thing.

But Ben wasn't stupid. If circumstances hadn't dramatically improved within the next three days, Ben was leaving the country.
His plans were already made.
A new - false - passport was already tucked away in a freshly packed suitcase, which was locked up in a storage facility in Wandsworth.
He knew that Mr Grant wanted to see him on Saturday night. The appointment had already been arranged, and he'd promised to attend.
The thing was though... Ben had already decided that if he didn't have the money, he would pick up his suitcase on Friday night, and be out of the country by Saturday.

If he went to the meeting on Saturday, the chances were that Mr Grant would have him killed. He knew that Mr Grant thought he would probably think that Mr Grant would let him off, on account of the fact that they went back a long way, and that Mr Grant really liked Ben.
However, the way Ben saw it was that Mr Grant had problems at home: the Russians and the Libyans were pushing into his turf, and the boys were already questioning if Mr Grant had the bottle to face up to them or not.
A couple of the boys were thinking of jumping ship.
If Mr Grant went slack on Ben, the boys would see it as weakness and that would be that. They'd lose respect for him, and in this game, respect was everything.
So Mr Grant would have no choice but to kill him. To set an example.
Which left Ben with no choice but to kill Mr Grant.
First. Before Mr Grant would kill him.
It would all get horribly messy.

Ben didn't like mess.
He didn't mind violence. A little torture. Killing people.
That was all fine.
The problem was that he genuinely liked Mr Grant, even looked up to him as a father figure of sorts.

The last thing Ben wanted to do was to be forced to kill him.

All of this made Ben quite angry.

Thanks to that fuckwit David who hadn't done his job properly, they were no further forward in finding the money and the envelope.

True, it wasn't his fault that they'd lost it, but Ben had made it very clear that it WAS his responsibility to find it.

Ben's team, Petrov especially, had searched high and low for it everywhere: underneath the cars, in the bushes, down the drains... in buckets, bins, dustbins... They had stopped and asked residents on the street, casually asked questions in the local shops.

Nothing.

Ben's instinct told him that the money had been lost in the square. At one point it had been there.

He still also believed that the money had probably been spent by now, but the money wasn't the important thing here. It was the envelope.

With any luck, though, Ben could still turn this situation around. Since taking David's finger as a souvenir - Ben's tenth finger this year which meant he was heading towards breaking his personal record for fingers-per-year - David had been working twice as hard.

The kick up the backside had worked.

David was trying really hard now, and if he found the envelope, instead of being angry and forced to kill Ben, Mr Grant would be pleased and grateful - and relieved not to have to lose a good man. Everyone knew that when Mr Grant was grateful, he was generous. Very generous.

So, fingers crossed - he could borrow one of David's for that part - by Sunday, he'd be a few grand richer, back in the good books, and sitting in front of his own TV watching Sunday football.

The alternative was not something he wanted to think about too much just yet.

Except for one thing.

If Ben was forced to leave the country because David hadn't performed, the last thing he would do before he left the square would be to kill the lazy bastard.

He'd make sure of that.

5.15 p.m.

Ray had not been out of the flat all day.

His hangover, instead of getting better, had just got worse.

He felt terrible.

So much so, that come 3 p.m. the choice was simple.

Either a few paracetamols, or the hair of the dog.

When Ray opted for the first, he was disappointed to find that the box in the cupboard in the bathroom was empty.
Emma had obviously had the last one and not got a new box...

Emma...

Ray went for the drink.
A cold can of beer from the fridge. His last one.
Dressed casually in his running trousers and a rugby top, he took the beer through with him to his den where he refreshed the Outlook link for the 100th time that day.
No other emails had arrived.

Ray had been thinking about it.
Rationally.
Perhaps optimistically.
It was beginning to look like he had got away with it.

Or was he just being stupid, assuming that others would check their emails as much as he did.
Randolph F. Best was a busy man. He might not get round to checking his emails for days, even weeks.
On the other hand, if that happened, Ray's email would be buried in spam and other emails by that time, and Randolph would never ever read it.
There was definitely 'scope for hope'!

The other reason Ray kept on using to justify his belief that he might have got away it was quite simply this: Ray had used Ghost to create an account and log onto a Brazilian version of Outlook. When R. F. B got the email, if he got it, to all intents and purposes it would have come from someone in Brazil.
There was no way that R. F. B. could track it to Ray in London.
The only danger was that R. F. B. read the email, passed it onto his security team, and asked them to track down the idiot who had sent it.
However, *even if* R. F. B. did that, Ray argued to himself, even the best people in MI5 would never be able to track Ray down from that account. Ghost virtualised and randomised every data packet so that to anyone who might be interested in Ray, he would be just a... ghost. Hence the name. No one would ever be able find him down and touch him.

Ray being Ray, though, he was constantly double-checking everything he did, and all his assumptions. Deep down Ray knew he was safe, but his being safe and him feeling safe were two different things.

Which is why, as an ultimate precaution, Ray had built his 'onion' alarm system.

Essentially, Ray's core network was protected by two outer networks. Each of these was effectively a DMZ, a demilitarised zone, with one of these DMZs acting as an outer DMZ to the other... a double DMZ.

At the ingress and egress to each of the DMZs Ray had put firewalls, NAT devices, Intrusion Detection systems, Intrusion Prevention Systems, you name it, he had it.

These DMZs sheltered and hid Ray from the outside world and made it impossible for other hackers to ever see his network, let alone hack into it, which would also be impossible.

However, being Ray, and being cautious, Ray did not want to leave anything to chance. So, within each DMZ and within his core network he had placed a network probe, a device that examined all the network traffic that passed through it and generated instant alerts if any 'strange' traffic was observed. These probes were linked to two flashing lights that were screwed into the wall above the network servers.

One was green. One was red.

The way the onion alarm worked - another one of Ray's inventions of which he was very proud - was the following: if the network probe in the inner DMZ detected that some rogue, unexplained traffic had successfully entered his network - most likely indicating that he was being probed or attacked by someone from outside who had already got through the outer DMZ and was now inside the inner DMZ - the green light on the wall would start to flash, and an SMS would be sent to his mobile.

This was the Den's equivalent of DefCon 2.

If the red light started to flash, this meant that someone had hacked their way through the inner DMZ and got all the way into the core network.

This was DefCon 1.

As well as an SMS to his mobile, his phone would start to ring and an audible alarm would go off in his bedroom.

Ray knew that if anyone ever, ever managed to hack into the second - inner - DMZ - which was impossible to do - that whoever succeeded in doing so, would also have the power to hack into the core network and get access to his crown jewels, his servers and databases.

Two things would happen if the red light ever started to flash.

Firstly, Ray would grab his hard drives and disconnect them from the core network, possibly removing them and hiding them underneath his floor boards.

Secondly, he would then run a special program he'd written called "*Scorched Earth*" which would automatically delete and overwrite all the data on any of his servers, laptops or network devices.

On no account would he ever, ever let another hacker get into his network and get access to his data.

Never.
Ever.
Would.
That.
Happen.

Chapter 18

London

October 2nd

10.00 p.m.

The tissue box was empty. The glass of wine needed refilling. Her life was a mess.
"My life is a mess!" she repeated to herself. A little drunk.
She was packed. Ready to go. Ready to run away.
Yet, instead of being blissfully happy with a new life stretching out in front of her, as the day had grown older, she'd become sadder, and sadder.
Her best friend had just left and her flatmate was out, and now she was left alone to face herself, something that she had been trying to avoid all day.

Emma was petrified.
Not of going to Canada, but of leaving London behind.
Actually, if she was brutally honest, that wasn't the truth.
The reality was that she was petrified of leaving Ray behind.
"Why hasn't he called me?" she sobbed to herself. "He hasn't even tried to contact me!"

She'd been over it a thousand times in her mind. She knew she was doing the *right* thing. She definitely was.
But what if she wasn't?
Ray had given them no chance to discuss it, to argue about it. He hadn't tried to 'woo' her back.
Not one single flower.
Which proved absolutely beyond a shadow of a doubt that the reason she'd split up with him was one thousand percent the right reason.
So why did it hurt so much?

Every time she looked at her suitcases she thought about Ray.
He didn't even know she was going.
She hadn't told him.
Maybe, just maybe he was planning to leave it a week before he would come charging round the corner on the back of a big white horse, all dressed in shining armour, and he would hoist her up onto his saddle and carry her off into the sunset.

And they would live happily ever after.

Except, obviously, there was one slight flaw with that whole fantasy.

Horses couldn't fly all the way to Canada, and that's where she would be by Saturday evening.

If that's what Ray's plan was, he would miss her. She would be gone.

"But will he miss me? *Does* he miss me?" she mumbled to herself as she dragged herself off the sofa to the fridge to get another bottle of chilled white wine.

Returning to the lounge, she curled her feet back up on the sofa and pulled her favourite cushion onto her lap.

The light on the phone was flashing. She hadn't noticed it before...Maybe it was Ray!

It was Paula, her friend, saying that she had got home safely and was looking forward to meeting her the next day for coffee as planned.

Putting the phone down, she stared at it. Telling herself it was not a good idea.

No good could come from it.

"But I have to tell him!" she protested. "Otherwise..."

She picked the phone back up and hit the little button with Ray's name on it and settled back into her sofa.

At the other end of the line, Ray's mobile phone began to ring.

There was no answer. Ray was not picking up.

Nervously, she sat up and dialled the number again.

Once again, it rang, but there was still no answer.

"Why is he not answering?" Emma asked herself, sitting up straight and impatiently dialling Ray's landline.

Once again the phone rang, but eventually went to voicemail.

Emma hung up, stood up from her sofa and started pacing around her lounge.

"Where are you Ray? Why are you not answering? Are you avoiding me?" she said loudly.

She stood for a second by the window looking out onto the street below, cradling her phone against her chest.

Her throat was tight, and she fought back the tears of frustration that were gathering in her eyes.

Suddenly her emotion changed, from sadness to anger.

With renewed emotion she dialled his number again and waited for the phone answering service.

"Hi, this is Ray. Please leave a message."
She swallowed hard.
"Ray, hi, it's Emma. I just wanted to tell you something...important...but you're not there. I'm leaving the country on Saturday. Going to live in Canada. I've got a job. They wanted me very badly so I'm going..."

She had intended just to leave a short message, but already she was starting to stretch it out, to talk too much... not wanting to hang up... She closed her eyes, took a deep breath and continued.

"... that's it. Have a nice life, Ray." She hesitated, feeling the temptation to say something more but thought better of it. "Bye..."

And then she hung up.

10:11 p.m.

Ray walked into his flat, closed the door and went straight to the fridge to put the cold beers in before they warmed up any more.

Two six packs, and a new bottle of whisky.

Enough to see him through the next few days.

As he took off his jacket and dumped it on one of the chairs, he thought again about his encounter with the man with the broken hand who had knocked on his door late that afternoon.

The man - what was his name? David? - knew that Ray knew something. In the same way that Ray knew that he was not telling the truth.

It was funny, Ray could almost sense that David wanted to tell him something more, but was hesitating to do so. At the same time, Ray had no intention of pushing him to tell him more: Ray hated drugs, they destroyed lives, and those who dealt with them were a force not to be reckoned with, but to be avoided at all costs. Ray was not going to get tangled up in the whole situation, and that was that. He wanted - and would have - nothing to do with it.

He would rather burn the twenty grand than give it back to a drug gang, and so long as he didn't say or admit anything, he would be safe.

Yet, there was something about the guy - he seemed a little desperate, that made Ray feel guilty.

"... *not doing the right thing*..."

The phrase from Emma jumped into his mind and started nagging him again.

Ray knew though that he *was* doing the right thing.

His every instinct told him to stay well clear, and that was what he intended to do. He had no idea what trouble the guy with the broken hand had got himself into, but it was his trouble, not Ray's.

Luckily he wouldn't have to go to work for the next few days. After lunch he'd had a brief email exchange with his boss. He'd told her that he would be working at home for the next few days, trying to crack the defences of the bank. He was close...Just needed a little more time. She seemed pleased.

"Little do they know..." he laughed to himself as he cracked open the first beer.

Checking his mobile phone on the kitchen table, he saw that it wasn't fully charged yet, so left it without picking it up.

As he walked towards the den to check the alarm lights on the wall and then to refresh the link on Outlook, he noticed the light blinking on his landline phone on the table in the hall.

Poking his head into the den, neither of the lights on the wall were flashing. He stepped into his den and quickly logged off and closed down all the servers. He was going to relax this evening, drink a few beers and clear his mind.

Stepping back into the hall, he sat down on the floor beside the table and picked up the phone. It was probably his sister who had left a message. He hadn't spoken to her in a while.

He pressed 1571 and listened to the voice message.

"Ray, hi, it's Emma..."

His heart skipped a beat, and he listened to what she had to say in disbelief.

"*What?*" he shouted aloud.

He hit '1' and listened to it again.

Letting the phone slide out of his hand, and fall into his lap, he stared into space.

"Going to Canada? On Saturday? SHIT!!!!!"

His mind was awash with emotion, and he struggled to make sense of what he had just heard.

He listened to the message again, focussing on Emma's voice as she said the words.

Her voice sounded strange. A little tense.

She sounded as if she was hating having to speak to him. To tell him the truth.

"*So, that's what this is all about. The whole time I was planning to marry you, you were planning a different life abroad!!!*"

Ray stood up and stomped around his flat.

Swearing. Shouting.

Not able to decide how to react.
Should he call her back?
Tell her not to go to Canada?
Tell her he loved her?

Then reality hit him.
Why bother?
What would he gain by telling her? Just more humiliation.
She had obviously been planning this for months. Maybe longer.
Behind his back, without ever discussing it.

At first the initial impact on Ray was great sadness, which slowly morphed to confusion, and lastly to anger.
A great deal of anger.
He thought of the ring he had planned to give her, the wedding he had planned... he remembered looking at possible places to go on honeymoon with her.
What a bloody idiot he had been!
Then another thought hit him.
Was she going alone?
Or was she going to live in Canada with someone else?

Balling up his fist he smashed it hard into the wall.
"FUCK!" he shouted aloud from frustration and pain, then examined the resulting cut across his bruised knuckles.

Walking through to the bathroom, he washed his hand in the cold water, and then rested his hands on the edges of the sink and took several deep breaths. For a few moments he thought of looking at himself in the mirror, but he couldn't do it. He couldn't face himself.
"Never... NEVER again!" he shouted.
In that moment Ray vowed he would never fall in love again.
Emma had been the one for him. At least he had thought so. He'd been a fool. And he would never go through it again.
Never. Ever.

Walking through to the kitchen he grabbed the bottle of whisky from the table and cracked it open.
Grabbing the same glass he had used the night before from the side of the sink, he poured half a glass and knocked it back fast.
"*Shit*!" he shouted again.

Carrying the rest of the first six pack through to the den, he settled into his seat and finished the rest of his beer as he powered up his laptop and servers and prepared to disappear into the world of cyber.

Taking rather longer than normal to type in the correct PIN responses from his SecurID tokens and log on - because he was already tipsy - by the time he managed to access Ghost and get back into his Outlook account in Brazil the alcohol was pumping through his veins and he was fuming.

Refusing to think of Emma, he was consciously looking for another route to vent his anger.

Finding his email inbox in his Brazilian account still empty, his anger rose another notch.

"Bastard! The bastard thinks he's got away with it!" Ray announced to the rest of the computers in the room, before cracking open another beer and drinking half of it down in several large gulps.

"Idiot. You bloody idiot. Just because you're '*famous*' and rich and powerful you think you can get away with killing people! Well I have got news for you, Mr R. Fucking Best!"

Almost blind with anger, Ray opened up the email he had sent before, copied the email address using Control C, opened up a new email and hit Control V.

Bingo! The personal email address of R. F. Best appeared in the "To" area.

Ray stood up, stared at the screen and then walked through to the kitchen, swiftly returning with the bottle of whisky and his glass, and poured himself another half glass.

All the time composing the new email in his mind, thinking of how to make R. F. Best pay.

"Aha...!" he chuckled to himself, as the answer dawned on him. "I'm a poet, and I don't know it..." He laughed. "Let the bloody games begin!"

Swigging another mouthful of whisky, he sat down in front of the keyboard, centred himself in his chair and started to type.

"I spy, I **SAW** her cry..." he wrote in the title section of the email, before moving down to the main body, "... And I know *why*!"

Ray sat back in his chair, surveying his handiwork.

He read the email twice.

"Short but sweet, Mr Fucking Best!" Ray approved his work.

Smiling, he leant forward and moved the mouse up to the left of the screen onto the toolbar and hit SEND.

Chapter 19

London

October 2nd

11.02 p.m.

Ferris saw the email come in, logged it and started to work on it immediately.

Anything that had to do with their contact was to be given top priority.

They had been monitoring Randolph Best for over a year now, nearly two.

Although Ferris hadn't been briefed on the original reasons for establishing the surveillance, last weekend he had been pulled into the office by his sector commander and told that the surveillance had to be increased.

He was one of only three who had been told the new reason for this: Randolph Best had killed someone: a beautiful Israeli model.

The death had been taken care of by a MOP, their nickname for the 'clean-up' teams that went in and 'sorted' difficult situations, normally arising from an accident, an assassination, or terrorist attack.

Only a few people knew that there had been a connection between Randolph Best and the deceased - officially now the victim of a fatal mugging, and on no account was it to be repeated or shared with anyone else in the agency.

Secrets within secrets.

However, Ferris was one of a few to have been told. First, because he needed to monitor any new communications to, from or between anyone connected with Randolph Best or the deceased model, to see if a link could be established. Second, they needed to ensure the safety of Randolph Best. When someone of his importance became involved in an incident, it was the job of Ferris's team to make sure they were aware of any HUMINT or Open-source intelligence that could provide any valuable information on the client or anything pertaining to him.

If anything happened in cyber space that could indicate a threat to Randolph Best, it was his job to spot it and report it.

In addition, the model who had been killed was Israeli. That made things more complicated.

She had served in the Israeli army and had a record.

She was already on their files.

Lastly, his sector commander was one of only two people that knew Randolph Best was already under surveillance. Ferris was the other.

"What you've been doing up till now is nothing to do with this, and will not be connected. Do you understand? From now, keep Project RH1 ticking along in parallel, but focus on Project Best Protect. As far as everyone else is concerned that's your main mission now. Only you and I know about RH1, understood?"

It was all a bit cryptic, but in his world, that was par for the course.

Ferris didn't give it a second thought.

More secrets within secrets.

The day before, he'd seen the first email come into R. Best's inbox. Randolph Best had opened and read the email several hours after receiving it.

As far as Ferris could tell, he'd subsequently taken no action as a result of it.

No phone calls and no replies to the email.

Admittedly it was a little confusing: "I spy, I saw her cry..."

There was no definite connection between the email and the murder.

Perhaps Best had read the email and also thought nothing of it. A random meaningless email that ended up in his inbox, but was probably a spam mail.

However, whereas Best would not have known it, there was an important piece of meta-data associated with the email that immediately drew Ferris's attention, and caused him to look at it in more detail: it had been sent and delivered from an anonymising program. Not TOR, something else. Something more complicated, something very clever, powerful and home-grown.

Which meant that whoever had sent the first email was clever, informed and deliberately trying to hide their identity.

The second email was more significant.

It was important for several reasons.

First, because there was obviously a connection to the previous email. It was the sequel to the prior one and provided more detail and clues as to the purpose of them both.

"*I spy, I saw her cry, and I know why!*"

The person who had sent it seemed to be indicating that they had seen a woman being distressed and knew the reason for it.

Ordinarily, the message would not get much attention, but given that there had been a death in such circumstances, it appeared to be hinting to some knowledge of an event that was possibly connected with the woman who had been killed, and was in some way being linked directly to the client.

Had the author of the email seen the client talking with the deceased model, possibly during a time when the model had been upset?

Was it in public?

Were there other witnesses?

As far as Ferris had been briefed, the death had occurred in private. They had not been outside in public together that night.

Was the client telling the truth?

Did the email allude to some information about the event that the agency did not yet know about?

Another reason that the email was significant was because it was the second email, possibly from the same author, which was also sent from an email account that had been managed using an anonymised browser.

Initial attempts to find out where the email had come from and the identity and location of the author had failed.

The popular conception of programs like TOR - the original and most common anonymising program - was that they were an effective way for users to defend themselves against network surveillance and traffic analysis. They believed that it gave users anonymity when online, that if you browsed and communicated when using TOR based programmes that it prevented others from learning someone's location and browsing habits.

Everyone who went to the TOR website could immediately learn that the onion routing project was a baby of research conducted and run by the U.S. Naval Research Laboratory. It was originally developed with the U.S. Navy in mind to develop a way of protecting government communications between government employees all over the world.

A future version of software that came from the project was released to the public, and soon people the world over were using it to secure their own personal identities and communications.

The belief - as promoted by the authorities - was that if it was good enough for government spies and employees to secure their communications and identities from surveillance, it was good enough for the thousands of people who also had something to hide and wanted to remain anonymous and protected from prying eyes.

Soon, clever forward thinking individuals outside of government circles were all using TOR browsers and software to surf the net and send emails to each other, secure in the knowledge that no one would ever know who they were, where they were, or what they were doing.

TOR made them invisible to the authorities.

Which is why, outside of the government, one of the biggest community of users to adopt TOR had been the criminal element. Terrorist and crime groups quickly became the main group to use it to communicate with each other, and to sell and buy goods -primarily drugs and arms.

What amazed Ferris was that even though most people knew that the TOR project was started and perpetuated for many years by scientists working for the US Navy, it didn't occur to them that perhaps it was not safe to use.

That maybe, although it stopped most people from seeing what you were doing, it didn't stop those who created the software in the first place from seeing everything you did.

Actually, it was a brilliant idea: create a program - create the myth that it made communications anonymous, and indirectly encourage everyone to use it. Soon those who had most to lose and most to hide would start using it, and the authorities had a clear view of everything they were doing.

It was their system. Bad guys used it. Bad guys were playing right into the hands of the good guys.

It reminded Ferris of the Enigma encryption system that the Germans had developed.

The British spies at Bletchley Park broke the German codes there and from 1941 onwards were routinely deciphering secret German communications. They kept secret the fact that they had cracked the codes for almost thirty years, during which time the Enigma system was effectively adopted and for many years used by numerous governments throughout the world in the belief that it was still uncrackable.

By not telling anyone they could read the codes, the British were able to read the secrets of other nations for many years. Even the secrets of their allies.

The truth about TOR, Ferris knew, was that like Enigma, the 'secure' communications were not *totally* secure. For those with the power and the capability and the trusted insight, anonymised communications were not so anonymous after all.

And the locations of those who used TOR were not as hard to trace as almost everyone believed.

For those who did not work for the people who had developed TOR, it was admittedly harder to do. However, it was not impossible.

All you needed was massive computing power, a few geniuses like those who had worked in Bletchley Park, and a lot of funding.

With those in place, the rumours were that it had only taken British agencies seventeen months to crack TOR, and put in place methodologies which allowed people like Ferris to uncloak those who had sought the invisibility TOR had promised to offer.

All it took was to have a minimum of three emails in a sequence for the UK intelligence agencies to be able to determine the location and identity of those who were using such anonymisation engines.

Using massive arrays of parallel computers the intelligence agencies would be able to capture and dissect vast amounts of metadata from the internet, and through using very powerful analytics algorithms, they would be able to trace and effectively triangulate the source of a communication by sewing together all the possible hops in a routed communication.

The process was helped by deploying 'Gretel', a programme that had been developed and inspired by the fairy tale story of Hansel & Gretel: as Hansel and Gretel had made their way deeper into the forest they had dropped a trail of bread crumbs along the way. The plan was that by following the path of these crumbs they would have been able to find their way out of the forest.

What Gretel did was the cyber equivalent of that.

Effectively, when a communication using anonymisation technologies was sent between 'A' and 'B', a small piece of 'malware' had been created which would append itself to such communications, and then periodically drop 'cyber crumbs' as it passed through the network attached to a communication. The 'crumbs' would then beacon out to its command and control centre, effectively shouting 'I'm here! I'm here'. The Gretel management program would then detect, locate and build a path from one crumb to another, which would then enable operatives like Ferris to track down where an email started or finished.

The person who had just emailed Randolph Best was not using the TOR program, but that did not matter. Admittedly, the system he or she had used was more complicated, and actually better, but their counter system should still be powerful enough and clever enough to overcome it.

Ferris knew that the way he described their solution to himself was not technically accurate. It wasn't that simple: his understanding of it was a gross oversimplification of how it worked, but for him it was the simplest way to describe and understand it. Purists would argue that Gretel did not work like that, but Ferris didn't really care.

All he cared about was that it worked, that he needed three emails in a sequence, and that in the case he was currently working on, he already had two. He had already engaged the power of Gretel to work on his behalf, its powerful processing capabilities crunching the numbers and running the analytics in the background for him even as he thought about it.

All he needed was one more email.

If whoever was taunting Randolph Best sent just one more email, they would have him.

In Ferris's experience, from now on, it would just be a matter of time.

Chapter 20

London

Thursday

October 3rd

10.05 a.m.

An alarm was going off in Ray's flat. A high-pitched, frequent 'Beep' bored its way deep into Ray's unconscious brain and prodded and pushed and shouted at him to wake up.

It screamed at him.

It took a long time to register, but when it did, Ray's eyes sprung wide open, and with a start he heard the beep again.

"Shit!" he tried to shout aloud and jump up and out of his bed but rolled sideways and fell onto the floor instead.

Gathering his thoughts, he pushed himself up from the ground and for a second forgot what he was doing and why he was suddenly awake, but then another 'Beep' sounded loud and clear and Ray was once again semi-alert.

Staggering towards the den, his heart pounding, he clumsily barged through the doorway and into the room, fully expecting to see either the red or green light flashing on the wall.

To his great surprise they were both inactive.

Nothing was wrong.

"Beep!"

It came from behind him. Confused, he turned, banged against the doorframe as he stumbled back out through the door and bruised his shoulder, stumbling and falling over.

Rubbing it vigorously with his left hand he squinted and looked around him.

What was going on?

"Beep!"

Looking up and following the source of the sound, Ray quickly found the culprit.

His fire-alarm.

The battery was running low again.

Ray swore aloud, laughed, and breathed a sigh of relief.

Then reaching for support to the table in the hallway he manoeuvred himself into a sitting position on the floor and took a few moments to recover from such a rude awakening.

"What time is it?" he eventually asked himself.

The clock on the wall told him all he needed to know.

The pain inside his head and his dry tongue and parched throat told him the rest.

A sudden memory of Emma's phone message, the emotional pain, the anger, the alcohol, sitting in the den, and then the email - which he had actually written and stupidly sent - all passed through his battered brain in quick succession.

"Fuck..."

Gathering himself and mustering more strength and determination to survive and cope with today's hangover, he eventually managed enough courage and willpower to push himself up off the floor.

The world began to spin a little.

He had got up too fast.

As everything slowly settled down and started to take on its normal, steady, position, Ray noticed the envelope on the floor below the letter box.

Bending down, picking it up and ripping it open, without really applying any thought to who it was from or what it may contain, he pulled out a single piece of handwritten paper from inside.

"*Dear Resident of Flat 6,*

I am sorry I disturbed you again yesterday, enquiring for a second time if you knew anything about my missing £20k.

Unfortunately, however, my gut instinct tells me that you do actually know something about it. Perhaps you even found it?

I may be wrong, but as a trader in the City who lives off his wits, my gut reaction is normally correct.

The truth is, I am in a very difficult situation. I cannot explain why, but I MUST find this money.

If you know where it is, I would ask you very humbly, that if you could help me get it back, that you would.

Quite literally, it would change my life.

Very possibly, it may save it.

David Anderson."

His mobile number and landline were both included at the bottom of the page.

As he read the words, Emma's voice echoed in his mind again. The same words.
Nagging him to do the right thing.

Ray dropped the paper onto the floor and stumbled through to the bathroom.
He needed a long, cold shower.

12.30 p.m.

Ray had checked his Outlook account a dozen times since the morning and there had been no new emails.
Perhaps all this stress was for nothing. Maybe the account was not active, or Randolph Best never actually looked at it.
Maybe Ray could send an email a day for the rest of the year and he would still get no response.
On the other hand, there was the very real possibility that Randolph Best had received his emails, had read them, and was already taking action to find out who the hell was taunting him.
Ray was under no illusions: a man of his calibre and importance would be able to call on the assistance of any number of Government agencies to help track Ray down.
Since he had already had the murder of the woman in his house 'cleaned up' by the authorities, Ray knew that getting someone to track him down would be all part of the same day's work for whatever agency Randolph Best had working for him.
Yet, when all was said and done, Ray was 99% confident that even if some spook agency did start looking for whoever had sent the emails, no one would be able to track him down, get through his network defences and then identify who he was.
99% sure.
1% unsure.
It was that last 1% that terrified him.

Come lunchtime Ray had become sick and tired of his grotty little flat.

What's more, he had run out of decent food and needed some lunch.

He was also contemplating logging onto his work and sending some emails, and just in case his boss decided to do a video conference with him, he thought he should probably go and by a new bag of shavers: he'd run out and his stubble was no longer of the 'designer' kind.

The nearest decent sized supermarket was about ten minutes walk away. Normally he would drive there, but at the moment he would definitely still be over the limit, so that option was out.

He'd have to go by foot.

As soon as he stepped out of the front door and the fresh air hit him, he realised that he was still a little drunk.

As he got older it seemed that the time it took to get over a hangover got longer and longer. It was not a good sign.

Alcohol-wise, Ray had probably never before drunk so much over a number of consecutive days, even compared to when he was in his last year at university and they had celebrated sitting the last exam.

It did not feel good.

He felt slightly unsteady and a little shaky as he manoeuvred the streets and tried to avoid the other pedestrians who streamed past him.

As he passed a local pub that was just opening, he contemplated nipping inside for another hair-of-the-dog, a quick wee 'dram', but decided against it.

Instead of making him feel better, there was the very real possibility that it could make him sick.

The supermarket eventually arrived at the soles of his unsteady feet, and incredibly he managed to round up a basket of fresh milk, bread, and several microwave dinners.

He was on the way to the desk to pay when he passed the newspaper stand.

Stopping in his tracks he stared at the front pages of the newspapers.

On almost every front page of all the newspapers, one photograph dominated.

It was a photograph of Randolph Best.

As he read the titles above and below the photographs, Ray's blood began to boil.

Pulling four different papers from the stand, he quickly paid for his groceries and left the shop as fast as possible.

Ray hurried home and got to the entrance to his street before his anger and impatience got the better of him and he couldn't wait any longer.

Parking himself on a public bench on the opposite side of the street from his house, with his back to the railings surrounding the exclusive, communal garden reserved only for the residents of the square, Ray pulled out the papers and began to digest the front covers of them all.

'Randolph Best Receives Knighthood From The Queen.'

'Years of public service finally repaid by Queen.'

'Most eligible bachelor in the United Kingdom is made a Knight in Shining Armour."

Followed by a headline from the Sun.

'Britain's Women Only Want the Best!', which claimed that Randolph Best had come top of a women's survey as the most wanted man in Britain.

On the second page of the Times, it went on to explain that following his knighthood, he had been invited to the Vatican to meet the Pope. Rumour had it that he may even be a hot runner for the next Nobel peace prize, for all the work he was doing to try to mediate between the warring parties in the Middle East and find a peace solution that they would all sign up to.

Ray read the newspapers in disbelief.

The man was a bloody saint!

Everyone in the world looked up to him, even the Pope!

Was Ray the only person in the world to know the truth?

No - he was not! RobinHood knew too.

And, of course, there were the British authorities who helped Best get rid of the body.

They knew too.

Although they were never going to tell the truth, were they?

An anger began to boil up within Ray.

The bastard could not be allowed to get away with this.

Someone had to do something. Someone had to reveal the truth and expose him for the murderer that he truly was.

It was time to stand up and be counted.

To do the right thing.

Ray got up from his seat, gathered his bags and crossed the street.

Ray had a plan.

He would release the video that he had taken to the world.

But before he did that, he was going to have a little more fun.

1.15 p.m.

As Ray put the key in the main door to the communal stairway and stooped down to pick up his bags of groceries, out of the corner of his eye, he saw David - the man who was chasing him for the twenty thousand pounds - turn the corner at the end of the street and start walking down the road towards him.

As he passed a white van parked near the entrance to the road, the two doors at the front of the van burst open and two large men jumped out. As soon as he saw them, David stopped in his tracks and froze.

The tallest, a big, burly black man in a smart blue suit, stepped in front of David, and gently but firmly grabbed him by the arm and escorted him to the back of the van which was facing toward Ray.

The other man stepped to the back, opened the rear doors, and stepped aside as the tall black man firmly but surely pushed David into the back of the van and climbed in after him.

As soon as he was inside the van, the man left on the street closed the van door behind him and then ambled to the side of the road, looking up and down the road, acting as if he was a look out.

The man glanced down the street in his direction, and Ray ducked sideways through his doorway and closed it behind him.

Hurrying up the stairs to his flat, he let himself in quickly and rushed to the window in his lounge which overlooked the square below, and from where he could see the top of the white van below.

The back doors of the van opened, and while Ray watched he saw David forcibly ejected out on to the street. He stumbled from the van, fell forwards but quickly recovered himself. He looked a little dishevelled and slightly shocked.

Brushing himself down while standing in the street, David turned and watched the white van drive off.

For a few seconds he stood there staring after the van, but then, to Ray's great shock, David lifted his head and stared directly up at Ray's apartment.

Just in time, Ray pulled back, stumbling back into his room, not a second too soon.

Sitting down in one of the chair's in his lounge, Ray thought about what he had just seen.

Either David had just done a drug deal with some rather shady looking characters, or he had been on the wrong end of some rough treatment.

For a second, just a second, Ray thought about the note that David had dropped through his letter box, begging for Ray's help.

Then the next second, Emma's voice was there again, telling him to do the 'right thing.'

"Bloody hell, woman! Leave me alone! Leave me in peace!" he shouted at his own conscience.

"You want me to do the right thing? Okay, I bloody will!" and Ray hurried through to his den, all thoughts of David now expunged from his mind and a fresh memory of Randolph Best filling it.

"You might have fooled the Pope, Mr Best, but you haven't fooled me!"

Ray sat down at his desk, logged on through his network defences, and started to plan exactly what he was going to do next.

1.25 p.m.

David closed the door to Chloe's flat, rushed to the toilet and threw up.

He paused for a while, hovering over the toilet bowl, wondering if he should just stick his head down the toilet and flush it until he drowned.

He couldn't go on like this.

David knew that he was almost at breaking point.

From out of nowhere they had pounced on him and forced him into the van.

"Where is Chloe?" the big black man had asked.

Ray had stared at him, speechless, panicking. What should he say?

"That was a bloody question, David. A question."

The black man hit him hard in the solar plexus.

David doubled over and gasped for breath.

"I'll ask again, politely. Where is your girlfriend? We know she didn't come home last night. And this morning she is not at work. Where is she?"

David coughed, clearing his throat and holding up his hand, signifying that the gang leader should wait... give him a chance to speak.

"I don't know," he lied. "I told her to leave work and not come home. Not to go back to work until I had found the money."

"And the envelope. AND the envelope David!"

"Yes, the envelope!" David nodded vigorously.

"So you thought you'd save her, huh?"

"Yes."

"Fine. Then we'll go and speak with your mother next. In Sheffield. No problem at all."

"Sheffield? How... how did you know?"

"You don't need to worry about that, David. Not now. All you need to know is that we have friends, colleagues, who run Sheffield. And it will only take a single phone call for them to visit Sally..."

"SALLY? HOW DO YOU KNOW HER NAME?"

The tall black man in front of him moved closer, his face only inches away from David's.

"This is your last warning, David. Tomorrow night, if you don't have the money, I will come for you. Personally. And if you run away, I will personally drive up to Sheffield and kill your mother."

"Tomorrow?" David's voice was shaking. "... And what will you do to me?"

The man laughed.

"Don't worry about that. If I were you I would worry what we won't do to you. For example, how many toes and fingers do you have left? How would you like to lose them one at a time? Slowly?"

David looked down at his bandaged hand.

"Why are you doing this to me?"

"Don't let's go through this again, David. You know why. Just get the money and the envelope and all this stops. Do you understand?"

Should he call his mother and tell her to leave Sheffield? Tell her to go on holiday?

What if he did? Would they kill his sister? His nephew?

Where would all this stop?

He sat on the bathroom floor thinking about his next move.

In reality, there was precious little more that he could probably do. He'd been to all the houses and flats in the square. He'd posted hundreds of flyers, and stuck posters everywhere.

If someone in the square had found the money, surely they would contact him.

Although, David already *knew* who had the money.

The more desperate he got, the more he tried to think of where else the money could be, the more his gut instinct told him that the man at No. 23 had it!

In spite of practically begging him to help - in fact, he *had* begged! - the man had still not said anything.

Had he spent the money?

Should David go and see him again and tell him it was actually not the money that was seemingly important: it was the envelope? "Just give me the envelope! Keep the bloody money!"

Or should David wait until the man left his flat and then break the door down and find and steal the money back himself?

Try as he might, David could see only one way out of the hole he was in.

He had to force the man with the money to give him it back.

But how?

The one thing that David knew that he could not do was to run away.

If he did, the people that were going to kill him, would kill those he loved instead.

In that moment, David knew one thing.

He was no longer a coward.

If the worst came to the worst, he would stay and face them.

He would not run.

Chapter 21

London

Thursday

October 3rd

3 p.m.

The glass of whisky stood on his desk, as yet untouched.

Ray had poured it out of habit as he had come through to the den, but realised now that he did not need it. Or want it.

After showering and shaving he had briefly logged onto work and was relieved to find that his boss was out of town. There was no need to fake it in a video call with her. He didn't have to pretend to be working or sober.

Instead he could relish his hangover in peace and carry on doing 'nothing' at CSD's expense.

Except this wasn't nothing, was it?

He was just about to bring one of the world's most powerful people to justice.

The only question was, how?

Emma's voice rang in his head: "*Do* the right thing!"

This time he didn't ignore it. He *was* going to do the right thing.

Ray was still furious. The anger pulsed in his veins. Deep down, somewhere in his fuddled brain, some part of him recognised the fact that the fury he felt towards Randolph Best was slightly overdone: Best had become a scapegoat for his anger and frustration with Emma.

The logic was simple.

Emma had destroyed Ray's life, and now he was going to destroy Randolph Best's life. Which made sense, because Randolph Best has destroyed his own girlfriend's life!

?

Or perhaps it didn't make sense, but actually, Ray did not care.

Randolph was still going to pay.

Unlike the past two days, Ray was determined to do this sober. This would be a premeditated strike for justice.

It reminded him of his days as an anarchist.

With what he knew, he was going to launch a massive strike against the ruling authorities.

Perhaps, if he handled this well and planned it properly, Ray could kill two birds with one stone. He could wound and expose Randolph Best in such a way that the knock-on effect would topple the government!

Ray had been sitting at his keyboard for the past thirty minutes. Thinking.

He was already logged onto his Brazilian Outlook account.

There were no new emails.

No replies from Mr Best.

And no flashing lights on the wall.

Everyone was good.

Twice Ray had started to write a long email, describing to R. F. Best exactly what he knew and making it very clear that he was going to post the video of the murder he'd committed on YouTube and spam the world so that everyone knew that it was there.

Randolph F. Best was the bloody Anti-Christ, and Ray was going to show and let the world know just why!

Each time though Ray had deleted the email after he had written it.

No. Just telling him what he knew would be too simple.

Ray had to play with him. Continue to tease him. Make him sweat.

Although it was clear that carrying on the way he had been going was not having any effect.

He had to rack it up a notch.

It should be subtle, but direct and to the point.

He thought about the thriller books that he had read, remembering the ones that were most scary.

It wasn't the number of words that you used, it was how you said it that drove the most chilling messages home.

Not quantity, but quality.

Short but sweet.

Deadly sweet.

A smile began to appear on Ray's lips and his fingers began to type.

The message was perfect.

After he had written it he stood up, went to the bathroom, made a fresh cup of coffee and then came back.

Staring at the words, he imagined how Randolph F. Best would react when he read the message.

It *would* make him sweat.

Perfect!

Ray lifted his right hand, extended his forefinger above the keyboard,... and hit send.

As the email winged its way around the world from the Outlook account in Brazil to Randolph's account in England, Ray repeated the email's contents to himself with a sense of pride.

His email was a classic.

Very simply the title of the email now read:

"I spy..."

Then, in the main body of the email he had delivered the payload.

"...I saw her ***DIE***!

R.I.P. Bayla Adelstein 1991-2015"

With the last line, Ray removed all doubt as to the power with which he now threatened Randolph F. Best.

Ray stood up, stretched and clapped his hands.
He felt good.
This is how a hunter must feel as he was tracking his prey.

The best part of it was that as far as Randolph Best was concerned, Ray was invisible.
In the cyber world which Ray ruled, Ray was a ghost.

3.05 p.m.

RobinHood's last doubt had evaporated with the latest round of public praise for Randolph Best.

At the best of times RobinHood's anger just boiled beneath the surface of his personality.

He'd never been able to hold down a job for long, had never had very many close friends, and nowadays, the only girlfriends he had came in magazines, or lived in very friendly houses in Germany which he would visit several times a year.

Called brothels.

His dissatisfaction with life fuelled his hatred of authority; quite consciously he blamed the authorities for almost everything that was wrong with his existence.

Now fat, overweight, frequently in excruciating pain, dying,... and spending most of his time in his own personal church, he had nothing to do but plan his part in the overthrow of the UK's government, the annihilation of as many of his fellow Londoners as possible, and how to hit the biggest bastards of all - the Bankers - a deadly blow from which the City of London would take months to recover, if ever.

He had been planning the cyber attack for months and the time for launching the attack was coming closer by the day.

If everything went well, he would launch the attack in less than two weeks. Perhaps sooner.

Today however, his anger directed away from the Bankers to 'Randolph the Wanker'.

As he read his profile in 'Who's Who?' he laughed quietly to himself when he saw that for a few years before entering politics, Randolph had been a Corporate Banker. A partner in one of London's top banks.

It helped firm his resolve.

Swivelling in his chair, he pushed himself across to another monitor and searched for the video file that he had copied from SolarWind.

Yes, true, SolarWind had asked him not to keep a copy, and yes, true, RobinHood had promised not to, but, hey... RobinHood was just being prudent.

He had kept a copy, just in case he might need it... In case a special occasion arose, like the one that had presented itself today.

Randolph Best had become the darling of the Western World.

But he and SolarWind knew the truth.

Sitting back in his chair, and watching the video, RobinHood's mind was thinking, calculating, planning.

Actually, it could all work out quite well.

First, RobinHood would hack into several TV stations - he'd done it before, no problem - and prepare to release the video of the murder so that it would play on TV stations across the world simultaneously at a time of his later choosing. He would build a small software program that would also simultaneously release the video to the media, including YouTube and Facebook, and all the major tabloids.

RobinHood would claim responsibility for it all.

The public would at first be shocked, but as the truth came out and millions of people across the globe watched the video and discovered the truth, they would respect RobinHood for what he had done.

He would issue a statement.

People would love him!

A week later he would launch the cyber attack which would knock out the City of London.

So many people already hate the bankers, that when they discovered that he also claimed responsibility for the attack, claiming revenge on behalf of the working man who had suffered through the recession while the bankers had become wealthier and wealthier, RobinHood would become a national hero! He was sure of it.

RobinHood was excited.

For the first time in years, he had a plan.

A plan which would make him happier, respected, loved and admired.

The last real hero that the British public had was Winston Churchill.

If everything went smoothly over the next few weeks, RobinHood would be the next.

3.10 p.m.

Ferris sipped his coffee and watched the computer screen in front of him. Through his dashboard he could monitor everything he needed to know about the three main cases he had been assigned.

Randolph Best was his top priority, which is why half of the dashboard covered activity that related to him.

Suddenly, one of the boxes on the top left of the screen started to flash. Putting his coffee down, he leant forward and touched the flashing box with his finger.

The box expanded and instantly took over the whole screen.

It was Randolph Best's personal email account.

Another email had arrived.

This in itself was not of great significance: he got about two emails every hour.

But when Ferris read the title of the email, he sat up straight, clicked on the email and opened it up: an action that thanks to their systems, they were able to perform without the real account holder being aware that their emails were being read.

"Bingo!" Ferris said aloud, reading the content of the email.

This was exactly what he had been waiting for.

The third email in the series!

The email was significant for another reason as well.

It was no longer ambiguous.

The person who had sent this email - his account name was just a number of no importance - had directly related his observations to the death of the Israeli model and connected her death to Randolph Best. He had not blamed Best for her death, but the insinuation was very strong.

In response to the receipt of the email, Ferris did two things.

Firstly, he picked up the phone and dialled through to his superior, informing him of the latest event.

Secondly, he toggled from the email account across to another dashboard that presented all the cyber toolsets at their disposal, and opened up Gretel.

He copied across the necessary parameters from the latest email, hit return and launched the tracker program.

Agent Ferris had already tried to run the program the day before, but after eighteen hours of crunching terabytes of data, if not more, it had drawn a blank.

They needed that third email to complete the 'triangulation'.

Now they had it.

Ferris opened up the Incident Management system, created a new ticket to describe what had just happened, and entered all the necessary details.

He looked at his watch.

Perfect. If all went well, Gretel should finish its run just after he got to work in the morning to start his shift.

With any luck, by lunch time tomorrow morning, the person who was behind this attack on Randolph Best would either be in a police cell somewhere in the world, or most probably dead.

Ferris tended to veer towards the 'dead' prognosis.

If the person had, as they claimed, seen Randolph Best killing the Israeli model, he or she would not be allowed to live.

There was too much at stake and the risk of the person taking their knowledge public was too great.

A thought occurred to Ferris, rapidly followed by a twinge of anticipation and excitement.

If the person who wrote the email lived in the UK, would Ferris be the person deployed and instructed to silence him/her?

He hoped so.

<u>Chapter 22</u>

London

Thursday

October 3rd

5 p.m.

Ray had not touched a drop of alcohol all day.

It felt strangely empowering. Not that he was an alcoholic... it had only been in the past week that he had really ever drunk so much.

It was just that his life was falling apart... *had* fallen apart... and today he was facing it all square on. Sober. In spite of all the things that had happened to him.

He had lost his one true love. Simultaneously he now also found himself at the centre of a conspiracy and scandal that could rock the Western world and bring down the British Government. He was also the only person who knew where the missing twenty thousand was,... and, *oh shit!*... he had committed one of the UK's worst ever cyber crimes!

In all the excitement and heartbreak of the past few days, he'd completely forgotten about that one.

Standing up from his sofa and walking to the window, looking down into the beautiful private gardens in the centre of the square, he thought about that last, minor thought: the bit about committing one of the worst cyber enabled crimes in UK history...

Was he a criminal?

Would he got to prison?

Thinking back on it now, he realised that he probably could.

For a very long time.

Shit!

Given everything else that was going on, this was probably something he didn't actually need on his plate to worry about just now.

How much had he stolen from the bank?

He tried to remember...You'd think he would remember something like that, wouldn't you?

Was it £500,000 or was it £5,000,000?

£5,000,000?

Bloody hell, it was just a matter of where to put the comma, but he couldn't remember exactly where he had put it.

At the time, he hadn't taken it that seriously.

Should he hack back into the bank and put it all back?
Tell them it was joke?

Then it dawned on him.

He hadn't actually accessed a single penny of the money - mainly because he had forgotten about it until now... ('How could I forget I'd stolen £5,000,000?')... and he'd practically not left the flat or had time to go and pick up the bank cards which gave him access to the accounts he'd put the money in.

Surely there was an argument that since he hadn't spent a penny of their money that he hadn't actually stolen anything?

Yet the thought that came to him next was even simpler.

The bank had been paying him to hack into the account.

All he'd done was demonstrate - admittedly on an unparalleled scale never before witnessed in the history of professional penetration testing - that anyone could hack into their bank and help themselves to their money... just as he had done.

All he had to do was go and collect all the bank cards, take them into the bank when he gave them his report and give them back.

He began to imagine his presentation to their Board of Directors: "Hi, My name is Ray Luck... blah, blah, blah... And now, before I continue and show you the results of my testing to see if your bank is secure or not, may I first ask you all... Has anyone here noticed that you may have lost... say... a small figure, like... five MILLION pounds?"

He'd wait for a pause... and then he would drop all thirty bank cards onto the table, invite each board member to take a few, and explain that each account contained between £16,700 or £167,000, depending upon how much money he had actually stolen..."Incidentally, I can't exactly remember how much I did take, but it was a lot of money and a lot of fun...!" Laugh, laugh.

The looks on their faces would be priceless.

Priceless.

Or at least £500,000 worth.

Below him, he watched as a very attractive young woman entered the park from the other side of the square and started to walk her dog.

She reminded him of Emma, interrupting his though processes and forcing his busy mind to move on to another topic.

Emma.

Should he call her?

Go round to see her?

Try to stop her going to Canada?

Heading back into his den he picked up his mobile from his desk, - quickly checking his Outlook account to see if Mr R. F. Best had replied yet - *he hadn't* - and then went back into the lounge and took up his position at the window again.

The woman was now standing on the grass near his side of the square. She had thrown a ball and the dog was chasing it.

Ray dialled her number without even looking at the keypad.

It rang five times and then she answered.

"Hi," Ray said, quietly.

"Hi," she replied. "I was wondering when you would call? Did you not get my message?"

"Yes, thanks, I did. But I wasn't in the right mood to call you back. Emma..." he paused, swallowing and trying to fight back the wave of emotion that seemed to come up from nowhere and threaten to engulf him, "... Emma came round and picked up her stuff."

"Were you there?"

"No, Sis, I wasn't here. The cow came round when she knew I would be out. Sneaked in behind my back... grabbed her stuff and left!"

"Cow? Do you *really* think she's a *cow*, Ray? I don't think you really mean that, do you?"

Ray choked. His sister was right. She was always bloody right. That's why he loved her so much.

"No," he replied quietly. "I don't."

There was a pause.

His sister said nothing, waiting for him to talk. She knew he wanted to talk. That's why he had called her.

"She's going to live in Canada. Permanently."

"What?" his sister replied, her voice raised. "When?"

"On Saturday."

"How do you know?"

"She left me a voice message. A simple few sentences... nothing fancy. Just a quick 'Hi, Ray, I'm going to live in Canada. Have a nice life!' "

"Was that what she said? Her actual words?"

"No... not exactly. But it was something like that."

"How long had she been planning this for? Did you know anything about it?"

"No."

There was a silence at the other end, before his sister came up with her summation, built and informed by years of wisdom and several very bad relationships.

"*What a cow!*" she exclaimed. Which gave Ray the answer to the question he had not even bothered to ask her: 'Should I call her? Beg for forgiveness? For mercy? Another chance?'

"Ray, perhaps you're better off without her. Move on. Find someone else."

Ray nodded without uttering any words.

His sister was right. He knew she was.

Ray only had one question left to ask.

"Why does it hurt so much, Claire? *Why?*"

9.10 p.m.

Having managed to remain sober for the entire day, Ray had decided that it would be a good idea to go to the gym for a detox. He'd had a swim, sat in the sauna, gone in the cold water plunge pool, and spent ten minutes in the steam room.

He'd come out a new man.

Fresh.

Invigorated.

Even clean shaven.

He felt great.

Until he got back to his street and found David standing at the bottom of the steps outside his building.

For a second he thought about turning around and going somewhere else to avoid him, but then David saw him and called after him.

Ray sighed.

"Blast!"

"Hi!" David said, almost apologetically as Ray approached him.

"Let me guess..." Ray replied. "You found the money?"

David shook his head.

"You know I didn't. Can we talk?"

Ray looked at him.

A twinge of guilt hit him. He didn't know why. This guy was involved in something that would just be bad news for Ray and Ray had sworn,

SWORN, NEVER to get involved with anything to do with drugs again. *ANYTHING!* Yet, Ray *DID* have his money...

"Five minutes. I'll give you five minutes."

"Where?"

Ray looked around him.

"Over there. In the park," he said, nodding towards the other side of the road.

They crossed the street, Ray walking first.

When they got to the entrance to the park, Ray typed in the code to the electronic keypad on the gate, and then pushed it open and walked in.

David followed Ray into the centre of the park, where Ray dropped his stuff and sat down on the grass.

"Five minutes."

David stood still, nervously looking around the park.

"Worried that your friends from the white van might see you?"

David gawped at Ray.

"I saw you this morning. Sit down."

David joined Ray on the grass in the dark.

"Shoot. The clock is ticking..." Ray instructed.

David took a deep breath, obviously gathering his thoughts for a moment.

"I'm going to level with you. Tell you the truth. I haven't got any more time to mess around. If I don't get the money back by tomorrow the men in the van will probably kill me. Or at least, they'll cut off the rest of my fingers."

Ray looked at his hand.

"They did that?"

"Yes."

David hesitated.

"The money isn't mine. It belongs to someone who wants it back very badly. I've offered to pay the money to whoever lost it with my own money, but they want THAT money back. I guess it's stolen money. Maybe they're scared of the serial numbers on the notes being discovered if someone spends them. I don't know. Anyway, they want it back, badly. They're forcing me to help them find it..."

"How did you get involved in this mess, if what you say is true, and it's not your money?"

"They thought I was you."

Ray choked.

"What?" he spluttered. "Me?"

"Yes. On Monday they kidnapped me off the street, they bundled me into the back of a van...took me somewhere quiet and then beat the crap out of me. They thought I had the money..."

"Why?"

"Someone told the men in the van they had seen a young man walking down the street about the same time the money went missing. He'd been carrying a brown bag and a newspaper, and a coffee. The men in the van hung out in the square looking for a young man who might fit the picture... they saw me... I fitted the bill...Bloody hell, I don't know why they thought it was me...but the thing is, they did. And then, when they'd beaten me up and it was obvious I didn't know what the hell they were talking about, they decided to use me to find it. I'm their eyes and ears in the square. Obviously it's easier for me to make enquiries, than a bunch of heavies in suits. People know me, or at least they recognise me."

"So why don't you go to the police?" Ray asked, being drawn into the problem even further.

"Because I can't. If I do, they will slash my girlfriend's face with a razor, disfigure her,...then probably kill her. I got my girlfriend out of here...she's gone...but the gang tracked down my family and are now threatening to kill my mum. And me. I've got until tomorrow night..."

Ray was silent.

He sat thinking for a few moments.

There was something about the way David spoke...maybe it was his body language, or the tone of his voice, ...or just the calm way he seemed to state the facts as if he had almost resigned himself to the inevitability of what was going to happen... whatever it was, Ray couldn't help but believe that he was telling the truth.

Which made everything a lot more complicated.

"Time's up." Ray said, starting to stand up.

David reached out to grab him, but as he looked up at Ray, his mouth forming some words to speak, he hesitated, closed his lips and withdrew his hand without touching him.

For a second their eyes met again, and in that moment Ray could feel the man's pain.

"This is all a bit heavy, ...David. Really heavy. I need time to think."

"What's there to think about? Either you know where the money is or you don't."

"Like I said, David, I need time to think."

"Fine. Take all the time you need. But don't leave it too long. This time tomorrow, I'll probably be dead. And if I am, it'll be your fault."

Ray looked at the man, nodded in acknowledgment and then turned his back and walked away.

Inside, he'd already made up his mind. He knew he was going to do the right thing.

The question was...how to do it?

Chapter 23

London

Friday

October 4th

6.55 a.m.

Ferris had come in an hour early. Ferris loved his work. He found it mentally stimulating, constantly challenging and extremely rewarding.

He was helping to defend his country, his loved ones and his way of life.

A new generation of spy, the cyber spy was probably more important, more efficient and effective than any 007 had ever been.

Ferris was one of the crème-de-la-crème. When the agency had first employed him he was already one of the best, but now, after years of further training and investment from the government, what Ferris didn't know about cyber warfare, you could probably write on the back of a postage stamp.

All last night he had been thinking about the Randolph Best case.

Would he catch his man - or woman? What would the program find for him over night?

Would it pinpoint the person behind the emails?

As well as wondering if he could be able to complete his mission and track this person down, Ferris had also started to wonder about the person's motivation.

Why were they doing this?

What did they hope to gain?

Was the intention to ultimately blackmail Randolph Best?

Would that be the next email to arrive: 'Unless you deposit £1million pounds in a bank of my choosing, I'll tell the world?"

Highly likely.

Although, at this stage, Ferris couldn't tell.

Given Randolph Best's esteemed position in society, blackmail could probably well be the ultimate goal of this activity, but for now it was not possible to tell. It could go one of many ways...if Ferris didn't catch him soon.

Which he would.

Ferris had decided that finding the person behind this threat would be his number one personal priority.

Disappointingly, when Ferris arrived at work the Gretel program was still chugging away, having not yet come to any successful resolution. The timer showed that it still had another hour to go, at least.

That had been ninety minutes ago.

The result was due any moment now.

Expectantly, Ferris watched the dashboard, willing the program to stop, and for the answer he needed to pop up on the screen.

The clock said he only had a few more minutes to go...the programme was coming to an end. It would be soon. Very soon indeed.

7.30 a.m.

Ray stirred, opened his eyes and was instantly wide awake.

He had had a terrible night.

An evening of fitful sleep, dreams and feeling terrible.

Mainly from guilt.

After speaking with David the night before, he knew he had no choice but to hand the money over.

Ray believed what the man had said. David was in big trouble. Serious trouble.

Ray had no doubt that the men looking for the money would probably kill David if he didn't produce the goods. Goods which Ray had hidden in his flat.

Which would make Ray responsible for David's death, if it happened.

Which it wouldn't, because Ray knew that he would have to give the money back today.

Being sober had its downside...such as realising that in spite of not wanting to get involved or have anything to do with any drug gang, he already was.

Ironically, although Emma would never find out, it had turned out that Ray was right all along.

The money was drug money, and the danger had been real.

Was still real.

The question was, how could Ray give the money back without getting dragged into the whole sordid mess and ending up dead in an alley somewhere?

It didn't seem to Ray that he could hand the money over to David and that would be the end of it...could it be that simple?

On the other hand, it could be that simple. If David didn't know who they were, once they had the cash, they could simply disappear and David or the police would never be able to track them down. So perhaps, they would just leave it at that.

After all, if they already had the money, and they then killed someone, that would just make things far worse for them... the police would definitely get involved...and they'd surely find a fingerprint somewhere...?

Ray could find arguments that went both ways.

One stream of thought ended up with both Ray and David dead as dodos. The other had them both having a relaxing beer on Saturday night, both looking back together on a week from hell that had been bad at the time, but which had passed.

Albeit with David having half a finger less.

After checking his Outlook account - which had no new emails - going for a quick jog, showering, and then making some scrambled eggs and bacon for breakfast, Ray decided that he would think about it some more.

He had David's phone number and address.

Was there a way that Ray could be more clever about this?

Could he come up with a plan that guaranteed both David's and his own safety?

Surely, there must be some way!

However, having spent the evening before thinking about it and going over it repeatedly in his mind, he still hadn't found an answer.

He would give himself until lunch time -12 noon - to think of something.

After that, if he hadn't thought of anything, he would just hand over the cash and keep every finger crossed.

Which would be one more than David had.

Ouch!

Knowing that he couldn't continue to do nothing for work, but not yet ready to face up to going into the office again, he called in sick.

"A virus...apparently. The doctor says there's a lot of it going round. I just have to wait for it to wash itself out of my system." He explained to his boss when he called the office. "But I stopped throwing up early this morning. I feel much better now. I could come into the office if you want me to. I've got so much to do..."

Surprisingly, his boss had insisted that he didn't.

"Stay at home and rest. Take the day off. I think you've overworked yourself on trying to crack your way into the bank. I know how much you hate to fail, Ray, but maybe it's not a bad thing that we can't get in to their systems. For once we've found someone who took all our advice two years ago after our last security assessment and who is now pretty secure!"

"I'd like to agree with you," Ray replied. "But I can't. I cracked it! Yesterday afternoon. I got in after all."

"Honestly?" his boss beamed.

"Would I lie to you?" Ray replied. "I'll start writing it all up on Monday. We can go see them next Friday and give our report to their management team then, if you want to."

As the conversation drew to a close, Ray knew that if they did go to see the bank next week, pretty soon he would have to make up his mind about the money he had stolen from them.

Would he tell them?

Or would he keep the five million pounds for himself?

He knew what Emma would say.

"Do the right thing!"

The thing was, Emma was gone.

She'd left him, and *she'd* done the wrong thing.

Ray was upset and still angry, and he knew it would just get worse, not better, as he thought more and more about her over the coming weeks.

Which is why, Ray knew, the only way to survive was not to think of her.

To forget her.

And move on.

There was one problem.

He had loved Emma. A lot.

And, try as he had over the past few days to block her out of his mind, whenever a sober thought of her passed through his brain, he felt an accompanying wave of pain and sadness.

The reason why, Ray knew only too well.

Ray was still in love with her.

Always had been, and always would be.

Even if she was in Canada and he never saw her again.

She had been the one.

8.25 a.m.

Ferris was beginning to get impatient. Every time the timer on the program showed that it only had a minute left to go, it would recalibrate itself and suddenly announce that it still had another ten minutes of processing to do.

It had done that several times, and now as the clock counted down from sixty seconds, the final minute, Ferris held his breath.

Was this it?

Was the program finally going to complete?

Would he know in just a matter of seconds who the email had come from and what their location was?

Ferris watched the last few digits on the digital clock begin to count down: ten, nine, eight...

Quite literally, he held his breath.

Five, four...

Three.

Two.

One.

The screen went blank, turned white, and then the final dashboard appeared with the summary of its run.

"Target undetermined. Location unknown. Insufficient data."

Ferris's heart sank.

"What?" he said aloud, "...but we had three distinct emails! This has never happened before."

For a few moments he sat there in silence, the significance of the message sinking in.

The strength of the anonymising program that the target was running was much greater than he had at first believed. As far as Ferris knew, this was the first time that Gretel had not managed to follow the breadcrumbs through the forest back to the origin.

For now, they were as lost as ever.

"Blast!" he said, thumping the table in front of him so hard that Agent Rees took off his headphones and turned around in the cubicle beside him.

"What's up?" he asked.

Ferris ignored him, picked up the phone and pressed three digits.

He was immediately routed through to his boss, now somewhere in the Middle East at the Peace Summit, where he was accompanying Randolph Best as part of his security contingent.

"Speak," his boss said.

"Sir, the program completed. The target is still yet unknown."

"What? I thought you said we had three emails?"

"We do. It's not enough. We need more."

"So what do you advise?"

"We need another email...," Ferris hesitated, reconsidering what he was just about to suggest, but then realising it was probably the best option. "Have you advised Unicorn already? Is he aware of the emails?" Ferris knew not to mention Best by name across an international connection, even though it was an encrypted and secure link. No one *really* knew how powerful the American surveillance systems were. Unicorn was Randolph Best's code name.

"Yes. I have. And he's read them. I cautioned him not to respond. That we were working on it."

"Sir, would it be possible to discuss it with him again this morning? I have a suggestion that would really help. If you could request Unicorn to respond to the latest email directly, we might be able to flush out a response. Perhaps prompt the target to send a fourth, possibly a fifth email?"

"I'm due to escort him to lunch. I can get his attention and speak to him then. Do you have any suggestions what he should say?"

"Yes. Tell him to reply and say that he doesn't believe whoever sent the emails. Suggest that he asks the author of the emails to prove his claim about what he saw. Something short but sweet, and slightly arrogant. Make the target angry. We need to force them to react spontaneously so that they make a mistake and we can flush them out."

"Agreed. But Unicorn is busy. Why don't you do it on his behalf?"

"Sir?"

"Just do it, okay? We need to catch this person soon. Do you understand?"

"Certainly." Ferris hesitated. "Sir?"

"Yes?"

"I have a request if I may?"

"The answer is yes."

Ferris frowned, surprised by the response.

"But I haven't asked the question yet, sir."

"I'm short of time. You want to ask me if you can take care of business once we know who we are dealing with, correct?"

"Correct, but how....?"

"As I said, so long as he/she is on UK territory, you are authorised to lead the sweeping party. I've already sent you the permission through the normal channels. Is that all?"

Ferris was almost speechless. His boss continued to amaze him.

Which is one of the reasons he had requested the transfer to this team originally.

When Ferris checked his emails a few minutes later, he saw that his boss had indeed already sent Form Z9 through, in anticipation of the previous run of Gretel being more successful than it had been.

Form Z9 however, did specify one condition.

Ferris was to try and bring the target in alive. Not dead.

Whoever it was that was sending these emails to Unicorn was very clever. Very clever indeed.

Rather than immediately dispose of him, the agency needed the target to tell them as much as possible about the details of the cyber or terrorist group to which they belonged, as well as information about the anonymising program they were using.

Whatever it was, it was very powerful.

The agency needed to understand what it was, how it worked, and if they could get a copy for themselves.

Ferris agreed.

Thankfully, after they had what they needed to know, Form Z9 also gave full permission for the target to be liquidated.

Ferris smiled.

Perhaps all was not yet lost.

Chapter 24

London

Friday

October 4th

10.45 a.m.

David sat in his bedroom looking through the photographs of the last time he and Chloe had been together on holiday.

He had just spent the past hour talking to her on the phone.

She was fine. Worried about David. Terrified that something bad might happen to him.

But she was safe.

His mother was also safe.

Or safer.

He had booked a nice weekend away for her, and a taxi had picked her and her best friend up an hour ago and both of them were now on a train heading towards Scarborough.

They would stay there for the weekend, and come home on Tuesday.

David knew he didn't have to worry about Chloe or his mum.

All he had to worry about was himself.

For a while he had considered fighting back when they came to get him.

Perhaps he could kill them before they killed him?

Unfortunately, David had never killed anything in his life before, and he didn't imagine he could start now.

How do you kill someone?

What do you do?

He didn't have a gun. Should he stab them with a kitchen knife?

He shuddered at the thought.

Should he call the police?

Perhaps.

Maybe he would.

The thought scared him.

What would happen if the police did arrest the gang, but they were then released?

Even if they did get sent to prison for a few years, nowadays people only ever served half of their sentence.

They would be out in a few years, if not months, and then they would be even angrier than they were now.

David knew that there probably was a solution. An answer. Somewhere.

But he was so scared, and mentally so terribly, terribly tired that he struggled to think. Everything was so confusing. Everything was taking on dark, sinister overtones.

He had tried so hard to convince the man who he still believed had the money, but in spite of his pleading, he had not budged or admitted to it at all.

Perhaps his instinct had been wrong after all.

Surely, *surely*, if he had been right, the man would have returned the money by now? What sort of person would keep it and watch as another man had his fingers hacked off and was possibly murdered?

No, David must have been wrong.

He looked at his watch.
Time was passing so quickly.
Soon it would be the evening.
They would come for him.
He would die.
He felt resigned to it now.

11.25 a.m.

Time was ticking by.
Ray paced his flat back and forward.
Thinking.
Pondering.
Practically praying…there had to be a way he could help David without endangering his own life, and also helping David to protect his own.

Yet, every scenario he could think off ended up, almost invariably, in the demise of any possible witnesses.

Ray knew these guys. They were ruthless.

Pushing thoughts about David to the back of his mind, he looked at his watch and realised it was time to check on his emails again.

Walking back through to his den, he sat down at his desk and refreshed the Brazilian Outlook account.

Nothing.
No response.

Since yesterday Ray had started to come to terms with the Randolph F. Best affair.

He was still as angry about it as before, but what could he do about it?

In spite of everything it was beginning to look like there was no one reading the email account he was sending his emails to.

The last email had sparked no reaction whatsoever.

If Randolph Best had read the email Ray was sure that he would have responded in some way.

But there was nothing.

He began to feel like an idiot.

He was getting incredibly stressed and excited about sending his cleverly worded threats to one of the most powerful people in the world, but it seemed he was just wasting his time.

What other options did he have?

To send the video to the press?

Hand it into the police?

Publish it online?

Publish it online!

Wow...why hadn't he thought of that before?

Surely that was his next, best option.

Actually maybe it was the only safe option he had.

Suddenly the screen in front of him moved, and Ray's heart jumped.

An email had just popped into his inbox.

Ray read who the email was from in almost pure disbelief. The name in the left hand column that identified the sender said, quite simply.

"Randolph Best."

And the title of the email was:

"Re: I spy."

Randolph Best had replied to his email!

Ray's heart started to thump hard against his chest, the adrenaline shooting into his arteries and instantly kicking in the primordial 'Fight or Flight' response.

Breathing deeply and with a shaking hand, Ray moved the mouse onto the email, pausing for a second before he finally decided to click it open.

The content of the reply to his message *'I spy, I saw her die!'* was three words.

"Prove it, asshole!"

12.35 a.m.

Emma stood above the River Thames, looking down at the cold, dark water flowing so quickly out to the sea.

She was standing on the Millennium Footbridge linking St Paul's Cathedral and the Tate Modern. She and Ray had walked over this bridge many times together.

When they had started dating, it was one of the first places that they had kissed.

She knew that Ray probably never thought about things like she did... he wasn't as romantic as her... but every time she saw a picture of the bridge she thought of that first kiss, and it gave her goosebumps.

Even now. Even today when she was leaving the country tomorrow.

She had come to London this morning to walk and think and to say goodbye.

She hadn't planned to come to this spot, but now she was here, she wasn't surprised.

It was a good place to be to think of Ray.

She missed him.

She loved him.

Still.

And yet, deep down, she knew there was no hope now.

She'd been dreading telling Ray that she was moving to Canada, because she was worried about his reaction.

On the one hand she was worried that he would come chasing after her, begging her to think twice, to take him back, pleading his love for her. And even more than that, she was worried that she might agree.

Her plans would be ruined, and she wouldn't move on with her life and experience any new adventures. Ray would win. She would lose. Or would she? Perhaps she would win everything she had ever wanted: Ray!

On the other hand, she was also scared that he would hate her. He would call her, swear at her down the phone, they'd have an argument and they would never talk to each other again. But she would go to Canada, and soon she would be happy?

The one thing she hadn't thought would happen when she finally plucked up the courage to tell Ray was ....'nothing'!

In all of her imaginings, Ray had reacted strongly. Either positively or negatively.

But at least he had done something.

And what had happened in real life? What had he done?

NOTHING!

She had got no reaction from him at all.

For a while her mind had gone into overtime, worrying about him.

Was he okay? Had he got her message? Or was he in hospital somewhere...?

She had a million different thoughts... She'd even almost got in a taxi and gone over to his house last night in the middle of the night.

In the end, her best friend had listened to her crying on the other end of the phone at 3.30 a.m. in the morning and persuaded her not to do anything.

It was quite obvious that Ray had moved on.

"Men," she had said. "They're all the bloody same. Honestly Emma, from what you've told me, you're better off without him!"

Perhaps she was right.

First thing tomorrow morning she would get on that plane, leave this country for good, and start a new life.

A life without Ray.

A new life. A better life.

Wiping away her tears, she looked up at the sun and closed her eyes.

She could feel the warmth upon her face and the sunshine dancing on her eyelids.

Smiling inwardly she repeated the little mantra to herself that she had been chanting all morning.

"A new life.
A *better* life."

If only she believed herself.

1.00 p.m.

In a matter of just a few short seconds, from opening the email response from Randolph Best to reading it and digesting its meaning, Ray went from being calm to incensed with rage.

He'd been looking for a response from R. F. Best, not knowing fully how he would respond, but seeing the words 'Prove it, asshole!' was something he had never expected.

Asshole?

"Bastard!" Ray had shouted upon reading it.

"Bastard! Bastard! ***Bastard***!!!!!"

Who the hell did Randolph FUCKING Best think he was?

Obviously Ray's email had not moved him at all! Instead of being cautious, wary, or even a little scared that someone out there knew his big secret, the bastard had actually doubted him and called him an asshole!

Ray jumped up from his desk and stormed about his flat, punching the wall several times, and repeatedly coming back into his den and reading the email over and over again.

He couldn't quite believe what he was reading!

"Prove it?" Ray shouted. "Don't you fucking worry mate, I will prove it. Beyond any bloody shadow of a doubt, *mate*, I'll prove it to the whole bloody world!"

His hands and fingers were shaking as he sat down at the keyboard and began to type a reply.

"FUCK YOU, ASSHOLE! WATCH YOUTUBE IN TEN MINUTES!"

He was just about to press return, and send the email when he caught himself.

He was breathing hard, and practically hyperventilating.

He read the email again, hesitating.

Inhaling slowly, he fought to control his breathing.

In....out...Innnnnn...ouuuutttttt......deep breath in....and now...a deeeeeepppp breath out.

Pressing Control A and 'Delete' he erased his message.

Standing up slowly, he returned to his kitchen and popped on the kettle.

He needed a coffee. A chance to step away and think rationally.

Why had Randolph Best replied like that?

Returning to the den, he checked the source email address just to make sure it did originate from the same place he had sent his email to.

The addresses corresponded.

He returned to the kitchen, switched the kettle off and made himself a strong, very black coffee.

"Shit!" Ray swore to himself.

He knew he needed to calm down. To think rationally. To plan what his response would be.

The last thing that Ray or SolarWind should ever do would be to shoot from the hip, and make a gut reaction response.

Ray took the coffee, marched through to the bathroom, stripped off and stepped into the shower, turning the temperature to cold.

As the water cascaded over his body, he focussed his mind and closed his eyes.

Think, Ray, *think*.

Plan. Think. Don't just react.

What would the best response be?

Why had Randolph challenged him like that?

Towelling himself down he walked through to the lounge, wrapping the towel around his waist. Resting one hand against the window, he looked out onto the park below.

Incredibly, as he gazed downward, out of the corner of his eye he saw David, standing at the side of the road, staring up at him.

For a second their gazes locked in on each other.

"Fuck off! Leave me alone, man, leave me alone!" Ray shouted loudly, thumping the wall beside the window frame.

Pulling back, he stepped backwards into his room and landed himself on the sofa.

He'd had enough of David.

Ray had given himself a couple of hours to try and think of a good solution to the bloody mess but didn't come up with anything. Dealing with David was the last thing he needed to have to deal with everything else that was going on.

He also felt very guilty. Ray knew that the right thing to do was to help the guy get out of the situation he was in.

Knowing what he did now, if he didn't help him, he'd be just as bad as the bloody drug bastards who were threatening to kill David in the first place.

Ray needed a clear mind, and couldn't afford to be distracted any longer.

Walking through to the hallway he picked up the paper from the table with David's phone number on it, and fished his mobile phone out of his trousers on the chair in the bathroom.

Typing in the number he sent a quick text to David.

"*I think I might know who has the money. Got a bigger problem just now, but will call you in a few hours when I'm done. Don't worry. I think we can sort this*!"

The moment he pressed 'Send' Ray felt a tiny wave of relief spread through him, and for a brief second he thought of Emma.

He squashed the thought immediately.

Tossing the mobile phone onto the table, he walked slowly back into the den.

A thought had just occurred to him.

Perhaps Best was actually scared? Perhaps he was just trying to take some control back from a situation which had the potential to turn into a nightmare for the world's most eligible bachelor?

And if Randolph was scared, perhaps he was just fishing to try and find out exactly what Ray knew?

After all, how was he to know that Ray wasn't bluffing?

The phone in his hall beeped. Ray ignored it. It was obviously a message back from David.

He could wait.

Right now he had bigger fish to fry.

The thing was, Ray had to take back control and *remain* in control. He had to be the one playing with Randolph, and not allow Randolph to play with his head.

Ray was the one in the driver's seat, not the other way round.

Ray was the Hunter. Best was the Hunted!

He tapped a message on the keyboard: "I spy," - the title header.

He began to play with the main message in his mind.

And then he had it.

He knew what he was going to do, and what he was going to write.

Chapter 25

London

Friday

October 4th

1.45 p.m.

David stood outside on the street, wondering whether in spite of everything, he should maybe try talking to the man in the flat one more time - he still didn't know his name.
He was looking up at the window, thinking about it when suddenly the man appeared, looked out across the park, and then downwards, directly into David's eyes.
The man looked angry. Very angry.
For a few fleeting seconds the man stared down at him, then moved back from the window and disappeared from view.
He was gone.

The man had seen him. He knew David was out there. And his sixth sense told David that the man did actually now believe his story.
So why was he not going to give him the money?
A thought occurred to David that he hadn't had before.
What if the man *did* once have it, but not now?
Perhaps he'd gambled it all away?
Given it away?

Feeling suddenly very lonely, and once again scared - the fear seemed to come and go in waves-, he decided that he needed to speak to Chloe.
Pulling out his iPhone from his pocket, he was just about to call her, when the phone vibrated slightly in his hand and a text arrived.
It was from an unknown number.
But when David read the message his heart soared, and he punched the air with joy!
"Yeeessssss!"

The message read:

"I think I might know who has the money. Got a bigger problem just now, but will call you in a few hours when I'm done. Don't worry. I think we can sort this!"

David looked up at the window, expecting to see the man standing looking down at him again.

No one was there.

David waited for another ten minutes then decided to go home and wait for the phone call that could save his life.

2.00 p.m.

"I spy" Ray had already written into the title of the email, which he followed by typing in slowly, "...As *YOU* killed her, I watched her die."

He thought about it for a few minutes longer, then hit 'Send'.

That was only the first part of his plan.

Next, he opened up his favourite movie making package - and imported the video of Best killing the Israeli model.

He selected a few of the best bits, cut them out, and inserted them into a short video clip, which he then interspersed with some text titles.

At the beginning of the thirty second teaser he created, he wrote "I SPY..." with text that reminded him of the beginning of a cinema blockbuster movie. The next few seconds were of the woman stripping, some passionate kissing between them, a short clip of him standing in the doorway with his face now clearly visible, followed by a few seconds of the fight scene and then her falling to the floor with the knife embedded deeply into her chest.

The last image on the screen was of her eyes staring blankly at the camera, hauntingly...before the credits rolled up:

**"British Government Members of Parliament Productions
Proudly Presents
'Death by Stabbing'**

**Starring
Bayla Adelstein as the Murder Victim
&
Randolph Best as The Murderer."**

When Ray played the video back, and then added a small sound track, he couldn't help but admitting to himself that it looked quite professional. It was short, but to the point, and he was sure that Randolph Best would absolutely love it.

He loaded it in an email, relieved that the final file compressed size was not too large for Outlook, and closed his eyes to think of a suitable message to go with it.

Actually, it didn't take long. A few seconds later the email was primed and ready to go.
It read:

"I spy..." in the header, followed by,
"Oh look, I watched the whole thing and recorded it...I wonder, who would like to watch this little movie first? The Pope, the Queen, or the great British Public? Perhaps I'll just send it to them all, courtesy of YouTube. Say goodbye to your career and 'Hello' to prison! Who, Mr Best, is the **ASSHOLE** now? ...You murdering bastard!"

Ray sat back, read the email several times, and thought it was pretty, bloody perfect. It certainly got the point across quite nicely.

He hit 'Send'.

3.00 p.m.

Ferris had just returned from a late lunch when the first email arrived. He read it and almost screamed aloud with pleasure.
"Brilliant!"
The idiot had taken the bait and fallen right into their trap.

"I spy... As *YOU* killed her, I watched her die."

Ferris sent a quick message to his boss.
"Email worked. Now have 4th email in reply. Will immediately initiate new run of Gretel with the new data."

After sending the message Ferris immediately got to work. He initiated Gretel, input all the parameters from the new email, and started the run.
Surely, this time it would succeed.
Noting the time, he filled out a ticket in the incident management system so that if he was not on duty when the run finished, the next agent would know to call him immediately. Only Ferris was now permitted to read the results that came from Gretel. It was strictly on a need-to-know basis, and nobody else apart from him needed to know.

Having completed the ticket, Ferris stood up from his desk, hit Control-Alt-Del to lock his screen, and then went to get a fresh coffee from the canteen.

3.30 p.m.

When he returned fifteen minutes later, logged back on to the console and went to take another sip from his coffee, he almost dropped the coffee carton onto his lap when he saw that another email had arrived.

He opened it up and read the message inside.
Ferris frowned.
Picking up the polarised blackout screen from beside his computer he placed it across his screen so that no one else apart from him - sitting directly in front of the screen- would be able to see any images on it.
Taking a deep breath, he clicked on the video file that was attached to the email.
"Oh....shit...." Ferris said aloud, as he watched the video play.

Without wasting another second, Ferris picked up the phone and connected with his boss.
"Sir, It's Ferris here. I just got another email. A fifth. There's a video attached to it. I've just watched it..."
"And?" His boss enquired.
"We have a problem. A big problem...I think you need to get to a secure terminal as fast as possible. You need to see this..."
"I'm just about to enter the Embassy with Unicorn..., this is not a good time."
"Sir, I must insist. You need to get to a secure terminal NOW! And make sure you take Unicorn with you. He'll want to see the video too."
"Why?"
"Because he's in it, Sir."

3.45 p.m.

Ferris was waiting for his boss to call him back.
In the meantime he had a difficult decision to make.
He was watching the Dashboard for Gretel and trying to decide whether to halt the program now, or let it run to completion.
Time was of the essence.
The author of the video was threatening to release it on YouTube.
The moment he did, chaos would ensue.
Right now, it was his job to stop that happening.

He had two choices: he could let Gretel run and hope that the fourth email was enough to help pinpoint the originator of the email. At best, the program would take several hours to complete. However, there was a possibility, Ferris conceded to himself, that even with four emails to work from, there might not be enough data.

But with five? Surely five would make the result a foregone conclusion!

It was almost definite that with so many discrete data points and all the information that could be distilled from the sea of metadata created by the five emails in combination with the magic that Gretel weaved, that they would be able to pinpoint exactly where the connections to the server were, from which the emails were originating.

So, should Ferris stop Gretel, add the information from the fifth email, and start it all over again?

The problem was, it might not be necessary, in which case he would lose the past forty minutes of run time that Gretel had already spent working on the problem.

On the other hand, he could pre-empt failure and promote certain success by starting it all over again from scratch...

The trade off was almost sixty minutes, and right now, Ferris knew that almost every second would count.

Deciding that 'Certainty' was better than 'Possibility', Ferris took a deep breath, hesitated for one second, then hit "Stop" on Gretel's dashboard.

A box and some annoying text appeared on the screen.

"Are you sure you want to abort this sequence?" the program asked him.

"Yes!" Ferris almost shouted as he clicked "Confirm".

It took another five minutes before Ferris had loaded up all the new data, primed the program and got it ready to track down the author to the emails.

He had just hit "Start" when the phone rang.

It was his boss.

As he picked the phone up, a new thought entered Ferris's brain.

"What happened if there wasn't just one person who was behind this? Maybe there was a group of people? In different locations?"

"So," the voice at the other end of the phone said. "I couldn't get Unicorn. He's still with the President of Egypt. But I'm logged onto the Secure Teamshare. Show me what you've got..."

"Certainly sir, but I think you'd better warn Unicorn afterwards...He's not going to like this, sir. Not one little bit...!"

Chapter 26

London

Friday

October 4th

4.45 p.m.

Ray felt good. Nervous. But good.

He was back in control. Only an idiot would not be scared once he opened up the video file and played it. By now Randolph Best would be shaking in his boots.

If he was at all human.

Which was part of the problem: whoever can kill in cold blood like that had to be insane, and an insane person didn't behave like normal people, did they?

Ray felt nervous...more nervous than before, because he knew that now he was in direct contact with R. F. Best that as soon as the video was viewed, it was highly likely that he would hand the file over to whichever government agency was protecting him, and that they would then start to try and find Ray.
Thanks to Ghost, they would not be able to do that.
Although he was still very confident they couldn't, it was that little nagging 1% uncertainty that still got to him.
Now that he'd sent that video, that 1% seemed to be much more significant than before.

He walked back into the den from the kitchen and checked the flashing lights on the wall.
They were dark.
"I need a break!" he said to himself, and then remembered what he had promised David.
"Shit...!" he swore aloud. "I forgot all about him."
Ray glanced quickly at his wrist.
It was late.

Would he be too late? Would David still be alive, or would they have come for him already?

Hurriedly Ray went through to the toilet, forced off the side panel that encased the left hand of the pedestal underneath the wash hand basin, and reached inside.

Pulling out a thick plastic bag sealed tightly with duct tape, he hurried through to the lounge and ripped the bag open.

Inside there was the brown envelope he had found last Saturday, a time that now seemed to belong to a different life long, long ago.

Taking the money out and dropping the envelope on the floor, he quickly thumbed through the money, counting it again to make sure it was all there.

It took him a couple of minutes to check it all, but he was relieved to find that he still had the full twenty thousand and the mice hadn't eaten any.

Grabbing his keys and mobile from the table in the hall, and starting out the door, he remembered that he'd heard a message coming in earlier.

Wondering if it was David chasing him for the money, he flicked to his messages and stared in disbelief when the saw that it was a message from Emma.

Stopping still in the stairwell, he opened it up.

"I'm leaving tomorrow. Good bye, Ray."

For a second he stared at the message in disbelief.

His hands were shaking, his mind a sudden mass of confusion.

Why had she texted him the obvious? She'd already made it abundantly clear she was going to Canada already - 'Have a *nice* life!' It was not the sort of thing he was likely to forget, was it? Was she just rubbing it in now? Or did it mean something else? Was there some sort of cryptic meaning behind her telling him again?

He was still trying to think what her message could mean and why she had sent him the message now, of all times, when the phone started to ring in his hands.

He hit answer and put it quickly to his ear.

"Emma? Are you okay? Why are you ..."

"It's David. Not Emma. Ray, that's your name, right? It was on your text message? Ray, it's late. You said you had the money. They'll be here soon...And if you don't give it to me quickly, it'll be too late! I'll be dead..."

"David..." Ray replied, trying to interrupt him, and immediately switching thought processes once again. "I'm on my way. I'm coming down the stairs. I'll be there in a moment."

"Where, Ray, where will you be?"

It was a good question. It would not be a good idea to hurry over to David's flat if the heavy mob were just about to turn up.

"Starbucks...the one opposite the tube station. In four minutes. Okay?"

When he got to the coffee shop there was a queue outside the entrance. Deciding not to join it, Ray stood to the side, and waited for David to arrive.

It was only a few seconds before he saw the man running round the corner at full pelt.

Ray stepped out, grabbed his arm and ushered him into the doorway of the next shop, now closed.

"Here." Ray said, thrusting the plastic bag at him. "It's all there. Count it if you want."

David grabbed it off him, the relief on his face almost changing his appearance completely. He even managed a smile.

Weighing it in his hands, David laughed for a second, and then looked Ray straight in the face.

"Where was it? Who had it?"

Ray felt himself turning a little red.

"It's not important now, you've got the money. Take it. Give it back to them, or do whatever else you want to do with it...I don't care. But with the greatest respect in the world, I never want to hear from you again. Or see you. Do you understand?"

David looked down at the bag, and then up at Ray.

He started to open the bag, but Ray grabbed his arm.

"Are you crazy? Not here...It's all there, I promise you."

"But..."

"When you get home, not now!" Ray reached out and touched David on the shoulder, lowering his voice and speaking to him calmly.

"It's going to be okay now David, honestly, it is. Just a few more hours, - hand that back, in public preferably - and you'll be fine." Ray smiled.

David nodded.

"I hope you're right."

"I am. I promise you."

Before David could react any more, Ray turned and jogged along the road, around the corner and back into the square and up to his flat.

5.15 p.m.

Having just checked his emails for the third time since he got home five minutes ago, Ray was about to start cooking something to eat when his phone rang.

He ignored it.

Ray just wanted some peace and quiet.

He wanted time to think about what his next step would be with Randolph Best. Was he really going to post the video on YouTube?

Did he really want to go through with it?

For the past few days Ray had been in a rage. He'd also been drunk for most of the time.

Now that he was sober...some of the alcohol fuelled anger had left his system, and he was a little calmer.

Not a lot.

But a little.

It was a good time to take stock of the situation.

Threatening Randolph Best was one thing...it probably did no harm as long as he was anonymous with no way of being discovered... but if he posted the video, he would bring the wrath of hell down upon himself, and the British Government would never give up until they tracked him down...

What they would do with him when they found him, probably didn't leave much to the imagination.

If they had already covered up the killing of the Israeli model, an ugly bastard like himself would not even make them pause for thought.

Ray would be dead.

If they caught him.

The answer was therefore, quite simple.

Don't get caught!

As he stirred some pasta and then added some sauce from a jar, he realised however, that it was already too late to go back.

Now the threat had been issued, and the gauntlet had been thrown down, the agencies working for Best would actually have no choice but to pursue him until they found him. If they could find him.

The thing was, they would never know if he would or would not carry out his threat, and the risk to them was too great.

They had to find him now. At all costs they had to prevent any possibility of Ray releasing the video.

In other words, like it or not, Ray was committed.

From now on he would never be able to live completely in peace.

For the first time since the whole affair had started, Ray felt a real twinge of fear.

He stopped stirring the pasta for a moment, and looked out of the window of the kitchen towards the setting sun. It was going down now. It would soon be dark.

Then Ray thought about the woman in the video. Her life-less eyes...and the lies the establishment had told about her death.

He thought of the 'hero' that Randolph Best had become.

He thought of Emma, and the life he had planned, but which now would never be.

He swallowed hard.

Then he thought of Randolph Best again.

And once again, his bile began to rise and the anger overtook him.

Ray knew he had it in his power to make Randolph pay, - to make the government pay.

Now he realised that he was committed, he knew that there could only be one victor, and Ray knew who that would be.

His name was Ray Luck.

Just then the phone rang again.

Unfortunately, Ray never heard it, a boiling kettle and some loud music on the radio drowning it out.

Ray served up his pasta.

He was starving.

Chapter 27

London

Friday

October 4th

6.30 p.m.

Ray had eaten his meal, chilled out and listened to some music,
When he switched on the television, the news was just finishing, and he caught the tail-end of the weather forecast.

The woman giving the weather tonight was very attractive.

Ray watched her, ignoring what she was saying and paying more attention to her dress, her eyes, her good figure, and the way she smiled at the camera and waved her arms almost sexily at the weather chart.

He had never seen her before. He probably never would again.

Ray had always wondered where the 'weather people' came from. It seemed to Ray that there were millions of them - every night you switch on the TV and the weather person had changed. Where had the last one gone? Where had the new one come from?

Why were there so many different people?

What happened to all the people who had had their moment of fame and been on national TV and given a weather forecast?

Was that it? Was their career over?

Only the sexy ones survived...the ones who fascinated men like Ray who watched them and not the weather.

Actually, perhaps that was the plan.

If you watched the weather-forecaster and not the weather, perhaps you would not notice how often they got the weather forecast wrong!

Ray's mobile started to ring again.
Sighing, he switched off the TV and walked through to the hall.
Picking up his iPhone he was surprised to see that he had five missed calls.

Two from David.
Three from Emma.

There were four voice messages.
Ray dialled in to pick them up. The first was from David.

"Ray, hi it's me, David. Where is the envelope? The money's all there but I *need* the envelope the money came in! Did I not tell you that the envelope is just as important, if not *more* important than the money? They'll kill me without the envelope! Have you still got it? Call me, back, urgently." There was a slight pause, and then, "...*Please.*"

Ray listened to the message and glanced at the floor through the doorway into the lounge where the envelope still lay on the floor in full view.

Shoot...he'd better take it to him right away... meet him back at the Starbuck's and hand it over.

The next message was from Emma.

"*Hi Ray, it's me, Emma. I'm going tomorrow,...to Canada... I... I just...Perhaps, maybe... I thought that...,*" there was a long pause. "*I'm sorry, perhaps I shouldn't have called. Take care, Ray.*"

Ray's heart skipped a few beats. He pressed a few digits on the phone and replayed the message again. And then again.

Bloody hell. What was going on?

Quick. He had to call her back... he would, in a second...

But first he'd listen to the other messages just in case there was another one from her.

The next one was from David.

"Hi, Ray, Please, please, call me back. I'm scared. They'll be coming over soon. One of the them just called me, asked me if I had the package. I said yes. They're coming over...they'll be here soon...Please, help me. Call me? I need the envelope!"

Ray listened to when the message was left, and looked at his watch.

Ten minutes ago.

Shit, he hadn't heard the phone ringing with the music on.

One more message to go. He typed in another number and let it play.

"Ray, it's Emma. I ...I can't go without seeing you again. I'm worried about you. Why haven't you returned any of my messages? Are you alright? I don't want it to end like this." Another pause, during which Ray's pulse soared to well over a hundred and twenty beats a minute. "*Ray, I'm coming over.* I'm near my tube station and I'm just about to go down and get on a train. I'll be there soon. Please be there..."

Ray's heart almost stopped beating.

The time at the end of the call was nine minutes ago.

She'd be there any moment.

6.31 p.m.

Ferris stared intently at the bright red digits on his screen as they slowly counted down from five minutes to zero.

The program had been coming to a resolution far faster than he'd expected - it had been the right thing to do to halt the previous run and start it again with the data from the fifth email added it. The extra metadata had given Gretel the oomph it needed to thread all the clues together and pin-point the location of where the data trail was starting.

According to the dashboard, there were only two minutes more to go.

Ferris stood up from his desk and paced his little cubicle, not for one moment taking his eyes off the screen.

The anticipation was almost killing him.

One minute to go.

"Yes," Ferris muttered underneath his breath. If the program had got this far at this point, it was highly unlikely to recalibrate the anticipated time to resolution.

This was going to be it!

Twenty, nineteen, eighteen...

Ferris took a seat in front of his screen again, and took a deep breath in.

Five, four, three, two, one.

The screen went dark for a few seconds, and then another dashboard appeared, complete with the crest of his agency and a picture of the Portcullis and the Royal Coat of Arms.

"Target data identified. Please input your credentials to view report."

Ferris pulled out the key fob from his pocket and in response to the various challenges on the screen, typed in his ID number, his PIN, and the number that was currently showing on his RSA token.

"Welcome back Agent Ferris." The screen announced.

"Do you wish to view the report on screen or download and save to PDF for printing?"

Ferris took the first option. He couldn't wait to print it off.

The screen flickered for a second, and then the report was there.

Ferris stared at the screen, and almost jumped for joy when he read the report.

It gave them everything he needed to know.

In fact, much more than he could ever have hoped for.

Ferris reached for the phone, punching in a few numbers and tapping the table with his fingers impatiently as he waited for the person at the other end to pick up.

"Simons here..."

"Simons, it's Ferris. The data just came in. I need you to drop everything and chase this down immediately. I'm forwarding you the data now. It's Code Red. Find me the address of where this bastard lives. As soon as you can. Remember, every second counts. Got it?"

6.44 p.m.

Ray was standing by the window staring down at the street below, in the direction of the tube station Emma would come from.

If she hadn't changed her mind, she'd be there any moment.

Would she really come?

Why was she coming?

Did this mean she might have changed her mind?

Was she coming back to him?

Or had she just forgotten something in the apartment that she was coming round to pick up?

What should Ray do?

Tell her the truth...that he still loved her? Beg her not to go?

Then a thought jumped into his mind that both scared and excited him at the same time: 'As soon as she comes through the door, get down on one knee, and give her the engagement ring!'

Ray smiled, his heart beating fast with excitement and nervousness.

Maybe things were going to be alright after all!

Just then an alarm began to ring.

At first - just for a moment - Ray wondered what it was. Was it the doorbell? A fire-alarm?

Then with a jolt and a surge of panic, Ray recognised it.

The last time he had heard it was months ago when he had last tested it.

The alarm was coming from his den.

Abandoning his stance by the window and rushing through from the front room, he pushed hard against the closed door to his den and barged inside.

His attention was immediately drawn to the flashing green light on the wall, and for a few moments he stood staring at it in disbelief.

The sound of the alarm pulsed every sixth time the light flashed, its din loud and grating, forcing Ray to quickly bring up the control dashboard on his laptop and then toggle the virtual switch for the audible alarm to the off position.

Slumping in the chair, Ray stared again at the flashing light, his brain struggling to understand exactly what it meant.

Clearly it signified that someone had managed to hack through the first two outer layers of his defences, passed through the outer DMZ, and his probe and Intrusion Detection System had now picked up anomalous network activity within the inner DMZ.

But how could they have done that?

Ray knew it was virtually impossible to do. It would take vast amounts of processing power to force their way through his defences, and to provide the right responses to the challenge questions they would be given. Ray had heard tell that the NSA and GCHG might have the power to do something like that, or alternatively there was a rumour that the security company that provided the tokens would automatically provide the security agencies with the capability to know the correct responses to any of the challenges that the authentication solution would demand a response to.

Ray had always been deeply suspicious that the rumours were true, but now, looking directly at the green flashing light on his wall, he knew they were right.

"I spy... As *YOU* killed her, I watched her die"

The words of his arrogant email flashed through his mind. He'd been an idiot.

How could he have been so *stupid*!

Ray had challenged a member of the British government, someone with full access to all the resources of GCHG, and now they had tracked him down!

As he watched the flashing light, the true severity of the situation began to dawn on Ray, and he felt the first edges of real fear.

He started to breathe deeply, panic now only moments away.

Ray gripped hold of the side of the table with both hands, knelt forward and began to breathe deeply, consciously trying to take control of the 'fight or flight' emotions that were pumping adrenaline into his veins and demanding a response.

In his nightmares he had practised for this moment, and planned what he would do if the day ever arrived when the lights began to flash and the sirens began to sound. But now it was actually happening, he was finding it difficult to remember exactly what it was he knew he was meant to do.

He took several long, slow deep breaths and then held it. Ray knew that his life was potentially in danger now and that he had to get a grip or in the very near future, that future may come to an abrupt and very unexpected end.

In, out, relax...
Innnn..., ouuttttt..., relax...
Slowly his mind began to clear.
He began to think rationally again.

Now that whoever it was that was pursuing him had managed to break through the outer defence perimeters and was marching around inside the inner DMZ looking for a way in past the next set of firewalls, Ray knew that it would probably only be a matter of time before they succeeded.

Having cracked the outer defences, with the vast processing power that they must have at their disposal to penetrate the outer firewalls, they would surely also be able to break through the walls of the inner perimeter. Ray didn't know how long it had taken them to track him down and then discover the correct passwords and pins to get this far, but whether it was only days, hours or minutes, at most it would only be the same amount of time again before they got through the last of his defences.

It could be tomorrow, tonight, in a few hours, or any minute now.

His gut instinct told him that it would probably be soon.

And once they did that, it would only be seconds before they would be able to identify his true location and his name...in fact everything about him: his age, mobile phone numbers, credit cards,...everything that identified a person in today's digital world.

Ray stood up from his desk, calm, and once again in control. "It's time to go," he said to himself aloud.
He looked at his watch.
6.55 p.m.
It was time to abandon ship.
Fast.
Ray knew his boat was sinking quickly and worst case, he had only minutes to escape.
From now on, every second would count.
He had to act fast, move quickly, and get out of the flat as soon as he could.

In real life he had only rehearsed it once, eight months ago, but now he was calm again, he knew exactly what he had to do.

Hurrying to his bedroom, he grabbed a sports bags from under his bed, one which already contained a long length of rope and a torch, and a number of other things he had preselected and always kept in there, ...just in case. Rummaging through his cupboard and chest of drawers, he quickly selected a range of clothes and underwear, his sunglasses and a hat, and then grabbed his passport, birth-certificate, some utility bills as a proof of address, and a few other documents from his hiding place underneath the sink in the bathroom.

Returning to his den, he unplugged his three external hard-drives, on which all his activity, personal documents, photos and computer programmes were kept and recorded, and grabbed the folder from his desk drawer that contained all the DVDs and CDs he used and had recorded, including the video of the murder. He dumped these in the sports bag. Next he gathered up all the USB drives he had, and anything else that might contain any information that he didn't want anyone else to see, and dropped them into the bag too.

Switching the shredder on, he quickly destroyed a handful of papers and computer print-outs he had on his desk, and then stepped back and made sure he hadn't left anything else that he shouldn't.

There was only one more thing to do...one more final, but drastic step, and he didn't want to do that until the absolute last moment... and only if the other light started to flash and the next alarm went off signifying that they'd penetrated his final defence barrier.

When that happened, within minutes a swat team from the police or some government agency would be streaming up his staircase and breaking down his door...

Ray looked again at the other light on the wall.

It wasn't flashing...*yet*.

Bending over his keyboard he brought up the interface to the program that he had written several years ago..., but never really thinking that he would have to use it in real life. He'd nicknamed it SCORCHED EARTH, and that explained almost exactly what it did.

In the eventuality that someone penetrated his defences, tracked SolarWind down and found out who he was and where he lived, forcing him to abandon his den and potentially run for his life, he would initiate SCORCHED EARTH: the programme would run through every IP device on his network and erase all memories and data and then write over them with random data.

Anything that wasn't in his sports bag or which he took with him would be lost.

Deleted. Erased. Burned.

He'd lose it all.

On the other hand, no one else would ever find it either.

The green "Start" button flashed on his screen, and Ray's finger hovered over the keyboard, hesitating.

He looked up at the other light on the wall. It was still dormant.

His finger trembled. Twitching.
Pressing the button, initiating the program...it was so final...
What if he was overreacting?
What if his second layer of cyber defences held out and were strong enough?
Perhaps he would wait a little longer...perhaps...

A loud banging noise on his front door startled him and made him jump. At exactly the same moment his phone started to ring.
Shaken and scared, Ray pulled out the iPhone and walked slowly towards the front door.
The name on the display said "David."
Shit...he'd completely forgotten about him.
Sneaking up to the front door as quietly as he could, he peeked through the peep-hole to see who was on the other side, holding his breath, half-expecting to see the police or...or...
Could it be *EMMA*?

It was David.
He grabbed the door handle and pulled it open, ushering David quickly inside...

"Why didn't you call me? I need the envelope...and I need it now!" David started demanding immediately, obviously very flustered and sweating profusely. Ray noticed that his hands were trembling. "They just called me...asked me if I had the money! I said yes, and they said they're coming straight over. When they find out I haven't got the envelope they'll kill me."
David's eyes saw the bag he had dumped in the middle of the hallway, now full.
"Are you going somewhere?" he asked, worriedly.
"What?" Ray asked, confused for a second. He followed David's eyes to the bag.
"Oh..., yes..." Ray replied. "I've got to get out of town. Believe it or not, I've got bigger problems than you. Way bigger..."
"Bigger than mine? They're going to fucking kill me! How can your problems be bigger than mine?" David demanded, reaching out and grabbing hold of Ray's arm. "Give me the envelope! Now!"
Ray shrugged his arm off.
"Listen, mate...I'm sorry..."
Ray started to apologise and was about to say he would get the envelope for him when there was another knock on the door. It was still ajar, and as both David and Ray turned around, Emma stepped into the hallway.

Ray stopped in mid-sentence, staring at her.

She looked gorgeous.

More beautiful than he had ever seen her...although as she opened her mouth to speak, he noticed that she was really nervous and her face was very white.

"Ray...," she whispered, then coughed to clear her throat. "Hi..."

She took another step into the hallway and then saw the bag on the floor.

She looked up at him, her eyes searching his for a thousand answers to questions that she wanted to ask.

"Emma..." Ray said quietly, stepping past David towards her and reaching out his open arms towards her.

At that exact moment an alarm started to blare loudly from his den, and a light started to flash behind him so brightly that they all turned to see what it was.

"Fuck!" Ray shouted aloud, spinning around on the spot and hurrying into his den, Emma and David following quickly behind him.

Ray stood just inside the doorway, staring wide-eyed at the red flashing light on the wall, the alarm so loud that they all lifted their hands to their heads and covered their ears.

"What's happening?" Emma asked, shouting to be heard above the noise. "What's going on? That's never happened before?"

Ray turned to her, and then looked across at David.

"Can you switch it off?" Emma asked. "It's deafening me!"

Ray glanced back at his desk. On one of the screens he saw the big green 'Start' button flashing that now implored him to initiate the Scorched Earth program.

On the other screen a big white number displayed on a black background was incrementing every second. In smaller letters above it a display read, "Time since network breach: 0.10," the number ten dominating half of the screen. "0.11, 0.12, 0.13..."

"Shit..." Ray said again, playing with the mouse and calling up a dashboard from which he could switch the audible alarm off.

With the room now suddenly quiet and everyone deafened by the silence, Ray turned to them both.

"You have to go. Both of you. *Now!*"

Emma's face dropped.

"Ray, Go? Why? You're scaring me. What's happening?"

Ray reached out and put one arm around David and the other around Emma.

"Go. Now! You have to go... Both of you! And **NOW**!"

Stunned and confused, David and Emma allowed themselves to be turned around and guided in the direction of the front door.

"Ray...? I need to talk to you! I..."
"Emma, go! I mean it...you have to leave! Now!"
They were at the front door.
Suddenly David dug his heels in and tried to spin around.
"I'm not leaving until I get the envelope!"
"You bloody are, " Ray shouted at him, letting go of Emma, grabbing hold of David and physically ejecting him through the doorway.

David was caught off-guard by the sudden show of force and stumbled forward through the door and just caught hold of the banister with his good hand before he almost fell down the flight of stairs.

"GO!"Ray shouted.

The door on the other side of the landing outside the flat began to open and old Mrs Simons, his octogenarian neighbour, started to come outside to see what the alarm was all about.

Ray hurried across the landing, smiled at her, and said, "It's okay Mrs Simons, everything's okay. But go inside now please, and don't come out whatever more noise you hear, do you understand? DON'T come outside!"

David was standing three steps down the stairs, his eyes begging Ray for help.

As Ray hurried back across the landing to his flat, he caught David's gaze and a thought suddenly occurred to him.

"David, you said they're coming over now? To get the envelope?"
"Yes..."
"Good. Tell them all about me. Tell them I've got it. I've given you all the money back, every penny, but when you get home, take some of the money out and hide it and then tell them that I've kept some of the money along with the envelope that they so desperately want, and that I'm not going to give it back to them, ...and tell them that if they want it they have to come and get it from me. They'll have to break the bloody door down though and search the flat from top to bottom because there is no fucking way I'm just handing it back to them!"

David's face went white.

"Why?" he asked. "I don't understand...they'll kill you!"
"Maybe. Maybe not. But whatever you do, David, don't come back with them. Find an excuse, anything...but *don't* come back up these stairs or it might be the last thing you ever do. Now go...leave! NOW!"

Without glancing back at him, Ray stepped back into his flat, pushing Emma back inside in front of him.

Placing both his hands on her shoulders he leant forward and kissed her gently on the lips.

"Emma, you have to go. *Now*. Honestly. Please...I'm sorry...I haven't got the time to explain just now... honestly I can't..."

Emma tried to speak, but Ray silenced her with a finger on her lips.

"Listen to me. *LISTEN!*" he commanded. "I don't know why you came over tonight, and I don't know what you want from me, if anything... but before I push you out that door in two seconds and close it firmly behind you, I need to tell you something. I fucked up. I know I did. You were the best thing that ever happened to me, and I lost you. But I love you. I always have and I always will."

Tears had started to roll down Emma's face. Ray was just about to say something else when a thought occurred to him. Momentarily he turned around and ducked down to retrieve something from the bag on the floor. Standing back up he turned to Emma and unrolled her clenched fist, forcing a small square box into it.

"Take this...don't open it yet, but if you haven't heard from me by the time you get on your aeroplane, take a look inside when you get to Canada. Not before! It's self explanatory. Okay?" he looked at her, and half-smiled, nodding to get her agreement.

She nodded.

"Good, now you *have* to go. You have to hurry. Some very bad people are coming and you have to be long gone before they arrive. If you stay here you could be in danger. If you pass anyone, don't stop and talk to them. As soon as you get home, grab your bags and leave the house. Don't go back. Go and stay with Paula for the evening. If I can, I'll come find you there. If I don't, you get on the plane tomorrow to Canada and never come back to England. Do you understand?"

Emma looked petrified. Her mascara was running and she was shaking from head to toe.

"DO YOU *UNDERSTAND ME?* PROMISE ME YOU'LL GO TO PAULA'S!"

She nodded...

"I promise..."

Ray kissed her gently on the lips. He felt Emma push forward, increasing the pressure, but before she could, Ray pushed her back, looked at her for one more second, and then spun her around, opened up the door and pushed her out.

He closed the door behind her.

"GO!" he shouted one more time, allowing himself a second more to look through the peephole to see that she was obeying him.

Outside, Emma stood staring at the door, squeezing the box in her hand tightly.

Then she turned, grabbed hold of the banister, and started to hurry down the stairs.

Ray's heart almost ripped apart as he watched her go.

Chapter 28

London

Friday

October 4th

7.03 p.m.

Ray knew that he had already taken too much time.

They would be here any moment.

Either the drug gangsters, the police or the Security Service.

Which would get there first, Ray didn't know, but either way it was likely that if they caught him, he wouldn't live very much longer.

He probably only had seconds to leave.

Grabbing a ski pole from the cupboard in his bedroom, and the folding metal ladder from the cupboard in the hallway, he unfolded the ladder and placed it beneath the trapdoor to the attic in the middle of the hallway.

Then hurrying back into the lounge he picked up the brown envelope from where it still lay on the floor, and then dropped it into the bag in the hallway.

Next, he climbed the ladder and pulled the trapdoor down.

Grabbing the bag from the floor he climbed up into the attic and dropped the ski-pole inside. He was almost up inside and about to close the attic hatch, when he remembered something important that he had forgotten.

Scorched Earth.

Swearing under his breath, he quickly let himself down again, hurried into his den, and without any further thought, clicked the mouse over the big, green 'Start' button.

Hesitating for a second to check that the program was running and to ensure that Scorched Earth had started to delete everything on his servers and any IP device on his network, he then switched off the monitors so that no one would see what was going on.

With the red light still flashing brightly he rushed back to the ladder, pulled himself up into the attic space and switched the light on.

Just then someone rang the buzzer on the steps outside the entrance to No.23, trying to get his attention.

The buzzer rang again and again, repeatedly, then suddenly stopped.

Ray swore again, cursing himself for not having practised the next step of his escape more than once or twice.

Grabbing the ski pole from beside himself, he reached down into the hallway below, holding onto the entrance of the attic as hard as he could with his other free hand.

He would only have one shot at this.

He took a deep breath.

Slowly, he leaned further down and extended the ski pole out in front of him. Pushing the top of the ski pole in between the flat bit at the top of the ladder and the first step down, he pushed the ladder slightly backwards then pressed down on one end of the pole and forced the other end of the pole up, locking the pole between the first step and the flat top of the ladder. The ladder was aluminium and very light. Slowly, very slowly, Ray started to lift the ladder up into the air, holding his breath all the time.

If the ladder fell, the game would be up.

He had to get this bit right.

Footsteps...he could hear the sound of heavy footsteps starting to come up the stairs in the stairwell, the heavy footfalls echoing up towards him.

Keeping his calm, he kneeled up slightly, freeing up his other hand. Carefully, he swapped the pole from one hand to the other, moving the ladder backwards beneath him, maintaining the pressure all the time.

As soon as it was beneath the opening to the attic, he started to lift it up towards himself.

When he'd practised it before, this was the most difficult part.

Slowly, very slowly, he edged away from the hole, guiding the top of the little ladder up into the attic space.

As soon as it appeared, Ray pushed the ski pole forward, jamming the ladder against the other side of the trapdoor.

Quickly, Ray knelt forward and grabbed it, pulling the ladder upwards and inside.

Even before he had breathed out, he grabbed the trapdoor and lowered it gently down, closing it and sliding home the bolt that he had added a few months ago to the inside of the lid.

Ray was now locked inside the attic.

Directly beneath him he could hear someone pounding on his door.

7.04 p.m.

Ben took the brown envelope out of David's hand and pulled out the thick wad of fifty pound notes. He flicked through the notes, not counting them, but using his experience of handling large amounts of money to guesstimate the amount. He estimated eighteen to twenty-two thousand pounds. It was about right.

Ben looked at the envelope. He turned it over in his hand and looked at the other side.

It was brown.

True.

But there was no blue tick on the back of the envelope. Where he had ticked every envelope to signify that he had counted the money inside and checked it.

David shifted nervously in his seat in the back of the car.

Ben turned round and looked at him.

"It's not the right fucking envelope, is it?" he said loudly, raising his voice. "You thought you could bloody trick us, didn't you?"

Before David could move out the way, Ben turned in his seat and threw a punch at David, hitting him on the side of his face and splitting his cheek.

David was pushed into the back of the seat, the minders on either side of him holding him tightly by his biceps and forcing him quickly to sit back up and in range of Ben's fist again.

"What the fuck are you playing at, David? Where's the bloody envelope?"

"He's got it." David shouted back. "The bastard in Flat 6 at Number 23 has got it!"

"What do you mean?"

"He gave me most of the money back, but not all of it. He told me to tell you that he'd kept some of it along with the envelope and that you could fuck off, and that he wasn't going to give you the other money or the envelope back. He said to say that if you wanted it back you had to go get it yourself. It's in his flat, but he isn't going to give it to you. He hates drug gangs...! And he swore that if I ever went near him again or he ever saw my face again that he'd call the police and tell them what was happening and give the money and the envelope to them."

In the back seat, one of the minders stifled a laugh, and the other smirked. No one ever told Ben or Mr Grant to 'fuck off', but now they had they knew it was going to get interesting.

Until now Adam Grant had sat quietly in the front of the car in the passenger seat.

He heard the men reacting and knew they were laughing.

Whether they were laughing at him, or Ben, he didn't know, but he knew he couldn't let such a remark pass without punishment.

Whoever was challenging his authority had to be punished, and it wasn't a job that he could let Ben take care of for him.

At times like this it was he who had to reaffirm his authority. He would make an example of whoever had the envelope and his money and who had disrespected him, and he would do it personally and in front of the gang.

Adjusting his gloves, and checking the gun and the knife in his pocket, Mr Grant opened the door and stepped out onto the pavement.

Bending down again into the car, he issued some instructions to the three men in the back of the car guarding David, telling them to follow him.

"...and Ben, you stay here. It's time I took over and finished this off personally. Keep an eye on our guest for me."

"...but I gave you the money back...and I've told you where the envelope is? You promised to let me go...."David shouted.

Ben hit him again.

"Shut up! Mr Grant is speaking!"

"No, Ben, that's fine. It's understandable. Our guest is a little concerned. Slightly worried, I imagine. But there's no need to be." Mr Grant replied in a quiet voice. "I'm just going to pop up and visit our friend in Flat 6 and if everything goes well, we'll be back down in a moment, with the envelope. And we'll let you go, as promised." He paused. "On the other hand,...if we don't get the envelope back...then I'll ask Ben to drive you somewhere quiet and kill you. Does that sound fair?"

At the entrance to No. 23 Mr Grant adjusted his tie then stood patiently with his hands crossed over in front of his stomach while one of his men used his tools to open the lock on the front door. Meanwhile, the other two men flanked him, keeping an eye out on the street, and making sure that Mr Grant was shielded at all times.

"Okay, we're in," the man with the lock-picking kit announced.

"You took your time, Harry." Mr Grant said, stepping past his henchman and into the building.

They hurried up the stairs, one of the men rushing up in front checking the door numbers. When they got to the top, it was the first one on the left.

Mr Grant leant forward and knocked on the door several times rather heavily.

He smiled at the three men beside him.

"Don't forget men, we're here because we were invited. I want you on your best behaviour please."

The men looked at each other, confused.

"Joking, obviously." Mr Grant laughed. "But no one touches the bastard who has my envelope until I've finished with him. Do you understand? This one's mine. No one disrespects my organisation and lives to tell the tale. Just make sure that he doesn't slip past me, okay?"

The men nodded. Smiling.

Mr Grant seldom got this involved anymore, personally, but when he did, it was always a lesson in sadism that few ever forgot.

They wouldn't miss it for the world.

7.10 p.m.

In the attic Ray knew that he had to act fast.

Opening up his bag he took out the torch, switched off the attic light and gingerly walked across the floor away from the entrance hall below to where the sloping glass window was at the rear of the building.

He opened the window up and after pushing the sports bag through and letting it drop onto the section of flat roof outside, he reached up, took the strain on his arms and hauled himself up and through the window.

Loud voices suddenly became audible beneath him.

He listened for a second. Someone was issuing instructions, and he could hear people moving quickly into and around his flat.

A wave of fear washed through Ray.

With shaking hands he pulled the window closed behind him, and pressed down on the bottom edge until he heard the catch click home behind him.

Gently he lowered himself down the outside slope of the roof until his feet touched the flat roof.

It was already dark outside, so Ray shone the torch down, picked up his bag and started to tip-toe across the roof in the direction of where Mrs Simons lived.

It was only a few metres, but for Ray, scared that someone underneath him in his den might hear his footsteps on the roof above, it was the longest walk of his life.

Not to mention the fact that only one metre to his left there was a fifty metre fall straight down.

7.11 p.m.

Downstairs, one of Adam Grant's henchmen finally managed to pick the lock to Ray's front door. With their guns drawn, they opened the door and searching and sweeping the space in front of them with their guns held up high in front of their chests, the four men stepped cautiously forward and into the flat.

Closing the door behind him, Mr Grant adjusted his gloves, mentally checking that all his men were wearing theirs too, and then pointed at his men in turn signalling for them to move forwards into the lounge, kitchen and the bedroom.

Adam chose the room with the flashing light for himself. He was hoping that he would walk in and catch someone by surprise, probably doing some sort of weird meditation or listening to music, but as he opened the door and stepped inside, he realised just how annoying the flashing light was: no one would chose to remain in that room for long, let alone find the experience at all relaxing.

The team moved from room to room, each person finding no one there.

A minute later they all met again in the hallway.

"Where is the bastard?" Adam Grant spoke loudly, his anger and frustration beginning to show.

"Petrov, what do you make of that?" Adam asked, pointing the den. Petrov stepped inside and came back out a few moments later.

"An office. Looks like we set an alarm off when we came through the door."

"I doubt it," Adam said, drawing on his quite extensive experience with burglar alarms from his earlier career as a thief. "It's something different. An alarm of some sort, but I don't know what for. Besides, if it was a burglar alarm, it would be outside the flat, not inside."

"What do we do now, boss?" Petrov asked, reassured that Mr Grant didn't seem to be at all concerned.

"We turn this place upside down until we find the envelope. Without touching anything and leaving any prints behind, mind. And whoever finds it gets a five thousand bonus. Seem fair?"

The boys smiled.

"But keep an eye out in case the bastard comes home. If he does, make sure he doesn't leave. I want to leave my initials on his forehead...for starters..."

Adam waved his hand briefly in the air and the team went to work. Adam stepped back into the den, and started going through the desk, the buckets, and cupboards. He picked up any books, opening them up and shaking them by the spines to see what fell out, and then dropped them on the floor.

In the other rooms cupboards were being emptied, buckets were turned upside down, and sideboards examined. In the bedroom, the pillows were turned inside out, the bed lifted up... his men knew exactly the sort of places people would hide things, both out in the open in full public view and in secret.

Methodically they started to go through the flat from one end to the other, turning a once habitable dwelling into what soon resembled a warzone.

7.16 p.m.

At the end of the road at the entrance to the square, four black vans stopped and blocked the street off. Simultaneously another four vans entered the square at the other side and parked, blocking the entrance from that side too.

No cars could now come or go.

Almost immediately the backs of six vans popped open and six men jumped down from each. The men who exited the first four vans were all fully armed, and kitted out in black uniforms, helmets, and Kevlar bullet proof vests. Each man carried an assortment of weapons and a supply of ammunition large enough to fight a small war, including MP5 sub-machine guns, Glock 17 9mm sidearms, NICO stun-grenades, and knives. Six men took up positions at the end of each street, blocking the entrance to any further pedestrian foot traffic, and locking down all movement into and out of the square.

The rest of the men immediately started fanning out across the square to take up pre-agreed positions in the park, the street, and from within other buildings in the square.

The men who jumped out of the last two vans wore an assortment of different civilian clothes.

One was dressed as a police man, another in the uniform of an electricity company, and a third as a pizza delivery man.

The rest were dressed normally.

They did however, all have one thing in common: they were each bristling with weapons and grenades hidden from view beneath their clothing.

While the others hung back at the end of the road, the pizza man walked down the street carrying a large pizza box, inside of which was hidden his MP5.

Turning at the entrance to No. 23 he hurried up the stairs and after checking that no one was watching or following him, he quickly started to pick the lock on the main door.

It only took him twenty five seconds, but by the time he was finished, the electricity man had come up the steps and joined him.

Pushing the door open, the electricity man disappeared into the building and using his torchlight, made his way quickly to the electricity junction box in the small cupboard that the plans of the building showed was located just underneath the stairs in the stairwell ahead.

Whilst he opened the junction box and found the fuse boxes for the flats at the top of the stairs, and the lights in the stairwell, the pizza man continued to hold the front door open as ten other members of the SWAT team made their way quickly down the street and rushed up the stairs into the building.

Within seconds, there were eleven men kneeling on the floor or flattened against the walls at the top of the stairwell outside of Flat 6, the home of Ray Luck, a professional cyber expert and ex-card-carrying member of the British Anarchist League and the Oxford 'Three-Ists Club'.

Ferris was in his element. This was his first live op in over six months, and as the excitement flooded through his veins, he realised again just how much he missed the thrill of real live combat.
Hopefully, after he had successfully led and completed this operation, he'd be trusted to lead other such operations in future.

First though, he had to catch Ray Luck.

At the top of the stairs the lead man put a listening device against the door and took a few seconds to determine what movement and activity he could hear from within the flat.
He could hear nothing. It all seemed quiet.
He signalled Ferris, and Ferris gave the command to place a small charge on the door and get ready to blow the lock.
As soon as it was in place, Ferris signalled to the men to put on their enhanced night vision goggles and spoke into the microphone on his sleeve, giving the order for the man below to cut off the electricity.

From this point on, everything would take place automatically.
Once the charge blew, the men would be on autopilot.
Suddenly everything went dark.
Simultaneously Ferris gave the signal to detonate the small charge and the men pushed back against the walls.
Ferris smiled.
"Sorry 'Ray', it looks like your 'luck' has just run out!"

7.20 p.m.

Inside the flat Mr Grant pulled out his phone and listened to the warning that Ben gave him.
It looked like a SWAT team of some sort had arrived in the square, had entered the building they were in, and were heading up his way.
Without any time to think, he signalled for everyone to stop everything and take up defensive positions.

Raising his finger to his mouth, he commanded them all to be quiet.

For a few seconds no one moved.
Guns drawn, primed and ready, they all held their breath.

7.21 p.m.

Up above, Ray had managed to make his way across the flat roof to the far end of the building, a journey that took him over the roofs of about twelve houses. Looking over the edge of the building he could see the top of the fire-escape that went from the ground to the top floor window of the flats at this end of building. Presumably, once upon a time, each of the different sections of the building had had their own fire-escapes, but for whatever reason now only this one still existed.

To get down to the fire-escape below him he would need to drop down about two metres, which ordinarily wouldn't be so far, and grab hold of the edge of the ladder pinned to the wall.

But at the back of the building, in the dark, with absolutely no margin for error, Ray was understandably a little scared.

Cursing his shaking fingers, Ray bent down and took out the length of rope from his bag.

Climbing back onto the main roof, and carefully and very gently shimming up the tiles, he reached a chimney stack and fed the rope around its base before tying it into a tight triple knot. Pulling on the rope and testing it, he manoeuvred back down onto the flat roof and stood up, pulling hard on the rope to make sure that it and the chimney stack would take his weight.

It was firm.

Next, he tied the other end around the handles of his bag and leaning cautiously over the edge he lowered his bag so that it dangled close to the edge of the ladder.

The bag disappeared below him, the rope stretching about half way down the building.

Taking several deep breaths, he lay down on his stomach and edged backwards towards the side of the building, gripping the rope tightly in his hands.

He was just about to commit himself to go over the side of the roof when he heard the first gunshots.

7.21 p.m.

As soon as the lights went out in the stairwell and the flats, the explosive charge went off, and the lead man pushed forward and kicked the door open.

From either side of Ferris his men streamed past him and into the flat, weapons drawn and sweeping in front of them.

Each of them carried Heckler and Koch sound-suppressed MP5SD automatic weapons, fully loaded and capable of devastating rapid fire in bursts of three rounds at a time.

Trained to seek out targets and threats and neutralise them, the SWAT team reacted automatically to the sight of the men immediately inside the flat who had their guns drawn and pointing straight at them, but who were now in pitch blackness, their eyes blinking and trying to acclimatize to the dark.

The first man in opened fire immediately, letting off a three-round burst of subsonic 9mm automatic fire that blew away the nearest man and pushed him back into the room behind him, into which most of his body exploded in a bloody mixture of flying flesh and shattered bones.

Almost simultaneously two of the men waiting for them and facing them inside the flat began to return fire blindly with their hand guns, the bullets hitting the first of the advancing SWAT team in the chest, and pushing him backwards into the men behind him.

But not before the second man entering the flat had himself depressed the trigger on his weapon and let off three trails of subsonic bullets that swept across the hallway, raked up the wall and cut one of the targets in half.

As the other men poured into the flat behind the first men who had entered, they immediately fanned out on either side of the door, simultaneously finding targets opposite them and firing at almost point blank range.

Unprotected, outgunned, untrained and not used to battle combat and unable to see in the dark, Adam Grant and his men were no match for those who had come in after them.

Both he and his last surviving henchman were forcibly smashed against the walls behind them with the momentum of the bullets fired only a metre away from them, large chunks of their bodies being ripped open and torn off by the force of the bullets entering their flesh.

Within seconds of the flat being penetrated, all four of them were dead.

7.23 p.m.

Up on the roof Ray tried to control his breathing. He had never felt his heart pounding in his chest so hard before.

He had heard four loud bangs come from his flat, and when they had started he had immediately looked along the edge of the building towards his rear window. For a couple of seconds a series of bright flashes had come out of the window from his bedroom. The bangs and the flashes had not been coordinated, and Ray didn't understand what was happening.

Whatever it was, it certainly was not good news.

All he knew was that people were in his flat firing guns.

Who were they shooting at?

The moment he asked himself that question he knew the answer: his plan had worked!

He thought momentarily of David and wished him well, hoping that he had taken his advice and not returned to the flat with the drug gang.

With any luck, David would be able to walk away from all of this and carry on his life as before.

Unlike Ray whose life may now never be the same again.

"*Ray Luck: Enemy of the State.*"

Ray fought to focus on the here and now.

At any moment they may guess where he was and come after him. He had to make good his escape while he still could.

Now. Before it was too late.

Wrapping the rope around his back, like he had once done when learning how to abseil on a school trip to the Lake District, Ray gripped the rope tighter and swallowed hard.

Slithering backwards on his stomach to the side of the building, Ray's legs passed over the edge.

He kept going.

One moment he was on firm ground, the next he was dangling in the pitch-dark fifty metres above the ground.

7.29 p.m.

A few moments before, Ben had wound the window down and was cautiously looking at the reflection in the side view mirror to see what was going on in the street behind them.

The limousine was parked two thirds along the street, facing the other entrance of the square, which like the entrance behind them that was closest to the entrance to No. 23, was now also blocked off by a small army of police or soldiers. Whoever they were Ben could not tell. All he knew was that all hell seemed to have broken loose.

He had seen quite a number of bright flashes and heard several loud gunshots coming from the windows of the top flat at No. 23.

So far, no one had come out of the building.

Ben was scared.

He turned furiously to confront David.

"You bastard, you fucking set us up!" he started to say, but didn't make it very far.

While Ben was looking out of the window, David had reached into his trouser pocket and taken out a can of the pepper spray that Chloe sometimes carried in her hand-bag when she went out with her girlfriends in London.

As Ben turned towards him, raising his gun and obviously going to point it straight at him, David had lifted the can and depressed the nozzle on the top, launching a jet of the spray straight into his captor's eyes.

The man immediately started to shout, automatically raising his hands to his face and pushing back from David against the dashboard on the passenger seat where he was now sitting.

As soon as he went backwards, David leant forwards and pressed the button on the dashboard that released the lock on the rear door.

Immediately, he dived for the door and pushed it open, stumbling forward and falling across the pavement against the iron railing opposite.

Pulling himself up with the help of the metal posts, he raised himself up first on to one knee and then up onto both his feet, heading towards the entrance to his stairs at No. 45.

Just as he passed the front door of the car, Ben threw it opened and stumbled out after him. With one hand wiping the tears from his eyes, Ben raised the other hand and took aim with his gun at David who was now only two metres away.

From this range Ben couldn't miss.

Two single bullets flew through the air, both hitting their target.

One passed through the top right shoulder, forcing the target to spin around and start to fall.

The second bullet passed through the left side of the skull, blowing the top of the head off and splattering a horrific mixture of blood, brains and bone all over the white plastered walls of No. 43.

Chapter 29

London

Friday

October 4th

7.30 p.m.

"Clear!" a voice called from the front room.

"Clear!" another announced from the toilet.

"Clear!" several others announced serially as one by one the rooms of Ray's flat were entered and searched for other targets.

Each room had been taken by a three man team, one standing to one side and pushing the door open, another standing directly in front of the door, primed to move in immediately the NICO 9 Burst 'flash and noise' stun grenade went off and started to bounce around the room, and another who stood behind him. The latter was responsible for taking the stun-grenade from its place on the back of the jacket of the man in front, holding it out briefly over the shoulder of the man in front and showing it clearly to him so that the man in front would know he was just about to throw it, counting down, and then tossing it in through the door.

As the grenade entered the room and went off, the men followed in after it.

Whereas those inside the rooms would be passively waiting or hiding and would be hopefully temporarily disabled by the bright explosions and concussive blasts, the SWAT Team would be moving quickly and aggressively, their action nullifying the effect of the grenades on them and allowing them to quickly overpower any resistance that they may otherwise encounter in the room.

Thankfully, there was no further resistance.

Within moments the flat was secure.

There were four dead.

Two of the bodies were no longer recognisable, their facial features either missing or so badly distorted that no visual identification would be possible.

A quick body search revealed something rather surprising.

One was carrying a very large amount of money in £50 bills. The other men were carrying guns, several knives and dark sun-glasses.

Before they had been messed up, they had all been dressed rather smartly, in expensive clothes, shoes, and designer watches, particularly the one who had been carrying the money and who no longer had a face.

Ferris had not expected this.

It appeared as if he had stumbled into the headquarters of a rather classy drug gang.

Unfortunately, Ray Luck, the man to whom the flat was officially rented, was nowhere to be seen.

Before calling in the rest of the team, Ferris had taken a moment to examine the flat himself.

Particularly the room at the back of the building that was filled with computers, servers, flat-screens and was currently illuminated by an annoying, flashing red light.

This was the room that most interested him.

It was obviously the centre of operations for whoever it was that had masterminded the attack on Unicorn - aka Randolph Best. There were several large servers, several flat screens to view data and images on, printers. Everything you would expect to see.

Except external hard drives or any laptops or tablets.

That worried Ferris.

It could be that Luck had backed everything up on the servers, hence why there were several of them - to provide redundancy. Or it could be that he had audaciously backed everything up in the cloud!

Ideally Ferris would have immediately liked to have started to ferret around on the systems to see what he could find.

Unfortunately, the large body count in the hallway precluded him simply sitting down and seeing what he could find. Any moment now the police would arrive and he would be consumed with bureaucracy and bullshit.

The main problem, however, was that the stun grenade that had been tossed into the room ahead of its penetration had destroyed the large flat screens: both had absorbed the compressive blasts, their screens smashed and splintered, and had then been pushed off the table onto the floor where they had received further damage upon impact.

The servers had also not come off well, but Ferris knew that so long as the hard-drives were not totally destroyed, they would still be able to recover all the files from them.

Ferris stared at the flashing light on the wall.

Almost miraculously it had survived the stun grenades and continued to broadcast a warning: although what that warning was about, Ferris was not sure.

While Ferris had just started to think about where Ray Luck could or might be, and what the relationship between him and the dead men in the hallway was, his mobile went off.

Ferris looked at the display to see who was calling him on his secure line, and immediately answered: it was his boss, Jacobson.

This was a call he had to take.

What he had to report was not good.

Ray Luck was still at large, and until they recovered the hard drives from the servers and examined the data they contained, they would not know if they had the video file of Unicorn murdering the woman.

Until they had both of them in safe custody, Ray Luck would remain one of the top threats to the survival of the British Government.

As of this moment, Ray Luck had just become the most wanted man in the United Kingdom.

7.33 p.m.

Trying to make as little noise as possible so as not to draw any attention to himself from anyone looking out of his flat's windows or to alarm any of the residents of No. 47, who in a worst case scenario might call the police to report a burglar, Ray had finally managed to make it safely down to the bottom of the fire escape.

Climbing down two metres to reach the metal ladder on the end of a dangling rope in pitch blackness above a fifty metre drop, had been the most scary thing he had ever done in his life - far worse than the experience minutes before of walking across the section of flat roof.

However, possibly not as scary as the next few hours may prove to be.

After having managed to find the top of the metal ladder and lower himself slowly down onto it until he could grasp it firmly with both hands and find solid footholds, he had then taken a few minutes to try and bring his breathing under control.

Going down the ladder he couldn't afford to put one foot out of place. He needed to be fully in control.

Still shaking like a leaf, he had then managed to slowly descend the ladder, one rung to another, eventually coming level with the bag, untying it and swinging it carefully across one shoulder, before continuing on down.

Now unbalanced, it was even more difficult than before, and he found that he could no longer look down, forcing him to 'sense' the position of the next rungs as he lowered himself from one rung to another rather than actually see them.

In total, it took him about five minutes to descend the fifty metres, and as soon as his feet touched terra firma, he looked up towards his bedroom at the end of the building, praying that no one had seen him.

Luckily, it seemed that no one had.

Getting this far, however, was not the end of it.

Now he was on the ground, he was in the communal garden that ran the length of about seven of the buildings.

To make his way to safety he had to cross the garden to the other side, climb up on top of a shed, ascend the high stone wall, and then drop down into the garden behind. Once there, he would be able to cross that garden, and then find himself facing the wall that separated that garden from a small mews behind it. If he could climb that wall, and get down safely into the small street behind, the only entrance to the street was from the main road which was on the other side of the buildings on the other side of the rectangular gardens that all the buildings around it shared.

By walking along the mews, he would come out onto the main road that ran parallel with the street where the entry to his building was, and from there he could catch a bus in any direction to get as far away from there as possible.

But right now, getting as far away as possible, in once piece, and still breathing, was Ray's main priority.

What happened afterwards would be something that Ray would figure out later, if he was still free and alive.

St. Cecilia's Square

7.36 p.m.

Within seconds of the shot being fired, both the bodies on the ground were surrounded by four members of the SWAT team that materialised almost mysteriously out of the bushes in the park and from behind parked cars in the streets.

The SWAT team split into pairs, each checking one of the bodies.

While one of the tall men in black kept his MP-5 cocked and pointed directly at the first of the bodies on the ground, the other approached it cautiously, and checked it for signs of life.

There were none.

The second bullet the body had received entered at an angle into the neck and had removed most of the flesh on the right of his spine, taking with it all the blood vessels including a piece of the jugular, ripping it out as the impact of the bullet had been absorbed by the body.

The bullet had done its job. The 9mm rounds the SWAT team carried were designed to bring any target down, the bullet spreading on impact and imparting its full momentum to the target, and ensuring that it did not pass through the body.

Their purpose was very different from soldier's bullets which were designed to pass through a target and carry on beyond it - hopefully then hitting a second or maybe even a third target in quick succession as it continued on in its trajectory.

A second SWAT team member probed the other body, this time quickly determining that he was alive and unharmed.

"Put your hands behind your back!" the SWAT team member ordered, quickly placing a plastic loop around the man's wrists and pulling it tight, locking his two hands painfully together.

"Roll over," the man ordered, the SWAT team stepping back, just in case the man had booby-trapped his body.

"Stand up and turn towards me!" the SWAT team member ordered.

The man who had been lying face down on the ground complied.

When he turned around towards the SWAT team, the three men raised their weapons high, the first man once again shouting.

This time it was a question.

"Why are you smiling?"

The man's smile made the SWAT team nervous. What did he know that they did not?

"I'm still alive and you just saved my life!" the man answered.

"What is your name?" the SWAT team leader quickly demanded.

"David," he replied. "My name is David."

7.48 p.m.

Ferris's job was done.

Before the IT Forensics team had arrived, and he had granted them access to the room with all the computers in, he had searched everywhere of relevance and removed a few objects for himself.

He felt uneasy about all of this.

There was something going on here that he didn't understand.

One of the men in his team had scanned the two faces of the bodies in the hallway, and uploaded the images to headquarters. Almost instantaneously it was confirmed that neither of them was Ray Luck. There was a possibility that either of the other two men with no recognisable facial features remaining could be Luck, but Ferris doubted it.

Their online database immediately announced that the two men were known criminals. Heavy duty members of one of the most dangerous and wanted crime gangs in England.

What were they doing in Luck's flat?
Did Luck work for them?
Was Luck a cover, a made up name?
Were the crime gang the ones behind it all, who, if they had not been killed, were intending to blackmail Unicorn?

"Ferris?" one of his colleagues asked, knocking on the door and requesting entry.

"Come. What's up?"

"I think you need to hear this," Agent White said. "This is David Anderson. He's a neighbour of the man who owns this flat. We just arrested him outside in the street. Mr Anderson has intel about Ray Luck and who these dead men are..."

It took twenty-five minutes for David Anderson to tell his story, and by the time he was finished, Ferris knew several things.

Firstly, Ray Luck had clearly invited the criminal drug gang and its leaders to his flat in the specific hope that they would get trapped by his men and either arrested or killed. It was evidently his way of helping David Anderson out of a situation that had got out of control and for which Ray Luck was partially responsible.

Secondly, it meant that Ray Luck had anticipated that they were coming for him.

He knew he had been rumbled.

Ferris turned to look at the flashing light on the wall.

In an instant, it all made sense: the flashing light, the lack of a laptop, external hard-drives, the freshly shredded paper that Ferris had found in the shredder. Ray had known they were coming...he had planned his escape and got out of there before anyone else had arrived.

As he was thinking, Ferris's eyes were scanning the contents of the computer room, his eyes noticing for the first time the blinking green light on the back of one of the monitors. It signified that the monitor was connected to the network...and although the screen was dark and broken, there was still some active communication that was going on...

With further recognition dawning on Ferris, he dived forward, pulling out all the plugs from the walls, switching off all the IP devices and servers still in the room.

He looked quickly at his watch, estimating the time it had taken for them to get here, and how much time had elapsed since they had broken through the second firewall and discovered who Ray Luck was and where he was operating from: it had been all of about fifty minutes.

"Blast!" Ferris shouted aloud, staring at the servers, cursing himself.

He wouldn't be able to have it confirmed until a few hours later, but already Ferris knew what the IT Forensics guys would tell him: the servers had been wiped clean. Overwritten with dummy data.

Luck had started a data-washing programme before he left, and all the time he had been standing in the flat, Ferris had been an idiot and let the program continue to run in the background.

His only hope was that he'd still managed to pull the power in time, and that somehow there might be some data left on a device somewhere which could still help them find Luck.

The third piece of intel that Ferris now knew was this: Ray Luck had got clean away.

He had known they were coming - demonstrated by the flashing red light - and had somehow managed to sneak past them all.

With the nearest tube station only five minutes away, he'd be well gone now, and there was no point in immediately pursuing him.

Ray Luck was obviously a very clever man.

It made Ferris more angry, and in some strange way, more excited to think that the chase was not yet over - and that in fact it had just begun.

Ray Luck was out there, and Ferris was going to find him.

Ferris knew that his escaping was only a hiccup in the process: ultimately, they would catch him, and probably very soon.

He was one man.

They had all the resources of MI5.

It would only be a matter of hours before Ray Luck would be caught.

Ferris smiled.

This hiccup would make the final victory that much sweeter, as well as giving him the perfect excuse to inflict a little more pain than necessary during the interrogation which he couldn't wait to enjoy.

"So, Ray Luck, your luck may not have run out yet, but it will. Very soon!" Ferris muttered under his breath. "That much I promise..."

7.55 p.m.

Ray dropped his bag onto the seat beside him at the back of the bus, keeping his head down and staring out of the window.

Before leaving the shelter of the cobbled mews and joining the hustle and bustle of busy London life on the main road beyond, he'd taken a woman's long black burqa body coat out of his bag and put it on, his body and face now completely covered, thus ensuring that his identity would be concealed from the CCTV cameras in the street and on the buses and public transport.

Ray knew that his life had now changed.

For how long, he didn't know.

He didn't have a plan.

Yet.

For now he knew that he had to live in the shadows and escape and evade capture at all times.

He was under no illusion as to the seriousness of the situation he was in.

He knew it was wrong, but he couldn't resist catching a bus that took him past the entrance to the square he lived in. As the bus had sat in the queue waiting for the lights to change outside the tube station at South Kensington, he had been able to see right into his square from the top deck of the bus.

What he saw confirmed everything he had feared: the square was blocked off with quite a number of vans and unmarked cars, and the street outside his house was swarming with fully armed SWAT teams.

They'd come for him just as he knew they would.

"*They*."

Who 'they' were he did not know.

There were no police cars. No regular signs of authority.

Whoever it was, it was not the regular police.

As the first bus he had boarded pulled off and drove on, Ray knew that he would never be able to go back to the square.

At least, not for a very long time.

The people who would now be taking his flat apart, bit by bit, looking for the video he had taken of Randolph Best murdering an innocent woman, knew what Ray Luck looked like.

What's more, they knew everything about him.

They would have copies of his birth certificate, his credit cards, his medical records, his school and university records, his phone records, and his last browsing habits on Google and Firefox before he had started to use Ghost.

Soon they would know details of all his friends, their friends...their medical records, their telephone numbers...

In this digital world, the government forces that were now looking for Ray would soon quickly discover every single aspect and detail about his life that there was to know.

In short, they would now know more about Ray than he did himself.

Ray knew that very soon photographs of him from his teenage years until today would be flying across the internet, any and all recognisable images of him being shared with every other government agency or police department in the world that might help track him down.

Computerised CCTV camera systems across the country would soon be programmed to pick up images from passers-by in the street and compare them with the photographs that they now had of Ray.

As soon as one camera - it could be a traffic camera, a camera in a shop, a CCTV camera in the street, anywhere - caught a view of his face in sufficient detail that it registered as a match to one of the known photographs they would now have of him, then he would only have minutes before he would be arrested.

Right now, Ray's appearance and identity were his biggest weaknesses and posed the greatest threat to him being caught.

Before the evening was over, Ray would have to vanish from the face of the planet: as the Phoenix rose from the fire, another person would have to rise from the embers of Ray.

Who? Ray did not yet have a clue.

Where would he take refuge? Likewise, another detail that he had not yet figured out.

For now, Ray knew that he had two goals.

Firstly, to get to Paula's and to see Emma before she left for Canada. With any luck - not his luck...luck that hopefully she would get from elsewhere - she would be able to catch her flight early tomorrow morning as normal. She had to get out of the country fast, before her name made it onto a watch list and she was picked up as she tried to board a plane.

Canada would be the best place for her.

Secondly, Ray had to stay free, and alive.

He didn't have a plan. Yet. But so long as he was free, he would have time to think of one.

In the next thirty minutes, Ray changed buses three times, zigzagging his way across the city towards Paula's house.

As he got closer and closer to his goal, his thoughts slowly began to crystallise.

Ray Luck, once the hunter who had taunted Randolph Best, teased and threatened him, had now become the hunted.

So long as he was free, the only power that he could barter with would be his ability to release the video of Randolph Best to an unsuspecting world and potentially topple the UK Government through the ensuing scandal.

Ray knew that it was a chess piece that if played correctly, would save his life. It was also the only chess piece he had.

Chapter 30

London

Friday

October 4th

8.45 p.m.

Ferris sat at his desk and cursed himself.
He had fucked up.
The mission was a total screw-up and after getting special permission to lead the operation, he had ballsed it up completely.
He had to redeem himself somehow and the best way to do it was to find Ray Luck.

Since getting back to the office he'd checked the few items he had quickly squirreled out of Ray's computer room, but discovered nothing of interest.
His only hope was that the servers and other network devices they had recovered would still hold some elements of information that could yield something - anything - of interest that could help them find Ray Luck.

Ferris had been overconfident and he knew that now.
Instead of reconnoitring the location properly and then covering all possible escape routes, Ferris had gone in hard through the front door. He had wanted to get there as fast as possible. In his haste he had forgotten to cover any rear escape routes.
How did that Latin phrase go? *Festina lente* - 'More haste, less speed.'

As soon as he knew who the gangsters were that they had killed, and why they were there, Ferris had realised that it was all a set-up.
Ray Luck had known they were coming, and he had escaped.
Standing there in the hallway with the blood of the gangsters beginning to congeal on the floor and the walls, Ferris had spent too much time worrying about getting the bodies out of the building before any police arrived.
The goal had been to enter the building quietly and snatch Luck without anyone knowing that they had been there.
Instead, the gun battle on the top floor had attracted attention from the people below, and Ferris knew that it would only be minutes before the police arrived.

After a few minutes thinking, he'd realised that the best option was for the rest of the team to leave and to avoid getting caught, and to let Ferris take the blame for everything else.

He knew it might be awkward at first, but then it would only be a matter of his boss making a few phone calls to clear it away with the management.

When the police arrived, the less said the better. With the backing of MI5 and the Foreign Secretary, Ferris would walk free within minutes without having to justify anything: it was a matter of national interest and any explanation for what had taken place there tonight was purely on a need-to-know basis.

And no one else needed to know.

The police would be powerless to act against him and his team, and Ferris knew that.

Once Ferris had decided to carry the can, and the others had left and he was alone in the flat, he had started to think more clearly again.

So, where had Ray Luck gone?

The rest of the flat had been checked, just to make sure he wasn't hiding in any cupboards, but he was definitely nowhere to be found.

Whilst standing in the hallway, thinking, he'd looked up and seen the trapdoor leading to the attic.

Grabbing a chair and standing on it, he'd tried to pull the trapdoor down but found that it was locked from within.

Which was curious.

Already in for a penny and in for a pound with the police, he'd taken out his Glock and shot the lock several times until the trapdoor had fallen open - not really worrying if Luck was hiding on the other side and might end up catching several bullets.

Reaching up and grabbing hold of the sides of the hatch, he'd hoisted himself up into the dark void beyond and immediately moved away from the opening and swept the attic with his gun.

It took a minute for his eyes to adjust and until they did he had to make sure he wasn't jumped by Luck from out of the darkness.

Luckily, as his eyes scanned the space around him, he noticed a light switch on the floor beside him and flicked it on.

A furtive few seconds scanning around him revealed an empty space.

And a ski-pole and a short metal ladder.

It was then that Ferris realised that he had been outsmarted, and how.

Staring down out of the skylight into the gardens beyond, Ferris traced the route that Luck would have taken, escaping over the walls and into the streets beyond.

He'd be long, long gone by now.

The sound of the ambulance had broken Ferris's contemplative spell.

Hurrying back through the attic space and dropping down into the space below, he'd come face to face with two-armed police officers, both of whom were pointing their weapons straight at him.

Ferris raised his hands in the air, and spoke calmly to the policemen, explaining who he was and inviting one of them to reach into his back pocket and take out his credentials.

As one of the officers complied, Ferris watched as a couple of paramedics rushed across the landing outside the open front door and into the flat opposite, and a few more armed policemen swept into his flat from the stairwell.

"What's happened? Has someone else been shot?" Ferris asked.

"No," the officer with his credentials' wallet replied, showing it to the other officer, and nodding at Ferris that he could take his hands down. "The old lady next door has had a heart attack. Looks like whatever happened here scared the life out of her..." the policeman said, waving at the bodies on the floor.

Ferris nodded. If the woman died, it wouldn't be on his conscience. Luck caused this and he was to blame.

"Could you answer a few questions for us first,...'Agent' Ferris?"

"It's Ferris, just Ferris."

Just then the police officer's radio buzzed.

The policeman answered it, and looked at Ferris critically as he listened to his commanding officer explain in no uncertain terms that he was to let the man Ferris just walk out of the door.

No questions asked.

Chapter 31

London

Friday

October 4th

9.30 p.m.

Ray got off his sixth bus, crossed the road and jumped onto another one going in the other direction.

Looking around him anxiously, he was now sure that no one had been following him. Which meant that for now, he was safe: hidden beneath the burqa no one would be able to identify him, even if a police officer walked right past him.

In today's political climate, no police officer in his right mind would stop and search a woman like 'him' without a full authorised stop-and-search warrant!

For now, at least, Ray was free to walk around without any immediate fear of capture.

He glanced quickly at his watch - although suddenly conscious that perhaps a woman dressed in a burqa may not do that and that such a simple action may draw unwanted attention - and upon seeing the time, he realised how late it was.

He'd have to hurry to Paula's and warn Emma about what had happened.

When he thought of her he felt a sudden pang of longing, and for the first time that night he remembered their kiss.

So much had happened so quickly.

Licking his lips, he tasted her lipstick and he felt a sudden longing for her.

During their short meeting they had exchanged few words, and Ray remembered that he had been quite forceful and rude to her.

They had kissed, and he had felt her need for him, but he had not let her explain why she had come to see him.

Was she having second thoughts about going to Canada?

Had she changed her mind about him?

Did she want to get back together?

At the thought of it, his heart surged, but within seconds his hopes came crashing down as he remembered that his world was now very different from before.

Ray's life was in danger.

People were looking for him - MI5 or MI6, maybe both - and when they found him Ray knew that the prognosis would not be good.

With a sickening feeling in his stomach it struck him again that Emma's life may also now be in danger.

Should he be going to meet her at all?

What happened if people were following him and he led them right to her, and they then captured them both?

For a second Ray considered heading in the opposite direction, steering well clear of Emma and making sure she was safe.

Then it occurred to him, that perhaps, if he did, she would not catch her flight to Canada tomorrow - if indeed she was still intending to go - so that she could stay and look for him.

"No," he thought to himself. "She has to leave the country. She needs to get out of here as soon as possible!"

Whether it was an excuse or the truth, Ray didn't argue, but in that moment he persuaded himself that going to Emma now, talking to her, and making sure that she got on the plane and escaped England the next morning was indeed the right thing to do.

Once she was out of the country she would be safe.

Paula's house was not far now.

Looking at his watch again, he estimated that in ten minutes he would be there.

In ten minutes he would see Emma for perhaps the last time in his life.

10.05 p.m.

When the doorbell rang, Paula and Emma exchanged worried glances. Paula indicated to Emma to go upstairs into the bedroom while she went towards the front door to open it, hesitating as she leant forwards to turn the handle: Emma had told her all about what had happened, and the way she had described it to her, she was in no doubt that there was something very serious going on.

When she'd turned up on her doorstep in floods of tears, Paula had just opened the door and let Emma fall into her arms.

It'd taken quite a while and a strong gin and tonic to get her to calm down and explain everything that had happened, and as soon as she had, Paula couldn't help but be seriously worried about Ray.

"Should we call him? To see if he's alright?" she'd asked Emma, but after thinking about it for a while, they thought they'd better leave it a little longer. Give Ray a chance to come to them first, before assuming anything bad had happened.

When the doorbell finally went an hour later, Emma slowly stood up from the sofa and then slipped upstairs to hide in the bedroom before Paula opened the door. Just in case it was somebody looking for her, and it was somebody that wasn't Ray.

Paula counted to ten, then slowly opened the door.
A tall woman in a burqa stood on the doorstep, looking directly at her.
For a second, Paula was caught off guard. This was the last thing she was expecting...
"It's me," a familiar voice said from behind the veil. "It's Ray. Can I come in?"
"RAY?" she gasped in surprise, stepping back and putting a hand to her mouth. She stared at the figure for a second, looking directly into the person's eyes, recognising the familiar twinkle that Ray always had. At the same time, he reached up with his left hand, revealing his face for a second before pushing past her into the hall.
Paula closed the door, and started to giggle.
"What on earth is going on? You look... "
"Ridiculous?" Ray finished the sentence for her.
"Perhaps..." she replied..."I mean, *now* I know it's *you*, you look ridiculous, but before...you didn't...you just looked like a Muslim woman...I would never have known.."
"Which is exactly the point." Ray replied, pleased that the disguise had obviously worked. "Is Emma here?" he asked, cutting to the point.
"Yes, sorry...she's upstairs...," she nodded towards the stairs. "Emma," she shouted loudly, "It's okay! You can come down. It's Ray!"

Emma appeared at the top of the stairs, just in time to see Ray clambering out of the Burqa.
Paula watched as Emma came down the stairs, not sure whether she should make herself scarce or whether Emma wanted her to hang around.
Emma came down and stood before Ray, tears running down her face, cradling herself in her own arms.
Ray reached out a hand gingerly to touch her face, and for a few seconds Emma held back, swaying away from his fingers.
But then she took a step forward, and as Ray's fingers stroked her cheek, she lifted her hand and touched his in sympathy.
They stood like that for a second, just looking into each other's eyes, Ray not sure if he was still a friend or now a foe.

Then Emma stepped forward and put her head against Ray's chest, and he wrapped his arms around her and held her close.

"Tea?" Paula coughed, losing her voice for a second as the emotion affected her too. "I think I'll go and make us all a lovely cup of tea. But first... maybe I'll just pop down the road to the petrol station to get some milk, and you can both catch up together in private in the lounge. It's more comfortable in there..."

Quickly grabbing her coat and keys, she let herself out of the door.

It wasn't far to the all night shop in the petrol station, but Paula walked very slowly.

Very slowly indeed.

She knew Emma and Ray had a lot of catching up to do.

10.25 p.m.

Emma sat on the couch beside Ray, her hands outstretched and held by Ray together in his lap. The tears still eased their way slowly down her cheeks, and Ray occasionally lifted a finger and gently wiped them away.

They sat in silence, Ray waiting for Emma to speak, and Emma waiting to know what to say, hoping that somehow she would understand her own thoughts and feelings and have a clue what it was that she actually, truly, felt towards this man.

"I'm so confused..." she eventually whispered.

Ray smiled.

He didn't know what else to do.

But when Emma looked up at him, she saw only concern and kindness in his eyes.

"I didn't think I would be sitting here with you this evening...talking..." Ray replied. "I didn't think I would ever see you again."

"I'm leaving for Canada tomorrow morning Ray...at least, I'm meant to be... I think I am...." she coughed, pulling a hand back out of his and wiping some more tears from her eyes.

She stood up, and walked to the window, pulling back the curtain gently and looking out, before turning around and looking at him. Studying him.

"What happened tonight, Ray? What's going on? I'm scared!"

Ray looked up at the ceiling, perhaps seeking some form of inspiration to guide him as to what he should say to Emma, the woman he loved. The woman that he knew he had to protect. At all costs.

"Something bad happened. Something bad."

"What? What on earth was going on?"

"I can't tell you, Emma. Not because I don't want to, but because I honestly believe that it's best that you don't know. The less you know, the better."

"Why? You're scaring me again."

"I don't want to, honestly I don't....but all I can tell you is that some people may be looking for me, and if they associate you with me, then they may want to ask you questions about me, and the less you know about it all, the better. They will easily be able to tell if you are lying or not...you're so transparent...you could never tell a lie even if your life depended upon it!"

"And will my life depend upon it?" she asked, quickly.

Ray hesitated.

"No," he replied. "But perhaps mine might."

Emma burst into tears again and started to walk towards Ray, her arms outstretched, then stopped abruptly and pulled at her hair with both hands.

"Is this about that money you found?" she asked, suddenly making the connection. "Is it drug money? Are the drug gang after you?"

Ray latched upon the gift she had just given him.

"Yes. It is."

"Oh dear...you were right! And I never believed you. I should have listened to you. You told me that it was drug money, and that it was dangerous, but I didn't listen. I'm so sorry..."

She crossed the room and wrapped her arms around him, cuddling him tight.

For a second Ray went with it, enjoying her warmth and the emotion, something he was not really sure that he would ever get from her again...and then he slowly put his arms on her shoulder and gently pushed her back.

"Please...sit down..." he said, his voice calm and steady. "I want to say something to you, and you have to listen to me."

She looked so lost and confused as he guided her to sit back down on the sofa. Her eyes were so big, so blue...so beautiful.

He swallowed hard, and knelt on the ground in front of her, taking her hands in his and resting them on her lap.

"I want you to know that I love you, Emma. I always have. I'm an idiot, and perhaps I don't deserve you, but I *do* love you. It's really important to me that you understand that! Okay?"

Emma nodded, her face white, her eyes questioning him.

Her lips opened to speak, but Ray rested a single, solitary finger on them, and spoke again.

"Good. Which is why this is really hard for me to say... but I think that you must get on that flight tomorrow and go to Canada. Get out of the country. You need to get as far away from here as possible, and leave as soon as you can."

"No, I can't leave you now! Not now!"

"Emma," Ray nodded slowly in front of her face. "You have to."

"No! I mean, before I came over this evening I was so confused...I didn't know what was going on in my mind, or what I was going to do...but now I know! I can't leave...not now!"

"You have to. You told me that I never did the right thing. Ever. Well, you have to let me do this. You have to let me insist that you get on the plane and leave..."

"You're sending me away? Now? Bloody hell Ray, this proves again that you never know the right thing to do... I split up with you, I came back to you, and now you're sending me away?"

"Emma, it's the right thing to do! Honestly! I need to know that you are safe. I need for you to be safe."

"No..."

"You have to go, Emma. *You have to*!"

"Wait, a second..." she said, standing up, and reaching into her pocket. "What's this for? Why did you give me this then?"

Ray stared at the little box in her hands. It was the engagement ring.

"Did you open it?" he asked.

"No, not yet..."

"Can I have it back?"

She stared at him, her mouth opening wide. Ray reached up with his hand to take it from her open palm, but she quickly stepped back, and opened it.

"Oh my God!" she said aloud, and then fell to her knees on the ground. "It's a ..."

"It's an engagement ring, Emma." Ray finished. "The one I was going to give to you last Saturday, after the special meal I was going to cook for you. But that was before you split up with me and walked out of my life...at least, I thought you had."

Emma stared at him.

"You were going to propose to me last Saturday? Ask me to ...marry you!?"

"Yes." Ray replied, and then added. "If you look at the receipt I probably left hidden under the ring setting in the box, you'll see I bought the ring a month ago. I've just been waiting for the right moment. The perfect moment."

Emma stared at Ray.

Slowly, she reached into the box, lifted the setting and took out the receipt.

"Wow!" she replied.

Tears were streaming out of her eyes now, but her look of confusion was slowly turning to one of joy.

"Ray, you want me to marry you? Honestly...this is not some sort of weird wind-up?"

Ray shuffled closer towards her on the floor where she was kneeling.

"Emma. This is really hard. More hard for me than I think you will ever, possibly realise. But 'yes' I was going to propose to you last week, and also even earlier on this evening...possibly...depending upon why you came to see me...but then everything went crazy, and now...now...it's not really possible! That's why I wanted to ask for the ring back. It's not the right time anymore..."

"What?" she asked, shaking her head, confusion returning to her voice. "I don't understand!"

"For all the reasons we just talked about. Because of what happened in the past few hours, my life is in danger now. And you have to leave the country as soon as you can!"

"Then you come with me too...I'll only go if you come too!"

Ray was about to reply that he couldn't, that whatever UK agency it was that was looking for him would be monitoring all the ports, just waiting to arrest him when he passed through security, but then he realised that he couldn't say that. It would take him down a rabbit hole he would never be able to get out of.

"I will..." he replied. Lying."You leave tomorrow, and I'll get my passport, and join you in a few days. There are a few things I have to sort out first. But you have to go tomorrow, okay?"

Emma's eyes searched his.

"You promise? You promise you'll come and join me?"

"Yes. I will. I promise. As soon as I can."

A smile began to spread across her face.

"Can..., Ray, can I put the ring on?"

Ray hesitated for a second.

"Is it okay if I say that I would prefer that you just take it with you? I want to propose to you properly...somewhere romantic and not just after I've been dressing up as a woman. This is all so fucked up. It's not what I planned."

She was looking at him now, hanging on his every word, the box with the engagement ring open in her hands.

Ray reached out and gently closed the lid.

"Please...take the ring. Keep it safe for me. I promise, I'll come to join you. And when I do, I'll take you to the Rockies or that tall observation tower in Toronto, or I'll get down on one knee on the side of the Niagara Falls? We'll do it properly. When I see you."

For a few moments Emma said nothing, then eventually she nodded.

"Okay," she said. "You win. We'll do it in Canada."

Putting an arm around his neck she reached out and pulled him closer to her.

She kissed him.

"Now..." she said, in a low, husky voice. "Let's go upstairs...if I'm going to get that plane, we don't have much time."

As they stood up and Ray followed her out the room, Ray bit his lips and swore in his mind.

Ray hated lying to Emma. Hated it. But even as he did, he knew that for once he *was* doing the right thing.

He just hoped that one day Emma would understand and forgive him.

Although Ray knew that there was a strong possibility that after tonight, they would never see each other again.

10.40 p.m.

Ferris put the phone down, fuming.

The warrants he needed to access the phone records and personal details of Ray Luck would not be available now until mid-Saturday morning. The situation was a complete mess.

He had put in the request via his boss as soon as he had identified the target as being Ray Luck and got his details, knowing full well that they would need all the information on him that they could get.

Bureaucracy made Ferris mad: it threw unnecessary obstacles in his path, preventing him from getting his job done - stopping him from protecting the country he loved and the citizens who lived there!

It was common knowledge that the UK Authorities collected all forms of electronic communication on its citizens, everything from the texts on mobiles, to phone calls and emails, but what was not such common knowledge was that if the authorities needed to access those records, they needed to have reasonable grounds and full authorisation from the Home Secretary to do so. Which meant bureaucracy, bureaucracy and bureaucracy...and by the time you got permission to start investigating anything, the bloody terrorist who you wanted to catch had absconded the country!

Ferris did have connections though. Unofficial connections, and he could 'make some things happen' while he waited for the official documentation to come through.

If he wanted to.

The problem was, Ferris knew that after tonight's fuck-up, he was going to be under a lot of scrutiny.

The last thing he needed was to actually catch the bastard Luck, and then lose his job for not following proper procedures and accessing Ray's electronic communications illegally.

On the other hand, if he didn't catch Ray, it was going to look really bad on him anyway.

Ferris thought about the implications of either action, juggling the consequences of both.

In the end, he picked up the phone and dialled a friend.

Fifteen minutes later he was looking at the text messages from Ray Luck's mobile.

It wasn't a lot. Not as good as getting access to his emails, and voice-records.

But it was a start.

A good start.

Although totally illegal.

2.30 a.m.

Ray and Emma stood by the door in the lobby at the foot of the stairs, hugging each other tight.

Emma thinking it might be for the last time in a week, and Ray knowing that it might be the last time ever.

Her flight was leaving from Gatwick in a less than three and a half hours' time, and she had to be there at the latest two hours before hand. She was cutting it fine.

Paula had agreed to drive her and she was already waiting outside in the car, letting them say their goodbyes in private.

"I love you," Emma declared for the tenth time in the past minute.

"I love you too, Emma," he promised back, "but you have to leave now. If you miss that flight things could get really complicated, and I *need* you safe and sound. Please...you have to go...now..."

Emma pulled back. "You're telling me to leave for the second time in less than twenty-four hours..."

"And both times to protect you, and because I love you...do you understand?"

"Yes."

"I mean, do you *really* understand?"

"Yes...yes, I do...I think..."

They kissed a few more times, then just as Paula opened her car door and started to get out and come towards them to hurry them up, Emma pulled away, smiled once more at Ray, and then hurried down the path to the car.

He watched as they drove off.

The intense feeling of sadness that he felt was like nothing that he had ever known before. He felt as if he was being ripped apart.

He wanted to go after her but he knew he couldn't.

Instead he closed the door, and sat at the bottom of the stairs, his head in his hands and his life in ruins.

Chapter 32

London

Saturday

October 5th

8.00 a.m.

Ferris sat in the car outside 10 Bluebell Gardens, the home of Emma Purvis, the girlfriend of Ray Luck.

Ferris knew it was a long shot.

He'd read all of Ray's text messages for the past few weeks and he knew that Ray and Emma had split up, the timing indicating that this had seemingly taken place before Ray would have seen the murder taking place online.

It was just a hunch.

However, Ferris knew that in a moment of dire need, with nowhere else to go, there was a strong possibility that Ray would still turn up at her doorstep and beg for her help.

A long-shot, but not such a long-shot that he should ignore it.

Ferris spoke into his phone, giving the signal.

He watched as a milkman walked up to the front door with a few bottles of milk, picked the lock and stood aside as a postman and another man quickly hurried in the front door and into the flat beyond.

Ferris crossed his fingers and prayed that his luck was about to change.

8.10 a.m.

"She got away without any problems. She's going to be safe." Paula promised Ray, as they sat together in the lounge of her house.

Ray smiled.

It had gone much better than he had hoped. After she had left he had started to think more deeply about his predicament and what lay before him, and he had begun to worry that he had perhaps been rather naive in hoping that Emma would make the flight without being arrested.

Fears which were thankfully unfounded.

"So," Paula eventually asked the inevitable. "What are you going to do now?"

"Get off the grid." Ray answered quite simply.

"What do you mean?"

"Disappear." he replied. "I have to disappear. Vanish."

"Vanish? You're not going to do anything stupid are you? Emma says you promised you were going to join her in Canada."

"I will. When I can. But for now, I have to disappear. So that no one can track me down and find me."

Paula was silent for a moment.

"You can stay here for a while, lie low, if you want?"

Ray smiled.

"Thanks. But no. They'll probably come and look for me here too. It's only going to be a matter of time before they turn up. You're one of Emma's best friends..."

"Ray," Paula interrupted. "Who will come looking for me? The drug gang? How will they know...?" she started to ask questions that Ray could not answer.

"You're right," he lied, again. "They won't. How could they? I'm just being paranoid. But it doesn't change anything though. I can't stay here. I have to leave. And soon."

Paula stared at him.

"Is this really serious, Ray? I mean, *really* serious?"

Ray stood up.

"I think it's time to go. It could be dangerous. Maybe...And the longer I stay here, the more you could be in danger....*maybe*."

Ten minutes later Ray walked out of the door, once again dressed as a woman.

Soon he had blended into the streets of London, and was gone.

8.12 a.m.

"What did she say?" Ferris almost shouted at the 'postman' after he came out of the house, angered by what he had just heard the man report.

"Luck or his girlfriend weren't there. The woman said that her housemate left last night, and said that she was going abroad for a couple of months. She'd paid the rent for the next three months in advance. She'd come back to the house in a bit of a state, grabbed her things and then left. She'd been planning the trip for a few months. Apparently."

"Blast! We missed her. But it may explain why she split up with her boyfriend. She was going abroad."

"The woman who shares the house was pretty upset about us breaking in. She demanded to see a warrant."

Ferris shivered. Things were not going his way today. They'd missed the woman, and now they could be in trouble for doing it: they didn't have a warrant.

"What did you tell her?"

"That a warrant wasn't required. And we weren't looking for her anyway, we wanted the other woman, a Miss Emma Purvis...and then we got out as soon as we could. I think she fell for it."

It was a lie. A warrant was absolutely needed, but Ferris didn't have the time to wait for it. He'd applied for it, but he wouldn't get it until later that day.

From now on he was going to do everything by the book. He'd already done too much without the proper authorisation, and now he was even more angry with Luck, he couldn't afford to get pulled off the case because of technical reasons before he'd caught the bastard. It would be several hours before the warrants he needed came in.

Ferris looked at his watch. It was still early, and he'd been up all night.

He made a decision.

"Martins?" he said into his phone. "You're in charge for now. Get everyone back to the office. I'm going home to get some kip. Call me as soon as the paperwork arrives. Okay?"

"Will do, skipper. As soon as..."

9.20 a.m.

The Right Honourable John Rowlinson pushed back from his desk in one of the offices high up in Whitehall, put his hands in his pockets and strolled over to the window.

Rowlinson had been playing these games for many years now and, to many people, he never seemed fazed by the activities and politics of the world in which he operated.

Unfortunately for Rowlinson, things were no longer exactly as they appeared. He was almost sixty-two years old, and the years of cigar smoking and drinking port at his club and the offices of all the various MPs he served had started to take their toll.

He was getting old.

Outwardly, he was still able to master his emotions, but internally, he was finding it increasingly difficult to control and overcome the stress that his interests in UK politics and his role in British Intelligence created.

Rowlinson was a wealthy man. A very wealthy man. So, in theory, he could walk away from this world at any time he wanted to. However, the truth was that he loved the job, and he loved his country. He knew that he had an important role to play in its defence, but more importantly the many 'private' interests that he served all had expectations of him that he simply couldn't abandon or neglect.

Especially those that concerned Unicorn.

He'd already been heading up a special 'activity' concerning Unicorn for several years now, and now there was all this messy business around the woman's death.

Whether it was by accident or design, he was ultimately responsible for both the surveillance and intelligence operations concerning Unicorn, and frustratingly, the new operation was clearly at odds with the first.

There was a real danger that if he didn't manage the new operation properly, it could expose the first one, and one or other of the two, maybe both, could come back to bite him hard.

Yet, strangely, that was part of the excitement and challenge that these activities used to have for him.

Ferris's file had just been sent to him by Jacobson, Ferris's boss. Rowlinson had just finished reviewing it.

Did Ferris have the capability to bring this Ray Luck in? Could he trust him to deliver?

Rowlinson was undecided.

For now he would let Ferris roll with the operation. Ferris's boss was going to give a report twice a day.

His boss had vouched for him and, in this business, that was something that Rowlinson respected.

He nodded, having made the decision for now.

Turning away from his amazing view of the London Eye and the Southbank, Rowlinson picked up the file and walked it over to the safe in the wall.

Once it was securely locked away with all the other files he had on Unicorn, he adjusted his tie and fished out his gold pocket watch at the end of its heavy gold chain. It was time to start the walk to Number 10. The Prime Minister was expecting him at 9.45 a.m. and Rowlinson did not want to be late.

10.30 a.m.

Ray sat on the top deck of the number 26 bus riding towards Waterloo. He'd already swapped buses twice. He'd decided that he was going to spend the next couple of hours just going backwards and forwards between Waterloo and Liverpool Street Station, while he thought about what his next steps should be.

One thing was clear to him.
As he had mentioned to Paula, he had to get off the grid.
From this point forth, Ray Luck would cease to exist.
Which meant that he could not use his credit cards, his phone, his email address, or his laptop.
He could not use anything electronic which the agency who was chasing him could use to track him down.
Frustratingly this meant that he would have to get another laptop: if the WASH program had not done its job properly, they would probably manage to find out the IP address of his laptop.
They would already have all his bank card details.
His phone calls would be monitored and the moment he switched it on, they would trace the location of his iPhone. Ray made a mental note to throw it into the Thames as soon as he could.
He couldn't call anyone who knew him. If he did, and they were monitoring his friends and family, they would trace him.
In the short term, these were all manageable, but the top issues that really bugged him were:
1: He would have to get another disguise. He couldn't stand walking around dressed in the burqa - he felt weird dressed up as a woman, and also a little disrespectful. He would have to buy a wig, some new clothes, and a false beard or moustache. Maybe even a false pair of glasses. Just being in London or any big city carried a significant risk. The police were everywhere. CCTV cameras were everywhere. If a clear image of his face was caught on a single camera, there was a strong possibility that alarm bells would start ringing on some people-tracking program in MI5 somewhere, and the police would be at the scene and arresting him within minutes.
2: How would he afford to live? He had no money... He only had about thirty pounds in his pocket, and since he had to pay for everything by cash, that wasn't going to last long.
3: Where was he going to go live? Living on the streets was not an option. There was a strong likelihood that the police might move him on, recognise him and then arrest him. Plus, Ray knew he wouldn't last long on the streets of London. He loved his home comforts too much. He'd probably end up shooting himself after a couple of days.
4: How long was this going to last?

The last question was the worst of all.
Right now, Ray could not see a way out of his predicament.

For now, Ray was on the run.

The longer it went on, the more likely it would be that they would catch him, and when they did, Ray didn't fancy his chances too much.

It was about 11.28 a.m. when Ray was looking out the window and passing by the Bank of England on the bus for the third time that day when the answer to his second problem came to him in a blinding flash of genius.

Stupidly, in all the excitement and fear of the past day, Ray had forgotten one very small, minor point.

A few days ago Ray had committed one of the largest cyber bank robberies in years!

Far from being poor, Ray was now rich and waiting for him in a series of rented PO boxes dotted across London there should be a pile of new VISA cards and PIN codes which would give him access to anywhere between £500,000 or £5,000,000 - depending upon how many zeros he had actually typed into the machine the other day when he was drunk.

None of them was in his name, and once he got hold of them, no ATM machine was ever going to ask for his identity.

All he had to do was go and pick them up!

Behind the veil of the Burqa, no one on the bus saw that Ray was smiling. For the first time in a week, perhaps his luck was about to change.

The mere thought of this made Ray laugh, because in that moment, it seemed so prophetic. It couldn't have been more accurate.

Ray Luck *had* changed.

From this point on he was going to be called Mike Denton, Stuart Groves, Peter Andrews or Hugh Grant: these were the names he had chosen for his alter egos and his new bank debit cards when he was drunk.

Ray had always liked the actor Hugh Grant, and when you are drunk, it's as good a reason as any to choose a new name.

Hugh Grant?

Why not.

Ray thought again about the money.

Unless he could find a way to resolve the mess he was in, and quickly, he was going to need every penny he had stolen.

The good news was that it was unlikely that the bank would ever find out who had stolen the money or when it had gone. There was a possibility that they would never even notice that it was gone.

The number of zeros he'd typed in would be crucial. If he had stolen £5,000,000 then he would never have to work again. He could assume one of his false identities and live any way he wanted.

With that much money he could buy a new passport on the black market and travel abroad. Go anywhere.

However, if it was only £500,000, it would not be enough to live a whole new life. The money would only last about ten years, and then it would be gone. He would only have that much time to make sure his new life was secure and that he had a good job and steady income by then.

That is, if he was still alive.

For now though, he needed to remain positive.
He needed to focus and think, and come up with a plan.

By 12.30 a.m. he had decided what he would do.
First he would have a cheap lunch.
Then he would buy his disguise, and then go to the first of the PO boxes he had rented in a 'MailBox' shop near Waterloo. He'd open up the envelopes he would find there, making sure he had about ten cards and ten matching PIN numbers. He'd leave the rest of the cards and pin numbers in the secure rented PO box. They would be safer there than him carrying them around with him.

Next he would go to a couple of ATM machines in Waterloo and withdraw five hundred pounds on each card from several different machines. Too much and it would draw unnecessary attention from the banks' automated systems. He needed to fly under the radar.

Then he needed to find somewhere to lie low for a while.

He thought of leaving London, maybe heading down to Brighton, or catching a train up to Edinburgh. He'd been there once before, years ago, and fallen in love with the place. He'd always intended to go back there, so now was as good a time as any.

He was still weighing up between Edinburgh or Brighton over lunch, when a much better idea occurred to him.

A much better idea.

It surprised him that he hadn't thought of it before.

He would go and visit RobinHood.

Chapter 33

London

Saturday

October 5th

12.15 p.m.

The paperwork arrived on Ferris's desk just as he was going to go for lunch. Forgetting how hungry he was, he immediately sat down at his desk again, picked up the phone and went to work.

Opening up the email that arrived almost simultaneously, he examined the electronic records of the warrants and checked that they were all in order. They were.

Using the permissions he had now been granted he and two of his colleagues immediately went to work pulling all the phone records, emails, text messages, bank records, academic and health records and all other forms of social media records that belonged to Ray Luck, his girlfriend, and several of his relatives. Once they knew who his friends and colleagues were, they would apply for warrants for them too, but they had enough to start with for now.

Some of the work they would do would be automatic, but a lot more of it would be manual. Their software could automatically trawl all electronic communications and look for specific information that they might need to know about, but the intelligence they often found most useful came from simply looking and reading all the basic communications they could access.

Ferris would start with communications that started around the time of the murder incident involving Unicorn last week, and then move forward from there. Afterwards, he would move backwards historically.

Within minutes he and his team had started to pull together an in-depth picture of Ray Luck's life, starting with two important facts.

First, Ray's girlfriend would now be on a plane to Canada. But if he wanted to intercept her when she arrived at her destination, Ferris would have to act fast. Which is why he picked up the phone, talked to someone he knew in another department and called in a favour: within minutes someone would be checking all the electronic flight manifests of UK citizens flying to Canada today. As soon they located Emma Purvis, his colleague would also speak to his contacts in Canada and have her followed when she stepped foot on Canadian soil. By the end of the day Ferris would know where she was living and what she was doing there.

Secondly, the intel showed that Ray worked for Castle Security Defence. The company was well known to their agency. Along with many other leading security companies, they had a partnership which went back years, mainly a one way street where CSD told them many interesting things in return for financial payments. Some of their employees were now even employed by his agency.

A quick phone call later, in spite of the fact that it was a Saturday, Ferris managed to get Luck's personnel record emailed to him by an overenthusiastic member of CSD's HR department who just loved to work with Her Majesty's Government. Well, at least she thought it was Her Majesty's Government, and Ferris was not about to explain the difference.

Luck's file confirmed what Ferris already knew.

Ray Luck was a cyber genius. One of the best.

So far, there hadn't been a network in the world that Ray Luck had not managed to hack into.

Ferris had already proved himself to be very smart, but reading the intel on him as it began to accumulate, Ferris began to realise just how smart Luck was.

Ferris smiled.

It would make it all the more sweet when Ferris eventually brought him in.

1.30 p.m.

RobinHood opened the door to his church and was, briefly, lost for words, the spell only being broken when the deep, brusque tones of SolarWind's voice came from behind the covered face inside the burqa.

"Hi, it's me, SolarWind. Can I come in?"

RobinHood laughed, quickly looking up and down the road to see if anyone else was watching them.

"I think you'd better."

He stepped aside and let SolarWind pass. As soon as he was in, he shut the door behind him.

"What the hell is going on? You must be in some serious shit to be wearing that!"

SolarWind was already busy clambering out of the burqa.

"That, my dear friend, is the understatement of the year." Solarwind replied. "Let's just say that the full might of the Empire is now bearing down upon my back, and I am now a full-blown fugitive of British justice."

RobinHood walked past him again, touching him gently on the arm and motioning SolarWind to follow him.

"Whisky?" he asked. "To calm your nerves while you tell me everything from start to finish..."

"They cracked my anonymising program. They tracked me down. Found me. Came after me..." SolarWind interrupted, throwing the burqa onto a chair and collapsing onto a couch.

RobinHood turned and stared at him in amazement.

"That's not possible..."

"That's what I thought..., I mean, I'd heard rumours...we all have...that TOR was so full of NSA-backdoors that it was unsafe,...and I did wonder if GCHQ or the NSA had the computing power to crack something like my Ghost program, but I didn't really think they could. But now I know. Now we ALL know."

"Bloody hell..." RobinHood exclaimed sinking into the couch opposite SolarWind and thinking about the anonymising program he had built for himself and was using every day.

"Do you think they've cracked mine too? That they're tracking everything I do?"

A dull feeling of impending doom began to spread over RobinHood. Were GCHQ and MI5 already aware of his plans? How much did they know? Had he been compromised too? Was he next? Would the same people who came after SolarWind be crashing through his doors and windows any moment soon?

SolarWind shrugged.

"No idea, mate. Maybe, maybe not. But if you're not on their radar I don't see any reason why they should. However they did it, it would have taken serious computing resources and assets, and that sort of computational power doesn't come cheap. Not the sort of resources you could afford to use on everyday people. Unless you've done something wrong that I don't know about? Or are about to?" SolarWind threw a questioning glance over at RobinHood.

RobinHood quickly shook his head and stood up from the couch, a grimace of pain momentarily passing over his face.

"I ...I need another drink...You?"

SolarWind downed the whisky in his glass and held out his glass for a refill.

"Just one more...but after that I'll need a coffee. I need to talk to you... I have to make plans. And I might need your advice."

"Sure. Anything. You know I'll help if I can. But why did they throw so much resource at you then? What did you do?"

SolarWind took the refilled glass from RobinHood's outstretched hand.

"Thanks...I'll tell you. I'll tell you everything. And then I'm going to ask you if I can hide out here for a few days until I get some other plans in motion. Until I figure out what the hell I'm going to do..."

It took Ray forty minutes to go through it all, answering all of RobinHood's questions, and filling him in on everything that happened since the last time they had met.

At the end of it all RobinHood whistled loudly again, as he had done several times during Ray's little speech, and then got up from the couch and began to pace the room.

"Shit, SolarWind. You're in deep shit. Deep, deep shit."

"Thanks. I know."

They sat in silence for a while, SolarWind wondering what RobinHood would say next, and RobinHood weighing up the significance of everything that had been said.

At the end of it, RobinHood almost whispered.

"Don't worry. We'll get through this. Together. And of course, you can stay here for a while."

SolarWind smiled for the second time that morning.

"Thanks. I really appreciate it! It'll really take the pressure off me for a while."

"Don't mention it. I'll try to help you if I can, and when it's all done, maybe your turning up here like this might also be good for me...I might need your advice and help on something."

"How? On what?"

RobinHood shook his head.

"One step at a time. First we'll put both our heads together and see if we can come up with a plan for you. We'll get you sorted first, and then we can talk about me afterwards. Okay?"

SolarWind nodded.

"Right," RobinHood announced. "Now, I think it's time I got those two big black coffees. Give me a moment. I'll be back in a second. Sugar?"

"Two please," SolarWind replied.

RobinHood nodded, and left the room.

He was gone for quite a while.

Chapter 34

London

Saturday

October 5th

10 Downing Street

The Prime Minister's Office

1.35 p.m.

The Prime Minister shuffled the papers on his desk, and waited for the tea to be poured and his assistant to leave the room.

Rowlinson looked around the office. He didn't like the way the Prime Minister had decorated it since he got back into power for a second term, but suspected it had less to do with the Prime Minister and more to do with his wife.

This was the fourth PM that Rowlinson had served. PMs came and went, but Rowlinson stayed.

They all needed him.

He understood that none of them would ever publicly acknowledge the work he did, and he didn't expect them to.

That didn't bother him.

So long as each PM understood the role they played in British politics, and didn't get ambitious or too cocky, then that was just fine.

Ultimately Rowlinson didn't work for the PM anyway. He worked for the people who put each Prime Minister into power, and could just as quickly remove him - or her- if the mood or the need dictated it.

Democracy was one thing. But the real world was another thing entirely.

"One sugar or two?" the PM asked as his assistant closed the door behind her as she left, her perfume hanging in the air and conjuring up a memory of the roses at the bottom of Mrs Rowlinson's garden.

She was a new assistant. Almost as beautiful as the last.

For a moment Rowlinson wondered if the rumours about the Prime Minister and his new assistant were true, and decided they probably were. Why would the PM break the habit of a lifetime?

"No sugar. Thank you, sir." Rowlinson replied. He was always polite and respectful to each and every PM, in spite of the contempt he had held one or two of them in. "I'm under strict instructions to cut down on my sugar intake. Doctor's orders."

"Aha...sensible. Very sensible. And appropriate. Very appropriate now we're going to pass that new law about sugar content in school foods. Sugar is a killer. There are no two ways about it."

The PM poured the tea and passed the thin china cup and saucer over the table to Rowlinson.

"So, I think you know why I asked you over here today?" The PM asked, getting quickly to the point.

"The Best affair?"

"Exactly. I would like an update from you, if possible."

"Did you not get my reports? You should be receiving two a day?"

"I certainly did. Thank you. However, there is nothing like the personal touch, is there?"

Rowlinson sipped his tea. Deliberately not replying. The game of silence. Whoever won it had the power. Rowlinson was an expert.

"So..." the PM continued. "What happened to this Ray Luck? How soon before you bring him in?"

"I cannot tell you that, sir. As I explained in my report this morning, he is currently at large. It's expected, given his experience and cyber skills, that he will be intending to disappear and avoid all forms of behaviour that would normally lead us to a subject of interest. I anticipate that it may be more difficult than usual to establish another contact that will lead us to him, however I am confident that we will be able to deal with him. If we can't contact him directly, we will do so via his immediate friends and loved ones. It's just a matter of time."

"Have we got time?" the PM asked quickly. "We can't allow Luck to release the video of Best and the woman. It has the potential to bring the government down."

"We understand that, sir. And that won't happen."

The PM leaned forward in his chair.

"And you are aware of the delicacy of the negotiations that Randolph is currently involved in? We can't afford for any scandal to come out at this time. Anything like this would destroy the talks, and it would be years before we have everyone back around the negotiating table. Bloody hell, John, the future of the Middle East depends upon what happens in the next two weeks. We've all worked far too hard for far too long to let anything interrupt the process now. If the video gets out it will wreck everything."

"We understand, sir. We won't let that happen."

"Good John. Thank you. I know you won't. I know you won't."

There was a pause. A moment when Rowlinson could sense that the conversation was not yet finished, and that the PM had not yet got to the real point that he wanted to make.

Rowlinson waited.

"I know you won't, John..." the PM repeated. "But should the unexpected happen, should this video get out before anyone had a chance to stop it...I want you to ensure that the Government is not affected."

Rowlinson sipped his tea, then slowly put his cup back down on its expensive blue and white saucer.

"I'm sorry, sir. This part I may not understand so clearly. I would just like to check what you are saying, to ensure that I understand your wishes completely. Did you just say that should the video accidentally get released, then *you* are *instructing* me that the Government must *not* be affected?"

The PM coughed.

"Yes, John. That is what I said."

"I see," Rowlinson nodded, taking in the full import of what had just been said and implied. Mostly implied.

There was another moment's silence.

The PM was looking directly at Rowlinson, his eyes steady as a rock. Rowlinson understood the PM completely.

"Thank you for the tea. It was delicious as always. Lapsang souchong?"

"I believe so. My assistant selected it. She knows a lot about tea. She's a clever girl. Very clever."

"And very beautiful, if I may say so, sir. Very beautiful."

The PM's eyes lit up, and if Rowlinson was not mistaken he was sure that for a brief second, the PM's face flushed a little pink.

As Rowlinson left the office after shaking the PM's hand, he smiled to himself.

The rumours were definitely true.

2.35 p.m.

Rowlinson was having a busy day.

His limousine had taken him directly from Downing Street to Freemasons' Hall, the headquarters of the United Grand Lodge of England and the principal meeting place for Masonic Lodges in London.

After putting on his ceremonial apron, and making himself presentable, he had entered the executive meeting room on the top level of the building, a room reserved only for the most special of occasions, and the most important meetings of all.

This was one of those times.

As Rowlinson entered the room, the eyes of ten of the most important, wealthy and influential members of British society fell upon him. They had been expecting him and he was fifteen minutes late.

"I'm sorry," Rowlinson apologised. "The PM was delayed."

"And?" one of the elder men asked, dispensing with any niceties.

"It was an interesting conversation. One which I trust you will respect me for, if I decline to disclose its content. However, I would say that I was surprised by the message I was given."

"Which was?" another of the most senior members demanded.

"That in all eventuality I should put the interest of the Government higher than the interests of Randolph Best."

"Meaning?"

"Gentlemen, it is not something that I feel I may discuss openly here. You may infer from it what you will."

"Enough of this nonsense," a younger member from the North of England retorted loudly, standing up and hitting the table with his fist. "You have been following and monitoring Best for almost two years now. We need to know what you have on him, and when you will complete the task you were given to do!"

Rowlinson met the man's eyes, someone whom he knew well and frequently came to verbal blows with, both here in the Lodge and also outside in the world that they had both vowed to protect.

"I will complete my task. That much I have sworn before The Lodge, even though it may go against some of the basic principles which I swore to uphold. I understand my role, and what I can contribute to it. And I will complete it, because I understand its importance. I will remind you all, however, that should I one day be judged by Him above, and by all the other members who have gone before us for breaking the Commandments we privately swore to uphold, it is I who will be damned. Not any of you. So please do not presume to lecture me about what I should or must do."

"We just question where your loyalty will lie in the tasks you now pursue, that is all. Upon first consideration, what you must do for us and The Lodge are diametrically opposed to what the Prime Minister asked you to do."

"Originally, perhaps." Rowlinson replied. "But now I am not so sure."

At the centre of the table, another man began to slowly rise from his seated position. As he did so, the eyes of the others in the room followed him and waited for the Worshipful Master of the Lodge to speak.

"Enough said. And there shall be no more doubt once you have again sworn before this Council that you will complete the task you were given."

Rowlinson's face began to turn red.

He stood.

Breathing heavily, it was as if he was counting to ten before he dared let himself answer.

"For those of you who can no longer recall the first oath I took before this same council, once again I swear before this Council that I shall."

As those seated at the table on the other side of the room began to talk animatedly between them, Rowlinson turned and walked out, quickly pulling his apron off and reaching into his pocket for one of his angina pills.

Until this afternoon Rowlinson had believed that he was trapped, with no possible way of completing both the missions he had been given.

Now, in spite of the stress the Council meeting had induced, there was hope.

As he made his way down through the building and back out to his waiting limousine, a plan was already beginning to form at the back of his mind.

A clever plan, and one that he was sure Mrs Rowlinson would certainly be proud off.

Chapter 35

London

Saturday

October 5th

The Church

3 p.m.

When RobinHood had returned to the room twenty minutes later, he was a little agitated. SolarWind was tempted to ask what was up, but decided not to. He had been sitting on the couch lost deep in his own thoughts, and hadn't really missed RobinHood at all.

The pair had then talked for over an hour, discussing a range of things, but focussing on two main topics.

First, how did the agency chasing SolarWind actually manage to break through his security?

Secondly, what was SolarWind going to do next?

As they both admitted, his options seemed extremely limited.

However, they were not daunted. At least, not yet.

Maybe it was part of the nature of all hackers to thrive on facing the seemingly impossible and still manage to find a way through or around any barriers that were put in their way.

For Ray, because it was not just an academic exercise - the future of his life was at stake - it was more stressful than normal, but at the back of his mind, Ray knew there had to be a way.

There was always a way.

Always.

He just had to find it.

"Like I said, you're welcome to lie low here for a while until you can figure out where you should go. I'm not too sure that it makes perfect sense for you to spend your time in the capital of England where there are probably more CCTV cameras per square centimetre than anywhere else in the world. You're just asking for trouble." RobinHood suggested. "But while you're here I think I could maybe do with your advice."

"On what?"

"A project I am working on."

"Which is?"

RobinHood smiled and shook his head.

"I'm not ready to tell you yet...I need to think about it a little more. Maybe tomorrow."

"No problem, mate. Whenever you're ready. I'll help out if I can."

"Will you?" RobinHood asked back quickly, a light twinkling in his eye.

"Certainly, why shouldn't I? Unless it's something really illegal..." SolarWind started to say, then quickly visualised the £5,000 that was currently in his pocket: before coming to the Church, SolarWind had spent the most lucrative few hours of his life, taking money out of bank accounts that had no upper limit for withdrawals - accounts which Ray himself had created while he was drunk. He could effectively take as much as he wanted. The only issue was that the more he took out on a single day from each account, the more likely he was to become a statistic on a bank report, and for his activity to be flagged up to a bank fraud squad.

The trick to robbing a bank, Ray reminded himself, was not to steal too much too quickly.

Have patience.

Take a little.

From many accounts.

And it. Would. Soon. Add up!

In this case, to £5,000.

If he did that a few days in a row, it would quickly grow: £10,000, £50,000, then £100,000!

"Sorry, SolarWind," RobinHood interrupted his train of thought, "but I actually have to go to work now...I've got a lot to do for this 'project' I'm planning. So, if you will excuse me, I'm going to disappear down to my cyber bunker for the rest of the day. Help yourself to food and beers in the fridge, and feel free to watch TV or rent a movie online. You can take the spare bedroom. It's the second door on the right past the toilet. Don't worry about me. I'll probably sleep downstairs tonight. I've got to work late."

"Are you sure you don't need any help now?"

"Positive, mate. Positive. But maybe tomorrow. See you in the morning."

9.30 p.m.

After watching hours of mindless rubbish until he could stand it no longer, Ray made himself a sandwich with food from the fridge, borrowed a book from the impressive 'library' that RobinHood had built for himself, and disappeared to his allocated room.

He was anxious, scared and his mind so full of thoughts that he thought it would take a long time for him to fall asleep, but after he settled down into the bed, mental and physical exhaustion overcame him and he only managed to read ten pages before the book fell out of his hands and Ray was asleep.

He slept fitfully and about three o'clock in the morning he awoke with a start from the middle of a terrible nightmare. He was dreaming about Emma and as soon as he opened his eyes, he knew instinctively that something was wrong.

Emma was in trouble.

Sunday

October 6th

10.00 a.m.

Ferris normally hated working on Sundays. It wasn't that he was a religious man, far from it, but it was the only chance he got to completely switch off. For him, peace and relaxation was pitching a tent beside a river somewhere, setting up his rods, and waiting for the fish to bite while he drank tea from his flask and watched the river drift past.

He would lose himself in the 'nothingness' of the outdoors.

His mind would be a blank and for hours on end there would be nothing to think or worry about.

He loved it.

Especially the pointlessness of it all: when he caught a fish, he would simply toss it back into the river, and wait for the next one.

To Ferris, actually catching fish was almost a distraction.

Ferris didn't tell anyone at work about his hobby, because he knew they would take the piss out of him for it. In the high-octane life that he lived in, his personal fetish was probably in the same league as being a train-spotter.

Today was going to be a special day. He had already packed his car by 6.a.m. and was about to set off to visit a river in Kent which he had never fished before, when his work phone went.

Ferris swore, and answered it.

An hour later he was having his retina scanned by the security system at work, having already typed in a pin number to a keypad, given a voice print and a finger print.

The light above the scanner turned green and the electronic door before him swished open.

Ferris stepped through.

Davis was waiting at his desk to break the bad news to him.

"So?" Ferris demanded, as he approached, furious about the way his day had begun but also concerned about what was so important that he had been dragged back into work for the seventh day in a row.

"Luck's girlfriend was arrested last night as soon as she got off the plane. They took her into custody in Vancouver. She's still there. They want to know what to do with her."

Ferris's jaw dropped.

"They arrested her? Why? Bloody hell, what on earth did they do that for?"

"I asked them already. They said it was a misunderstanding. They've apologised."

"Shit. I just told them to find her and follow her. Take a few photographs. Find out where she was going to live. Keep tabs on her."

"They interrogated her."

"They did what?"

"They asked her about Luck. Well, when I say *ask*..."

"Stop. Stop right there. I don't want to hear any more. We don't even have a warrant to have her arrested. Let alone intensive questioning..."

"I suggest you'd better get a warrant pretty sharpish."

Ferris slumped down in his chair, shaking his head.

"Fuck." He swore again. "Bloody Mounted Police. Tell you what, right now I'd like to mount the head of whoever is responsible for this on a spike!"

"It gets better..."

"How?"

"She was hurt during the interrogation, and she's demanding to see a lawyer."

"Brilliant. Just bloody brilliant."

Ferris shook his head again, turned to the computer and switched it on, swiping his fingers over the scanner and speaking into the microphone for authentication by matching another voice print.

"Okay, Okay. What's done is done." Ferris said, turning back to Davis and becoming more focussed. "We've got a situation to deal with here, and we have to do it. First things first. They haven't granted access to the lawyer yet, have they?"

"No."

"Good. Make sure they don't. Get the warrant drawn up and approved quickly. I'll concoct a reason for it and send it to you in a minute. We'll have to create some additional reasonable grounds for our suspicions about her. Unfortunately for Miss Purvis, she just became an international terror suspect, and she just lost most of her rights. Understood?"

"Yup. Got that."

"Second... we need photographs of her in custody. I'm going to need them to help reel Luck in. Now we've made the mistake we have to take as much advantage of it as possible."

"I'm on to that too."

"Good. Lastly. Get me a coffee. Please. Black, three sugars. It's going to be another long day."

12.00 noon

Ray slowly opened his eyes, the smell of bacon assaulting his nostrils and enticing his taste buds to go haywire.

He loved bacon.

Looking at his watch he was shocked to see how late it was.

He lay back on his pillow and stared up at the stone arch that curved over his bedroom and formed an intrinsic part of his high ceiling. Ray admired the tasteful way the character and features of the church had been retained and made part of the design and layout of the modern home that RobinHood had transformed the church into.

Bright sunlight streamed through the amazing stained glass windows high up the wall, and Ray studied the figures and tried to guess what story the window was telling. It looked like the parable of the five loaves and two fishes. Or was it two fishes and five loaves? Biblical stories were not his strong point. Instead of going to Sunday school he had spent his time building his own computer and learning to program it.

Ray found it curious that for someone who did not believe in God, RobinHood had gone to so much trouble to maintain and respect the integrity of so much of the building.

Or was it just that RobinHood had taste and a good eye for architecture? The man was obviously brilliant at so many other things.

As soon as that thought had passed, another erupted with a blinding flash in his mind.

Emma!

He suddenly remembered the dream that had woken him in the middle of the night. It had seemed so real.

He couldn't remember what the dream had been about, and was unable to recall any imagery from it, but he was filled with the feeling it had left him with.

A horrible feeling. Something terrible.

Once again, his heart raced, and he felt fear. Fear for Emma.

Something was wrong, he was sure of it...

"SolarWind?" RobinHood called out, followed quickly by a knock on the door.

"Tea? I've got a fresh cup for you here, and breakfast is on the go..."

Ray reached for his clothes, having slept the night naked as he normally did, and quickly pulled on some trousers.

Jumping up he opened the door and was greeted by a beaming RobinHood.

"Good morning. I didn't disturb you because I thought you could probably do with all the sleep you can get, so that you've got a clear head to think later. Tea? Sugar?"

"No. That's fine as it is." Ray replied, accepting the cup as RobinHood handed it across. "Thanks."

"Two minutes, and I'll put your breakfast on a plate. I've made you a good fry up? You're not a vegetarian are you?"

"No. If it moves, I'll eat it. So longs as its dead."

"Me too."

RobinHood watched SolarWind sip his tea from the corner of his eye as he served up the breakfast onto the plates and carried it across to the table in the large, tasteful kitchen-diner.

"There you go, Ray. I hope you enjoy it!" RobinHood said, watching his guest for his reaction.

At first there was none. Ray picked up the knife and fork, and like a little boy, immediately surveyed the goodies on his plate: two rashers of bacon, two eggs, mushrooms, two sausages, some baked beans, and two pieces of toast.

He was just about to pop some sausage in his mouth, when it dawned on him what RobinHood had just said.

Ray looked up at him, his eyes wide open.

"You know my name?"

"Yes. Ray Luck."

Ray blinked.

They'd known each other for years, and until now neither knew who the other really was. It was an unwritten rule that they should respect each other's anonymity.

"How?"

RobinHood walked to the island that separated them from the kitchen area, and picked up a newspaper from the black, polished, granite surface.

He walked back to the table and placed it on the table so that Ray could see the front page.

It showed a large photograph of Ray.

The story that surrounded it detailed the search for 'Ray Luck', the most wanted terrorist in the UK.

There was even a reward of £50,000 for handing him in.

Ray stared at the paper, dropping his knife and fork on the table and grabbing the paper.

RobinHood drank some coffee and ate his breakfast while he waited for Ray to finish reading it all.

When he looked up and stared at RobinHood, his face was as white as a sheet.

"I know. It's bad." RobinHood acknowledged.

"Bad?" Ray almost choked. "It's a bloody disaster. What the hell am I meant to do now?"

"Don't get caught. Stay out of sight. Stay off the grid, and don't leave a single e-crumb that they can trace." RobinHood quipped. "By the way, you're on the news too. I saw you on BBC and ITV this morning. And I guess you're also in the other papers. It seems like it's a national campaign to find you."

"Shit...my mum...she'll die of fright...and my sister. I've got to tell them..."

"You can't. They'll be waiting for you to do just that. Her phone and communications will be bugged. They'll trace any connection you make with her..."

"I know, I know..." Ray said, standing up from his seat and beginning to pace the room.

"Eat. Your breakfast will go cold. We'll think about this together. Calmly. The government is banking on you doing something crazy if they put enough pressure on you, which is why you have to do the opposite. You have to outwit them. Constantly."

Ray turned and looked back at RobinHood. The man was right.

"Sit." RobinHood gestured again. "I have an idea for you."

Ray walked back to his seat and sat down, obediently.

"I can help contact your sister. Probably the best way to do it is to contact her via a friend. Where does she live? Do you have any friends who live close to her?"

Ray picked up a piece of toast and looked at it, before taking a small bite.

"My sister lives in North London," he said. She goes to the same pub almost every Sunday for Sunday Roast with her friends." Ray looked at his watch. She'll be there for another two hours probably..."

"Good. I'll go to her. I'll tell her everything's ok."

"No. You mustn't speak to her directly. I'll write you a note. You hand it to the barman. The note will have her name on it. He knows her...she's a regular. He'll give it to her. It'll only take you an hour to get there...if you leave soon."

"Sure. No problem. I can do that for you."

Ray smiled.

"Thanks. I'll write the note for you in a moment...But first, I'd better think about what on earth I'm going to say to her... and I'd better polish this off, or I'll make the cook angry."

RobinHood laughed. "Too right. He slaved over the stove for hours. By the way, here... " He said, picking up an envelope from a sideboard behind him, and tossing it across to him.

"What's this?" Ray asked, turning it around and looking at it. A big white envelope with the British Gas logo on the front.

"My name. It's Andrew. Andrew Grentham."

Ray stared at the name on the front, above the address of the 'The Church'.

"Now I know who you are, you may as well know who I am. Although, having been here last time, I wouldn't be surprised if you hadn't already checked out the deeds at the Land Registry. Anyway, you can call me Andy."

Ray smiled, then stuck out his hand and offered it to Andy.

"Nice to meet you!"

They finished their breakfast, Ray wrote the note, and then Andy disappeared.

Thirty minutes later Ray was sitting alone in the church watching the BBC News on TV.

Top of the hour, the main news story was about him.

For almost five minutes he watched the newsreader warn the public about the top terrorist that now posed the biggest threat to British lives.

"Help us find him, soon. Before he strikes," was the plea.

Ray watched in fear, then made it to the toilet just in time before he vomited.

Chapter 36

London

Sunday

October 6th

The Church

6 p.m.

Andy returned just after 6 p.m.

After seeing the photographs of Ray's sister on Facebook, he'd easily been able to spot her in the pub. From outside looking through the window he had watched the young man he'd given the note to hand it to the barman, and the barman immediately call her name.

She had got up, walked to the bar, and accepted the note.

At that point, Andy had left.

"Thanks for that, Andy." Ray said.

"No problem."

They sat in the lounge, Pink Floyd's Dark Side of the Moon playing in the background from some amazing hi-fi.

"So?" Andy asked, tossing a beer over to Ray and cracking open one for himself. "Any thoughts on what you're going to do next?"

"Not a lot. The future's looking a little dim at the moment. I can't see a way out of this."

"You can't think like that. There is always a way. You know that, Ray. There's ALWAYS a way. You just can't see it yet."

"I know. I know you're right."

They sipped their beers.

"You know, what I need right now is a new identity. Or two... Do you know anyone who can help me get one?"

Andy nodded.

"Perhaps. I have a few connections. It's just a shame you need it so soon. If you only had some more time, you could have my identity."

Ray looked at Andy.

"What do you mean?"

"I mean, I'm dying. Or so the doctors assure me. I've only got a couple of months, six months tops."

"WHAT? Are you joking?"

"Joking? You think I'd joke about something like this?"

"No... no. Sorry. I didn't mean..."

"I know. Don't worry about it. It's not your fault. It's not anyone's fault. Cancer just seems so random."

"I'm sorry, Andy...I don't...I don't know what to say."

"Thanks..."

"I mean, honestly...I can't believe this. Are you winding me up?"

"No. Actually, I'm not."

Ray stared at Andy, searching his expression and his eyes for a hint that this was all a weird joke, but finding none.

Andy's face said it all. He was telling the truth. Andy was going to die.

There were a few moments' awkward silence, Ray trying to come to terms with it all and not knowing how to really respond. Eventually Andy continued.

"Anyway, like I said, it's a shame you can't wait until I'm gone. Or maybe you can? Maybe you could lie low here for a while, until I'm gone...then just take over from me afterwards. I've not really got any relatives or anyone to miss me, so nobody else would notice."

"Are you serious?"

"Probably. I hadn't really thought of it until I mentioned it just now, but maybe it's not such a daft idea after all."

Ray was shaking his head. Not because he was discounting the idea, but more because he was finding it all too much to take in.

"Think about it Ray...as long as I die at home, you just hide the body. Don't tell anyone I'm gone, and then you take over everything I have. If you don't, the bloody taxman will take it anyway, and the last thing I want is for the government to have everything that I spent my life trying to build for myself. You'd be doing me a favour. Really. You should think about it."

Ray looked at Andy, his mouth open but no words coming out.

"Maybe I should sweeten the deal by admitting that I'm rich, Ray. I've made a lot of money. *Taken* a lot of money...from banks... I've hacked into the biggest banks with the best security and I've been helping myself for years. I'm loaded...but I can't spend it. I just haven't got the time or the energy. When I die, you could have it all!"

"I can't believe we're having this conversation. I don't want your money." Ray laughed. "I probably don't even need it either. I got drunk last week, and you know what? I was so fucking angry with everything that I hacked into a bank as well. I took a lot, but I was so far gone I can't remember if it was five hundred thousand pounds or five million."

Andy laughed.

"What? The good, righteous 'SolarWind' went rogue and crossed over to the dark side?"

"Sort of... but when I sobered up the next day, I wasn't happy I'd done it."

"But now, it's a godsend, right?"

"Too right. I've got access to enough cash to live off for quite a while. I'll be okay. But that's not the problem. The problem is that unless I'm careful I'll get caught, arrested, and then I'll almost definitely just disappear."

"Which is why you have to disappear first. Now."

"I know...And I have...You know I stood in the middle of the Millennium Bridge yesterday and threw my phone, my SIM cards, credit cards and identity cards into the Thames, in a bag full of stones. As of yesterday, Ray Luck died. The problem is I just don't know what the new person is going to be like...who the new 'me' will be."

"So, what about Andy? You don't fancy being me? Living in a church?"

Ray looked around him. Andy's house was amazing. There was no doubt about that.

"No disrespect, Andy. But the answer is 'no'. I don't want to have to wait for you to die...I mean, I don't want you to die! And anyway, six months is too long. I have a life to get on with now ... *sorry*...I mean, I've promised I would get over to see Emma as soon as I could. We're going to get engaged. Did I tell you?"

"Yes. And, it's okay. I understand. You can't hang around like a vulture until I drop dead. I know."

"Exactly. Although, to be honest, at this moment, I don't know WHAT I'm going to do."

"One thing's for sure. For now, until you can think of a plan, you have to lie low. In fact, it's probably better if you don't even step outside the front door. It's far too risky."

"Like house arrest? No way!"

"No, like hiding. For now, you have to hide."

7.00 p.m.

Randolph Best pushed the door open and stormed into his office in Whitehall.

He'd just got back from the airport. It was a Sunday evening, but he had no one to go home to: back in his house in South West London only his live-in housekeeper was waiting for him, but he'd already called her and told her he'd be a little late.

The trip to the Middle East had gone well. Much better than expected.

At long last, peace, finally, seemed like it could be on the cards and within their grasp.

For now though, for the first time in years, he actually had something more important to take care of. According to Jacobson, who led his security entourage, someone had been trying to blackmail him with a video of the woman's death and was threatening to release it on YouTube.

Until now, with his mind occupied by other matters and continuously surrounded by very important dignitaries whom he couldn't afford to ignore or snub, he'd left it in Jacobson's normally capable hands.

However, in the car back from the airport Jacobson had informed him, after Randolph had enquired, that the matter was still far from resolved. They had come back to his office now to discuss it further.

"He got away? You almost had him and you let him escape?" Best had exclaimed, slumping into his red armchair behind his desk.

"Yes, sir. He knew we were coming, and eluded us via the fire escape at the back of the building he was living in."

"The fire escape? He got away down the fire escape and you hadn't got the rear of the building covered? Are you the British Security Service or is this the Keystone Cops?"

"My man moved in with his team at the earliest possible moment. We didn't think Luck knew we were coming. We assumed we would catch him by surprise."

"Unbelievable. Bloody unbelievable." Best said loudly, standing up again and moving across to stare out of his window onto the Cenotaph below.

On this side of the building, the Cenotaph dominated the view. Best had always thought that it rather focussed the mind: it made you think about the consequences if you got your overseas policy wrong: war!

"So, who is 'your man' on this one? Do I know him?"

"Dominic Ferris. He's a good man, but you don't know him."

Best turned back from his view and faced Jacobson.

"Okay, so he escaped. Are you onto him yet?"

"Not yet, but we have a few hopeful leads." Jacobson replied, not wanting to say anything about the girl in Canada.

When all this was done and dusted, some Mounted Policeman in the Rockies was in for a sharp shock.

They'd already had two fuck-ups in this affair. There had better not be another. Jacobson believed in the Ferris boy, and wanted to help him if he could: he reminded him of his younger self, but if he messed up again, Jacobson would drop him like a stone.

"Get this wrong, and the government falls, do you understand Jacobson?"

Jacobson nodded.

He knew. Only too well.

When he left Best's office ten minutes later, he immediately dialled the private number of Jonathan Rowlinson.

"It's Jacobson. We just got back."

"Finally."

"I'm sorry. The meetings all went rather better than expected. We were delayed. The Palestinians were eating out of his hands."

"Doesn't sound good. Is this going to be a problem?"

Jacobson hesitated.

"I don't know, sir, to be honest. It could be."

A moment's silence.

"Okay. We need to talk about this. Meet me at my club in an hour's time."

Jacobson hung up and swore, then dialled Ferris.

"Anything? No? Right, you've got twenty-four hours. I don't care what you do, but whatever it is, just do it. And fast. Everyone's getting jumpy. We need some positive news. Do you understand?"

Ferris understood.
And he had a plan.

8.30 p.m.

Rowlinson's club, The No. 11 Club, was the most exclusive club in London. Few knew about it, and those who did were only told about it by other members, mostly only once they had been preselected to join.

And if you were asked to join, you did not refuse.

Although it was possibly also the most expensive club in London, the people who were members of No. 11 were not concerned about such trivialities. Indeed, most of them had probably not actually touched money themselves in years. They got others to handle their pecuniary affairs for them.

Rowlinson was a regular at No. 11.

It was where he did most of his business. In fact, a place like No.11 was in many ways not dissimilar to the Roman Forum, just a lot more exclusive. It was in the quiet rooms and corridors, sitting comfortably in their red, leather armchairs and drinking port or brandy, that a lot of the most important business transactions in the world were made.

The people who frequented No. 11 were amongst the wealthiest and most powerful people in the world, and to them, the market place never closed.

Every conversation was an opportunity to buy, sell, or learn.

Or to influence.

To change and fashion the world into a better place for them.

Not necessarily for others, but definitely for their interests.

The powerbrokers at No.11 swayed markets to behave as they wanted them to. They made deals with each other so that once they stepped back outside the walls of No. 11 the members would use their influence and power to influence policies in governments around the world. It wasn't unknown for small wars to be started in far flung corners of the globe, simply because the brokers in No. 11 deemed that to be the best way to change a country and alter it so that they could sell more, buy more or improve their influence of the people in that market place.

The members of No. 11 didn't take kindly to do-gooders who changed the world to be a better place at the cost of destroying a market place.

Money *was* their world.

And the world was *their* market.

Unlike some other private clubs in London, its membership was not restricted to Englishmen, ...or even Englishwomen.

The rationale behind this rule was simple: wealth and power were not limited by skin colour, creed, race or gender.

Randolph Best had never been invited to join No.11, in spite of his influence and power. He did not qualify: for two reasons. First, because his power was mostly political, and depended upon the whim of the electorate. A simple mandate could sweep away his ability to influence and remove him from the world stage. Secondly, his politics were not supportive of the goals of the other members.

Randolph Best was a peacemaker.

He was a good man, someone who sought, above all else to improve the lives of human beings across the globe.

On the other hand, Best and the Members did share a common trait: they were all passionate about their beliefs and worked tirelessly to achieve them.

Unfortunately, Best's passion to make peace in the Middle East was now beginning to yield tangible results.

For the first time in decades, real peace was a threatening possibility.

His latest trip to the region had proven disastrously successful.

In short, the Members were not happy.

"Come!" Rowlinson shouted, putting down his paper and watching as the door opened and Jacobson walked in.

"Aha... good to see you," Rowlinson opened, his disposition friendly and relaxed, still managing to hide the growing stress within him.

Rowlinson was now serving three masters: the Prime Minister, the Members of No. 11 and the Lodge. Two of them wanted something very similar, but the Prime Minister, although less powerful, by nature had more visibility. Officially, his Government also paid for Rowlinson's services, although what they paid was minuscule in terms of what he got from the others, unofficially.

Lastly, there was also himself. His own conscience.

Over the years Rowlinson had made it a personal policy to conceal from everyone else around him what he truly thought and believed.

To everyone who surrounded him, Rowlinson was an enigma.

He preferred it that way.

It made people nervous. Respectful. Subservient.

There were few affairs where Rowlinson let his personal interests sway his thinking or actions, but this was one such case.

When Rowlinson had seen the video it had made him furious.

It was like an exploded bomb: powerful, potentially devastating, but if used properly, perhaps useful.

Rowlinson shook hands with Jacobson and then waved him to a chair.

"Shall I pour?" he asked, indicating the tea set on the sideboard.

"Lapsang souchong?" Jacobson asked.

Rowlinson stood, and moved across to the sideboard.

"Naturally," he replied.

After pouring the tea and gently placing the beautiful china cup on the small table beside Jacobson, Rowlinson returned to his chair with his own cup and took a few small sips.

"Aah... wonderful. So refreshing." Rowlinson said softly.

Jacobson smiled.

"I'm glad you could come," Rowlinson said. "We have much to discuss..."

10.30 p.m.

Ray sat at the back of the train carriage, huddled in a seat in the corner, his new laptop open on the fold-down table in front of him.

He and Andy had spent a long time earlier that day talking about the need for Ray to stay off the grid...and to avoid any form of electronic communication that could be traced to Ray Luck.

Ray knew that the UK and US governments had tremendous capabilities to listen to all known forms of electronic communications, with an incredible ability to narrow down and focus on any particular Subject of Interest - or SOI in the vernacular of the intelligence community.

It was thought that with today's technology they could find anyone they wanted, incredibly quickly.

No one really knew exactly how they did it, or how good it was, but there was almost no doubt that such capability existed.

Perhaps the capability was exaggerated, but after the speed with which they had blown away his defences earlier on, Ray did not want to take any more chances.

He and Andy had agreed that Ray still needed to use the communications networks, but only ever with new, assumed false identities, never in sight of a CCTV camera with his face clearly visible, and never speaking directly into a telephone or mobile, just in case they now had the capability to listen in and match voice patterns.

Andy reckoned that the Ghost program that gave them some form of anonymity on the internet was still safe to use for accessing the internet, but never from the same place twice, and never if it was used to communicate directly with someone.

Andy also suggested that in future, all access to the internet using Ghost would additionally have to go through a virtual sandbox, of which the hacker community had posted many on the web, thus ensuring that any data or files accessed or viewed would only ever open up in a virtual environment: should any cookies be downloaded or malware inadvertently launched when exploring the web - which could perhaps be deliberately pushed to them by the agency tracking them - the sandbox would automatically refresh itself and wipe itself clean, immediately expunging the malware.

Ray had also promised Andy that he would never ever attempt to surf the web, or contact anyone whilst anywhere within a ten mile radius of the church.

Which basically meant that if Ray wanted to do anything on the internet or wanted to contact anyone in any way, he would first have to leave the safety of the church, don the burqa and get as far away as possible.

Whilst mulling over the various options, Ray hit upon the idea of using the national train network to help mask his locations and identity and at the same time get him access to the web.

Which is why now, quite late on a Sunday evening, Ray was heading out of London towards Peterborough and logging on to the free thirty minutes of Wi-Fi onboard the train using an old laptop onto which they had loaded a copy of Ghost.

Once he got to Peterborough he would catch the next train back again to London, and to be safe, after using the laptop on the return trip too, he would throw the laptop away.

Next week, using Ray's new found wealth and continued access to free cash, he would start buying new tablets or laptops by the dozen, each one cheap, but powerful enough to run Ghost.

The carriage he was sitting in now was almost empty, and very few people were walking up and down the train.

Luckily for Ray, no one seemed interested in paying the slightest attention to the woman in black huddled over a laptop.

Which was perfect, and his obscurity allowed Ray to focus and concentrate on what he had to do before his free Wi-Fi ran out.

Ray didn't have a plan. Yet.

He knew he had to have one, but for now, he couldn't for the life of himself figure out how he was going to get out of the shit he was in.

All day long he had been walking around with an overwhelming feeling of dread pressing down on him, and he had developed a habit of looking back over his shoulder every few minutes to see if he was being followed.

He was becoming paranoid, although perhaps rightly so: there was a fifty thousand pound bounty on his head, everyone WAS out to get him, and the entire population of Britain *was* on the look-out for him.

How long could he expect to stay undetected?

Plus there was MI5, and probably a million other secret agencies sniffing after his blood.

Shaking his head, and taking a deep breath, he finished logging onto the Wi-Fi and then accessed the internet through Ghost.

At this point, Ray could only think of doing one thing that made any sense and wasn't too dangerous.

He couldn't log onto his own real email accounts. That would be too risky.

The only thing he could think of doing that had any validity and made any sense was to log back onto the Outlook account in Brazil and see if Randolph Best or the agency working on his behalf had sent him any new messages.

Shaking, his heart pounding in his chest, and sweating under the burqa, Ray logged onto the Outlook account and held his breath as the Inbox opened up and appeared on his screen.

There was a new message.

A single, solitary communication, from Randolph Best.

The title of the email shouted at Ray, conveying a simple message, that he was now the hunted and Randolph the hunter:

"Ray Luck - *Where are you?***"**

Ray stared at it on the screen, his mind numb and in panic.

What would it say?

Should he open it up?

Was it some form of electronic trap?

Looking around him and peering around the edge of the seat to see if anyone was watching him, he considered his options.

1: Do nothing.

2: Open it up, flag his position on the train - somehow, although he couldn't think how this could possibly happen, given all his precautions - and then get arrested by storm-troopers pouring into the carriage from a million different hiding places...

3: Open it up, read it quickly, and then close it down, hopefully without setting off any alarm bells, and not endangering himself.

Ray knew that the truth was probably somewhere between the second and the third options, but he knew that to do nothing was also not an option. After all he had come all this way to access his email just in case there was a message, and now there was, he had to see what it said!

It was then that Ray saw that there was an attachment.

What was it?

Was it malware?

A tracking program?

A .exe file?

Ray was now twice as scared.

He knew he had no choice but to click on the email and open it up. He couldn't *not* do it.

Swallowing the bullet, he clicked on the title and held his breath.

The screen jumped a few times and then slowly loaded the new email screen.

There were four words in the email:

"Watch Emma say 'Hi!' "

Ray scrolled the email up and down on his screen just checking there were no words or content.

Nothing.

He stared at the attachment in the space beneath the header, a movie file, the words beneath the file inviting him to download and play it.

Knowing that he couldn't actually download anything to his laptop, only to the sandbox in the cloud somewhere, Ray was not worried about malware actually getting through to him, but he was still nervous.

When he clicked on the link to download the file to the virtual sandbox, would something else happen that he couldn't predict?

Ray shook his head and swore aloud, and then immediately looked around to see if anyone had overheard the man's voice issuing obscenities from underneath the burqa.

There was no one near him.

"Blast..." Ray muttered again, feeling slightly faint.

He knew that the longer he thought about it, the more unlikely he was to click on the file and play it.

Yet, he also knew that he had to do it, and doing it now, via Ghost using a nameless Wi-Fi connection on a disposable laptop was his best chance of ever viewing it.

Ray breathed in deeply again, bit the bullet and clicked the file.

It immediately began to download to the virtual cloud space, buffer and play.

As soon as the video file appeared, Ray clicked on the bottom right hand icon to make it play full-screen.

The video showed a room, at first dark, but then slowly brightening.
There was a chair in the centre of the room...and a person sitting on it.
The person had a bag over their head.
Their hands were tied behind their back.
On a wall behind the chair there was a flag: it depicted a large red maple leaf on a white background with a red vertical stripe on either side. Ray recognised it immediately. It was the Canadian National Flag.

Ray began to shake.

The room had dark walls, a dark floor, and no windows. Apart from the flag and the chair, it had no features.

A single light bulb hung down from the ceiling in front of the chair, about a metre above the persons head.

The screen went dark. Through his earphones Ray could hear footsteps.
Then the screen lit up again and the bag had disappeared from the person's head.

It was a woman.
Curly hair.
Attractive.

Crying.

The camera zoomed in.
The woman's face grew larger, began to occupy most of his screen.
There were bruises on her face.
A cut above her eye.
And fear.
A look of fear in her eyes that Ray had never seen before.

Fighting the urge to vomit, and struggling to overcome the dizziness and nausea that engulfed and threatened to overwhelm him, Ray stared at the person on the screen.

As the woman opened up her lips to speak, Ray felt his heart inside his chest begin to tear open.
The woman on the video whispered three words,

"Ray, help me!"

And then the screen went dark.

Chapter 37

London

Monday

October 7th

The Church

01.30 a.m.

Ray opened the heavy oak, arched main door to The Church and stepped inside.

Closing it quickly behind him, he slipped into the lounge and took off his burqa and then hurried to Andy's bedroom.

The door was locked, but Ray could see a light coming from underneath the door.

"Andy? Are you still awake?" Ray asked.

There was no answer.

"Andy? Are you awake?" Ray asked again, this time louder.

Still no reply.

Ray knocked on the door loudly, this time with a sense of urgency.

When a voice said Ray's name from behind him, Ray almost died of fright.

"You looking for me?" Andy asked, then burst into laughter when he saw Ray jump out of his skin.

"Bloody hell...where did you come from?" Ray asked, spinning round to see him.

"I was working downstairs. I saw you come in on the internal CCTV, and then watched you try to wake me up."

"Good. I need to talk to you."

"Actually, I need to talk to you too. I have a technical problem I definitely need your advice on..."

"Not now. Later, yes. Definitely yes, but not now. Something's happened... Something bad..."

Andy looked at Ray and could see the frustration and pain in his eyes and motioned him back towards the lounge.

As Ray turned to start walking, he noticed Andy flinch, his eyes screwing shut as if in extreme pain.

"What's up? Are you okay?"

Andy reached out for the wall to steady himself, breathed in deeply and then exhaled slowly.

"I'd like to say that I was okay, but the truth is that I'm not...it's the cancer. In the past couple of weeks it's started to get much worse. The pain comes and goes in waves...I haven't had much for the past few days, but this evening...it's been quite bad. The pain killers help though. A lot. Although I'm told that as the cancer gets worse, the pain gets worse too."

"Sorry...I didn't realise it was so bad already..."

"And why should you? I didn't tell you...and I've been dosed up most of the time so I've not felt so bad. But I've been working and I forgot to take my latest dose."

"Listen, you've got your own problems to deal with. I've already burdened you enough with mine. Let's forget it. Maybe you should take your medicine and get some rest."

"Rest?" Andy laughed. "In a few months I'll be getting all the rest I need. No...I need a whisky...and I think you need one too."

"Should you be drinking if you're on painkillers?"

"So, what, you're my doctor all of a sudden? Telling me what I can and can't do?" Andy laughed back.

"No...I didn't mean it like that. I just meant that..."

"Don't worry. I'm winding you up. While I still can. Anyway, enough about me. Let's get those drinks and you can tell me what's happened. Obviously something major."

Ray let Andy go first and then he followed him through to the lounge, walking slower than normal. Or was it just that Ray was paying attention for the first time to how Andy walked?

Andy poured two drinks then handed one across to Ray. A very large whisky. Taking his own and sitting down slowly in his usual armchair, Andy nodded at Ray to start explaining what was going on. "Okay...come on then, tell me what happened!"

Ray explained it all. Told him about the message, the video. And what the woman had said.

"And you're sure it was Emma?"

Ray stared at Andy.

"Don't be stupid. Of course I'm sure it was Emma!"

"Sorry...I'm just checking. How could they have got to her so fast?"

"I don't know. I said goodbye to her just as she was leaving to go to the airport. They can't have picked her up in this country, because I don't see how they would have known she was going to leave...I mean, how did they know so quickly? They only found out about me the day before."

"They could have rushed some warrants through to get access to your emails, found out about your girlfriend..."

"But on my e-communications with her we didn't discuss online, via text or on the phone that she was going to Canada...They couldn't have got that from my communications. They would have had to get a warrant to intercept hers too...and that takes time. I just don't see..."

"Maybe it's irrelevant. The main point is that they have her now."

"But who has her? Who?"

"It has to be the agency who is after you. Only they would have got permission to have the warrants issued to track your comms, and then got the Canadian authorities to arrest her in Canada."

Ray listened to what Andy was saying, and was silent for a while. Thinking.

"Okay...so they have her. And it looks like they're treating her roughly. From what I saw, they may even have been torturing her..."

"Unlikely."

"Why?"

"They could get in a lot of trouble. Way too much trouble. This is Canada you're talking about, right? Canada. Not terrorists in Iraq. And why would they want to anyway?"

"Exactly. That's exactly my point? Why?"

The answer, however, was obvious, and they both already knew it.

"So, what...they're expecting me to give myself up and come in?"

"Looks like it."

"A trade, me for her?"

"Probably."

"Can I trust them to let her go?"

"No. You can just hope they will."

"Fuck... what the hell am I going to do? If I hand myself in, they'll kill me. That's almost certain."

"But not before you give them the film back, right? And prove that it was the only copy!"

"Yep. That's obvious." Ray nodded. "They want the film. And my guaranteed silence."

"It certainly looks that way. Just now. But that doesn't mean to say that it's the only way. There has to be another. I mean, you and I know that there is ALWAYS another way. The problem is that we just need to find it!"

"And fast!" Ray agreed.

7.30 a.m.

When Ray had eventually lay down in his bed at three in the morning, he was sure that he would not sleep. His mind was awash with emotions. He couldn't stop thinking about Emma, about the images of her that he had seen. Her words to him replayed and echoed in his mind over and over again.

"Help me. Help me. HELP ME. RAY, HELP ME!"

When the first rays of sunlight eventually filtered through the window and woke him, he opened his eyes and was surprised to find that he had slept again.

As he turned his head to look at the time, he felt the grogginess in his brain and realised that the whisky he had consumed so copiously before he made his way back to his bedroom had at the very least had some beneficial medicinal benefit.

For a few hours it had helped him to forget.

To shut off the sound of Emma pleading for help that he was powerless to give.

As he stood in the shower with a curtain of cold water raining down upon him from above, pricking his senses and helping him to shrug off the tiredness and a possible hangover, he remembered the plan that he and Andy had hatched earlier that morning.

Never, NEVER let the enemy take advantage of you or press you into a corner.

Always, ALWAYS fight back. Do the unexpected. Come at them when they expect it least. Never retreat. Always advance.

Brave words, all of them, which did contain elements of a winning strategy. Words which had inspired Andy and Ray to decide that the best course of action was for Ray to go on the offensive.

He would get back on another train, log back onto Ghost and his Brazilian email account, and play the video of Emma one more time.

Ray knew that he couldn't download the video, which he knew was probably what the agency was banking upon too. However, Ray could film the video while it played on his laptop, and then Andy could enhance it with this wizardry in his cellar, just as he had done with the video of Best murdering the woman in the first place.

Then when Ray had the video of his girlfriend being tortured by presumably MI6 or the Canadian Secret Service...whoever they were....he would release it on YouTube and go public with it. He'd kick up a shit-storm the like of which the British Government had never seen before.

All the time, he would have the video of Randolph Best in his back pocket. His trump card.

He could only play the trump card once, but so long as he had it, the Agency, MI5, *whoever the hell they were*, would be petrified that he would release the video. He had to use it wisely. So long as he had it, *HE* had the power. Not them.

So, instead of walking into MI5 and handing himself in, he would publicise the video of Emma and demand her release on Social Media, simultaneously threatening Best via Outlook that unless Emma was released immediately, and publicly, that he would then also post the murder video on YouTube.

It was a game of bluff. On both sides.
Yet, if Ray kept his cool, he knew the cards were still all stacked in his favour.
If only he could keep calm. Keep thinking.
And stay sober.
He couldn't afford to make any more stupid mistakes.

Just after 10 a.m. Andy returned from the local PC superstore, having bought a box of cheap tablets and laptops, using one of the debit cards that Ray had lent to him, along with its PIN number.

Not wanting to waste another precious moment, Ray was already dressed and ready to leave the house.

As he watched Andy lug the box into the house, Ray noticed that today he was walking slower and was obviously in more discomfort. Ray made a mental note to discuss his illness with Andy when he got home, and to learn more about the cancer that was killing him.

Was Andy really as rich as he claimed to be?
If not, if it was a matter of money, getting better treatment...maybe Ray could help? Maybe Ray could pay for some private medical care?
It was just a thought, but maybe one that was worth further consideration.
Later.

After grabbing a tablet, inserting a new 32Mb memory card, testing it and making sure that he knew how to film with it, he left the church and made his way as quickly as possible to Kings Cross.

Once there he looked at the Departures board and chose an Intercity leaving in the next thirty minutes, and then quickly bought a return ticket to York.

He had no intention of going that far, but from now on, in everything he did, he wanted to introduce an element of unpredictability.

By 11.45 a.m. he was sitting in a half-empty carriage as the train pulled out of the station.

It took five minutes to boot up the laptop, load up Ghost and go through his security precautions.

His tablet fired up and ready to film the video as he streamed it onto his laptop screen, Ray connected to the free Wi-Fi, signed into his Brazilian Outlook account and waited for his Inbox to load.

11.50 a.m.

Ferris had been sitting by his terminal logged into the mainframe all day long. He had been monitoring the e-tag that he had put on the latest video he'd sent to Luck.

He'd been sitting at his desk for almost two days now, managing operations and the team trying to track Luck down, and waiting for Luck to open yesterday's first message and watch the video of his girlfriend being questioned and treated rather roughly in Canada.

Jacobson's instructions had been clear.

Step it up. Locate Luck. Bring him in.

Dead or alive.

But only dead IF they had the original copy of the video he'd made of Best murdering the woman, and ONLY IF they knew he hadn't made lots of copies and set them up for automatic release if they brought him in against his will.

Jacobson didn't care how he did it.

He didn't want to know.

However he had indicated, off the record, that getting it done was more important than how it was done, which Ferris had interpreted as carte-blanche to do whatever he needed to do.

The idea to make the most of the botch job carried out by the Canadian police was his own.

Sometimes you just need to do what it takes, and to make the most of whatever situation you find yourself in.

Be inventive. Use your initiative. Be creative.

After a little bit of rough questioning it was obvious that the woman wasn't going to speak without more coercion. At this stage, Ferris didn't think that was such a good idea. She was probably a completely innocent party in all of this. She had insisted that she and Luck had split up and that he had broken her heart.

In fact, that was the reason she had decided to start a new life.

Ferris did actually buy that part. From the text messages he had read from Luck to her, there was no reason not to believe it.

Yet, although he didn't intend to do any further harm to her - yet, Luck did not have to know that. Ferris would use her as the bait to lure Luck in.

On top of it, Ferris knew that his options were limited.

She was his best hope.

He had posted the link to the video to Luck, gambling that when he watched it for the first time he would not think of filming it on the screen. Ferris knew he would not download it to his laptop for fear of it carrying a Trojan. However, it was a gamble. A gamble that could go badly wrong.

If Luck filmed the video and posted it, and did some social media around a claim that the Canadian and UK authorities had arranged the wrongful arrest and torture of an innocent UK citizen, there could be huge international ramifications, and Ferris would be skinned alive.

He was in enough trouble already.

Which is why he had placed the e-tag on the first video and waited patiently and hopefully until Luck had read the email, gone for the bait and then watched the video.

He'd let him watch it a couple of times to let the video sink in, and for Luck to be able to memorise the images.

Then, thirty minutes later he had deleted the original video from the hosting server and replaced it with a second with the same URL.

Then he had started waiting for Luck to watch the next one.

Incredibly, he hadn't.

At least not yet.

11.58 a.m.

Ray's Inbox loaded and the emails he had received from Randolph Best appeared on the screen.

His heart leapt a few beats when he saw the email from yesterday on the screen, and switching the Tablet on, and setting it up to record the video, Ray clicked on the video file.

The screen went blank and then slowly an image materialised from the blackness.

It was a picture of an empty chair.

Just a bloody empty chair, with a Canadian flag hanging on the wall behind.

Ray closed the email, opened it up and played the video again.

It was the same video, the same empty chair.

Ray stared at the video, wondering what was going on.
He closed the video, and looked at the email.
It was definitely the same email as yesterday, the contents still saying

"Watch Emma say 'Hi!' "

He checked the time signature and confirmed it was the email from before.
What had happened to the video of Emma?

It only took him a second to realise that although the URL must be the same, whoever had sent him the email had obviously somehow replaced the original video with a second.
Why?
To get his attention? To make him worry?
Where was Emma? What had they done with her?

Ray was still staring at the screen when a second email suddenly appeared on his screen.
Ominously the title read,

"Hello Ray. How are you?"

Ray's heart skipped a beat.
Breaking out into a cold sweat Ray suddenly felt as if the train carriage was closing in all around him.
Looking first at the empty seat across the aisle from him and then quickly scanning the rows of seats in front, he checked to see if anyone was watching him.
No one.
He already knew that there was a CCTV camera almost directly above him, which is why he had chosen the seat he was sitting in, because from that angle, with the laptop screen angled slightly down, the camera would not be able to see what the woman in the burqa on the seat below was looking at. Ray was deliberately sitting in the blind spot.
He took a few more deep breaths, and then returned to the email.
Clicking on the email title he opened it up and read its contents.

"Missing your girlfriend, Ray? Wondering where your girlfriend has gone? If she is still alive? Don't worry. Too much. She's okay for now. We'll let her live for another 72 hours. And then we'll kill her.
Or maybe we won't.
You see, we're nice people. Reasonable people.

We only want you.
And the video.
So, if you hand yourself in to the police within 72 hours we'll set her free.

Of course, if you don't, you will never see her again.

Which is interesting, because Emma tells us that you have split up with each other. That it's over?

If that's true, and you don't love her, then leave her to us. We'll take care of her for you. Permanently. I told you we were nice people!

But if you do still love her, look at your watch, right now, and synchronize it with me.
You have 72 hours to do the right thing.
Don't be selfish Ray.
Save your girlfriend's life.
The clock starts now."

Ray read the email and looked at his watch.
It was 12.05 p.m.

Chapter 38

London

Monday

October 7th

The Church

1.35 p.m.

Ray sat alone at the end of the empty train platform.

He didn't really know where he was, or when the next train back to London would be.

After watching the video, as soon as his train had arrived at the next station, Ray had stepped through the doorway and got off.

He was in a daze, his mind numb and his body so stressed, that he felt as if his head could explode at any moment. Unable to think, or feel, or to pay attention to anything that was happening around him, Ray simply sat and stared into space, thinking of Emma.

Had they harmed her?

Where was she?

What had they done to her?

Would they really kill her?

Or was all this just a game of bluff?

Ray had read the email a million times, and watched the last video again and again.

The image of the empty chair was emblazoned on his brain, along with the Canadian flag mocking him on the wall behind it.

Ray had never felt like this before. It was a strange feeling: somewhere between panic and insanity.

None of this made sense.

How could all of this be happening?

Just over a week ago - was it only a week? - he had been planning to pop the question and ask Emma to marry him, and now...*now*? Now she was on the other side of the world, kidnapped, and he didn't know if she was even dead or alive.

And himself?

Ray Luck?

Ray Luck was the most wanted person in the UK, perhaps in Europe.

Everyone, everywhere was looking for him.

But now he had no choice.
They had won.
Whoever 'they' actually were.
He would have to give himself up.
Yet again, they had proved themselves to be smarter than he was.
Cleverer. Sharper. More cunning.
What hope did Ray have?
None.
Now, he only had one choice, which was no choice at all.
To save Emma's life, he would have to give himself up.

2.35 p.m.

It was two hours before a London bound train had stopped at the station, and Ray had managed to pull himself together enough to climb on board.

When someone had passed him in the corridor on the train and offered him - 'her' - a hot tea or coffee from a mobile food trolley, he had grunted a 'yes' in reply, and then dropped a five pound note onto the trolley while the attendant was preoccupied with filling a cup with hot water.

When offered some change, Ray had shaken 'his' head. The attendant duly dropped the tip into a plastic cup marked 'Tips', and smiled.

"Here you are, Ma'am. Enjoy your trip."

Ray had taken the cup, his head down, and avoided the attendant's gaze.

As the attendant handed over the cup, he briefly noticed the thick, manly fingers of the woman in the burqa, but within seconds had turned to another customer and carried on his service.

"Excuse me, would you like any tea, coffee, or snacks?"

Drinking the tea seemed to revive Ray somewhat, bringing him back to the land of the living, and calming him down.

Slowly he began to think rationally again.

Once again be began to become aware of the world around him, the black burqa which covered his body, and the rucksack that was lying on his lap.

When the tea was finished, he realised how hungry he was, and slowly made his way down to the buffet car, where he pointed to some food, and offered a twenty pound note to pay for it.

This time he remembered to expose as few of his fingers as possible, pointing at the food he wanted so quickly that the attendant in the buffet bar saw and thought nothing odd about the woman in front of him.

Carrying his rucksack on his shoulder, he found an empty toilet en route back to his seat and locked himself in it. Pulling down the burqa from his head so that he could eat freely, he gobbled the food down, and drank the other cup of tea.

Lifting the burqa to his waist, he opened his trousers and relieved himself in the toilet. Afterwards, he smoothed himself down, readjusted everything so that once again Ray Luck could disappear under his disguise, and then returned to his seat.

He was feeling much better now.

The food and the tea had worked wonders.

This time, as he sat down and thought about Emma and his predicament, his thoughts began to flow freely and easily.

It dawned on him then exactly, what now had to happen.

To free Emma and save her life, Ray was going to give himself up.

Ray was under no illusions what that meant: almost without doubt, once they had him and they had the video, they were then going to kill him.

2.45 p.m.

When Ray used the key Andy have given him and let himself into the church, Andy was in the lounge lying on the couch.

He seemed to be in a lot of pain.

His eyes were slightly glazed over, and when Ray spoke to him, his speech was slightly slurred.

"I'll be better in ten minutes or so..." Andy replied. "I just took some stronger drugs...the pain is getting worse. Sorry."

Ray sat down beside him.

"Can I get you something? Do you need anything?"

Andy winced, screwed his eyes tight shut and then answered, "A new body?"

Ray shook his head.

"Sorry pal."

Andy opened his eyes.

"How did it go? Did you get to film the video? Have you got proof of what they're doing to Emma?"

Ray shook his head, and then told him everything that had happened.

"Bloody hell..." Andy replied, reaching out to the top of the couch and trying to pull himself up into a sitting position. "Looks like we're both going to die now, doesn't it!"

"You don't mince words, do you?" Ray replied.

"I haven't got the time to." Andy answered truthfully.

Silence.

"But..." Andy said, lowering his legs over the side of the couch. "It's always surprising how things can change, how quickly perspectives can alter. Half an hour ago, I felt like I was going to die, and that I couldn't survive another moment because of the pain. But now? Shit, these drugs are amazing. Now I feel good. Not brilliant, but not bad. Better than I have done for days!"

Andy stood up and patted Ray on the shoulder.

"Ray... we mustn't react too quickly. Don't give up yet. There is always another way. Always..."

"You keep saying that, but how? They've got Emma. They've given me an ultimatum." Andy looked at his watch, and mentally counted down the hours he had left before they'd threatened to kill Emma. "Sixty nine hours and ten minutes to go. If there is another way, we'd better think of it soon."

"I'll make us both a cup of coffee. We need clear heads."

"Clear heads? What are you on just now?"

"Morphine."

"And you have a clear head?"

"I was speaking relatively."

Ray laughed, and then immediately felt guilty. Andy noticed it.

"Listen, I think you need to step back a bit from all of this. Stop looking at this bottoms up, and take a more global view."

"What the hell are you talking about?"

"You need some distance."

"And how do I get that? Have you been listening to me? I've probably only got three days left to live before I get tortured and then murdered, and even then, if I do give myself up there's no guarantee that they will set my Emma free."

"Then we have to come up with something else to barter with. You have to find some way of trading something with them so that they will be forced to let her go free."

"What?" Ray asked. "The video? The master copy?"

"Perhaps. That's the obvious thing, isn't it."

"They want that anyway."

"I know. All I'm saying is that we need to use it somehow. At the moment, they've got Emma. You've got the video. But is there anything else? Think about it."

"Something to trade?"

"Yes," Andy replied, as he hobbled around the kitchen and made them both some coffee.

"I think it's a good idea if you think about something else for a while. Give your subconscious a chance to mull this all over. It'll come up with something. Trust me."

"What? Are you some sort of mentalist or something?"

"Sort of. I studied NLP - Neuro Linguistic Programming for a few years. I know how powerful the subconscious is. It's like a massive computer program. You give it a task, set the program running and it'll tick over in the background until suddenly it just prompts you with the answer. At least, that's what my experience has been of it. Just when you least expect it, the solution is there. Right before you. Plucked right out of thin air."

Ray laughed.

"It's pretty unlikely."

Andy reached out to Ray and offered him the coffee.

"Let's try it. Anyway, I want to ask you for your help on something. Something completely different."

"Like what?"

"Let's go downstairs to my den. I want to show you something..."

Five minutes later they were looking at one of the displays in Andy's den.

Andy pointed at the screen.

"This is the one...I just can't seem to get into the applications running on this server. It's been hardened, I've tried every vulnerability and exploit I can think of, but without any joy. I was wondering if you had any tricks up your sleeve that could help me get admin rights for the system?"

Ray stared at the screen, at the prompt asking for login credentials.

Coming down the stairs, Andy hadn't said much about what he was trying to do. Simply that we was trying to hack into a target, had managed to get past most of the defences and find the server he wanted to compromise, but that try as he might he could not find a way onto the server. Ideally he wanted to log on, bump up his user privileges and grant himself full admin rights so that he could then do anything he wanted to.

What he wanted to do, Ray didn't ask.

As soon as he saw the prompt sign flashing away, asking him to log on, it was like waving a red flag at a bull.

"What system is it?" Ray asked, nudging Andy and telling to get up from the seat and let him take his place at the terminal.

Andy started to answer Ray's questions one at a time.

For Ray, it was exactly what he needed at that moment: an opportunity to rest his mind and focus on something else for a while.

For those who loved to hack and probe and explore the cyber defences that corporations, organisations and governments tried to put up in front of them, sitting in front a terminal and stalking security defences in cyber space provided the same mental escape that other types of people got from fishing, or hill-walking or painting.

Very quickly Ray was lost in another world, the experience made even better by the fact that Andy was not able to do what he was asking Ray to help him with.

Ray felt a hand on his shoulder...

"Sorry... you're going too fast...what are you doing now? That's Russian isn't it?"

"Yes. I've just logged on to a server that belongs to the Gorgon Hacker Collective, one of the most sophisticated cyber groups to emerge from Russia last year. It's resources are amazing...and they have a list of thousands of zero-day exploits that are not yet publicly known. It's like a menu book for constructing persistent targeted attacks against Western Corporations."

"Wow...how did you find out about them?"

Ray laughed.

"It's just one of many I dip into every now and again. These guys are probably state-sponsored, and have way more resources than I could ever have. I just find it amazing that their own security is so lax, that I can get in without really trying."

"So, what are you looking for?"

"I'm just checking to see if they have any information on vulnerabilities within the operating system running on your target server. Anything that we could exploit... *Bingo!*" Ray said suddenly.

Leaning forward to examine what was displayed on the screen, Ray went quiet as he scanned and digested several pages of information, mostly all in English, the international language of hackers.

Andy said nothing. He knew exactly what Ray was doing and that he needed his full concentration.

"Okay...gotcha...now, let me try something..."

Andy watched in awe as Ray went to work.

"Any chance of another coffee?" Ray asked after a few minutes, not looking up from his activity.

"Sure... now?"

"Yup. Now's good."

"Okay, fine. Coming right up." Andy answered slowly, mesmerised by what Ray was doing. He didn't want to miss anything.

"And,...is there any chance of a biscuit?" Ray added.
Ray turned and looked up at Andy and smiled.
Andy got the hint. Ray wanted to be left alone.

Hurrying so as not to miss too much, Andy climbed the stairs, made the coffees and returned as soon as he could, but he was already too late.

As he entered the room, Ray was sitting on the black swivel chair, facing the door, his legs and arms crossed and a smile beaming from one side of his face to the other.

"And voilà! You're in!"

Ray stood up, took his coffee and gestured for Andy to take his seat back.

"You're really in? So fast?"

"Yes...and oh, by the way, I've already taken the liberty of making you a Super-User. You're in control now...do whatever you want."

Now it was Andy's turn to be lost in his cyber world.

Pulling the chair up closer to the screen, Andy quickly scanned the display and saw that he was indeed now a user with Super-User admin rights.

"This is incredible...How did you do it?"

Ray laughed, and tapped the side of his nose with a free finger.

"That, my dear, would be telling, would it not?"

And with that, Ray turned and left the room, taking his coffee with him and leaving Andy behind to get on with whatever he now wanted to do.

Now the hack was over, the adrenaline was leaving his system and a terrible feeling of impending dread was beginning to weigh down on him again.

When he got upstairs, he went to his room, locked his door and lay down on his bed.

Closing his eyes, he pictured Emma in his mind, and thought of what he had to do.

Ray was under no illusion as to what was going to happen to him as soon as he handed himself in.

What he found interesting was that even though he knew he was probably going to be killed, he wasn't for one moment thinking that he wouldn't do it.

It was a no-brainer, and he knew he would sacrifice his life for Emma's in the blink of an eye.

What he was most upset about however was that if she was set free, and he was murdered, then they would not spend their lives together. He wouldn't get the chance to propose to her. To marry her. Or to have children together.

It was for this reason, that slowly his thinking finally began to change.

There had to be another way.

There had to be.

Ray just had to think harder to find it.

He closed his eyes, concentrated and began to search the universe for the answer to his problem.

Chapter 39

London

Monday

October 7th

The Church

6.10 p.m.

Ray hurried towards the door, sweating underneath the burqa. Amazingly no one had paid him any attention as he had run through the crowd of policemen towards the fire-exit at the end of the room.

Coming to the door, he found the exit was locked with a heavy chain and padlock.

He tried kicking the door several times, trying to force it open but without luck.

A voice suddenly shouted at him.

"Stop!"

Ray turned to see several of the policemen looking at him and starting to run in his direction.

Turning around again to face the door, he looked down and found that somehow he now had a pair of heavy-duty wire cutters in his hand.

Losing no time, he quickly reached forward and cut through the chain, before launching himself at the door, pushing it open and diving through to the other side.

The room beyond was dark and cavernous.

"Emma!" he shouted aloud, his voice bouncing around the room and coming back at him from all sides.

Suddenly the lights in the room came on, at first blinding him with their intensity, forcing him to squint with his hand over his eyes until his pupils adjusted to the light and he could see again.

He was standing at the edge of a large empty hangar.

In front of him, about thirty metres away there was a single chair.

Lying in front of the chair on the floor, sprawled out on the cold concrete was a body.

Even from where he was standing Ray could tell that it was the body of a woman.

Sprinting across the hangar, Ray came to a stop a few feet from the body.

She was lying face down, her clothes soaked in blood, her legs and arms bent at some ridiculous angle that made her look like a rag-doll, and not a real human being.

Ray bent down, grasped her shoulder and gently but firmly turned her over so that he could see her face.

A slow, long guttural scream started to build up within him, and was finally released just as several heavy hands grabbed him from behind and pulled him backwards away from the body.

He was too late.
Emma was dead.

"Nooooo!!!", Ray screamed and came quickly to a sitting position, his body shaking and still trying to fight off the invisible hands that were holding him.

He looked around the room and blinked several times.

The image of Emma in his mind quickly began to fade, but the feeling it left within him terrified him to the core.

There was a knock on the door, "Are you okay? Ray, what's up?"

Ray jumped off the bed and grabbed the door handle, letting Andy in.

"Sorry, I must have fallen asleep. I was dreaming about Emma. I dreamt that they had killed her already."

"It was just a dream. Don't worry, but you had me scared there for a moment. I thought that something had happened."

"What time is it?" Ray asked, glancing at his watch and seeing the answer before Andy replied. "Bloody hell, have I been asleep for almost three hours?"

"Yep. You needed it. Now you will be able to think a bit more clearly. Come through and get a coffee. I've just made myself one, and was about to cook something."

Ray followed Andy through to the front room and plonked himself down in front of the large, fifty-five inch LED TV.

The news was on.

A couple of moments later Andy brought him a coffee.

Just then a familiar face appeared on the TV, dominating the screen.

"There are still no reports of Ray Luck, the man police identified yesterday as being the most wanted man in Europe. If you have any information on his whereabouts or if you think you have seen him, please dial 999. Mr Luck is described as being very dangerous, and on no account should any member of the public approach him by themselves. The police have also just announced that there is now a reward of £100,000 for anyone who can provide any information that leads to his arrest."

Ray looked across at Andy, his face as white as a sheet.

"It's the third time I've seen you on TV today. You're famous, pal!" Andy laughed."What number did they say I should call for the reward...?"

Ray's eyebrows lifted higher, and for a few seconds the confusion showed in his eyes.

"I'm joking you idiot. What would I do with another £100,000? I'm not going to be alive long enough to spend it!"

Ray crushed up a napkin and threw it at Andy.

"It's been another busy day for Randolph Best," the TV presenter said, immediately catching both Ray and Andy's attention. "After being praised in Parliament for his successful visit to the Middle East last week, Mr Best, who is now widely tipped to be on the Queen's next Honours List, was warmly received by the nurses and doctors at Great Ormond Street hospital, where he came to visit the sick children and pass on a personal cheque which he had donated privately. We don't have the exact figure of the donation but it's rumoured to be a six figure sum.

The TV was then filled with pictures of Randolph Best as he toured the hospital and met some of the children.

"...At one point, according to the nurses who were nearby, the plight of one of the little children who Mr Best met during his visit, moved him to tears. It was reported that in a departure from the planned schedule, in private and off-camera he sat on the child's bed for quite a while holding his hand, talking to the little boy and his parents, and doing everything he could to cheer up the child, who was apparently very homesick."

"According to the boy's parents afterwards, Mr Best was genuinely overcome in a rare show of emotion for such a high profile politician. Afterwards, he refused to talk with any more of the press, slipped out of the back of the hospital into a waiting car and left without any further discussion."

"And now for the weather..." the newsreader said, smiling and shuffling the papers on his desk.

"What was all that about?" Ray said, staring at the television.

"What do you mean?" Andy asked.

"I don't know. I'm not sure," Ray said, his words tailing off into nothing.

"It really pisses me off," Andy said. "A carefully planned PR stunt to promote Best in the 'best' light. And it worked. If only they knew what we knew! The mob would lynch the bastard!"

Ray stood up and walked across the room to the TV set, resting his hand on top of the screen, turning to face Andy with a quizzical look on his face.

"I don't think that was a publicity stunt. It makes the man look weak, not strong, and in his role I don't think that's a good thing."

"I don't understand what you're getting at. Where's this leading?"

"I don't know. I'm just thinking aloud...There's a thought tickling the back of my brain and I want to know what it is..."

"Ray, the bastard has your girlfriend and is threatening to kill her..."

"Or does he? I mean, if everything they say about him is true, would he actually order someone to torture or kill a defenceless woman?"

"Are you kidding me? You saw him kill a woman already!"

"Yes. In a heated argument, after sex... "

"Ray, what are you getting at? I'm really confused right now."

"A little light just went on in my brain. I've been trying to think all day about what my next move is. Like you said, there is always a way. There has to be a way. So I've been thinking about it, trying to find an angle, an idea, anything. And then I just saw that piece of news and something went 'bing' in my mind. There's something here, I know it."

Andy walked slowly over to the chair and sat down, grimacing in pain as he did so.

"Like what?"

"I keep telling you, I don't know yet. Help me with it, will you?"

"Okay. So, let's try."

Ray took a few steps and sat down beside him.

"What did they just say about him being in the Middle East last week on a State Visit?"

"I didn't catch it, but it sounds like he was abroad doing what we pay him to do..."

"Which means that he was really busy and probably didn't have the time to watch his emails every second?

"Yes..."

"In other words, the emails I got back last week, the exchange of communications that led them to tracking my location down and breaking into my flat...that was all done by MI5, MI6 or whatever other agency it was, right?"

"Yep."

"And Best probably didn't even know much about what was going on?"

"No...he would have had other things on his mind."

"And when Emma flew to Canada, Best was probably travelling back from the Middle East?"

"Yup?"

"So he probably didn't order for her to be arrested and tortured?"

"Probably not."

"Although he could have sanctioned it. Maybe, but a little voice at the back of my mind is telling me that he probably knew nothing about it. Perhaps he still doesn't even know anything about it."

"Maybe not..."

Ray stood up, and started to pace the room.

"The thing is...we both know that he killed the woman, because we saw it...we've got it on film...but everyone, and I mean everyone is constantly going on about how wonderful he is, and how sensitive this guy is..."

"He's a bloody politician! Everything is one big act!"

"So why didn't he come out the front door of the hospital and let the cameras see his tears much more publicly?"

"I don't know..."

"And neither do I, but his actions, who he is, who he's meant to be...and what we saw him do...there's an alarm bell going off in my mind somewhere - a very quiet alarm bell mind you - but it's the only thing I've got right now, so I'm going with it, okay? Actually, thinking aloud, I think there are probably two aspects to this. First, I think what I'm saying is that I just don't think that he would order or sanction the treatment of Emma like this..."

"So?"

"So I think if he knew about it, he would stop it. Secondly, he's got too much to risk if it came out. If we started to put some really negative stuff about Emma and his involvement in this out into the press, even though he would immediately deny it, he would be scared about some of it sticking to him and ruining his image."

Andy's expression changed. He was beginning to see the angle Ray was developing.

Ray walked across the room, poured himself a glass of fresh water and was about to start to drink it, when he put the glass down and walked back to stand in front of Andy.

"We've been talking to the wrong person. He hasn't been reading my emails! Maybe he's never ever even seen them! I've been talking to the agency the whole time!"

"I agree..."

"Right, so we've got to change course. From now on we only talk to Best. I need to talk to him directly. Tell him what's been going on with Emma. Make some sort of deal with him!"

"Are you still going to hand yourself in?"

Ray frowned and shrugged his shoulders.

"Probably. But I'm going to make a deal with Best first. The more I think about this, the less I think he's behind it or would support it. He's committed murder, yes, but my gut instinct's telling me that he would never be involved with what's happened to Emma, and if he knew, he would stop it."

"Possibly."

"A 'possibly' is better than anything else I've got right now. Which means that it's our only plan."

Andy nodded.

"But," Ray paused, "as with a lot of great plans, there's a pretty massive problem, isn't there?"

"Which is?"

"How on earth do we get to talk to Randolph Best directly without the Security Service listening in or stopping us?"

Chapter 40

London

Monday

October 7th

The Church

9.30 p.m.

Ray and Andy had eaten dinner in silence, sitting at the breakfast bar in the kitchen, facing each other, but both lost in their own thoughts trying to figure out what to do next.

Andy had noticed that Ray was developing a habit of looking at his watch every now and again, and he knew that it was because he was counting the minutes ticking by until the deadline would expire.

Outside the rain was pounding down hard, and occasionally a lightning bolt lit the sky and thunder crashed somewhere in the distance. Far away, but still incredibly loud.

As if the air was not charged with enough tension already, the storm brought an extra sense of urgency and energy with it.

Soon both plates were empty, and still neither of them had spoken.

The sound of the thunder was getting louder as the storm moved closer, closing in on them and hunting them down.

Without warning, the lights flickered, went out for a second and then returned.

Ray jumped to his feet, ready to react, and half-expecting some SAS-like storm troopers to pile in through the windows and try to overpower them.

Nobody came.

Suddenly Andy spoke aloud.

"Shit...I might have it! I might just have it!"

"What do you mean?" Ray asked, turning his attention away from the doors and windows and onto Andy.

"Do we know where he lives?"

"Best? No..."

"No, problem. I can find out!"

"How?"

"From my database or my network."

"What database?"

"You're good at stuff, and so am I. I'm not completely useless. What good's an anarchist if he doesn't know where all the important people live, or at least how to find someone else who does know where he lives."

"So what's your idea? What do we do once we find out where he lives? Go and visit him?"

"No way. Too risky. He'll be heavily guarded. Tell you what...give me half an hour and let me see if my idea could work. If it can, I'll tell you all about it."

Ray looked at his watch again.

Time was running out.

"Sure..."

"Don't worry, I think I'm on to something. Wait here..."

Ray watched as Andy slowly hobbled out the room and down to his den. When he left the room, Ray looked at his watch again.

It was 9.45 p.m.

10.00 p.m.

Canada

Emma shivered.

Her tears had long since dried up, but the fear had not left her.

They - whoever 'they' were - had given her a few tablets to take, and she had pretended to swallow them, but as soon as they left the room again, she spat them out and crushed them with her feet.

Her cell was small, dark, and cold.

But the food they had given her was fine.

At first she couldn't touch it, because food was the last thing on her mind.

Luckily they had left it in her cell, and when the hunger eventually had overcome her, she had eaten it cold and quickly, gulping it down.

A few hours later they had given her a cup of coffee, and some doughnuts.

Her bruises hurt, but she didn't worry about them.

All she could think about was the video they'd made of her.

Would Ray see it?

Would he hand himself in?

Would they kill him?

If they set her free, and he died, would she ever be able to forgive herself?

If only she had been stronger.
Then perhaps Ray would still have a chance.

If he died, it would be her fault.
She closed her eyes, and thought about their last kiss together, and longed for the future together that Ray had promised her.
Would she ever see him again?

She heard footsteps.
Holding her breath, she stared at the door handle.
It began to turn.
Then the door opened and two men stepped into the room.

"Please, no..." she whimpered, but the men just smiled and ignored her plea.

10.30 p.m.

"Ray, come on, I've got something to show you!" Andy announced as he emerged at the entrance to the lounge. "Come on down."
Ray looked up from the piece of paper on which he was scribbling down random thoughts and ideas in an attempt to come up with some sort of plan for how he could maybe contact Randolph Best and have some sort of conversation with him.
So far he had written down three ideas, and scored them all out.
The reality was he couldn't see a way to do it, short of going to the Houses of Parliament and waiting outside the door until he arrived one day.
Jumping up, he eagerly followed Andy back down to the den.
"Here...take a seat," Andy said, waving to the chair beside him.
"What have you got then?" Ray asked, eagerly.
"His address for starters, at least where I think he may be living when he is in England. And...this is the bit I'm proud of - I think I might have an idea how we can contact him."
"How? And how did you find out where he lives?"
"The Electoral Register. Simple as that."
"That's all public information?"
"Don't be daft. It wasn't *that* simple. But in a democratic society, it's amazing what information the government will give you, if you know what to ask, and how!"

"You hacked the Electoral Register?"

"Absolutely. He votes just like anyone else and his address is listed in the database just like anyone else! And by the way, I found out where you live as well... No. 23, St Cecilia's Square, right?"

Ray nodded, not knowing whether to be pleased or not.

"Thought so...right, so according to the same database, our friend has a penthouse flat in London in Lindhurst Square in Mayfair, one of the most exclusive addresses in London, and a large house further out in the suburbs. He also has a grace-and-favour home called Chevening in Kent, which is the official residence of the Foreign Secretary, but according to the Press, he hates the building and only ever visits it when he has dignitaries from abroad visiting him there. He spends his time shared between his penthouse flat and his own private house in Surrey. "

"So, what's the plan? We go and visit him?" Ray asked, not questioning for a second that Andy had got it right.

"Visit him? No. That would be way too risky. Anyway, I've a much better idea!"

"Which is?"

"Have you ever heard of a Smart Meter?"

"Yep, I've got one at home. It's an electronic meter that was installed in my home to provide automatic readings of my electricity usage to my electricity provider."

"Yes, well, that's what they've told you it's for, but it does a ton of other things too. Things that you might not exactly be pleased about, if you knew what else it was also doing. But that's exactly why they *don't* tell you what it can do. Anyway, the important thing for us just now is that it's really a computer that sits right at the heart of any house, connected to all the wiring and power lines, with connections to any internal Ethernet networks. For those with the right skills, i.e. me and you, we can get access to the Smart Meter from any laptop in the house that takes electricity out of the wall socket and is connected to the national grid. Once you're connected to the Smart Meter and you hack into it, then incredibly it's not too difficult to actually traverse the Meter and get access to the electricity providers themselves, their networks and any partners, suppliers or businesses that connect to them."

"Yep, I'd heard that and read about it, but I haven't tried it myself yet."

"You should. It's dead easy. Anyway, that's just one side of the story though. The thing is, it works both ways. It's also possible for the electricity provider to monitor and access and even control practically everything you do in your house, so long as it's IP enabled. Which is part of the reason they're installing them in people's homes in the first place. From a commercial perspective they will soon start offering people services where you can dial into your house from anywhere in the world and switch your heating on, or turn the lights on and off, or switch your TV on, turn music up and down, and even get onto your computer and work remotely on your home computer."

"I know..." Ray agreed. "They run IP communications over the electricity cables just like you do with the Ethernet cables that connect computers and laptops together to make normal networks."

"Exactly..." Andy nodded, pointing to the screen to draw Ray's attention to the display on it. "Which is why I hacked into the National Grid headquarters and tracked down the details of the Smart Meter that has been installed in Randolph Best's house in Surrey, the place where he is most likely to be. If we have no success there, then we'll try his flat next, but my idea was that I would use the details to hack into the Smart Meter in his house in Surrey...but, and you won't believe this... I didn't have to. I found that once I was in the National Grid's network, it was possible to get straight from the National Grid to the local energy supplier and connect directly into the Smart Meter in Randolph Best's house with Super-User Admin rights. The Smart Meter let me straight in...See!" and Andy pointed to the GUI on the screen again. "That's me, in control of Randolph's Smart Meter."

"You're kidding."

"Would I joke about something like this? This is too good to be true. It just shows you what a joke the whole security system is that they have in place. This is the first time I tried it and I'm straight in!"

"But how did you do that?"

Andy laughed. Feeling quite smug with himself.

"Do you want me to do it again? To show you?"

Ray laughed.

"Yep. Please. Mr Cyber God. That would be extremely cool of you if you did!"

Andy frowned.

"*Please!*" Ray imitated a little kid, begging for extra sweets.

"Watch and learn, my little apprentice! Watch and learn!"

Which is what Ray did.

He watched.

And he learned.

In fact, what Andy did was truthfully, actually, very 'cool', and Ray couldn't help but feel a little admiration for what Andy achieved.

Soon they were back in, just where they had been before.

"So what do we do now?"

"Okay..."Andy took a deep breath then carried on, "...the next step is to get onto the internal network in Randolph Best's house. I want to see if there are any computers connected to the network or surfing the internet..."

"Go for it..."

Andy nodded, flexed his fingers in mid-air, and then turned back to his keyboard.

Ray watched as he started to type on the keyboard, at first trying to memorise what Andy was doing, and how he was doing it, but then realising he was typing too fast and that he couldn't keep up.

He turned his attention back to the monitor.

"Aha..." Andy exclaimed. "See that...there's three devices on the network at the moment...Let's see what they are..."

Ray pulled his seat closer to Andy, who typed a string of commands onto the keyboard.

"There's a laptop, a burglar alarm and a heating system. I'm tempted to play with the burglar alarm and set it off, just for fun, but I guess we can leave that for another day. Let's see who's on the laptop..."

Andy typed another set of commands and queries into his browser, this time Ray now recognising everything that Andy was doing.

The screen filled with the Inbox tray of an Outlook session, their screen now replicating the screen of the laptop that the person on the other end was using.

"Aha...someone's doing email."

As they watched they could see the person at the other end click on *'New'* and start to write a new email. In Spanish.

Ray pointed to the name of the person who was sending it.

" María Sáenz. Who's she? Have we got the right place?"

"Don't know. I think so..."

Andy started typing furiously on the keyboard, and a new window opened up which he dragged across to a second monitor.

"Look, this is the camera on her laptop...it's switched on and looking straight at Maria."

The image showed the head and shoulders of a pretty woman sitting with a towel wrapped around her body, obviously having recently stepped out of the shower.

"Nice looking..."Andy commented. "Shame about the towel."

"But who is she?" Ray asked.

"Let's find out..."

Andy next logged onto Facebook and searched for María Sáenz. Four names came up. One of the pictures beside the names looked a little like the Maria they were watching on the other screen.

Andy clicked on the link, and started perusing her Facebook pages.

Comparing the pictures of the woman on the Facebook pages with the woman on their display they quickly confirmed that it was the same person. Her photographs on Facebook showed that she was a very pretty woman.

"Can you read Spanish?" he asked.

"No," Ray replied. "French yes, Spanish no."

After a couple of minutes scrolling through her pages he gave up.
"There's no obvious connection to Randolph Best."
"Try LinkedIn," Ray suggested. "Or Twitter."
Andy logged onto LinkedIn and repeated the search.
This time there were just three names, one of them showing a photograph they'd seen on the Facebook pages.
This time it was written in English.
It only took thirty seconds to find what they needed to know.
Maria's career history immediately revealed that she was a House Keeper who had worked for some very famous people.
And she was now working for Randolph Best, her latest client, as a live-in house keeper who kept Randolph Best's property in order, probably cooked his meals, and did his washing and ironing.
"Bingo!"
"So, what do we do now?" Ray asked.
"I'll get her to go and get Randolph so that you can speak to him. Then it's up to you. You'd better start thinking about what you're going to say to him."
"How are you going to do that?"
"I don't know...let me think for a moment..."
Andy stopped typing and looked away from Ray, focussing on something on the other side of the room, thinking.
A few minutes past.
Ray was watching the video feed of Maria, at the same time still following her typing emails on her laptop.
She suddenly got up, moved away from the laptop. As she moved she dropped her towel.
"Look!" Ray said loudly, pointing at the screen.
"Wow...she's gorgeous, "Andy quipped, staring at the naked Maria as she started to brush her hair.
"Forget that...if she stops doing stuff on the laptop and switches off, we're sunk. Do something quick! Get her attention back."
"Okay, no pressure...let's try this..." Andy flexed his fingers in the air like he had done before and started typing away again.
"What are you doing?" Ray asked.
"I'm interrupting her Outlook session and taking control of her laptop. I'm going to write text onto her screen that she can read and so we can talk to her directly. But first I'll make the screen flash on and off and make the laptop play some music, so we can get her attention and get her to come back to see what's going on. Look, on this display window I'll make it so we can see exactly what she can see on her screen."
Andy opened up another window on the other display beneath where they could already see the video feed of the now naked Maria; he then typed

some text strings into his terminal, and suddenly they could see her laptop display.

Ray watched as Andy made Maria's laptop go to YouTube and start playing some loud punk music from the 1970s that was certain to get her attention. Just to make certain Andy adjusted the volume on her laptop so that whatever was playing blared out uncomfortably loud.

A second later, under Andy's direction the screen started to flash, alternating between black and white.

The effect was immediate.

Maria turned to her laptop, stared at it, and immediately came towards it, naked as the day she was born.

Andy typed a few words on her screen.

"Hello Maria!" it read in Spanish, in very large words that dominated the display at her end.

From their hideaway in Andy's den they could see the immediate shock in her eyes. She stared at the screen and sat down in front of it.

Randolph Best's House
Surrey
10.42 p.m.

María Sáenz stared at the laptop screen in disbelief.

The screen had stopped flashing.

Her name was written on the screen in large letters, and it was saying hello to her in Spanish:

"Hola, María Sáenz!"

Beneath the words, there was a box with the words, "Please reply" written in small letters in it in English.

Her heart began to start beating faster. What was happening?

The ugly loud music that had been playing a few seconds before had stopped, and it had now been replaced by some beautiful Spanish music with Flamenco guitar in it.

New text appeared on her screen.

"We are sorry to disturb you Maria. Are you okay?"

Maria blinked and stared even more intensely at the screen.

After a few moments her hands moved to the keyboard and started to type a reply in the box provided: "Yes. I am fine. Who are you? How is this happening?"

She hit return.

A moment later a reply appeared.

"Please do not be alarmed. I am a friend of Randolph Best. I need to speak with him urgently. Is he at home this evening?"

Maria was confused. She frowned, and typed a reply.

"Señor Best? Yes, he is at home. Who are you?"

10.45 p.m.

In the room underneath the church, Andy turned to Ray.

"Can you remember the name of the woman that Best murdered? It was given in the paper..."

"Nope... Google the newspaper article..."

10.46 p.m.

"My name is Bayla Adelstein. I work for the British Security Service. I need to speak with Randolph Best urgently."

Maria nodded.

The British Security Service?

It made a little sense.

Only they would be able to take over her computer like this.

She typed in a reply.

"What do you want me to do? Why do you not call him on the telephone?"

The reply came instantly.

"The telephone network has been bugged. I cannot call him, but I need to warn him immediately. He is in danger. Please can you go and fetch him and tell him he needs to come to your computer immediately."

She replied, "You wish me to bring Señor Best here now?"

"Sí. Por favor."

Maria sat back from the computer for a moment, her mind a whirl of thoughts.

Some more words appeared on the computer screen.

"Maria, his life is in danger. Please fetch him now."

Maria stood up, nodding and speaking aloud in Spanish: "Yes, I will go and get him now..."

10.49 p.m.

As she turned and left, Andy whistled.

"If only I wasn't dying and I wasn't so bloody fat...she's gorgeous. Her breasts are amazing!"

Ray ignored the comment.

"What do I say if Best comes? What do I do then?"

"That's not my problem mate. The moment he turns up, I'm going to leave the room. I've done all I can to help you. From now on, it's down to you."

Ray nodded, mumbling a thank you under his breath, but trying to think as quickly as he could what he should say to Best if this worked.

If Best did come, the next few moments could mean the difference between life and death for Emma, ...and for him.

If he fucked up now, they were both dead.

Chapter 41

London

Monday

October 7th

Randolph Best's House,

Surrey

10.58 p.m.

Randolph Best was relaxing in his bath, sipping a glass of his favourite malt, when there was a sudden knock on his bathroom door.

In a second, Best went from being so completely relaxed that he was almost on the edge of sleep, to being on the highest state of alert.

His brain, although slightly dulled by the whisky, immediately processed the threat: it was low...

The door was unlocked. If someone had wanted to threaten him, they would have quickly opened it and burst in through the door, catching him unawares. Instead they had knocked politely.

Almost immediately the knock was followed by a female voice: Maria's. What did she want?

Why was she disturbing him during his bath?

For a fleeting second an erotic thought past through the grey matter of his brain. It was however, quickly dispelled by the urgency of her next words.

"Señor Best. Please. You must come. There is an emergency. The woman on my laptop says you must come. Immediately."

"An emergency? On your laptop?" Best replied, loudly, beginning to raise himself out of the bath. "What do you mean?"

"I am sorry, to disturb you Señor Best. And it is very strange, but there is a person talking to me on my laptop who says she knows you. She say she work for UK Security Service. I ask her why she not call you on the phone, and she say the phone is, is *'bugged'*? She say she cannot speak to you on phone, but you must come as is emergency. Your life, she say, is in danger!"

Wrapping a towel around his waist and reaching for the dressing gown on the back of the door, he turned the handle and stepped through to face Maria.

She was standing there, with nothing but a towel wrapped around her presumably naked body.

For a second Best was taken aback by the sight of his housekeeper, unashamedly chosen by him personally from many others because of her looks and his immediate sexual attraction to her at the time of the interview.

"Come..." she said, "Please..."

Best finished tying the belt on his dressing gown, drawing it closed, and started moving past Maria towards her quarters.

"Did this woman give a name?"

"Yes," Maria replied. "She say her name was Bayla Adelstein."

It was if a lightning bolt had just exploded in the room.

Best stopped in his tracks, and turned to Maria.

"Bayla Adelstein?"

"Yes. She say you know her. She is your friend?"

11.06 p.m.

Ray almost couldn't believe it as he saw Randolph Best suddenly drop into the chair in front of the screen.

His face now occupied the full screen on the largest display in Andy's den.

Ray watched Best's eyes as he started to scan the screen of the laptop in front of him.

He watched as his lips began to move, but couldn't hear him speak.

Was Best trying to talk to the computer?

Beside him Andy stood up from his chair and pushed the keyboard across the tabletop towards Ray.

"Good luck. I'll be upstairs."

Ray glanced at him, but accepted that perhaps it was best if Andy just left him to it now. Adjusting the position of his chair slightly and raising his hands to the keyboard, he began to type.

"Mr Best, welcome. Are you speaking to me or to Maria? I should say that I cannot hear you. Please type on the keyboard for us to communicate with each other."

Ray watched as he saw Best move closer to the laptop at his end and begin to type.

"I was talking to Maria. Who are you?"

Ray replied, "May I first suggest that perhaps it is better if Maria were to leave the room? I wish to speak with you in private."

Without looking away from the screen Ray saw Best say a few words, presumably to the woman.

"We are alone. Maria has left. Now tell me. Who are you?" Best demanded to know.

"Bayla."

"Don't be stupid. That would not be possible. Bayla is no longer a friend of mine."

Ray hesitated, then committed himself.

"Would that be because you murdered her, Mr Best? With your own bare hands, and a very large knife?"

Surprisingly, very surprisingly, Best did not flinch.

It was not the reaction that Ray had expected. At the very least he would have expected him to appear flustered or scared.

Instead, Best quickly typed a reply.

"I never murdered Bayla. Who are you?"

"Oh, but I beg to disagree, Mr Best, you see I know that you did."

"I did not."

Ray breathed in deeply. Who was meant to be under pressure here? Him or Best?

In for a penny, in for a pound...

Ray typed his bold reply.

"I spy, Mr Best, I *saw* her die!"

11.08 p.m.

Randolph Best watched the reply appear on his screen.

"...I *saw* her die!"

To all intents and purposes whoever was communicating with him just now seemed to have seen the video and the murder. However, there was no proof yet. He couldn't react or acknowledge the accusation in any way until something more specific was said.

He typed his reply.

"Unless you identify yourself this instant, I will switch off my computer and end this madness."

Randolph Best waited, wondering what would happen next.

The reply that came back surprised him, both in its immediacy, and its openness.

11.10 p.m.

Ray stared at the screen. Sweat was running off his forehead and he felt nauseous. His mind went blank.

What should he say?

He swore loudly.

A picture of Emma filled his mind.
Emma hated lying. She always did.
Maybe the time had come to stop lying. To stop running.
Ray suddenly felt tired. Exhausted.

Ray made a decision.
From now on he would just do the right thing.
He would tell the truth.

Arrogance and stupidity had got Ray and Emma into the position they were in now... Every time he had tried to do something smart he had just dug himself deeper and deeper into a mess that now was going to claim his life in a few days time.

The fact that he was going to die was something that subconsciously he had already accepted.

This was all about Emma. About giving her the chance in life that she deserved. About *saving* her life.

Taking a deep breath, Ray's fingers began to type his reply.

11.13 p.m.

"Mr Best, my name is Ray Luck. I am a cyber professional. I was searching the web one day when I was bored, carrying out some idle video surveillance using a program I developed for use in my profession as a Cyber Pen Tester, and a video feed of yourself and Bayla Adelstein accidentally got captured by my search algorithm. I must confess that I watched yourself and the beautiful Miss Adelstein have sex with each other... at that point I did not know who you were, and I was a little drunk. Please don't be shocked. I know I shouldn't have, but I did..."

"At first it was interesting, and erotic...but then you started arguing with each other, and I watched in horror as I saw you kill her."

"At first I didn't know it was you or who the woman was... but then it was reported in the papers that Miss Adelstein's body was found in a street. I recognised her immediately from the video. When it was reported that there was evidence that the murder had been committed by a drug dealer who was then found dead from an overdose, I got angry."

"I didn't know at that point that you were involved. The image of you on the screen was dark, and your features were not discernible...so I used a graphics package to clean up and enhance the video file I had recorded of the murder. Fortunately - or perhaps unfortunately for me, given everything that has now happened since - when the software had worked its magic on the video, everything became crystal clear. You were now clearly visible.

There is no question that it's you in the video. I sent you the file, did you not see it?"

Best replied: "Yes, I did. Continue...please..."

The man who claimed to be Ray Luck continued his confession.

"What I have just written is all true. I am being honest and completely candid so that in what I say next you know that I am not lying. I was an idiot to come after you, to imagine that I could get justice for your murder of Miss Adelstein. I was wrong...but I was driven by the obvious injustice that was taking place, and knowing that there was some sort of high-level cover-up taking place."

"Stop! Please...for a moment," Best replied quickly. "I did NOT murder Bayla Adelstein! It's important that we are clear on that. Do you understand?"

There was no immediate reply. Ray Luck was obviously considering his next step.

It came a moment later.

"You say you did not murder Miss Adelstein. I saw you do it, but that is NOT why I am contacting you now. The reason I need to speak with you so urgently, and in this way, is because the Security Service has kidnapped my girlfriend and has threatened to kill her at midday on the 10th October unless I hand myself in. Which is what I will do. However, ...first..."

Best began to type his reply immediately, interrupting Luck's flow.

"Kidnapped your girlfriend? I never authorised that and I know nothing of this. Believe me! What is her name and when did this happen?"

"Emma Purvis. On Sunday afternoon. She flew to Canada and as far as I can tell she was kidnapped by the Security Service as soon as she arrived there. I have received emails and videos of her after torture, with her begging for her life and urging me to surrender. If I give myself in and hand over the video, I'm told you will set her free."

"I don't know about this. I didn't authorise it."

"The thing is Mr Best, I know that if I hand myself in, you will kill me to keep my silence. And I accept that. But, I am worried that you will not keep your side of the bargain. That you will also kill my girlfriend, irrespective of if I hand myself in or not. Mr Best, I have to be honest with you, I'm struggling with all of this. Part of me says that I should hold out, that I should blackmail you further with the film of the murder in which you are the star. I mean, I could just threaten to release it on YouTube, Twitter and every other social media site in the world so that your life will be ruined. I can create so much trouble for you that it doesn't matter how much you deny it, your public image will be ruined for life, and the government will fall because of the cover-up they so obviously supported. But there's a risk. A risk that you'll kill Emma as soon as I release the video. In which case we both lose. I lose Emma, and you lose everything you have: your fame, your Nobel Prize, your beloved position in the government, your career. We both lose everything we value. I don't know what to do, Mr Best. So I thought I'd ask you. You see, this afternoon I watched the news report of you at the children's hospital and for a moment I saw a spark of humanity in you which I can't believe can exist in a person who would be so evil to kill my Emma in cold blood. I'm confused. I don't know what I'm dealing with here. And then I realised that for the past few days I must have been exchanging emails with some agent in the Security Service and not you. Maybe you didn't even know about the emails that I've sent to you or the replies which someone sent to me on your behalf? Maybe I've been talking to the monkey and not its owner... So, before I decide on what my best course of action should be, I wanted to talk directly with you. To see what you've got to say for yourself. To find out if you know what's been happening to Emma? To find out if I can trust you to swap my life for Emma's."

Randolph Best watched the last few letters appear on the screen and then sat back.
This was all getting way out of control.
He was so angry that his hands were shaking. He'd left it to the Agency to take care of all of this, and they'd screwed it all up.

Best admired the honesty of the man on the other end of the line. He also didn't underestimate the capability of the man, and his intelligence.
He knew that the 'frank' confession that Luck was giving to him just now was not only a brave thing to do, but it was also the act of a man who was facing death and had very little to lose: the most dangerous type of adversary you can encounter.
Best had to tread very carefully. The man had been pushed into a corner.
One wrong word, one false step and Ray Luck would release the video and the Walls of Jericho would all come tumbling down around him.

11.20 p.m.

Ray felt defenceless.

He'd come clean. Told the truth. And now he was waiting for the reply.
Ray didn't actually know what to expect.

He knew that Randolph Best would be scared of the threat of the video being released: Best was gambling that Ray still cared about what happened to Emma: if Ray didn't, Best would be toast!

Best was clever. He would know that he hadn't won yet: that Ray could still destroy everything he stood for, if he wanted to.

Best's answer began to appear:

"Mr Luck, I appreciate your honesty and candour. I understand that in response you will expect me to be honest with you, and that you will weigh up every word I write. I also understand that in spite of how it seems, there can be no clear winner here: you believe that we both have the power of mutually assured destruction within our own hands. Do you agree?"

Ray was surprised by the question, and caught a little off guard, but still managed to reply with a quick "Yes, I do."

"Then there are several things I need to convince you of.

First, I need to assure you that I did not authorise the detention of your girlfriend and that I know nothing about it. Secondly I need to promise you that once you hand over to me the original copy of the video and can assure me that you will not release it or publish it, then she will walk free, with no further harm."

Ray's heart skipped a beat.

"Thirdly, I need to convince you that I did not murder Bayla Adelstein. Which I can do quite easily, face-to-face. When we meet."

Reading the words, Ray knew that nothing new had been said that could guarantee Emma's life was secure. They were just words. This had been a waste of time.

Also, Best was protesting his innocence, which struck Ray as very odd and stupid, given that Ray had the video of the murder and had witnessed it with his own eyes.

The truth was that Best was still asking him to meet him with no further assurances than he already had.

Ray was just beginning to think that Andy had been right and making a direct appeal to Best had been a waste of time, when the next words from Best arrived.

They were not what he had expected. In fact they were quite surprising.

11.21 p.m.

After locking her bedroom door, María Sáenz picked a book of the shelf in her bedroom and hurried into the bathroom. Taking no chances she then also locked the bathroom door before opening the book and taking out the small mobile phone which she had hidden within the space cut from inside the pages of the book.

Nervously she switched the phone on, listened again one more time to make sure that she could not hear her boss for any reason, and then selected the only number that was on the phone. She pressed dial.

"May I speak with Ferris?" she asked. "This is Sáenz. I have an urgent report to make."

Chapter 42

London

Monday

October 7th

The Church, London

11.22 p.m.

Ray sat in silence, rereading the message from Randolph Best for the third time.

"Ray, I know you approached me directly to gain some confidence that I will spare the life of your girlfriend Emma, and I realise that by just saying 'we must meet' you gain no assurance from my words. I also know that without assurance you could release the video and by doing so destroy my career and bring the government down. I know I need to give you some assurance. Which is why I say the following: I wish to invite you to come to meet me in London at my private flat in the heart of London. It is where you claim to have seen Bayla Adelstein being murdered by myself. When you come, I will prove to you that I did not murder her. I will also explain to you why you must on no account, release the video to the public. For now, I can only inform you, without proof, that there is more to all of this than you realise. You will understand when I show you. To assure you that this will not be a trap and that my intention is pure and trustworthy - even though you have already admitted that you are willing to sacrifice your life for your girlfriend's - I would like to suggest that you do NOT bring the video with you. Instead, using your IT and cyber skills, I would suggest that you set up the video to automatically release and publish to the world if I do not set you free again after we have talked. This way, we remain at detente. We both retain the capability of mutually assured destruction, but I gain the opportunity to convince you of my innocence and to gain your trust. Under these conditions, will you agree to meet me tomorrow at 9.45 a.m.? I have a Cabinet meeting in the morning that I cannot miss, but as soon as it is over, we should meet."

Ray was just about to start to read it all again for the fourth time when three words appeared at the bottom of the screen.

"Please trust me."

Ray typed his reply.

"On condition that you assure me that Emma will be looked after and definitely not questioned or beaten again, and that you send me a picture of her taken with today's newspaper to prove she is still alive and okay, then I will agree. Send me the photograph and the address by 9.00 a.m. As long as I get it, I will leave for the address you give me. In the meantime I am going to follow your suggestion and make preparations to automatically release the video tomorrow lunch time at 12.00 noon."

The reply was immediate.

"Which email address should I send the photo to?"

Ray hesitated, and then replied with an email address that he had made up and sometimes used to hide his identity when hacking. He knew that there was no real connection from it to Ray Luck, and that there was therefore no way that it would be being monitored by MI5 or MI6.

And even if they were somehow monitoring it and had connected it with him, Ray had nothing more to hide.

Tomorrow he would hand himself in. Even if he did manage to persuade them to set Emma free, Ray was certain that he was going to be killed once he traded the video of Emma.

It was a macabre thought, but an honest one - after tomorrow Ray would have no more secrets to keep, or any further need of email accounts.

The dead do not write emails.

11.59 p.m.

The Church

Ray walked into the lounge upstairs and without asking, walked over to Andy's drink cabinet, took out the bottle of whisky and two glasses, pouring two large drams.

Andy watched him.

"The ice is in the fridge. Two cubes please."

Handing a glass to Andy, Ray sat down heavily on the couch and took a swig of his drink.

"It's rather fitting that I ended up spending the last day of my life in a Church."

Andy stared at him.

"So, it didn't go so well then?"

"It went. How well I don't know. It's all a bit weird," he replied, then went on to explain everything that had happened, finishing with, "...which is why either way, today is my last full day in this bloody shit, but wonderful world. In every scenario, I hand myself in, they kill me and they get off free. The only question is, if they let Emma go or not."

Andy pondered his next words.

"Forgive me for being rather selfish...but I need to know...what's it like knowing that tomorrow you're going to die?"

Ray stared at him, and then laughed.

"I never thought I'd hear you asking me that question. You're the one whose dying. Officially."

"If I wait it out, it'll probably not be for another few months, maybe a little longer. I was told to watch out for the symptoms I've now got, and from here on in, it just accelerates. I'm shit scared, although maybe I don't show it, but you...you're just carrying on as if nothing is wrong!"

Ray slumped back in this chair, and looked at the whisky in his hand.

"Fuck. This whole thing is so fucked up!" He took another swig from the glass. "To be honest, I'm trying not to think about it too much. I haven't got a choice really. I love Emma. I'll do anything to save her. If she was here in the room right now and someone tried to shoot her, I'd dive in front of her and take the bullets. Without thinking. Which is what I'm doing tomorrow. I'm probably more scared that if I stop and try to think about what I have to do, then maybe I won't do it. Maybe I'll bottle out and run away. Then she'll die because of me, and I won't be able to live with myself and my conscience and I'll probably kill myself anyway, the only difference being that she'll be dead too. At least if I do what they tell me, maybe there's some hope that one of us will get out of this alive."

Andy was quiet.

Then after a few moments he whispered something that at first Ray didn't quite hear.

"I'm not going without a bang."

"What did you say?"

"I said, before I go, I'm going to do something that will make everyone sit up and take notice. In fact, it's going to happen this coming Friday. Thanks to you."

"What are you talking about?"

"I mean, if it wasn't for you, I would just die and nobody would remember me, but thanks to your help last night, this Friday morning I'm going to pull off the biggest cyber attack the world has ever seen. It's been years in planning. If you hadn't helped me I'm sure I would have figured it out eventually, but that was before I got diagnosed with 'death', before the quacks told me that if I didn't pull a finger out soon, nothing was going to happen."

"Andy, I don't get you. What the hell are you talking about."

Andy turned and looked at Ray, his face cold and almost expressionless.

"There was a time when I thought that you and I would have made a great team...actually you proved it last night, by helping me to hack into the National Grid's main server farm. When you were a proper card carrying anarchist, I really looked up to you, and believed that you had the potential to be 'the man', the bloody hero we all needed. But then you fucked off, got all loved up, moralistic, and gentrified. Went to the dark side, and became good!"

Andy's voice was getting louder, his face turning a little red.

"Which I don't regret." Ray said. "For me, it was time to move on. So I did. For the record, I've always respected you too. And yes, I agree, had I stayed an anarchist, then we would have made a great team. But I didn't. Anyway, what's this attack you've got planned for Friday?"

Ray took another sip from his glass of whisky, suddenly wanting to get really drunk but realising that wouldn't be a good idea. Tomorrow he needed to be on form when he met Best so that he could negotiate Emma's safe release. Somehow.

Andy started to push and pull himself up from his sofa. Once he was on his feet, he walked to the kitchen bar, grabbed the bottle of whisky and poured himself another drink.

"Friday? What am I going to do? Hah! Wouldn't you like to know!!! Normally I'd be tempted to say, 'Wait and see!' but given that you'll probably have been murdered by then, I may as well tell you now."

Ray didn't smile back. At the mention of his death, he felt the first twinges of panic, and his heart skipped a couple of beats. He took a deep breath.

"True, so...?"

"Okay, since you asked so nicely. On Friday, a day which will be forever remembered as British Banking's Black Friday, I am going to destroy London's Banking system. I'm going to take away all the trust from the system so that no one will ever touch British Banks again with a barge-pole."

Ray whistled. If Andy managed to do that, he would certainly go down in history.

"It's been years in planning, and months in the making... I only had a few wee hiccups along the way, including the one you fixed for me earlier on, for which I will always remain truly grateful, by the way. In future, every time I think of you I will say a mental 'Ta!' "

"So, what are you going to do? How are you going to destroy the Banking System?"

"That would be telling, wouldn't it, but I'll give you the highlights, shall I? The bankers have to be stopped. They're bastards. All of them. Rich fucking bastards. They don't give a shit about us, or anyone else. It's all just *me*, me, me, and my bonus. I hate them..."

"You're not alone there pal, you're not alone!"

"...Yeah, but, unlike everyone else, I'm actually going to do something about it. I've spent the best part of a year creating a massive botnet across America, Europe, Russia, China and Australia, and at 11a.m. on Friday morning, they are going to launch a series of staggered distributed denial-of-services attacks on a whole range of banking centres, servers, and applications, I'm going to kill the stock market, kill the banks trading applications, shut down cash flows, prevent people from getting access to money...any service that has got the word money or cash in it, I'm going to bring to a grinding halt. You should see the banner that I'm going to post on the servers and all the PCs in all the banks: it's brilliant! I spent days designing it. It's a really snazzy graphic - 'RobinHood was here!' But that's not all..."

Ray couldn't believe what he was hearing. He could tell that Andy was deadly serious, and he knew that if Andy said he could do it, then he would be able to. This wasn't some sort of crazy story. This was a real threat, and it was going to happen.

"There's more?"

"Yup. Sure is. I'm going to shut the City of Westminster and Canary Wharf down completely. I'll make them wastelands."

"How?"

"I'm going to cut all the power. At 12 noon, just when the banks will think they have begun to understand what has hit them, and all of the malware that I've sent in via phishing attacks has started to spread and take effect, I'm going to shut down all the electricity. I know that a lot of them will have their own emergency generators, but I've thought of that too. Almost all the banks use the same supplier of generators, and lo and behold, would you believe it...they all have a couple of very useful vulnerabilities in their software which I've spent the past few months preparing to exploit. It's already done. I just went to the manufacturers' sites, hacked into them, added my own private malware to their own software updates, and gave them all several months to make sure they would all download and update the software, thereby installing my malware."

"It's going to be brill. As soon as I turn off the part of the National Grid that supplies most of London, the power will go off and their generators will kick in, and my software will start to run. "

"And what happens then?"

"Aha..., at least three of the five major types of generators used to produce emergency power will self-destruct. Catastrophically. To be honest, my plan isn't completely perfect, because the other two major types of generator may continue to work. I'm just gambling upon the fact that even if they do have power, none of the operational systems will work anyway either because of my malware, or because of my DDOS attacks."

"Bloody hell, Andy. It sounds amazing, but how can one person do all that?"

"I'm not just one person. I'm RobinHood! The best bloody hacker in Olde London Town!"...and don't you forget it, pal, okay?"

"Tell me again, just how are you going to switch the electricity off?"

"How much do you know about the whole phenomena about the convergence of IT and OT?"

"IT and what?"

"Operation Technology. OT is to Industrial Networks as IT is to business and computer networks, except OT has been around for a whole lot longer. OT is the stuff that makes Industry work. It's the name given to all the processes, software and hardware that people have been building for hundreds of years since the industrial revolution. The thing is, industrial plants and utilities both use OT to make them work. Historically, everyone had the sense to keep OT networks and systems completely separate from the outside world, so that no one could interfere with them, or play around with them. But in the past ten years all the profit hungry managers of the big corporations that run our industries have started demanding that in order to maximise profits they need to modernise industrial control centres and start merging IT with OT...which basically means that they start connecting the industrial plants to the internet. With me so far?"

Ray nodded.

"Great. Because for hackers like us, that's just like waving a red flag at a bull. The thing is, industrial systems were never, ever, designed with any concept of network security like modern businesses were. Words like 'IT' and 'cyber attack' just weren't in the dictionary of any of the guys who designed these things. So what's been happening recently is that overnight an oil company or an electricity generation company starts making it possible for remote industrial sites to start talking together over the internet and sharing data with headquarters....either over the internet via VPNs, or across secure IP enabled WANs etc...and bingo, suddenly all the industrial processes upon which society depends are immediately exposed to all the prats like us who just can't wait to launch a cyber attack against them, or send them our malware so that we get control and can take over their systems. Which is exactly what you helped me to do with the central servers in the National Grid. Once you helped me get in, I just installed a couple of my own software programmes, and reprogrammed and rescheduled the systems. At lunchtime on Friday, I've arranged it so that the national grid will redirect all the electricity away from all the financial centres in London, and the bits that surround them. Then at 12.10 pm, the databases will start to delete themselves, and then the servers will shut down and go off line. I've done the same to the back-up server farms that the system will hand-over to when things start to go down. Basically, even when they know what the problem is, they won't be able to do anything about it for weeks. Maybe months!"

"How did you know how to do all of that?"

"I've been planning this for years. Working on it for years. Three years ago I got a job for six months working as a contractor for the National Grid so I could learn how it all worked and what I would need to do. I'm telling you, this is going to be great. I was originally planning to launch the attack in about six months' time, but as soon as I was diagnosed, I had to move it all forward. Luckily I've managed to get it all done. I'm ready. All I have to do is effectively press 'go' on Thursday night, and the next day it will all happen automatically. Out. Will. Go. The. Lights. And. It'll. Be. *Adios*. To. London as the banking capital of the world!"

Ray was thinking about what Andy was saying. Not about the bankers, and the billions of pounds they would lose, but about everything else that would be brought down as collateral damage.

A sudden picture of Randolph Best visiting the children in Great Ormond Street hospital popped into his mind.

"No..." Ray almost shouted, "Actually...*you can't do that*. Hitting the banks is one thing... I mean the systems they use, their computers and software applications....all that's fine, but you can't take out the power to the wider areas. If you do, lots of people will die. People in hospitals on life-supports, people getting stuck in lifts. People stuck in ambulances in the grid-locked traffic on the way to work. Workers underground. And if you take out the power grid for a long period of time, the generators will eventually run out of fuel, and if the streets are all blocked with cars, because the lights are all stuck at red, then new supplies will not get through...Have you ever read that book...CyberStorm? It'll be just like in the book, when a cyber attack took out New York!"

Andy smiled and then gave a short laugh..

"You've asked several questions there? Do you want an answer to them all, or just the most important...?"

"This isn't a game, Andy, people are going to die!"

"So," Andy replied. "We're all going to die. You perhaps tomorrow, me in a couple of months time, if I last that long. Or maybe sooner...What do I care if a few others die too? Someone needs to take some positive action. So I will. It'll be my legacy!"

"Your legacy?"

"Yes. I want to be remembered. Everyone wants to be remembered."

"Maybe, but not for killing people!"

"People dying will be the side-show to the main event. People will remember me for the biggest hack in the world: the most destructive cyber attack ever. Anarchists the world over will look to me. I'll be like the best anarchist ever! The one that brought down the banking system. The one that destroyed the British Government. I'll be a god in their eyes. People will talk about me for decades to come."

Ray was staring at Andy now, not able to believe the words that were coming out of his mouth.

The look on Andy's face had changed. His pupils had widened and he was looking at Ray but seeing past him, through him, into the distance somewhere, visualising thoughts of misled glory that he had somehow managed to evoke in association with mass-murder and wanton destruction.

The images of the children in Great Ormond Street hospital flashed into Ray's mind again.

It was to Great Ormond Street that his brother had been taken when he had been given the drugs in the school playground by a stupid boy who had stolen them from his big brother and thought he was being clever by sharing them out with his friends. On top of that, the drugs looked like 'Smarties'; the kids had no idea just how powerful and deadly they would be to someone so young. The doctors had tried to save him, but failed. They had fought for his life for days, and fought hard. For years Ray had wondered if with better equipment and better resources they would have been able to save him, but when he grew up and learned more about what had happened, he had realised that it would probably have made no difference. The damage inflicted on his brain by the drugs which his brother had so foolishly taken was so severe that nothing would have made any difference: if he had come out of the coma, he would have been a cabbage. Reluctantly he had later realised that his dying had probably been a blessing.

Yet ever since then, Ray had had a soft-spot for the amazing doctors and nurses at Great Ormond Street, and several times during his life he had participated in fund raising activities to help raise additional funds for the work they did. The thought of Andy killing the children in the hospital, the thought that Andy was going to put lives in danger and that he didn't even care about it, was making Ray see red.

Ray had to try and stop him. To make him see sense.

He stood up and went to pour another drink for them both, giving him a few moments to think.

"Why are you an anarchist?" Ray asked Andy, handing over the drink to him.

"I hate authority."

"Me too, but that doesn't mean I want to kill people."

"We're getting repetitive."

"Do you like living in Britain?"

"Yes, it's the best country in the world."

"So why do you want to destroy it?"

"The fact that Britain is the best country in the world, doesn't mean to say that it's as good as it could be. It could be better."

"Like how?"

"Without the bankers. The wankers. The tossheads that fucked us all and got rich from it?"

"But you got rich from them, didn't you? You stole the money back. You're a millionaire."

"I took a share back on behalf of the people, that's all."

Andy looked at Ray quizzically, as if he was about to say something else but had just forgotten it and was looking for inspiration as to what it could have been. He was obviously starting to get quite drunk - a combination of the alcohol and the painkillers he was taking.

"Andy, if you shut down the City and ruin the banking industry, you'll take away the jobs from tens of thousands of workers who depend upon the banking system to survive. They're just normal people like you and I, not rich bankers. They don't deserve to be hit. Their families will starve. And if the banking industry collapses, and there are thousands without work, the housing market will get swamped with a glut of houses in London that no one can buy, made worse by the likelihood that interest rates will most likely skyrocket as well. The housing market will collapse, the country will go into recession, and we'll never recover because you *fucked* the banking system. You'll destroy the country, its people, and its future."

Andy smiled and laughed, giggling in an almost childish way.

"I do all that myself? Just little old me?"

"Yes. It'll all be down to you. All the misery, the desperation, the destruction and the deaths. You'll be the most hated person in the country, maybe even in the world if we topple everyone else into a global recession too, which is highly likely if London dies."

Andy downed the rest of his glass of whisky and waved it in the air for a top-up.

"Hated? No, that's not good. Not good at all. Anyway...fuck...I took too many of those bloody new pills today, I'm feeling really dizzy..."

Ray quickly filled up his glass with some more whisky.

"Drink this. It'll help steady your legs."

Andy laughed again.

"You know? You might be right. You might just be right. I might be hated. I might kill some people... but you know what? I actually don't give a flying fuck... The more the merrier I say! The more I fucking kill, the merrier I'll be! And I won't be dying alone then. I'll be going with some company!"

"Why? What do you mean?"

"Well,...you see...I'm too much of a bloody coward to face a slow, painful, fucking awful death...so come Sunday, after I've seen how it's gone on Friday...I'm probably going to top myself. Kill myself. You know, a bit of suicide never did anyone any harm..."

"Suicide? Shit Andy, this is crazy! Why do so much damage and then just leave?"

"Like I said, I'm a bloody coward...and I can't stand the pain anymore."

Ray stood up, putting his glass down on the kitchen island.

"I can't listen to this anymore..."

"You're just jealous. Bloody jealous. Angry that I can do this and you can't!"

It was Ray's turn to laugh, "Me? Jealous of you killing people?"

"Nope...jealous that I'm going to be more famous than you, the great SolarWind."

"Great? I don't think so. See where my ability got me and what it's done to the person I love."

At that point Andy's eyes began to close. The alcohol and the drugs were proving to be too powerful a cocktail.

Ray watched as Andy slid down onto the sofa and then rolled off it onto the floor.

When Ray was sure that Andy was out for the count, he bent down and put a pillow under his head and turned him onto his side, just in case he was sick.

Ray picked up his glass again from the island, and sat on the sofa opposite the now snoring Andy.

What the hell was he going to do?

Tomorrow he was going to probably die. The life of his girlfriend was in danger, and now he had just discovered that Andy was going to kill himself on Sunday, and that on Friday he was probably going to sound the death knell for Britain as everyone knew it today, at the same time as causing an indeterminate number of deaths.

Deaths which Ray could prevent if he could somehow stop Andy from launching his attack.

But how?

And did he have time to stop him?

Ray looked at his watch.

It was 3.20 a.m.

If he was going to do something, he would have to do it fast.

In less than seven hours Ray would be meeting Randolph Best, and the strong likelihood was that he was not going to be walking out of that meeting free, or alive.

Seven hours?
For what he would have to do, it was not enough time.

Chapter 43

London

Monday

October 8th

The Church, London

08.30 a.m.

Unable to sleep on what was possibly going to be his last night alive on earth, Ray had spent the evening with his eyes open: he wanted to see the world, while he still could.

For a while he had thought about calling his mother, but then realised that it would only upset her, and that he would possibly put her in danger.

He thought about calling his sister, and then for similar reasons, decided against it.

In the end, he had found some paper and a few pens in the kitchen and spent several hours writing letters: one to his mum, one to his sister, and a long one to Emma.

He had spilled his heart out to them all, thanking them for whatever he could think of to thank them for, and telling them repeatedly how much he loved them.

To Emma he expressed his regrets for a life possibly not spent together, and apologising for messing it up for both of them. In the letter he told her the truth about everything that had happened, who the people were that had kidnapped her, and the deal that he was making with the devil: if Emma got to read the letter, the deal had been well-made, and if she didn't...then they would both be dead.

That was something Ray did not want to think about.

Afterwards, Ray had watched the sun rise, and spent the early morning thinking about his life, his achievements, and his failures.

There were many regrets.

Many things that he would have liked to have done differently.

He had always assumed that he would have had more time.

Time to correct many of the mistakes he had made. Time to do things differently.

Time to live longer.

It was not right that his life was going to be stolen from him, that Randolph Best was going to claim another victim - him!

But one of the major regrets in his life was Emma. Not having married her last year. Not having bought a house together. Not having had a baby with her.

She had often talked about the children she would have one day: a boy and a girl.

"I like the name Alice for the girl, but I can't make up my mind what the boy should be called. Maybe I'll leave that one up to my husband!" she had said.

He remembered her words well.

He also remembered her other words: "You wouldn't know the right thing to do..."

This time however, he knew exactly what he had to do.

What he had to do, in order to do the right thing.

He was going to sacrifice his own life for Emma's.

There was no fear. Just acceptance. And determination.

By the end of the day, come what may, Emma would be free!

08.35 a.m.

A Plumber's Van

Whitehall

Central London

Ferris had just spent one of the worst nights of his life, wondering if the next day he would still have a job.

Late the night before he had been dragged from his bed by an urgent phone call with Jacobson, who was more angry than Ferris had ever heard him before. A few minutes before that, Rowlinson had called Jacobson, demanding that within an hour, they should have a new video of the Emma girl in Canada holding a newspaper, proving that she was still alive, and healthy, i.e. not dead.

Apparently Best had been tipped off and was furious that he had not been fully briefed on the situation.

Rowlinson had taken a bollocking. Rowlinson had promptly passed the bollocking down the line, and Ferris had been the last person to receive it.

However, as Jacobson had started to crucify him on the phone, Ferris had played his master-card.

He'd told Jacobson everything that María Sáenz, Best's housekeeper, had told him late last night.

"Did you manage to find out what the communications between the person on the laptop and Best had said?"

"No. There was no way to track it. It was totally invisible to everything we've got."

"Any idea who it was?"

"Luck." Ferris replied. "It had to be. Unless it was Rowlinson?"

"I'll check. But I don't think it was him. If he or I had wanted to talk with Best we would have just picked up the phone."

"Exactly. Which is why I think it was Luck."

There was a moment's silence.

"Okay. Luck obviously contacted Best directly, cutting us out the loop, and he must be the one that told Best about his girlfriend. He's probably trying to cut a deal with Best directly. Where's Best now?"

"Still in his home," Ferris had replied, assuming that since he had not been informed otherwise, the permanent twenty-four hour tail was still watching and waiting somewhere outside the Best mansion.

"Good. I want you to follow him tomorrow. Don't let him out of your sight. But first get me the video of his girlfriend and the newspaper, and make sure that from now on it's only caviar and champagne for her. No more rough stuff, okay?"

"Are we going to release her?"

"Possibly. But whether or not she's alive at the time, will depend upon what happens over the next twenty-four hours. Best is up to something, and I don't know what. Send me the video within the next two hours."

The video was made and delivered with thirty minutes. They even had time to force Emma to put some makeup on.

When they told her that her boyfriend was still alive, she had smiled.

And that's when they filmed her.

It looked good.

After only a few hours sleep, Ferris had taken personal command of the covert watch team, who for the past two years had been following Randolph Best wherever he went.

Today, Ferris was the one sitting staring at the LCD screen with his head bowed, and monitoring the video feed of the people coming and going out of Downing Street.

As soon as Best emerged, he and today's two man team were going to follow him everywhere he went.

Wherever he went.

The Church

London

08.45 a.m.

Ray had often wondered what it would be like to die. Those last few moments before life slipped away. Curiously, as a child, he had often wondered if all those people who had their heads cut off during the French revolution...as their heads fell into the buckets, could they still see? Would they look back up from the bucket and see the guillotine towering above them and know what had happened? He had read on the internet that some experiments had once been conducted that showed a human head could remain conscious for about thirty seconds after being separated from its body.

So, when did death occur? And what was death?

As the minutes had slowly ticked by in the Church, earlier that morning between three and four a.m., Ray had had some very dark and strange thoughts.

Perhaps, as he was lying on the bed, he had actually momentarily drifted off to sleep, dreamt for a few seconds and then woken up again.

He couldn't really tell.

Every few minutes he would look at his watch, and do a quick mental calculation how much longer it would be before he met Randolph Best.

It was weird.

Even though he was ninety-nine percent sure that the best he could hope for from the meeting was an assurance, a promise, that Emma would be set free, there was that odd one percent - was it called hope? - that encouraged the occasional thought to flit through his mind, that maybe, just *maybe*, he could somehow still get out of this alive.

Together.

With Emma?

Unlikely though.

Very unlikely.

It was Ray Luck versus the British Government.

Ray versus the establishment.

Ray had always been a realist, and on his last day on earth, he wasn't about to change now.

So, how would they kill him, after he had handed over the video?

A bullet? A chop to the neck?

Poison?

For a few moments, Ray's tired brain started to try and remember all the ways that James Bond had killed people. Maybe he would die just like one of the bad guys in the films?

When Ray started to think of his parents again, and his mother, Ray began to fight back the tears.
He re-read the letter he had written to his mother, then sealed it tight: there was nothing more he could think of to add. How many times could he tell her he loved her?
The answer of course was, simply, 'never enough.'

He thought of his father.
If he died, would he see his father again, ...very soon? Do the dead meet the dead?

Then earlier, around five a.m. Ray's thoughts had wandered back to Andy and the devastation he was planning for London.
At the back of his mind, Ray had to admit to himself that there was something to respect at the scale of the hack, and the planning and execution that must have gone into it. Yet, somewhere along the way Andy had completely lost the plot.
Ray remembered the look he had seen in Andy's eyes.
Was it madness?

He felt sorry for Andy because of his illness...but Ray couldn't understand Andy's desire to kill others and take them with him.
Life was precious.
Life was good.

Ray swallowed hard, and breathed deeply.
Fuck, he didn't want to die...

Then there were Emma's words again, about doing the right thing.
Do the right thing.

Ray had begun to think about that, Emma's words ringing over and over again in his mind.
He thought about Andy's plan.
He thought about the 'bastards' - the bankers - who actually probably did deserve everything they might get, but not the innocent people of London, the City of London, the best capital in the world!
He loved London. Always had.

Which was why he still lived there now...*had* lived there...

There was a certain irony about these thoughts and feelings that were not lost on Ray. He loved London, the UK, everything about being British, and yet it was that same Britain - or rather the British Establishment - that was about to kill him.

So why did he want to defend it?

It was a good question, but which Ray knew there was only one answer for.

It was simple.

Andy's plan was just wrong. Murder was wrong. Death was wrong.

And Ray knew that he had to do his best to stop Andy from going ahead with his plans.

Somehow.

But what should he do? What *could* he do? There was so little time left.

No time to do anything really, apart from hand Andy in.

Ray thought about that. A lot. But realised that he couldn't do it.

'*You never double-crossed a cyber-bruv.*'

In the end, Ray sat down and wrote one last letter.

To Andy.

"Don't do it, Andy," or words to that effect. "*Please* don't do it!"

Ray pleaded for Andy to retain his self-respect. He'd been a good anarchist up till now, a brilliant, well-respected cyber black hat/ hacktivist/ hacker...

Why throw his hard-won reputation away by putting himself in a league of common murderers?

Did Andy want to die? Obviously not, so why then force death upon others?

Don't be a bastard.

A cold-blooded, murdering bastard.

Rather, surely it was better to die a noble death? Ray stumbled over those words. What did 'noble' mean? How could any death be noble?

Ray tried to find clever words, a convincing way to persuade Andy to step back and take a fresh look at what he was planning to do.

Was this *really* how he wanted to be remembered?

In the end, Ray left the decision up to Andy, but offered him an olive branch in return: an idea.

Instead of the destruction and misery which would be the legacy he was planning, why not just fix all the ATM machines in London to empty all their money out to everyone passing in the street?

And to post a message on the screens telling everyone it was a gift from RobinHood, paying back to Londoners, the money the bankers had stolen from them by causing the financial crash.

Surely that was a better way!

If he did that, he would get his revenge back on the banks and everyone would remember Andy for what he did in a positive way, and possibly even *mourn* his death when his obituary was finally placed in the papers in the months to come, ...instead of cursing his name, and being happy that the bastard had died.

Ray read the letter again, sighed deeply, then sealed it and stuck it to the television screen with some sellotape.

He looked at his watch.
8.55 a.m.
It was time to check his email and then go.

Chapter 44

London

Monday

October 8th

The Church, London

09.02 a.m.

Leaving the house just before 9.a.m. and once again wearing his burqa, he walked out of the church, and closed the door behind him.

Perhaps, just perhaps, there was a slight possibility that Ray might come back there later that day, but Ray knew that the possibility of that happening was slim at best.

In all probability, Ray was walking into a trap.

During the night he had thought about setting up the video to release automatically and play on all the social media sites later that day, if he didn't manage to make it back and stop the countdown from happening, but in the end he had decided against it.

If they killed him and Emma, what would Ray benefit from doing it?

All of a sudden, revenge did not taste so sweet.

Ray didn't want revenge. He didn't want to bring down the government.

He just wanted it all to end.

He was tired.

So tired. So bloody tired.

Anyway, there was one major point that prevented Ray from doing it.

He couldn't.

To do it, he would have to arrange it all from the computers and servers in Andy's house.

The spooks would trace the cyber traffic back to Andy's house, and he would be arrested.

And if that happened, Ray would be just as bad as Andy: as Ray died, so would Andy.

Ray would be responsible for his death too, because once they had Andy there was no way that they would kill Ray, then let Andy off.

In other words, the best Ray could do would be to bluff Randolph: to pretend that he had set the video up to automatically publish itself to the world if Ray didn't stop it, ... and then just see how far he could go with it.

The Underground

Central London

Ray had been naughty.

As he had left the church, he had 'borrowed' Andy's mobile phone.

On the underground somewhere between Charing Cross and Tottenham Court Road he'd gone online using Andy's browser - courtesy of the Wi-Fi now available everywhere on the Tube, and logged into the email account he'd given Randolph Best.

The beauty of going online on the underground was that they'd never be able to track any signal to a CCTV camera in a specific carriage, and figure out it was him.

Anyway, it was a fictitious email account, and there'd be little chance of tracking it back to Andy. Or himself.

As he waited for the email Inbox to download, Ray wondered why he was even taking any precautions.

If they arrested him as soon as he met Best, taking precautions now wouldn't matter, and if by some slim chance they didn't arrest him and he somehow walked out of the meeting, then that would only happen if he'd managed to strike some sort of deal with Best, and he probably wouldn't need to hide out anymore anyway.

What Ray was doing this morning was a gamble, a single throw of the dice. The odds were stacked against his survival and he knew it.

The Inbox of his email appeared.

Ray held his breath.

Top of the list was an email from Randolph Best.

With an attachment.

Ray hit the link and opened it up. The message was short.

"Emma is alive, and well. We must meet. Please come to my London flat at 10.15 a.m. Ask for me at the Reception Desk and give your name. You will be expected."

There was an address, somewhere near Mayfair. The nearest tube station would be Bond Street.

Ray breathed out slowly, his pulse racing, his face sweating under the Burqa. He felt slightly nauseous.

Clicking on the attachment, a short movie file opened up and began to play.

Ray's heart skipped a beat when he saw Emma. She was sitting on a chair, smiling at the camera and holding up a newspaper. The camera zoomed in to the newspaper until Ray could make out the date: it was yesterday's.

Suddenly Emma's face filled the screen.

"I'm fine, Ray. They're treating me much better now. Good food. Even a glass of wine. They've said they're going to release me, later. I'm not allowed to say anymore, except that I love you. Ray. *I love you*!"

The video flickered, and died.

After wiping the tears away from his eyes with the edges of the veil, watching the video four more times and changing trains once, Ray stood up and caught the escalator up to Oxford Street.

Emerging into the open air, Ray looked up at the bright blue sky above and blinked a few times.

He thought of Emma again and tried his best to ignore his fear.

Randolph Best had done what he'd said he would do.

From where he was now, it was just a short walk to Mayfair.

Mayfair

Ferris sat in the back of the plumber's van, studying screens and listening with his headphones.

From Downing Street they had followed Best as he had driven his own car - a red Porsche, through central London to his flat in Mayfair.

Doing what he was told, Ferris was watching him like a hawk.

They had seen him go into the building.

From there, it had all gone dark.

A private security company managed the building where Best's penthouse flat was, and they did a good job of regularly sweeping the building for bugs and unauthorised cameras.

Over the past few years, Ferris's team had given up trying to outsmart them.

For now Ferris and two other members of his team would just have to watch the entrance doors and wait.

If he made any private calls they could pick them up: they had been monitoring his calls and communications for the past two years, and Best still knew nothing about it.

He'd been inside the building for ten minutes now, and there was no indication he was going to leave anytime soon.

Ferris was used to waiting and watching the entrance to Mayfair Villas.

In fact, it was only a few weeks ago when he had watched Bayla Adelstein walk in through the door, never to come out again, alive.

The Church

9.45 a.m.

Andy stood in the shower, cold water thundering down upon his skull, his tongue a large piece of leather that ached and throbbed at the back of his mouth, his brain a pulsating mass of dead cells that ached every time his heart pumped.

"Shit..." Andy swore to himself, as he turned under the jet of cold water and was racked by a wall of pain. Now the veil of the alcohol was beginning to lift, the pain was beginning to crush him.

Not bothering to dry himself, he stepped out of the shower and hurried as fast as his pathetic body would allow him, through to the kitchen where he had left his medication.

Grabbing hold of the tablets and injections, be crashed onto the sofa, and loaded the painkillers into his blood as fast as he could.

Slowly the pain subsided, and his brain began to clear.

Andy smiled and almost laughed.

He'd just discovered the perfect cure for hangovers. Shame he wouldn't live long enough to market it.

As the pain left, and a semblance of being and feeling normal began to return to Andy's cancer ridden body, he saw for the first time the letter that Ray had taped to the television.

Hauling himself up out of the sofa he retrieved the letter, turned it over a few times in his hands, and then ripped it open.

Laying the letter on the granite of the island and smoothing it out with one hand, he steadied himself against one of the chairs and read the letter.

For the first time since he woke he thought of Ray.

Obviously the man had gone. Probably to his death. It was unlikely that Andy would ever see him again.

Andy frowned as he read the letter, swearing a few times, and laughing at the naivety of the man who had written it.

"Fucking idiot!" Andy swore aloud. "Idiot!"

Did Ray think that a few words on a piece of paper could take away all the years of planning? Alter a course which was destined to guarantee Andy a place in the history books? Make him the most feared and powerful hacker in the world?

Fuck, no.

Andy laughed. There was, after all, some irony to the situation.

If it wasn't for Ray, Andy wouldn't have been able to execute the best part of the plan. It was only thanks to Ray that so many people might die.

Andy crossed to the sideboard and poured himself another glass of whisky. The hair of the dog. Just a small glass. Just enough to take away the edge ...of reality.

It was a shame in a way, Andy thought to himself, because genuinely he did like the man. Ray Luck was actually an okay guy. It was just a shame he was such a pussy. A wimp. A fool.

Not like himself. Strong. Determined. Righteous.

Thankfully, in spite of being drunk, Andy had managed to refrain from telling Ray the best part of the plan. The pièce de résistance.

Actually, there were two best parts of the plan...one new and exciting that Ray himself had thrown into the mix without Andy even thinking about.

The other, something that Andy had always wondered if it was possible, but now knew was.

A couple of months ago Andy had managed to hack into the servers and programs that controlled the Thames Barrier. Over and over again he had watched the dashboards and control panels as the barriers had been raised and lowered, and he had figured out just exactly how it was done.

Although he hadn't yet done it himself, he was almost 99% confident that on Friday afternoon, about the same time as high tide, he was going to be able to lower the Thames Barrier.

Which without doubt at this time of year and according to the tidal charts, would lead to London being flooded.

In his mind, Andy could almost hear Ray whimpering about how many people would die as the waters cascaded down into the underground tunnels and drowned commuters and tourists in their thousands.

Wimp.

"And what *was* wrong with that? We all have to die some time!" Andy thought to himself, more realistically.

And the gift that Ray had given him?

"Hah!" Andy laughed, carrying the glass of whisky and the bottle with him down to his underground den in the vaults. "The video!"

Andy had already got it all planned out.

Originally he had planned to start Friday with a bang by publishing the video to the world at 8.45 a.m. A precursor to the rest of the day's activities. A day that the world would never forget, and many Londoner's would never survive.

Ray Luck was a fool. Ray had trusted him and believed him when Andy had said that he had not copied the video and that he had deleted the recordings he had on his servers.

"What the fuck? Did you think I was going to pass that gift horse up? Idiot!" Andy swore aloud, the whisky already beginning to mix with the river of fresh painkillers flowing in his veins. "By Friday evening, after everyone has seen the video and found out the truth, the British government will be in turmoil, and may already have fallen! Just when a panicking London will need strong leadership, when the city and the financial world is reeling from my cyber attacks, and the city has been flooded. By Saturday the government will be destroyed, and so will London!"

Andy laughed, and leaned against the door to steady himself as he fiddled with the key to open the door, pressed a fingerprint against the scanner and then typed in his pin code.

Andy wasn't an idiot though. He knew that with Ray disappearing this morning, - off to meet Randolph Best and possibly his maker shortly afterwards! - that perhaps he'd better move things up a bit. Instead of waiting till Friday, maybe he should release the video this morning.

Like now.

Just in case Ray struck some sort of deal, and then came back, safe and sound, with his fucking girlfriend set free, or something...

Whatever...

And actually, *ACTUALLY*...it might not be such a bad idea after all. If Ray released the video today, *this morning*... then firstly, it would really, *really* piss that smarmy bastard Ray Luck off completely. And secondly...(another large sip of the whisky)... it would make double sure, triple, even quadruple sure that the bloody government would be gone by Friday. And that would absolutely, fucking *ABSOLUTELY* guarantee that the chaos he would cause on Friday would have its desired effect with no one in control to stop it!

"Sounds like a plan, Stan." Andy said to himself as he sat down in his black swivel chair in front of the Starship Enterprise, and started planning to go boldly where no other hacker had ever gone before.

Drunk. Dying. Desperate.

And once again in pain.

Topping up his glass and taking another sip of his whisky, he blinked, cleared his eyes, and tried to remember just what he had to do to publish the video online.

He knew he'd already partially set it up to go...but he just couldn't remember at that very moment, exactly what else he had to do to make it happen.

Closing his eyes, he gripped hold of the edge of the chair and let another wave of pain wash over him.

That scared him.

For the first time ever, even the combination of the drink and the drugs wasn't able to mask the agony he was in.

As the wave of pain passed, it had the unexpected benefit of clearing his head, and suddenly he remembered just what he had to do.

Actually, it wasn't much. It would only take about thirty minutes!

10.10 a.m.

Mayfair

Ray stood across the road from the entrance to the address that he had scribbled down from the email which Best had sent him.

As Ray had expected, the building oozed wealth: a prime address in the centre of London, flash cars parked outside, and not one but two doormen at the front of the building, each wearing a smart red suit and a hat.

As he stood watching, several other women in burqas with children walked into the reception area, the doormen tipping their hats and smiling at them. Probably rich oil money, maybe wives of Arab Sheiks. Ray would blend right in, without raising an eyebrow.

Ray looked up, scanning the front of the building, guessing which of the flats would be Best's.

He would find out sooner rather than later.

The traffic was surprisingly busy, and Ray had to dodge in and out of the cars as he crossed the road.

He headed straight to the front entrance, walking with purpose and confidence, pretending as if he lived there.

The two doormen at the front of the building scanned him quickly as he walked towards them, and one of them stepped towards him.

"Damn," Ray thought to himself, "They're going to stop me."

"Good morning, Ma'am," one of them said. "Can we help you?"

Ray stopped, momentarily wondering how to react. He looked quickly around, and noticing a CCTV camera up above the entrance, he quickly looked away from it.

"I'm here to see Randolph Best. He's expecting me." Ray replied, suddenly even more nervous than he'd been.

What if they stopped him now, and he didn't even get as far as meeting Best?

He'd already scanned the streets around to see if there were any obvious signs of police or anyone else suspicious who could be waiting for him, but it had all seemed fine.

The doorman was obviously surprised by the male voice that came from behind the burqa, and was momentarily taken aback. But only for a second.

"Your name?"

Ray noticed that this time around he didn't say Ma'am or even Sir.

"Ray Luck."

Without further hesitation the doorman raised his arm to his mouth and spoke to his sleeve.

"Mr Luck is here. I'm bringing him in," the doorman said, then looked up and focussed on Ray. "Please come with me, Mr Luck."

The man nodded at the other doorman, and as Ray followed the first man in through the main door to the building, the other doorman followed right behind.

The first doorman walked across to a room behind a large, marble reception desk, the door opening in front of him as he approached.

The first doorman stepped through, and Ray followed him, noting that the second doorman remained outside in the reception area.

Inside the room a large man with a military style crew cut, wearing a smart black suit was waiting for him.

He had an ear-piece in one ear, and as he opened his arms out towards Ray, Ray noticed a gun-holster hanging down underneath his arm inside his jacket. In one hand the man had an airport style metal detector. He waved it gently at Ray.

"Please. Step this way. I need to search you."

Ray hesitated.

"Mr Luck, it's standard precautions for anyone who enters Mr Best's private apartments unescorted. Please comply," the man urged.

Ray nodded, shrugged his shoulders and stepped forward.

The security guard - Ray wondered if he was Security Service, the police or some form of private security - coughed, and nodded towards the burqa.

"Excuse me, Mr Luck. May I ask you to remove your...robe."

Ray looked down at his black burqa, having forgotten that he was wearing it.

Taking it off, he let it fall to the ground.

He stepped forward and lifted his hands, watching the security guard's eyes as the man stepped forward and started scanning Ray's body and clothes and patting him down.

The detector beeped a couple of times and Ray had to empty his pockets, and then remove his shoes, replacing them after they had been checked.

Finally satisfied, the man stepped back, and requested some ID.

Ray handed him the passport that he had been carrying with him since he'd started out on the run.

The security guard scanned the picture on the passport and scrutinised Ray's face.

"Please tell me where you were born and your date of birth?" the man suddenly asked.

Ray was surprised. They never did this at the airport!

He answered.

"And now, what school did you go to and how many A-levels did you get?"

"Why do you need to know?"

"We don't. We know already. We know everything about you Mr Luck. We just need to check that you know. That you are who you say you are."

"Five. Four A's and a B, in case you want to ask that too. And Milford High."

"Thank you."

"Did I pass?"

The man stared at him, acknowledging the stupidity of the question and cautioning him against further silly remarks.

"Mr Best is expecting you. I will take you to him now."

Ray felt a sudden rush of relief. As soon as he had been taken into the room, he was sure that he was going to be arrested, there and then.

The tall security guard waved his hand slowly towards the door, indicating that Ray should walk back out.

Bending down and picking up the burqa, Ray complied.

As he walked out the door, the doorman led the way towards a lift, and the security guard walked closely behind.

At the lift, the doorman swiped a card through a card reader and the lift door opened.

They all stepped inside.

This was the other moment that Ray was dreading. Would they press "B" for basement, take him downstairs to the garage and bundle him into the back of a waiting car, or would they press a number and take him up into the building above to one of the apartments.

Ray swallowed hard, gripping the burqa tightly in his hand.

The security guard stepped around Ray, pressed a finger against a panel on the wall of the lift - some sort of fingerprint scanner - and then typed in P2 onto a keypad below the scanner.

"P?" Ray asked, almost without thinking.

"Penthouse." The security guard replied monotonically. "Mr Best's private accommodation."

Ray smiled.

He'd got past the first hurdle. He was in the door.

Chapter 45

London

Monday

October 8th

Mayfair

10.15 a.m.

Ferris sat outside in the van studying a rerun of the video for the third time.

There had been something funny about the way the woman in the burqa had been stopped outside the entrance. Both doormen had been immediately on the alert, and when one of them had challenged her, he'd spoken into his microphone, and then personally escorted her into the building.

It was almost as if they'd been waiting for her.

From this angle in the van, Ferris couldn't see the front of the woman, but when he zoomed the video in to study the face of the doorman, he'd noticed a surprised look appear on his face, just after he'd spoken to the woman.

Ferris wanted to get a closer look at the woman.

He switched the CCTV feed to the one that came from the camera above the entrance. They'd long since bugged the camera, and now routinely recorded everyone going into the building, on a four hour loop.

Ferris wound the latest recording back to the moment the woman first appeared in shot, and studied what he could see of her face.

Zooming in closer he noticed something odd.

Although the pixelation was poor, and he couldn't make much more out, Ferris could swear that the woman had blue eyes.

Blue eyes?

And she had white skin.

That much he was sure about.

Was it common for women from the Middle East to have blue eyes? Possibly.

Ferris didn't know.

After that the woman disappeared, following the man inside.

Still, there was something odd there that Ferris couldn't quite put his finger on.

He turned to the notebook on his laptop and recorded his thoughts, and described what had just happened.

Just in case it was significant later on.

Ferris trusted his instinct.

Something had just happened, of significance.

What that significance was Ferris did not yet know, but given time, Ferris would figure it out.

10.23 a.m.

Mayfair

When the lift opened on the tenth and top floor, Ray followed the security guard out, flanked by the doorman.

They stepped out into a short hallway, with an impressive looking door at either end of it.

The security guard turned right, walked six steps towards a door and stopped.

He turned to face Ray.

"We'll be standing outside. Right here. Mr Best gave strict instructions that you were to be left alone."

"Thank you," Ray replied, not really knowing what else he should say.

"I need to warn you, just in case you were thinking of trying anything stupid once you got inside, Mr Best knows how to handle himself. If you made a move, did anything silly, Mr Best could kill you in a second without thinking about it. Do you understand me? That's why he's so confident about seeing you alone. He's not scared of anyone. I know who you are, Ray Luck. If I hear one thing wrong, I'll be straight through that door, and I'll take you out with one shot. DO. YOU. UNDERSTAND?" The man warned again, this time slightly opening his jacket and showing the gun in the shoulder holster.

"Completely. Do anything silly, and I'm dead. Don't worry. I won't."

"Good."

The security guard looked at the doorman and nodded slightly at him, before turning around and ringing the doorbell three times in quick succession, slipping a key in the door and opening it up.

"In you go," the guard ordered. "Mr Best will be waiting for you in the drawing room. Turn left and walk to the end of the hall."

Ray smiled, nervously, and still carrying his burqa, stepped into the hallway beyond.

The security guard closed the door behind him.

Ray walked down the corridor slowly.

A voice called out.

"Ray? Please come through..."

Ray stopped for a second, the sound of his heart pounding against his ribcage so loud that he was convinced that whoever the voice belonged to must be able to hear him.

He gathered his wits, and then continued forwards, coming to a door and then pushing it gently open.

He stepped into the room beyond.

It was a large room.

Opulent.

Spacious.

A high-ceiling, with a grand, white marble fireplace with three comfortable sofas edging a large, plush, hand-woven Persian carpet in front of the hearth.

Two large arrangements of flowers stood on a marble table against the wall on the left, filling the room with the smell of roses and lilies.

Light flooded into the room from the right: large, spacious windows, before which stood a large, grand man.

Even from the several metres away, Ray was surprised by the aura and charisma that exuded from the man.

He was tall, powerfully built, straight-as-a-rod, tanned, and handsome.

Very handsome.

"Ah...finally, we meet!" the man said, turning towards him and stepping forward, hand outstretched. "Randolph Best. Pleased to meet you. And you must be Ray Luck?"

The man oozed charm.

With every pore in his body, Ray wanted to hate this man, but he was already finding it difficult to do so. The man was a cold blooded murderer, Ray knew, but still, it was easy to see how he had risen through the ranks to become one of the most powerful men in British and world politics.

"Hi. Yes. Ray Luck, that's me."

"Good...Listen, sorry I didn't meet you at the door. I was just checking down outside. Looking at the traffic. It's very busy today for some reason. Very busy. It's not normally like this though."

"The traffic?"

"Yes...oh, sorry, I know that's not what you are here to talk about. And neither am I. Please, let's take a seat. I'll pour us some tea, shall I?"

"Tea?"

"Yes. Or do you prefer coffee? Or something stronger?"

"No. No. Tea would be fine..."

"Good, please, why don't you make yourself comfortable?" Randolph Best gestured for Ray to take a seat on one of the sofas. A subtle gesture. Half way between an invitation and a command.

Ray complied.

Best sat down close to him and reached to the table at his side and started to pour tea into two cups.

Ray couldn't stand the civility and normality anymore.

What was this? A mind game to overpower him? To show who was in command? Or was this just the way the upper class did things?

"I have to warn you, Mr Best, that I have set up the video of you murdering Bayla Adelstein to be automatically released at 2 p.m. today. I've set it to release on all the major social media channels, and to be sent by email to the top UK and foreign newspapers and TV channels. Only I can stop it from happening. And I'll only do that if you release Emma, ...and myself..., in time for me to stop it."

"Very good. I understand, Ray. It's very enterprising of you, and very clever, and exactly what I asked you to do, if you recall. Do you mind if I call you Ray?"

"Call me whatever you want. I don't care. So long as you release Emma."

"Milk? Sugar?"

"Just milk...what's going on here?" Ray couldn't take it any longer. "What's with the tea and biscuits? You murdered someone, you've kidnapped and tortured my girlfriend. And all you want to do is drink tea?"

"Wrong, Ray. You're wrong on every count." Best put down the teapot, and turned to face Ray more directly, giving him all of his attention. Ray looked straight into his deep blue eyes, and for an instant, saw something. A flicker of emotion.

Was it fear?

Or something else.

Perhaps anger.

The moment passed and it was gone.

"Ray, I invited you here today for a reason. Several reasons actually. I wanted to talk to you in private, and to show you something, personally. For your eyes only. You see, you have just accused me of several very, very serious things, and none of them are true, and I am going to prove it to you."

"What do you mean?"

"I didn't murder Bayla Adelstein. Not at all. And I didn't have anything to do with kidnapping your girlfriend Emma. Don't worry, I've already ensured that she will be okay. As soon as you told me about what had happened, I made some enquiries and have ordered that she should not be harmed. Furthermore, once we have concluded our conversation here, so long as we part friends, not enemies, then she shall be set free immediately."

Ray listened to every word Randolph Best uttered. He knew now that Best didn't mince words.

"She'll be set free? As soon as I leave?"

"You have my word...as long as you and I reach an understanding, and I can convince you that I didn't murder Miss Adelstein."

"But I saw you. I saw you kill her. I watched you with my own eyes!"

"Aha... there we have it! You see, you saw me kill her, but you didn't see me murder her."

"What? What do you mean? Please, stop playing games..."

"Ray, I mean, yes, yes you are right. I did kill her. Yes I did. But no, I didn't murder her..."

"Semantics. Stop playing games with words. I saw you bloody murder her!" Ray said, raising his voice and jumping to his feet.

Randolph Best looked up at him, and studied his face for a second.

"Please, ...please sit. I have something to tell you. Something you may find difficult to believe, but something that is nevertheless completely true."

Ray hesitated for a second, but Randolph Best's eyes were locked with his and didn't waver. Almost from sheer force of will, Ray felt the need to sit down...to do as he was bid. He hated the feeling.

"Please, Ray. Sit, and relax. And I think we should both have a drink. Forget the tea,...I need a brandy. And you?"

"What...? A drink? No...Actually, fuck it. Yes, please. A large brandy would be good."

Ray sat down.

What the hell was going on here?

Best stood up and stepped away for a few moments, making his way to a drinks cabinet in one of the corners, and returning quickly with two glasses of brandy.

"Here you go. Cheers."

Ray took the glass, and watched as Best knocked his whole glass back in one.

"Okay. So. No more word games, just straight talk, okay?" Best said, sitting down again and relaxing back into the sofa.

"Please."

"Ray. I didn't murder her. I loved her. And I did kill her. But only because she tried to murder me. It was self-defence. Purely self-defence."

Ray blinked.

Shit, he had never thought of that.

"Ray, I've now seen your video. I hadn't seen it all properly before, because I was travelling...in the Middle East, on government business, trying to finalise the peace deal. And in the video you can only see me approaching her from one side. I can understand why you thought that I had murdered her...but the video is misleading. What you can't see is that she had a knife in her bag, and that as I approached her she pulled it out and lunged at me. I just reacted, grabbed the knife and defended myself. There was a struggle, and I was forced to fight for my life. It was a close call..."

"But you're a trained killer...I've read all about you, and the muscle man at the door drummed it into my head before he let me in that you could kill me without blinking if I tried anything stupid...She would have had no chance... Even if she had attacked you, you didn't need to kill her..."

"She was a trained assassin, Ray. I didn't know it until too late. And believe me, it was either her or me. She was good, very good. She almost got me. I was just a little bit better, that's all. I was lucky."

"An assassin?"

"Yes. We believe she was working for an Israeli Intelligence agency."

"Mossad?"

"Perhaps. It hasn't been confirmed yet."

"Are you joking?"

"No."

"Bloody hell..." Ray looked at the glass of brandy in his hand, then quickly downed it all in one. "And this is true? All true?"

"Yes. Honestly. Which is why I invited you here today. To prove it to you. You see, it was in the room next door where I killed her..."

"Here? In this flat?"

"Yes. But before I show you anything, you and I need to talk about something. Something of national security. And of global importance. Something that could and will affect the lives of millions, maybe billions of people."

"What do you mean?"

"Do you love your country, Ray? I know that you used to be an anarchist, but from what I understand you've been steering away from that recently and have become a good citizen. Your colleagues at CSD speak only in the most glowing terms about you..."

"What? You've spoken to the people at CSD?"

"Ray. We know everything about you. Of course we have. I needed to know more about you. At this point in time, you have the potential to bring down the British government and destroy the peace process in the Middle East. Your actions could cause the deaths of thousands, maybe millions, and set the world on a course towards a third world war from which it would be very difficult to ever recover. Of course we had to know everything about you!"

Ray stood up.

"Wooahh! Steady on. You're going way too fast. What the hell are you talking about? Third world war? Destroying the peace process? What on earth are you going on about?"

"Ray, it may sound hard to believe, but the night you saw me defend myself against Bayla Edelstein - with whom incidentally I had fallen in love and by whom I was completely fooled, but that's another story - the night you saw me kill Bayla..." Best coughed, and momentarily looked upwards, before fixing his gaze back on Ray... his voice once again steady, "was the night you inadvertently became a pawn in world politics. And may I say, one of the most powerful players on the world stage. And you still are. Until you agree not to release the video, and delete it."

"I don't understand. How can what I do be so important?"

"Don't worry. I'll explain. But first, please, let's go through to the bedroom where I killed Bayla, and I'll show you the truth behind what you think you saw."

Chapter 46

London

Monday

October 8th

Randolph Best's Flat

Mayfair

London

10.45 a.m.

The moment they entered the bedroom, Ray recognised it. He'd seen it a hundred times before, every time he had watched the video.

He walked quickly over to where the large SMART television used to be against the wall, although now there was none.

"I learned my lesson," Randolph said. "People always say it's not good to have a TV in the bedroom, and they were right..."

Ray looked down at the floor where he had seen Bayla's dead body, her face and eyes so void of life, staring so vacantly at the camera which had fallen on the floor beside her.

"I can't believe I'm here." Ray said.

"I'm glad you are. At least now you can find out the truth. If only the bloody idiots at the SIS had arranged this all earlier, none of the rest of this would have been necessary."

"SIS?"

"The Secret Intelligence Service...what used to be called MI6. This is an international issue, and comes under their jurisdiction."

"Why?"

"Bayla was a spy. She'd tried to destroy the peace process in the Middle East by killing me..." Randolph's voice tapered off again. Ray took a moment to look around the bedroom.

"New carpet?"

"Yes. There was a lot of blood. They ripped it out and incinerated it somewhere."

"Can I look around?"

"Sure."

Ray walked over to the bathroom from which, in the video, Best had emerged in semi-darkness, the images of which he'd had cleaned up and enhanced by Andy.

Randolph gave Ray a moment to absorb the room, the scene of the so-called crime. He watched Ray walk around the room. Ray was about to move over to the window and look out when Randolph warned him.

"No...please, don't go there. Just in case anyone see's you."

"Who? Who would be looking?"

"I'll tell you in a moment. But first, can I show you something?" Randolph asked.

"Come over here, and look up there..." Randolph said, pointing to a wall light, high up on the wall near the door frame through which Ray had just passed to go and look in the toilet and walk-in shower.

"What am I looking at?" Ray asked, a little confused.

"It's a light. But it's also hiding a camera. Part of the internal CCTV that I have in every room. No one else knows about it. Only you. And look, there's another one here in the walk-in wardrobe..." Randolph took a few steps into a small room that led off the bedroom, and pointed at another light, "...and over here...just beside the entrance door."

Ray followed him over and looked at the light on the wall beside the entrance into the room.

"CCTV?"

"Yes," Randolph replied, seeing a little light switching on inside Ray's mind. He already knew what Randolph was going to say next.

"And they were all working the night you murdered Bayla?"

"Killed Bayla! In self-defence! And yes, they were. Come over here, I want to show you what they recorded."

Randolph walked over to the bed, and lifted up a pillow, pulling a laptop out from underneath. He opened it up and put it on the bed.

Ray stood beside him.

Randolph asked, "Ready?" and then pressed play on the movie file that appeared on the screen.

"This is what the camera beside the doorway near the bathroom caught. At the beginning of the video sequence I am in the bathroom just behind and underneath it. In a moment you'll see me step out and walk across to her...the rest is obvious. I'll let you see for yourself."

Ray watched transfixed as he saw an image of the woman in the centre of the screen.

She was getting dressed.

Once again Ray was reminded of how attractive Bayla Adelstein had been.

"She was beautiful, wasn't she?" Randolph said, softly.

It was a strange question. Given the circumstances. Then without making any comment in reply, Randolph added, "I loved her."

Ray half-turned to look at Randolph standing beside him, but his attention was immediately drawn back to the screen by Randolph's voice, shouting something in the video. Unseen, the voice came from the bathroom, just as Ray remembered in his version of events.

Bayla was dressed now, and was bending over her overnight bag, taking something out.

"Look...see there!" Randolph said, pointing to the screen.

Bayla had just removed a long knife from inside her bag and had slipped it into the side of her bag. Ray saw the blade flash momentarily in the light.

She stood up straight.

"Please, come back here!" she shouted to Randolph, who was still in the bathroom.

"Where are you going?" Ray heard Randolph ask. "You can't leave. Not now."

"I go!" Bayla shouted back at him, Randolph still off-camera, directly underneath and slightly to the side of the camera. "You bastard. I leave now."

Ray saw Randolph emerge from the doorframe underneath, and walk across the room towards the woman. Unlike in his version, this time Ray was watching Best from behind, the woman on the other side of the room. However, the position of the camera on the wall to the side of the doorframe meant that the view of the woman and Randolph as they came together was slightly from the side.

"Don't go. There's something else I have for you," Randolph said, just exactly as Ray remembered.

He saw Bayla hesitate.

"Perhaps, " she replied. "Come here..."

Beside Ray, Randolph stiffened, in anticipation of what was going to happen next.

"Watch carefully," he said, unnecessarily, from his side.

On screen, Ray watched Randolph move towards Bayla. He slipped his hands inside her coat, pulling her gently towards him.

The handbag around Bayla's neck slid forwards over her shoulder and in front of her.

Best and Bayla were both kissing, and Ray could once again hear the sounds of what had previously sounded as though Bayla was getting aroused and lost in the moment.

Except in this version of events, Ray could clearly see that Bayla was faking it, making sure that she was distracting Randolph's attention.

Ray saw that Bayla's eyes were wide open, and he watched, almost in disbelief, as her free right hand reached forward and into the side of the bag which had swung in front of her, quickly pulling out the long knife.

As in Ray's version of the video, what happened next, happened very fast.
Bayla stepped back from Randolph, creating a small distance between them, and giving her room to manoeuvre the knife.
Although Ray couldn't see Randolph's face, he heard him shout something - he still couldn't make out what - at the same time reaching out and grabbing the knife which he had just seen.
No, Randolph had gone for the woman's wrist, not the blade.
He saw him grapple with the woman over ownership of the knife.
Bayla had tried to manipulate and push the blade towards Randolph's chest...
Randolph had taken the power of her thrust, reversed it and the blade, and pushed back...
It was over in a second.
Bayla had screamed. Randolph had shouted something, which was still indiscernible, and then Bayla had fallen against the TV and crumpled onto the floor.
Dead.

Ray stared at the screen. Dumbstruck.
And empty.

He had got it all so wrong.

11.15 a.m.

Mayfair

Ferris looked at the video of the woman in the burqa emerging from the tube station and turning to walk towards Mayfair.
Using one of the apps in his surveillance system, he had loaded up a map of all the CCTV cameras in the area, and searched for all video images which included a woman in a burqa in the past hour.
There were a lot, but together he and his team had managed to trace the steps of the woman in the burqa all the way back to the tube station from which she had emerged before turning outside the exit and making her way down to Mayfair.

To be honest, after all that effort, Ferris had not gained any new intelligence. He had hoped that he would have been able to see something else, something, anything, that might have given him some useful intel.

There was something about the woman in the burqa. Something odd.

Ferris's instinct was seldom wrong. Little alarm bells were still going off inside his head, and Ferris was determined to figure out why.

Splicing all the video feeds together, he watched the woman walk all the way from the tube station to the front of Best's apartment block, following her along several long streets and past twenty different cameras.

True, she did walk a little strangely, not as gracefully as most women he knew, but perhaps she was wearing high-heels which made it difficult to walk, or her shoes were too tight.

Maybe she wasn't wearing shoes at all.

As she approached the apartment block on the other side of the road, she entered a blind spot and disappeared from view for quite a while.

Maybe she had gone into a shop? Or sat down on a bench?

Although she had only been just across the street it had taken a long time for her to cross the road from the last position they had seen her in.

What had she been doing?

Just standing there?

Eventually she had crossed the road through the traffic and approached the doormen.

Ferris watched the two doormen approaching the woman.

One doorman said something.

The woman replied. Once again Ferris noticed what appeared to be a slight look of surprise on the doorman's face.

He then raised his wrist and spoke into the microphone, and then said something back to the woman before they all went inside.

Why did they all go inside? Why not just have one doorman accompany the woman?

Ferris rewound that part of the video, called over his colleague from the other side of the van, and pointed at the screen.

"Davis, you're the best of all of us at lip reading. I can't make it out. Can you make out what the doorman is saying to the woman?"

The other agent looked at the screen, rewound the video and played it back a couple of times.

"I'm not completely certain. I think the doorman has an accent of some sort. But right at the beginning, here, he says 'Good morning, Ma'am. Can we help you?' "

Ferris nodded. It made sense.

"But, here... when he raises his arm and speaks into his microphone, it gets confusing. I think he says, '*Mrs* Luck is here. I'm bringing *him* in,', but when he speaks to the woman in the burqa, he definitely says, 'Please come with me, *Mr* Luck'."

Ferris swore.
Five seconds later he was on the phone to Jacobson.
Six minutes later, Jacobson was in a van and heading over to Mayfair with a special ops team of eight men.

11.20 a.m.

Randolph Best's Bedroom

Penthouse Flat

Mayfair

There was a second video: taken from the angle of the CCTV camera on the wall near the entrance door to the bedroom, it clearly showed that Bayla Edelstein had pulled a knife and thrust it out towards Randolph. Her intention had been all too clear.
She had tried to murder him.

It was obvious from the video that the woman had known exactly what she was doing. If Best had not been an expert at self-defence, and had not reacted instantly to the flash of the blade that he had seen, he would have been dead.

"She was a spy." Randolph said calmly.
"How did you meet her?" Ray asked.
"At a party, six months ago. We flirted. She asked me out. I was impressed. I said yes, and we'd been dating ever since."
"So if, as these videos so clearly prove, you only killed her in self-defence, why the big cover up? Why not just tell the truth?"
"I never showed the videos to anyone else. I didn't need to. No one else knows about them, or the CCTV system. Only you. The cameras are my secret. But I did tell everyone the truth about what happened, and no one had any reason to disbelieve me. Why should they?" Best replied. "Listen, do you mind if we go back to the other room now. I don't particularly like being in here. I always use the other bedroom now."
They walked back to the other room.
"A drink? I'm certainly having another one."

"Please," Ray replied.

He waited in silence for Best to join him and hand him his drink.

"Ray, I'm going to tell you something now that you must promise NOT to tell anyone else. Normally you would have to sign the Official Secrets Act before I said this to you, but given the circumstances in which we find ourselves and granted that you are currently probably the most wanted 'terrorist' in Europe, it seems a little stupid insisting upon it."

Ray smiled. His first smile for the past few weeks.

"Do you know anything about the Peace Process in the Middle East, and the activities that I have been spearheading for the past five years?"

Ray shook his head.

"No, I'm sorry, but no. To be truthful."

"That's a shame. I thought that as an anarchist you would be politically motivated and aware?"

Ray began to turn a little red.

"That was a while ago. I just hate authority...people telling me what to do. But I haven't had the time, or the interest really, to follow other people's problems. We've got enough in our own country."

"Which is fine. You live a busy life surviving from day to day, and we can't expect everyone to pay attention to everything that goes on outside the UK, can we? Anyway, my father was born in Egypt and I have always had an interest in the region. My mother was Jewish. Can you imagine that? An Arab marrying a Jew? Anyway, it made for an interesting upbringing. Technically, it makes me Jewish too, but my parents were very liberal and they wanted me to form my own opinions. I grew up in England, but I spent years travelling and living in the area, and then I went to university and joined the British Army."

"SAS?"

"Yes. Although that came later. And then I entered politics. Years ago I believed that the next big World War was going to start because of the developed world fighting over assets in the Middle East, but now I've changed my mind. I believe that unless we solve the problems in the Middle East, we're looking forward to decades of regional conflict throughout the Middle East and into an ever increasingly developed Africa. Wars between different countries, ruling families, different religions...but a lot of it, a lot of it starts with the conflict between the Arabs and the Jews. Between two opposing ideologies that don't *have* to live in conflict with each other, but do. We need to help them find peace, and take away the excuses for war and unrest and civil disturbance that a lot of power brokers in the region use to justify their own personal goals."

"And what happens if we don't?"

"Over the next few years you will see tens of millions, maybe hundreds of millions of people displaced from their homes through war and civil unrest, famine, starvation or persecution. And they will all head north to Europe. Looking for a better way of life. To the European Union. To the United Kingdom. We won't be able to stop them. We're talking about a mass migration of people the like of which the world has never seen before. Of course, Europe won't be able to support all of them. Economically or culturally. Our societies will begin to change. Slowly at first, but then faster and faster. There will be increasing unrest and unhappiness; as we fail to integrate the arriving masses of lost, lonely and desperate people into our cultures, our societies will fragment, and then one day we will wake up to find Europe being ripped apart at the seams and Western European Civilisation a thing of the past." Best stopped, thought for a moment, and then continued. "We have no choice. We have to help those who live in the Middle East to find peace amongst themselves. Their problems are our problems. We live in a global village now, and they are our neighbours."

"And how do you do that? How do we find peace?" Ray asked, surprised by his interest in what Best was saying.

"There are a lot of problems that need solving. But one of them is to get official recognition for the State of Palestine."

"I thought it was already a country..."

"No it isn't. A lot of other countries in the world recognise it has the right to be a country, but most of the Western World and the big players don't. There was a United Nations General Assembly resolution in 2012 which gave Palestine non-member state observer status in the UN, but even with that and so much recognition around the world, Palestine is not yet eligible to join the United Nations as an independent country. It's not a country. Yet."

"Yet?"

"It will be soon. If the all the progress we have made in the past few months continues. The signs are very positive. It could just be a matter of months!"

"Why are you telling me all of this? What's it got to do with Bayla Edelstein?"

"Because she tried to kill me to stop the Peace Process. To stop me attending the meetings last week in Cairo, Tel Aviv and Iran."

"Wow..."

"The thing is, and whether you believe me or not is up to you...it actually doesn't change things much either way, but I was in love with her. I didn't suspect for one moment that she was what she was..."

"And what was she?"

"Jewish. And working for an ultra right wing orthodox group that would do anything to stop the peace process. Until last week, I thought her name was Yara Hakimi. An Arab. I fell for it completely. We fell in love. We spent time together. Although I never told her any official secrets, she may have picked up from me a few pieces of information that could have been of interest to her group. Possibly. She certainly couldn't have got any closer to what was going on than by being with me."

"This is heavy stuff. Way more serious than I thought..."

"It gets worse, Ray. Which is why I am telling you all of this. Please, let me finish, so that you can see the bigger picture here. The thing is, after she tried to kill me..."

"To assassinate you?" Ray suggested.

"If you want to call it that, yes...anyway, after I killed her, I told the authorities everything. We discussed it and then after much careful consideration we decided that we couldn't go public with it. It was only by sheer luck that we found out her true identity. She was screened when we started going out together, and all her records backed up her claim. To all intents and purposes she was who she claimed to be ..."

"So, was she working for Mossad?"

"I can't say. And you don't really need to know. Suffice it to say, that after she died we found out who she really was, and that her real name was Bayla Edelstein, an Israeli. There was no way that we could admit that I had been sexually involved with an Israeli undercover agent, who possibly has - had direct access to the Israeli government. That in itself would wreck the peace process. All the people I've been talking to recently, Heads of State and Royal families, they would question my judgement, my loyalties, my motives. Five years of work would be wasted. The peace initiative would be over. Everyone would go their separate ways, and those lurking in the shadows would take full advantage of it all. The region would descend into chaos and there would be war. Almost guaranteed."

"I can't believe what I'm hearing..."

"Please do. Make up your own mind. But please try and see what I am telling you is the truth. So, basically, in the end, we covered up her death. We knew people would be looking for a body...there was a small leak. Someone let it out that she was dead...so we had to produce a body. But we managed to create a convincing story around her death that no one could officially question. Apart from you."

"Me?"

"Yes. You have the video. A recording of what really happened. You know the truth, or at least a version of it that you believed to be true..."

"Until now."

"So, you see, if you release the video, then everything goes pear shaped. Bayla Edelstein wins. Everyone who is opposed to the peace initiative wins. And the world loses."

"No pressure then. No pressure..."

"Ray, it's not a joke. This is totally serious. I don't want to force you to just 'say' you won't publish your video, because I know that at any time in the future you could just change your mind and do it. I truly want you to see the bigger picture, to understand what would happen if you did release that video. That's why I'm telling you all this. To help you understand."

"But you've kidnapped my girlfriend and had her locked up somewhere in Canada. How am I meant to feel about that?"

"I didn't order that. I told you that already, and hopefully now you will believe me. Ray, I really wanted to meet you this morning, personally. I'm a good judge of character and I needed to see you and size you up. I wanted to see what type of person you are. And from everything I've seen this morning, and from the initiative you took to contact me, and the things you told me then and how you said them, not only can I see that you just wandered into this whole mess completely by accident, but I am convinced that you are NOT a terrorist, as the agency would have had me believe. And I actually believe that you are a decent person. Who will do the right thing. Which is why in one minute I am going to do two things. First, I am going to call the agency that is managing the detention of Emma, and order them to release her immediately, with an option to fly her home today to the UK for free, if she wishes. And then secondly, I am going to call the Prime Minister directly, and tell him that you pose no threat to the UK and that he should rescind all messages about you being a terrorist and issue you a complete pardon. After that you will have your life back. And then you can decide what you want to do about the video..."

It took four minutes for Best to do exactly as he had just said he would for Emma. While Ray listened, he heard him call and issue stark instructions to someone who was apparently in Canada and liaising with the Canadian authorities concerning Emma's detention. Emma would be released within the next ten minutes.

Unfortunately, when Randolph tried to call the Prime Minister, he was not available to speak. He was apparently on a direct call to the President of America and did not want to be interrupted.

Randolph told him it was 'urgent' that the PM should call Randolph straight back on his private phone, ..."as soon as possible."

When Randolph hung up, he looked at Ray.
Expectantly.
"I'm doing all I can, Ray."
"Okay, okay. I know you are." Ray stood up and moved about the room. "This has all got way out of control. Listen, I know now, having seen the videos that you have, that you never wanted to kill her. In fact, you're lucky to be alive. And I get all the stuff you are telling me about the Middle East peace initiative. And there's no way that I want to cause any problems with

it. So, basically, you have my word that as soon as I have spoken to Emma and I know that she is free, that I will delete all the files."

"And you will never show them or release any hidden copies at any point in the future?"

"As long as Emma is okay, I promise."

"Excellent. Can we shake hands on it?" Randolph said, extending his hand.

Ray took his hand in his.

"So long as Emma is unharmed, I will never release the video. I promise."

They shook hands.

Ray returned to his seat and sat down.

Now the pressure was off him and Emma, it seemed hard to believe that everything might just work out after all.

No sooner had he thought it, than a new thought occurred to him: what was he going to do about Andy?

In a few days' time, Andy was going to destroy London, the banking system, and cause many unnecessary deaths.

Should he tell Randolph all about it?

Or should he try harder to stop Andy again.

What was 'the right thing to do'?

Andy was a cyber-bruv. You never ratted on a cyber-bruv.

But did that apply here?

What Andy was planning to do was way off the scale!

"Mr Best, may I borrow your phone? I urgently need to talk to someone."

"My mobile? I want to keep the mainline free in case the PM calls us back..."

"Please... that would be great."

Best fetched his phone and gave it to Ray.

"Can I step into the corridor and make a private call?"

Best nodded.

Andy's phone rang ten times before it was answered.

"Fuck me, I thought you would be dead by now!" Andy said as soon as he heard Ray's voice.

"I'm alive. They're not going to arrest me. The whole thing was a big mistake. Best didn't murder the woman. *She* tried to murder *him*... assassinate him, and he just defended himself. She was a spy trying to stop the peace process..."

"And you believed it all? Bloody hell, Ray, you know they're just fucking with your head..."

"Have you been drinking again? Are you drunk?"

"Drunk? Yes. Again? No. I never sobered up!"

"Did you get my letter?"

"The whiny piece of crap in which you begged me not to destroy London or kill anybody? *No*...I didn't get it!"

"But you read it all, right?"

"Fuck off, Luck. I'm chuffed it's all working out roses for you and that woman of yours...what was her name...? Angela?"

"No. Emma. Maybe you shouldn't be drinking so much with those drugs you're taking. You know you passed out last night?"

"It's either that or the pain. So fuck off, okay? Now, I've got to go...I'm very busy... things to do and all that..."

"Wait! " Ray shouted. "Andy...Listen, I'm coming home. We need to talk. You can't launch that cyber attack against the banking system and there's no way I can let you take out the National Grid on Friday. You can't kill people just because you're going to die!"

"No? You fucking watch me pal. Now fuck off!"

The phone went dead.

Ray stared at the phone in his hand.

What should he do now?

Go back to the church and try to talk to Andy again, or 'do the right thing' now. Perhaps he could tell Best all about what Andy was going to do, but try to cut a deal with him so that, because of the special mitigating circumstances concerning Andy's cancer, they'd go easy on Andy and not put him in prison to die. House arrest maybe. But nothing more.

He'd try one more time.

He dialled the number again.

Andy answered.

"What the fuck do you want now?"

"One minute. That's all. Please don't hang up..."

"Ray, piss off. You're interrupting me. I'm just about to put on a little show for you. I think you should switch on your TV - BBC One will do fine...or go to YouTube... Now you're all pally-pally with your new mate Mr Best, it's all down to me now, ain't it?"

"To do what?" Ray shouted, his hands beginning to tremble.

"Your fucking video, that's what. *It's time to show the world*...Give me five minutes, and I think the world will be able to see it, ...everywhere..."

Andy hung up.

The door to the lounge opened and Best came towards him.

"Is there a problem, Ray? I heard you shouting. Is there anything you need my help with? Is there something you need to tell me?"

Ray stared back at Best.
He heard Emma's voice whisper to him, "Do the right thing, Ray. Do the right thing!"
Ray swallowed hard.
Andy had left him no choice.

Chapter 47

London

Monday

October 8th

Selfridges

11.40 a.m.

Eva Baczkowski looked at herself in the mirror in the toilet of Selfridges.

In five minutes she was going to have the final interview with the HR manager for the job of her dreams.

She'd already had two interviews that morning, and both had gone well. Eva couldn't believe her luck.

Since coming to England everything had gone so well.

She loved it here!

As she adjusted her lipstick, smoothed down her dress and checked her hair, appraising herself one final time, she thought for a second about how pleased her mother would be if she got the job.

She would be so proud.

Eva would be so proud.

"Please, please, *please* let me get the job!" she prayed silently in her native Polish mother tongue.

She checked her watch.

She'd better hurry.

If all went well, in less than fifteen minutes she could be starting a new life!

11.41 a.m.

A Plumber's Van

Mayfair

Ferris's face lit up like a Christmas tree.
He couldn't believe it. He'd just struck gold.

After all the fuck ups, all the mistakes, with what he'd just heard, he was going to redeem himself in spades.

For the past two years, long before Unicorn had killed the Israeli spy, Ferris had been monitoring and following him.

All his personal communications were routinely monitored.

Occasionally they learned about something which seemed to interest those above him, and which excited Jacobson.

This certainly would.

Ferris had just started listening to a phone conversation made using Randolph's mobile.

He'd expected to hear Best talking to someone.

Just a few minutes before Best had talked to the section head in Canada, and then immediately afterwards he had called the Prime Minister from his landline.

But then someone had called a number in London, which according to the map on his screen, was a Church in Stratford.

When the phone was answered, Ray Luck had come on the line!

Bingo!

As the conversation played out, Ferris started to get excited. This was brilliant.

Ferris had just uncovered a plot against the banking system and the Critical National Infrastructure: someone was going to take out the National Grid!

Then suddenly the man at the other end hung up.

Ferris looked at his watch. Jacobson and the special ops team should arrive in Mayfair at any moment.

Ferris was still wearing the earphones when a light on the dashboard started flashing. Ferris selected the link and started listening in again.

Ray was calling the man back.

Two minutes later Ferris was on the phone to Jacobson.

"The shit's about to hit the fan. An accomplice of Ray's is about to release the video of Adelstein's murder to the world. I reckon we've got minutes."

Two minutes later a helicopter took off from central London carrying eight men.

It's destination the church in Stratford.

11.45 a.m.

Whitehall

Rowlinson picked up after three rings.

He listened patiently as Jacobson explained the sequence of events that were unfolding, and assured him that everything was being done that could be done.

"And where are you?"

"I'm on the way with the ops team to visit Randolph Best to apprehend Ray Luck."

"Good. Good. And where did you say this Church is?"

"Stratford. The team will be there within minutes."

"Excellent." Rowlinson replied. "Excellent. Tell them to secure the area, and the suspect there. But tell them NOT to touch anything. Nothing at all. Do you understand?"

"Yes."

"Good. I'm on my way over there too. Text me the address."

At the other end of the call, Jacobson frowned.

"And Jacobson..." Rowlinson continued. "Once you get to Mayfair, don't go in until I give you the all clear. Stand down, until I say go? Do you understand?"

"But Luck could get away again..."

"I said do nothing, until I give you the authority and direction to go in. Do you understand me?"

"Yes, sir. I understand." Jacobson replied.

But in truth, he didn't.

11.47 a.m.

Randolph Best's Penthouse Flat

Mayfair

Randolph Best closed the front door to his penthouse flat.

Two minutes before there had been a series of loud knocks. It was the security guard standing outside in the corridor, guarding the door with the other doorman.

They had heard the shouting and wanted to know if everything was okay.

Best had opened up, showing them Ray in the corridor and promised them that everything was fine.

In fact, he gave permission for both men to return to base.

"The threat from Ray Luck here is over." Best rested his hand gently on Ray's shoulder. "It's been a terrible misunderstanding. When he leaves here this morning, he'll be a free man again. He no longer poses us any threat."

"You are ordering us to stand down, sir?" the agent in the suit questioned him.

"Yes sir, I am. But thanks for your help. I appreciate it."

The two security guards looked at Best, and then at Ray, then nodded and turned towards the lift.

Best turned to Ray.

"So, who is this man you were shouting at just now. Do you think he will go ahead with the threat?"

"I don't know. I think so. He is a fellow hacker. We met years ago. We shared similar interests..."

"Anarchy?"

"Exactly. I grew out of it. He didn't. He was the one that helped me clean up the graphic files so we could see your face - at first the image was too dark to make you out. He must have kept a file on his servers. He promised me he'd deleted it. When I went on the run a few days ago, his was the only place I could think of going. He put me up and hid me. Nobody would know about him. We got on well. I thought he was a friend. But now it looks like he was just using me."

"So, what can we do about it? If he releases the video we still lose everything."

"And Emma? And me?"

Best didn't hesitate.

"I gave you my word that she'd be released. You heard me talk to Canada already. And the same goes with you. As soon as the PM calls back, I'll request that he clears your name."

"Why can't you do it?"

"I'm the Foreign Secretary, not the Home Secretary. I need to get the PM onboard. Don't worry. It'll be fine. But now, I think I need to call someone. I have to inform the SIS what your friend is about to do. Maybe we can stop him. Block his internet access, and prevent him from..."

"That wouldn't work. Everything would have been hosted and programmed in the Cloud. All you can do is send somebody round to try and prevent him issuing the command which will instruct his cloud-based programmes to publish the video, but once he issues that instruction it will be too late. I think it probably already is. Anyway, there's something else I also need to tell you! Something that could be *even* more important.

Something which would have an immediate direct impact on our national security and our economy..."

Just then the phone rang, interrupting them. Best glanced at the display and recognised the number of the caller immediately.

"Prime Minister? Is that you? Thanks for calling back so quickly, but I can hardly hear you. Are you on your mobile? Okay, good. That's better..."

Ray listened as Best first of all reported to the PM about his meeting with himself, and then requested the PM to immediately arrange a cancellation of all terrorist alerts regarding Ray, with immediate cancellation of any charges against him.

"He's here right now...may I hand the phone to him?"

Ray was caught off-guard.

One moment he was the enemy of the state, the next the Prime Minister was congratulating him for his bravery and honesty, and apologising for the mess that both sides had got themselves into.

Ray was speechless. He stumbled his words, said a few stupid things that he'd always be embarrassed about, and pushed the phone back towards Best, mouthing, 'We need to talk...quickly...!"

Ray could see that Best was trying to get off the phone, but the PM was now engaging him in something else, a matter of state that was obviously important.

Ray pointed towards his watch.

"Prime Minister, I'm sorry to interrupt you, but there's been a development. We may have a problem..."

Again Ray heard Best starting to engage with the PM, explaining the problem with the video that could be released at any moment.

Ray was growing increasingly impatient. All the time that Best was talking to the Prime Minister, realisation of the magnitude of the problem that they were facing was growing inside of Ray.

Ray was getting scared.

What if Andy brought 'Friday' forward? He was obviously unstable now. What if he flipped and changed the day the attack was going to be launched? Would he do it today? Tomorrow? Was Andy even planning anything else that Ray didn't know about?

And what happened if Best sent a SWAT team in to capture him, Andy heard them coming and then set everything off now. Immediately!

After all, he'd have nothing to lose.

Ray had to tell Best everything.

Everything.

And now!

He pointed at this watch again and made a face at Best, who was still talking to the Prime Minister.

Ray's impatience grew and grew until eventually he leant forward and put his finger down on the receiver of the phone Best was talking into, cutting him off from the Prime Minister.

Best stared at him.

"What the hell do you think you're doing? That was the Prime Minister of the United Kingdom you just cut off..."

"I'm sorry, but I need to tell you everything. And *now*. The video is only one thing. The other things that Andy is planning to do are far, far worse...we have to stop him. *Now*..."

11.53 a.m.

The Church

Near Stratford

Rowlinson accepted the helping hand as he climbed down from the helicopter, and was then quickly ushered into the black car which was waiting to rush him from the recreation park he'd landed in to the church only two minutes away.

"The house is secure, sir." The man who had helped him explained. "There was one occupant. He claims to be a Mr Ray Luck, but our records show that he is a Mr Andy Grentham. He was apprehended in a room in the old vaults of the church, which is obviously his command centre of operations. As far as we can make out he's half drunk and high on drugs."

"What was he doing when you moved in? Did he resist?"

"There was no resistance. He just stared at us. Watching. To be quite honest, he's pretty far gone, sir. But he was sitting in front of several computer terminals. He claims he was just about to bring the government down. To 'show the world the truth', whatever he means by that."

"Where is he now?"

"Still in the room, handcuffed to the door. We have not touched anything, just as ordered."

"Excellent. How many are inside?"

"Six."

"Pull them out from the cellar. I only want you and I downstairs, with two men upstairs. Keep your sidearm handy, just in case. The others should take up positions in the neighbourhood, but maintain vigilance."

"Yes, sir," the agent replied, before speaking into his radio and issuing several commands.

By the time Rowlinson followed the agent into the church, the other agents had taken up their new deployments as ordered.

As soon as Rowlinson entered the computer den in the vault downstairs, the agent who was supervising the man handcuffed to the door, left and disappeared upstairs.

Rowlinson was alone with the man and the agent in command.

Rowlinson turned his attention to agent beside him.

"I'm sorry, could you please get me a coffee from the kitchen. I'm desperate for some caffeine."

Rowlinson saw the hesitation in the agent's eyes.

"Don't worry. I'll be okay for a few minutes. He's not going anywhere."

The agent looked at Andy, and then nodded, and quickly left the cellar.

"What is your name?" Rowlinson asked Andy softly, moving to the end of the room and sitting down in the leather chair in front of the computer screens.

"Fuck off..." the man slurred in reply.

Rowlinson laughed.

"That's a rather odd name. I thought you said it was Ray Luck?"

The man's eyes, half-closed and glazed over, opened slightly.

"Yep. That's me. Ray Luck."

"Or maybe not. Ray Luck is a well known cyber expert. But from what I can see here, you're a bit of an amateur..."

The man's eyes opened wide.

"Bastard!"

"Who? Me or Mr Luck?"

"Both of you. You're both bastards."

"You're probably right, Mr Grentham. Or can I call you Andy?"

"Can I call you 'cunt'?"

"If you wish. I don't mind. Now...let me see, what is it that we have here?

What is it exactly that you are trying to do?"

Andy was silent.

"My men tell me that you were saying something about 'bringing the government down?' And 'showing the world the truth?' Am I right? Do you think you're capable of doing that? You look pretty much the worse for wear, from what I can see? I guess that must be the combination of alcohol and the drugs you're taking to ward off the pain that's slowly crushing the life out of you? Am I right?"

Andy raised his eyebrows.

"Oh, don't worry. I know a lot about you Mr Grentham. I read your intelligence file on the way over, along with your medical records, and a few other little bits and pieces of information we've accumulated on you over the years. In particular I find it very interesting that in the last few weeks or months of your life you are still dreaming about pulling off the biggest cyber attack in the world. I find that very interesting indeed. To be quite honest, although we know a lot about what it is you are planning to do, we don't yet know it all. So, I'm here to cut you a deal. If you tell us everything that you were planning to do this Friday...aha, *yes*, we do know about the date...well, if you share your little plans with us today, or tomorrow, then we will make sure you get the morphine and the other drugs that keep your pain at bay. We're nice that way, Mr Grentham. Honestly, we are. However, and there is always a 'but' in life, don't you find? - until you tell us, we won't give you any access to medication or medical help. But we'll respect your right to privacy and put you in a cell to sleep your hangover off. Alone. Without any drugs. In a padded cell where no one can hear you scream. Does that sound fair?"

Rowlinson only had to look at Andy once to see the terror in his eyes. The threat of living without pain relief was more than he would be able to bear. Sure, while he was drunk, he might hold out for a few hours, but from what Rowlinson had learnt from the medical report he had read, he was sure that it would only be a matter of hours before Andy Grentham started to scream and plead for painkillers and tell them everything they needed.

Who needed torture, or water-boarding, when you had mother nature on your side?

Rowlinson turned his attention back to the computer terminals. He scanned the screens, quickly taking in the information they presented him with.

"So, Mr Grentham. It looks to me like you were about to initiate a program on this terminal which would load the video of Mr Best murdering that poor woman, onto the internet, and so that it would also play on national television services?"

As he spoke, he turned and watched Andy's face for recognition. He saw it immediately in the slight flicker of his eyes.

"So, what exactly happens if I click on here? Does it initiate your program...? *Yes?*" Once again Rowlinson saw the recognition in the man's eyes.

"So, why didn't you do it? Having second thoughts about the repercussions of your actions? Too scared to do it?"

Rowlinson watched the man on the floor, cowering in the doorway. He saw the confusion and conflict of emotions boiling away within him.

Rowlinson's tone changed. His demeanour becoming more serious and slightly menacing.

"You do realise, you slimy little fucking toad of a man that you are, that if you did press this button, you would destroy the career of Randolph Best, one of the most respected men in the world? You would destroy the entire peace treaty initiative in the Middle East! And you would bring down the government in a matter of days! Is that what you want? Eh?" Rowlinson said, raising his voice.

"You're the cunt. Not me. You fucking bastard. You just haven't got the balls to do it, have you?"

Andy looked up, fighting the alcohol and the drugs, and trying to stand up but quickly falling over again.

"Don't fucking worry. You might not have the balls, but I do!"

And with that, in one swift movement, Rowlinson turned back towards the computer screen, moved the mouse and clicked on the bright green 'Go' button.

Seconds later, the program that Andy had written, automatically started interrupting many popular TV channels, and replaced their schedule programming with a video whose graphic content shocked all those that saw it. At the same time, the video of Randolph Best murdering Bayla Edelstein began to start playing on social media players across the world.

Within minutes, it had gone viral.

Chapter 48

London

Monday

October 8th

Selfridges

12.01 p.m.

As soon as Best had got off the phone with the Prime Minister, Ray had started to tell him about the cyber attacks that Andy was threatening to launch that coming Friday.

Randolph Best stared at him in disbelief.

"Are you sure about this? Certain that this is not just something he made up? You said he's dying and on heavy medication? Hacking into the banking system is one thing, but the rest? He would have to be a psychopath to want to do that."

"Perhaps he is. And maybe the fact that he's dying has altered his ability to think rationally, but I don't for one minute think that he's making this up. He's been planning this for a long time. This is real. And this is going to happen, unless you stop it."

"Friday?"

"Yes."

"Shit!"

Before Randolph could properly react to the news that Ray had just given him, the phone which he was still holding in his hands, began to ring.

Best looked at the calling line display, not wanting to be interrupted by anyone less than God at this point in time.

"Prime Minister? I'm so sorry we were disconnected..."

"Have you seen the news? Are you watching the TV? If not, switch it on *NOW!*"

"Which channel?" Randolph asked, immediately reaching for the remote control on the coffee table and pointing it at the large SMART TV on the wall.

"Any channel. It's on them all..."

The screen came alive and Best immediately flicked it to BBC 1.

As soon as he saw the first image on the screen, he knew that their worst nightmares had just come true.

Ray stepped closer to the screen, and stared at the image of Randolph Best walking out of the bathroom towards Bayla Adelstein.

Best flicked the channel to ITV, and then Channel 4.

The same image was playing on them all.

It was Ray's video of Best killing Bayla Adelstein.

Ray turned to Randolph.

"This has got nothing to do with me! Andy must have released the video. He did it! Shit...he bloody did it!"

Best's face had drained of all its colour.

The voice of the Prime Minister had got louder.

"You told me just now that the situation was resolved? That the threat was over! How the hell did this happen, Randolph? Do you KNOW WHAT THIS MEANS?"

Randolph took a deep breath, the colour slowly beginning to return to his face.

Ray could see that behind his eyes, Best was already beginning to think.

The SAS soldier in him was taking control.

He had already begun to accept that the situation was now different - the threat landscape had changed: the video had been released. Best had to accept it. The question was now, what next?

"Prime Minister...please, tell me. Who have you spoken to since our call?"

"No one. Not yet..."

"Have you given the order to rescind the arrest warrants on Ray Luck and remove the watch order on him?"

"Not yet...I haven't had a bloody chance..."

"Not good. What about this...the video...who else has called you about it?"

"No one...I was watching the news and this just came on...Bloody Hell, Randolph..." the Prime Minister shouted as he continued watching the video play on the TV screen. "You just murdered that woman on prime time TV! The whole world just saw it! Shit. Shit...we're screwed, Randolph. We're all screwed! ...Randolph, I've got to go. Get over here to Downing Street immediately. Be here in ten minutes!"

The Prime Minister hung up.

Randolph stared at Ray.

"Look at me one more time. I'm going to ask you a single question, and I want you to know that I am trained in NLP - which, to the uninitiated, is Neuro Linguistic Programming. We learned it in the SAS. Basically I can ask you a question, and if you lie, I can tell. And believe me when I say that I *can* tell. If you lie to me now, I'll hand you in. If you tell me the truth, I'll help you get through this. Did you have anything to do with releasing this?"

"No. I made the video. I gave it to Andy. He promised me he'd deleted it. But the rest is just like I said it was. He threatened me just now that he would release it, and now he has. I'm sorry. I'm so sorry!"

"Good. You told the truth. I can see that. So now we have to plan your next move. I have to go to 10 Downing Street. My worry is that as soon as anyone sees you, they'll either arrest you, or shoot you on sight. Don't forget, until the PM gives the order for you to be cleared, everyone is still looking for you, and you are still the most wanted terrorist in the UK. But I'm afraid that as of right now, I've got bigger fish to fry, than to look after you. Perhaps the best thing for you to do just now is to hide in my flat, and stay out of sight?"

"That sounds good to me. Can I talk to Emma sometime?"

"Emma? Oh...yes... I'll call the agency in Canada and get her to call you here in the flat."

Randolph walked over to the window, looking down at the square below.

"Blast, the traffic is still really heavy. I need to get to No 10. as soon as possible..."

Best's voice suddenly tailed off.

"Oh dear,...I think you may have a problem, Ray!"

"What do you mean?" Ray asked, alarmed, walking towards the window.

Randolph raised a hand, cautioning him to stay back.

"Remember what I said. Stay away from the windows..."

"So what's going on?"

Randolph looked down at the road below. The back doors to two white vans parked on the other side of the road had opened, and a group of men had poured out of each of them. They were all fully armed. 'SWAT' squads. One, perhaps two. Best counted ten men in total.

He immediately recognised one of them.

Jacobson.

Best shivered.

When Randolph turned back to face Ray his expression had changed. Ray couldn't work out what it meant. Was it anger, or was it fear?

"Ray, I never told you the complete story. About the Peace Initiative. Perhaps I should also have told you that the Israelis are not the only ones opposed to the peace process. There are other groups, including powerful factions in the UK and Europe...powerful groups of businessmen and politicians, who also oppose what I am trying to achieve."

"Who?"

"I can't tell you. It's classified. But just remember what I've told you. *Everything* I've told you. Whatever happens, I promise you that I am your friend. I will support you. But now, you have to go. You have to leave here. Fast. People are coming. Now. And I'm worried that if you get caught with me now, then things are going to get very complicated, and very dangerous. If you stay, you could get killed. If you leave you could get killed. But I think I have an idea."

"What?"

"I read the file which described how you escaped from your flat in London when the security services came for you. You went up and over the roofs?"

"Yes.."

"You're going to do it again now. Come with me, quickly. There's a trapdoor in the bathroom. It'll take you into the attic, and from there there is a little window that opens up onto the roof."

They started to talk as they walked.

"Once you are on the roof, you have to walk across all the roofs, and through a roof garden, until you get to the end of the street. There's a fire escape at the very end. Get down it as soon as you can. And stay low as you walk across the roof. Don't let yourself be seen from the street. And watch...be careful...it's a long way down! Don't fall."

They were standing in the bathroom now. Best cradled his hands together and gave Ray a leg up to the ceiling, enabling Ray to grab the ring on the trapdoor and pull it down. There was a ladder inside. Best pushed Ray back up again, and Ray pulled the ladder down. He climbed up it quickly.

"Where can I contact you again?" Ray asked, looking down on Best from above.

"I don't know. Stay low until this is over. I will tell the PM all about this as soon as we figure out how to keep the lid on everything and save the government. When that's done, we'll issue a statement on the TV putting you in the clear...Come to Downing Street then. I'll arrange with the police to let you through."

"Okay. I'm sorry about all this mess. If it wasn't for me..."

Best looked up at him. His face serious.

"Actually Ray, I'm beginning to think that this is perhaps not about you at all. It could be that all of this is not as innocent as it seems."

"What do you mean?"

"I mean, those others that I mentioned, who don't want the peace treaty to succeed?"

"What about them?"

"Perhaps... they...."

Best turned and looked over his shoulder. He had just heard the bell on the lift ping. The elevator was just arriving.

He looked up at Ray.

"Go. *Now*. And quietly. They're here. Close the lid after you. And good luck!"

Ray took one last quick look at Best beneath him, and then pulled the trap up.

He didn't stop to listen to the sound of Best closing the bathroom door and hurrying back into the lounge.

Within seconds Ray was across the attic, through the window and out onto the roof.

Eva laughed aloud in the car. She hadn't been as happy as this for years.

Just over thirty minutes ago she had been offered the job of her dreams: a saleswoman in Selfridges in the perfume department.

Every day she would be surrounded by beautiful people. Beautiful smells. And beautiful women.

The traffic in front of her was slowing down now.

In future,...when she started her job, she would catch the London Underground to work. Driving to the interview this morning had been a mistake. A big mistake.

But now the interviews were over, she was in no hurry. She could relax. She pushed back in her seat and began to daydream. She started to think about her new job.

And her new life.

Eva laughed again.

Today was definitely, definitely her lucky day!

Keeping low, Ray walked slowly and as steadily as possible across the roof. Where he was now, the roof sloped upwards at an angle of about forty-five degrees, but further ahead it levelled off, and there was what seemed to be a roof garden surrounded by a low wall.

Luckily it had not been raining, and the roof was not wet or slippery. Otherwise Ray would almost definitely not have been able to creep across the roof as he was doing now.

When he was younger Ray had no problem climbing trees, but the longer he lived, the more uncomfortable he got with heights.

Knowing that he was over six floors up, Ray couldn't bear to think of what lay below him, and he kept his gaze steadfastly ahead towards the roof garden, and beyond, towards where Best had promised him there was a fire escape.

For the second time in almost a week, Ray was walking across the London skyline. Fleeing for his life.

Knowing that if just one foot slipped, he would fall to his death.

Over twenty-five metres below.

Chapter 49

London

Monday

October 8th

Randolph Best's Penthouse Flat

Mayfair

12.25 p.m.

Best stood in the hallway, and looked at the CCTV camera display beside the door. There were now eight people standing outside in the corridor.

When the lift had arrived for the first time, five men had stepped out, fully armed, and covered in body armour.

Jacobson had waited for the lift to return to the ground floor and come back up carrying some more men before he had knocked on the door.

Best took a deep breath and opened it.

Six minutes earlier

In the moments before the SWAT team had bundled out of their vans and headed across the road towards the building where Best's flat was, Rowlinson had called and talked to Jacobson.

Wearing earphones, Jacobson had listened to Rowlinson bark his orders down the phone.

"This," Rowlinson had explained, "is where it all comes to a head. And where you and I earn our money, and serve our country. Not the tosspots in power, but the establishment that has made and kept our country great for century upon century. Do you understand?"

"Yes," Jacobson had muttered.

"And this is when you must remember your vow. The one you took when I had you initiated to the Inner Lodge."

There was a pause.

"And this is where you get to redeem yourself for the balls up you've made of this so far. This has been a two year history of fuckups. But don't worry. I've sorted it. I've fixed it for all of us. We can all still be heroes, and honoured by the Lodge for the precious work we are doing. All you have to do is carry out my orders exactly as I will give them to you now. Without question."

Jacobson listened to his orders.

He nodded. Hung up.

And then took his headphones off and turned to Ferris.

"Ferris, I need to talk to you for a few moments in private. Please step outside the van for a second."

Three minutes later, after being fully briefed, Ferris and Jacobson crossed the road. The rest of the SWAT team followed.

"Jacobson?" Best commented, acting surprised, as the door opened and Jacobson stepped forward. Best raised his hand to signify that Jacobson shouldn't enter his flat. "The Prime Minister just called me. He needs me in Downing Street immediately. I was just leaving."

Jacobson carried on forwards, Ferris and the SWAT team pressing on in behind him.

They now filled the inside corridor of Best's flat.

Randolph made a show of putting his jacket on.

"Sir, we need to talk." Jacobson said, feigning respect for the man that he had hated for the last two years.

"Why? Did you not hear me? I'm in a hurry. There's a national emergency developing and I have to get to Downing Street. *Immediately!*"

"Where is Ray Luck?" Jacobson asked, his voice calm and monotone.

"Who?"

"Ray Luck."

"And who the devil is he, when he's at home?"

"The man who entered your apartment at just after 10.16 a.m. this morning. Dressed as a woman. The same man who is an international terrorist and currently wanted by every security agency in Europe. The very same man who made the video that is currently being played on every major TV and Social Media channel in Europe. The video that shows you murdering Bayla Edelstein."

"Oh...that man." Best replied, knowing that it was now obvious they had been watching his flat for the past two hours.

"So, where is he?" Jacobson asked again.

"I don't know. He seems to have left. Just before the video started playing across the world. I think he was worried I would kill him."

"Which is why you asked the Prime Minister to pardon him, I suppose?"

"You've been listening to my private communications. Communications between the Foreign Minister and the Prime Minister are top secret. You should know that."

"But we are the Security Service, and our job is to protect you. Our warrants enable us to listen to every word you speak. And *you* already *know* that."

Jacobson smiled at Best and raised his eyebrows, then clicked his fingers in the air. Four of the men immediately peeled off and started to search the apartment.

"Please, while these men find Europe's most wanted terrorist, why don't we go through to your lounge and watch whatever we can find on TV. Your snuff video, for example..."

Jacobson gestured with his hand, and for a moment Best considered resisting, but then thought of the priceless paintings on his wall, and the Persian carpets which Jacobson's thugs were about to trample all over.

"This way..." Best replied.

Jacobson and Ferris followed, Ferris indicating that only one of the men should escort them into the lounge.

As soon as they entered the bright, beautiful room, all eyes were drawn to the TV. The scene was a reporter standing outside the entrance to Downing Street. Already a small crowd was gathering. Incredibly, someone was already waving a large placard which was demanding the resignation of the Cabinet, claiming an international cover up.

"Murderers!" a couple of people were chanting.

"Is this your work, Jacobson?" Best asked, turning to Jacobson and addressing him directly.

Jacobson immediately looked shocked. Suddenly the tables were turned. What did Best mean? The video? Or the placards? Or the demonstration? Did Best *know*?

"I'm not a fool Jacobson. I know all about you. And the group you work for."

Jacobson walked into the middle of the room, not answering Best's question.

One of the SWAT team entered the room and reported to Ferris.

"There's no one else here. The flat is empty. "

"Impossible," Ferris replied. "He's got to be here somewhere."

"Were the car parks monitored? Maybe he slipped out with the other agents when they returned to base, hidden in the boot?" Jacobson suggested.

Best turned to Jacobson.

"How do you know? Was one of my agents working for you too?"

For a second Jacobson wondered about the answer. Maybe one of them did. And perhaps Ray had actually escaped that way.

Jacobson looked across at Ferris. His look said it all.

"*You fucked up again Ferris. It's the second time you were outsmarted by Luck.*"

Ferris began to turn a little red, his anger and hatred towards Ray Luck ready to boil over.

Jacobson turned to the leader of the SWAT team.

"Giles, remain here with Ferris. Just in case I need you. But first, dismiss the rest of the team. Send them back to base."

The man quickly left the room, issued a few orders, and within seconds the other members of the SWAT team had left the flat.

"Good," Randolph Best said, "I don't want to appear rude or unwelcoming, but can I insist that the rest of you also now leave please. I really have to hurry now. The PM will be furious if I don't show up there soon."

Best gestured towards the door, now blocked by Ferris and Giles, who had just returned.

Instead of complying, Jacobson moved towards the large windows, and looked out and down towards the square, his back turned towards Best.

"Did you see us coming? Is that it? You were ready? You helped Luck to escape?"

"What do you mean?"

Jacobson turned around, his hand extended and now holding some form of gun, which he immediately fired at Randolph Best.

Randolph Best fell to the floor.

12.28 p.m.

The traffic wasn't going anywhere fast, but Eva was no longer in a hurry. She had done well this morning. She was proud of herself.

She couldn't wait to call her parents and break the good news: that would be the first thing she would do when she got home.

Another reason that Eva was excited about the job, was that one of the perks entitled her to get a very good discount on clothes and perfumes from Selfridges.

As soon as her first month was finished and she had got paid for the first time, Eva was going to treat herself.

She deserved it!

The sky was blue this morning. Bright blue. There were no clouds.
It was a beautiful day.
Eva looked up...

12.28 p.m.

Ray had managed to scramble half-way along the roof, and had now come to the low wall that surrounded the roof-garden.
He climbed over it and hurried across the garden to the other side.
As he hurried, he stepped through a puddle of rain water, which had pooled on the waterproof surface of the patio.
Reaching the other side of the garden, Ray hoisted himself up and put his foot on the other side of the wall, which was once again a sloping roof rising to his right, and falling to oblivion on his left.
As he let himself down onto the other side, Ray looked back over his shoulder, checking to see if anyone was following him.
Seeing no one, he let go of the low wall and turned in the other direction.
From where he was he could see the end of this section of the roof.
The fire-escape must only be thirty metres away.

As Ray put all his weight on his right foot, the rubber sole of which was still wet from the water from the roof garden, his foot slipped, and went out from under him.

Ray started to fall, the edge of the roof only two metres away...

12.28 p.m.

Randolph Best hit the floor hard, and immediately started to convulse and thrash around on the ground.
The 1500V electric shock delivered by the taser which Jacobson had just fired at him, dropped him like a rock, incapacitating him immediately.
Still holding the gun, Jacobson stepped closer.
Lifting his finger off the trigger, he waited for Best's body to start to recover so that he would be able to hear what Jacobson had to say to him.

Slowly, Best stopped convulsing and slowly opened his eyes.
"Don't move, or I will press the trigger again. It's only on low, but next time I will turn it up. How does 2000V sound? Not good? Then be quiet

and listen to me, you big shit. You think you're so clever. So smart! Don't you?"

Best just stared at him, his mind still clearing.

"You're a fool, Best, an idiotic fool. We've been following you for two years now. Two years. Two years of my life wasted while you try to balls up the world. Listen to me, you Arab loving bastard, no one wants Palestine. No one. Do you hear? God gave Israel to the Jews, and that's the way it's going to remain. It's the natural order of things. The way it should be. The way it was promised that it would be. Today is the day that I complete my vow to the Lodge, and today is the day that once and for all, this nonsense stops. Do you understand me? Yes? Then bloody NOD if you understand me, you bastard!"

Best didn't nod.

Instead, he started to raise himself up onto his elbows, and moved as if he was going to lurch forwards towards Jacobson.

Anticipating such a move, Jacobson applied more pressure to the trigger of the taser, and once more Best fell to the ground, writhing and squirming at Jacobson's feet.

With his free hand, Jacobson turned a small knob on the gun, and increased the power of the charge wracking Best's body to 2000V.

Jacobson turned to Ferris.

" Do it." He said, his voice cold, and without emotion. "Do it *now*!"

Ferris nodded and beckoned to Giles to help him.

Ferris moved quickly to the large windows and opened them up wide. The room was immediately filled with the noise of the city and the sounds of the horns blaring loudly from the cars stuck in the traffic jam below.

Ferris looked briefly at Jacobson and he nodded again. This time a little impatiently.

Signalling to Giles, both men then bent down, and made ready to grab Best.

Jacobson released his finger from the taser's trigger, and pulled hard on the wires and the barbs embedded in Best's chest, removing them with one quick yank.

Ferris and Giles immediately grabbed Best, and hoisted him to his feet.

Moving fast before he started to recover, they pushed him towards the window and the fresh air.

Gaining a little momentum, as soon as Best's waist hit the edge of the window sill, Giles pushed hard on Best's back from behind, and Ferris bent down, scooping up both of his legs.

As Best's upper torso started to bend forwards through the window, Ferris lifted his legs off the ground and hoisted them up and out of the window.

One moment Randolph Best was in the room with Jacobson, Ferris and Giles.

The next he was gone.

12.30 p.m.

Eva looked up.

At first the black object that seemed to separate from the top of the building above her had no real form. It was just black. Initially small, but quickly growing larger.

As she stared at the object, time seemed to slow down, and her mind fought rapidly to make sense of the anomaly with which it was presented.

Different shapes and comparisons swept through her head, but none of them made sense.

Until, with a shock, one memory registered in her mind, and struck a chord.

She suddenly remembered an image from a television programme that she had seen on television a few weeks ago, from a documentary on the BBC recounting the terrorist attack on the World Trade Center in New York.

The image was of what the English documentary had called 'the falling man'.

Eva's eyes widened.

Adrenaline shot into her veins, and she gripped the steering wheel in panic.

She didn't have time to scream.

A head and a torso punched through the top of the car and the windscreen, smashing into Eva with the force of a falling elephant.

The body of the falling man merged violently with Eva's, crushing her head and pulverising her rib cage and internal organs, which exploded and splattered like a squashed tomato all over the inside of the car.

The traffic light in front turned to green.
The sky was blue today. Bright blue. There were no clouds.
Outside the car, some pedestrians began to scream.

Chapter 50

London

Monday

October 8th

Mayfair

12.35 p.m.

As Ray Luck reached the bottom of the fire escape, he tensed his body and jumped the last six feet to the ground.

Immediately curling into a ball, he rolled forward across the ground, spreading the momentum and impact of the fall.

A moment later he was on his feet, heading away from the back of the building across the garden.

At the end of the garden he scaled the side of a summer house, hopped onto the wall behind it and then dropped into the mews on the other side.

It had been a close call. He'd almost slipped and fallen to his death, but thankfully, he'd just managed to catch the edge of the small garden wall and pull himself back up.

Apart from that one small 'mishap', Ray was getting rather good at this: he'd almost perfected the technique of escaping down the back of buildings.

If he never managed to get back his normal life, then perhaps he should consider becoming a cat burglar.

As he hurried down the cobbled mews he quickly checked that he still had his wallet.

Good.

He knew that there was at least five hundred pounds in there.

At the end of the mews he found himself in a main street. Hailing a passing taxi he jumped in.

"Where to, mate?" the cabbie asked.

"Kings Cross please." Ray replied.

Out of breath, sweating, the adrenaline still pumping through his veins, Ray settled back in the taxi and closed his eyes, shielding his face with his hands.

With any luck, the cabby wouldn't pay him any attention.

With this traffic it would take about thirty minutes to get to Kings Cross train station.

What he was going to do when he got there, Ray didn't know, but for now it gave him half an hour to get his breath back and think what his next step could be.

Without his burqa, Ray was visible to everyone.

Still the most wanted man in Europe, it was surely just a matter of time before someone recognised him.

12.46 p.m.

Jacobson put down the landline in Randolph Best's front room. He had just called an ambulance, and informed the police about Best's unfortunate suicide.

"We'd come to arrest Ray Luck, - the terrorist - who we had believed to be in Best's apartment, but as we entered the building from below, we saw Randolph Best beginning to clamber out of the window. We rushed upstairs, and called to him from the door. He didn't respond, so we picked the lock and opened the door and hurried into the lounge. Unfortunately, we didn't make it in time. He'd jumped before we got into the room. From what we can gather, he'd been watching the news, and he had seen the footage of himself murdering Bayla Edelstein being broadcast to the world. I can only presume that rather than face the scandal that will ensue, he took the easier option of committing suicide..."

The police promised to be there immediately.

"Don't worry. We'll wait." Jacobson had agreed.

"Such a shame," Jacobson said, smiling. "Such a tragic, but rather useful end to two years of surveillance! Rowlinson will be delighted! I must admit, when Rowlinson ordered this, I was rather sceptical, but now...well, it all seems to have worked out quite nicely, don't you think?"

At first, when Rowlinson had given him the order to terminate Randolph Best, Jacobson had been shocked. It seemed too audacious a plan, but Jacobson had to admit to himself now, seconds after they had completed the plan, just how clever it actually was.

There would be no comeback.

The media and the police would now assume that Best's death was suicide, committed within minutes of the murder of Bayla Adelstein going public.

In one fell swoop, Rowlinson would satisfy the wishes of both his main stakeholders: the Lodge, and the businessmen and women at the No. 11 Club. Even better, the publication of the video would blacken the government, and the rumours of a cover-up - which would be fuelled and encouraged by his own team would lead to the collapse of the government. Jacobson knew that Rowlinson would see to that.

Rowlinson hated the Prime Minister, as did most of the members of No. 11. It had long since been their hope that one day he would be replaced.

Today Rowlinson would help create that situation, manipulating public opinion and events until their wish came true.

Rowlinson would be a hero, and Jacobson knew that some of the glory would be passed down the food chain, to him.

Lastly, Ferris's help would not go unnoticed.

Jacobson had long since known that he could trust Giles, ever since he had helped Jacobson in some rather illegal activity in Iraq, but now he could add Ferris to his list of trusted accomplices, a man who carried out his orders, without question, no matter how peculiar or illegal those orders may at first seem to be.

As Jacobson waited for the police to arrive, he watched the TV and drank some coffee.

For a brief, passing moment, he wondered who had been in the car in the road below which Best had so completely destroyed when his body had landed on it.

Collateral damage.

Regrettable, but necessary.

Then the moment passed, and Jacobson turned his attention back to the TV.

According to the weather forecast, the sun would still be shining at the weekend.

Now the Best fiasco was finally over, he could hopefully get in a good round of golf.

13.15 p.m.

The journey to King's Cross was painfully slow. Which was good. It gave Ray some more time to think.

Unfortunately however, when he eventually got out of the taxi, he still did not know what he could or should do.

He had to find somewhere to lie low.

But where?

And then he had it.

His own flat.

The last place they would expect him to go, would be there. It was too obvious.

Of course, he wouldn't walk in the front door, just in case someone was actually watching the place. Instead, buoyed by his recent success of escaping over roof-tops and across buildings, perhaps he could do it in reverse and climb up the fire escape, cross the roof and then break back in through the attic windows?

If the flat was empty, he could hang out there for a few days, maybe even eat his own food and drink his own beer!

On the other hand, if someone was there, he could do an Anne Frank, and hide and sleep in the attic, without them knowing.

Standing in front of St Pancras, and wondering what on earth he should do, it did seem like a really good plan.

Mainly because it was the only plan he had.

He was just about to flag another taxi and hop in, when his attention was caught by the image now showing on a large flat screen TV in the window of a shop on the other side of the road.

It was a picture of Randolph Best.

Ray crossed the road, darting in and out of the traffic, a sinking feeling in his stomach.

By the time he got to the other side, his worst nightmare had been confirmed.

According to the large text that formed the title to the news segment and ran across the top of the screen, Randolph Best had just committed suicide.

Ray stared at the words and felt his world begin to cave in on him.

This couldn't be happening.

Breaking out into a cold sweat, Ray stepped into the shop and listened to the broadcast.

Ten minutes later he left the shop with a brand new radio, some batteries and a pair of headphones.

13.30 p.m.

Hurrying along the road until he found a small park, he found himself an empty piece of grass to lie on, put the batteries in the radio, put the headphones on and lay down, stretching himself out. Hiding in full view of everyone.

Tuning the radio until he caught a news station, Ray closed his eyes and covered his face with his hands, listening to the broadcaster explain what had happened.

It seemed too incredible for words!

Although not yet officially confirmed, apparently, within minutes of Ray escaping from the flat, Best had opened the window and jumped out, crushing a car and killing a commuter trapped in the traffic below.

There was a lot of talk linking his death to Ray's video which had now been seen on most of the major TV channels in the world, and had been downloaded or watched over twelve million times on social media channels, breaking all sorts of records for something going so viral so fast.

The verdict was already out, even though there wasn't even a jury to hear any of the evidence: Randolph Best had committed murder, the British Government had covered the story up, and then after the video had been leaked, the Foreign Minister to the UK, the Right Honourable Randolph Best had committed suicide.

The Prime Minister was due to make a statement later that afternoon.

People were already calling for his resignation.

The Israeli Ambassador had demanded a full inquiry and an apology for the murder of one of their citizens, and already, doubts were being cast on the peace process. At this rate, it would be unlikely to survive the next few days.

Ray had soon heard enough.

He had no chance now.

What was he going to do?

And what had really happened in the flat after he had left?

Ray couldn't accept or believe that Best had killed himself. There was no need to do it, and when he had been there with Best in the flat just an hour before, suicide was the last thing on Best's mind.

So, if Best hadn't committed suicide, then there was only one rational conclusion left.

He had been murdered.

In fact, given the timing of it, there was no doubt that the people who had killed Best had to have been the people that Best had thought were coming for Ray.

Or maybe Best had got it wrong from the start: it was never about Ray. Maybe the people had been coming to murder Best.

Were they acquaintances of Bayla Adelstein? Had they seen the video and come to finish the job that Bayla had started?

Thoughts went round and around in Ray's head.

He struggled to see any way he could get out of the situation he was now in.

It all just seemed too much.

If only Ray had managed to stay in the flat a little longer, and somehow hide, and then see who had actually come to get Best? Maybe if he had stayed in the attic, he would have been able to overhear the conversations that went on below.

Then the irony of it all dawned on Ray.

Once again, there had been a murder.

Once again, only Ray knew the truth: Best had not committed suicide; he had been murdered by the people who had come to the flat.

And now there was some form of cover-up going on.

In fact, it was even more ironic than that: if the truth didn't come out, it looked very likely that the British Government would fall.

Ray Luck, an anarchist who couldn't stand authority, was the only person who could save the government.

Only Ray knew the truth.

Unfortunately however, Ray didn't know who the murderers were.

If only he could have seen what had gone on inside the flat after he had left!

Who were the people who came? Who killed Best? And why did they do it?

In the midst of his despair, just as Ray was close to giving up and admitting it was all way too much for one man, and that there was nothing he could do, a small sequence of four letters entered Ray's mind.

Four letters that Ray knew could help save his life, the career of the Prime Minister and the future of the British Government.

C.C.T.V.

Chapter 51

London

Monday

October 8th

CSD Offices South West London

22.30 p.m.

Ray had changed his mind. For what he now needed to do, climbing up the back of his building and breaking back into his own flat would be too difficult and too risky.

Instead, he would go somewhere else. Somewhere where no one would expect him to be. And somewhere that would have all the resources he needed, to do what he wanted to do: the offices of Castle Security Defence in South West London.

It was a good plan.
After ten o'clock the offices would be unmanned.
Alarmed, yes, manned no.
True, they may have disabled his badge, but Ray wasn't worried about that.
He had a spare. One which no one else knew about: about six months ago he had lost his badge, and the receptionist, a new person, had issued him a temporary card and PIN number.
That night he had worked late, and when he had left the office, the reception was empty, and he had signed his temporary card back in at the front desk, but kept the card.
No one had ever chased him for the other card. For a security company, their internal security was way too lax.
He'd used it several times since then, and each time it had worked, the last time being only a few weeks ago. The best part was, the card was in his wallet.

His authentication token would probably have been disabled, but for what he wanted to do, he didn't need it.
Ray was going to use the computers in the research lab, open to anyone, but with no access to the corporate network, and only able to surf the internet.

Which was all he needed to do.

Watching from the car park as the security at reception finally left, he walked slowly around the building to make sure no one was working late. By this time it was always empty.

If anyone needed to work late, why do it from the office? They could just log on from home.

In fact, nowadays, most of the office was empty all the time anyway. In reality, the reasons for actually coming into an 'office' to work were all slowly evaporating. The benefits of 'unified communications' and video conferencing meant that you could work from anywhere in the world, and still stay in constant contact with your colleagues.

Tonight, Ray was banking on it.

After convincing himself that there were no suspicious lights on in the building, he hovered on the edge of the car park in darkness away from the CCTV for another ten minutes, just to be sure.

After a while it started to rain, and Ray's fingers began to get cold.

Which was bad news for someone who needed to type quickly.

It was time to go.

Walking up to the building, he kept his head low, covered in a hoodie that he had bought that afternoon so that he could avoid London's infamous CCTV cameras and the hawkish eyes of any police that he might pass in the street.

When he came to the door, he swiped the card through the door scanner, typed his PIN number on the keypad and held his breath.

The light turned from red to green.

Ray pulled the door open and stepped inside.

No alarm went off.

Carrying the bag of food and several cans of coke which he had brought with him, to keep him nourished and awake all night, he walked to the back of the building and down the stairs into the lab area, tucked away conveniently in the basement.

Tapping the entry code into the pad on the wall beside the door, he heard the door click and he pushed it open and stepped inside.

Closing the door behind him, he flicked the light on, and looked around.

Within minutes he was seated at a table, a test laptop opened up in front of him, and a can of coke in his hands.

It was going to be a long night.
Ray flexed his fingers, closed his eyes and began to think.

Castle Security Defence Offices in South West London

10.55 p.m.

Ray knew that time was not on his side. He was confident that under normal circumstances he would be able to do what he had to do, but these were not normal circumstances.

Basically, he only had until tomorrow morning when the first shift came in, to save the country, and possibly his life.

And in between, he had to do one of the best hacks he had ever done.

He knew it was possible, because he had watched Andy do exactly the same thing only two nights before.

Once the four little letters, C, C, T and V, had appeared in his mind, the rest of his plan had materialised within seconds.

CCTV was about to become his best friend.

Earlier that day he had realised that in order to save himself and make any further progress, he needed to know what had transpired in Randolph Best's flat after he had left.

Who were the people who had come in after him, and what had they done to Randolph Best?

And why?

If only he could have been there to witness it all...like a little fly upon the proverbial wall!

It was then that he had remembered Best pointing out to him the CCTV cameras hidden in the walls of his bedroom; he remembered Best stressing that no one else knew they existed, and that no one else knew of the videos which proved he had not murdered Bayla Edelstein.

Almost definitely there were other CCTV cameras throughout the flat.

And if there was one in the lounge, or in the hall, and he could get access to the CCTV camera footage, then maybe, just maybe, he could see and hear what had gone on, or at the very least, identify who the people were who had come into the flat and murdered Best.

It was a funny feeling.

Ray was both excited and scared.

Scared, because if he couldn't do what he needed to, he had no other plan.

Excited, because what he wanted to do now, he had never done before, and if he succeeded, **IF** he succeeded, the payback would be amazing.

Stealing the money from the bank was one thing, this was going to be another.

For a hacker, this was going to be as good as it gets.

This evening, his life would depend upon his hacking skills and his ingenuity.

The plan was simple.

Following the example of Andy, he was going to hack into the National Grid's network, and from there jump to the local energy supplier to Best's penthouse apartment in Mayfair. Once there he would try to connect to the Smart Electricity Meter in Best's flat, hopefully with Super-User Admin rights just like Andy had managed to achieve when hacking into Best's house via its Smart Meter. Once he got into the flat, he would jump onto the IP network and look for the CCTV system and the server where all the videos were stored.

He would first find the videos of when Best defended himself against Bayla Adelstein, download them and save them onto one of several USB Flash drives he had bought this afternoon.

Then, he would look at all the other CCTV footage that had been recorded today, and see if he could find the answers to any of his questions.

And if he could?

Then Ray Luck would be a very, very lucky man.

No pressure then.
No pressure.

The secret to doing this, and doing it right, was to stay calm. To divide the activity into phases, and conduct each phase, one, at, a, time.

By 11 p.m. Ray was ready to go.
He began to type.

Within minutes, Ray had become focussed. He slowly blanked out the rest of the world, his attention concentrated solely on the cursor on his screen and the little white letters that popped up whenever he hit the keyboard.

To Ray, hacking was like driving a car.

His subconscious and his years of experience doing exactly what he was doing now, took over.

Autopilot switched on, and Ray disappeared into his other world.

His virtual world.

He began to fly.

To soar.

Across the Ethernet cables, the LANs, the WANs, the Internet Gateways; it felt good to be back, to be on the 'offensive', to be SolarWind again.

Yes...

It. Felt. Good.

Getting access to the headquarters of the National Grid was not simple. Andy had made it look easy, but in truth, it was quite tricky.

They had several layers of defence: the most modern firewalls, intrusion detection devices, one active intrusion prevention system, web-gateways, SIEMs...the works. Everything you would expect them to have. And more.

The strange thing was that when Ray had stood behind Andy in his den in the church, watching what Andy was doing and trying to remember the techniques and the IP commands he used, he didn't think that he had taken it all in. He'd thought that Andy had been typing too fast, and was working too fast for Ray to see what he was doing.

But now, as he retraced Andy's steps, he found himself reacting automatically to the challenges that the security defences threw at him; he found that he could recall command strings that Andy had typed, and procedures that he had followed. When once prompted for a password, Ray had remembered exactly what Andy had typed in: it was a default password - basically a password which had been shipped with that component of the system, and never changed by any one in their IT department. Andy had said that he had got it from one of the many hacker forums that listed all the standard default passwords for computer devices and industrial components - basically, you went to their website, entered the name of the device you wanted to hack, along with the name of the manufacturer, and it responded with a list of all the known default passwords for that software, device or server. The incredible thing was that mostly, it worked!

As it did now.

' *Chrysanthemum&14£*'.

And bingo, he was in.

SolarWind flew past the security defences.

It had taken him almost an hour to get into the network of the National Grid. But once there, the other phases began to fly past quite easily.

Soon he was in the network of the local energy supplier.

Even sooner he had located the details of the Smart Meter installed in Best's flat, and then connected directly to it.

Literally, all he had to do was find it in the list, let their ever so friendly GUI present him with several options and then choose the one he wanted from: *'Install, Delete, Update, Connect.'*

'Connect' seemed liked a good idea, since it was being offered to him on a plate.

So he clicked on it, and it did exactly what it said it would.

How friendly!

Within seconds he was on the Smart Meter in the penthouse apartment.

Less than three minutes later he was on the internal network in Best's house.

And shortly before midnight, he was looking at all the active IP devices on Best's network.

Ray smiled.

"*Show me the money....show me the money...*" he whispered to himself, drank the last of his second can of coke, and dived straight back in.

00.15 a.m.

Ferris showed his pass to the detective at the door to Randolph Best's flat. He saw the recognition in the man's eyes that he was a spook, and his resentment that with the letter of authority Ferris had just waved in his face, the detective had to let the spook into the apartment so that he could trample all over his crime scene.

The detective knew Ferris's type: they thought they were above the law, that they could do things without following the proper procedures, that they were immune to the tedious hum-drum processes that he himself had to follow on a daily basis.

The worst part was that it was true. He could.

"Come in. Sign the book. Don't touch anything. And let me know when you leave, okay?"

Ferris nodded. And promptly ignored everything he had just been told.

Ferris couldn't sleep. He couldn't stop thinking about Ray Luck.

How the hell did he get away from the flat without them knowing about it?

There was no way he could have got out of the front entrance without him seeing it, and when they had checked the CCTV cameras afterwards, they were able to see the security guards get into the lift on the top floor, take it down to the basement, get in their cars and leave. No one had followed them. No one had surreptitiously been bundled into a car, and carried out from under their noses.

They had seen Ray Luck walk into the house. They had not seen him leave.

Ferris had spent the rest of the day bugged by a simple, stupid, nagging question at the back of his mind.

Was it possible that Best had a 'panic room', a secure vault that he could disappear into if he ever felt under threat?

Was it hidden, somewhere...maybe in the walls?

Had Best put Ray in his panic room and hidden him there?

And once he was inside, had Ray heard or maybe even seen everything that had gone on?

Did Ray know the truth? Could he incriminate them?

Was Ray maybe even still there? Just waiting for the police to leave?

Ferris knew that such places were equipped with enough food and water for someone to hide inside and hold out for days.

The idea of the panic room made sense. It certainly explained Ray's disappearance.

Which is why Ferris was back in Mayfair now.

He wanted to know what had happened to Ray Luck, and he was going to find out.

And if he was still there in the flat, if Ferris could find him, he was going kill him.

Chapter 52

London

Monday

October 9th

Castle Security Defence Offices in South West London

00.20 a.m.

Now he was on Randolph Best's home network, the first thing he wanted to find was the application controlling all the CCTV cameras, and the server where all the video files were stored.

It wasn't hard.

The Internet-Of-Things had found a welcome customer with Randolph Best: already there were quite a few things in Randolph's home environment that were IP enabled; by conducting a quick scan of all the IP devices on the network, the responses starting flooding back from heating systems, Smart TVs, an alarm system, a lighting system, a music system, two laptops that were connected to the internal Wi-Fi, a router, a firewall, several VoIP phones, the Electricity Smart Meter, ten CCTV cameras, two external hard-drives, and two servers. The first server seemed to be full of personal files and information, most of which at a quick first glance were heavily encrypted. For now, Ray left that well alone. Being accused of stealing governments secrets was not something that Ray needed just now.

The second server had a number of applications running on it, one of which was a popular application which Ray recognised: a CCTV management system.

Ray opened it up, found an elementary backdoor to the program - which made a mockery of the security claims of the company - and pulled up the dashboard which showed the video streams coming from the active CCTV cameras.

"Bingo..." Ray said, bending forward and studying the images from the cameras.

Ten images.

He immediately recognised four of them: two that were streaming images directly from the lounge of Randolph Best, and two that came from the bedroom where Best had killed Bayla Adelstein.

There was another one in the kitchen, two more in the other bedroom, one in the hallway, and one in the dining room, and one looking out from above his front door towards the lift.

Ray was impressed.

He initially focussed his attention on the output from the CCTV cameras in the lounge.

As Ray had expected, the apartment was still full of police and forensics, who were going over everything with a toothcomb, searching for fingerprints, and looking through Best's personal effects.

Three of the forensic team were working on the area around the windows, through which Ray presumed Randolph had made his exit.

Then one of the images, of a man in the second bedroom, caught his attention.

The man seemed to be going round tapping the walls.

It was as if he was looking for something.

What if he found the CCTV cameras?

Ray pulled his attention away from the CCTV dashboard, and looked at the file management system, quickly discovering where the videos files were being stored.

"Good," Ray whispered to himself, almost as if he was scared the people in Randolph's flat would hear him. It seemed as if all the video files were backed up for a month before automatic deletion.

He went into the directory, and found the video files saved on September 28th, and searched using the time function for activity recorded around 10.00 p.m. that night.

Although he was tempted to watch the different files which showed Bayla and Randolph talking together in the lounge, and then moving through to the bedroom, he did a fast forward and selected the two CCTV camera video files that had recorded the activity in the bedroom.

He started to download all the images which the CCTV cameras had recorded from 11.00 to 11.30 p.m. to the F drive on the laptop - the large USB Flash memory drive he had brought with him - knowing that this timeframe would have caught the murder from both the angles Best had showed him.

Ray watched as the files started to download. The download seemed to chug along, taking ages.

As he waited, Ray opened up another window and went back to the CCTV video file storage, and looked for images recorded earlier that day, from 12.00 p.m. to 2.00 p.m.

Opening one of the video files up, which started at 11 a.m. that morning, he moved the time cursor to 12.00 p.m. and saw Randolph Best and himself in his lounge, staring at the TV.

It was hard to believe that Randolph was now dead when on the video feed he was so very much alive!

Ray fast forwarded the video, seeing himself and Randolph dart around the room like in some old fashioned Charlie Chaplin movie, waving their arms around wildly and making exaggerated faces.

Soon they had left the room. This was when they had gone to the bathroom and Ray had climbed into the attic.

He kept the video winding forward.

Suddenly Best was back in the lounge again.

He was accompanied by a couple of men, one in a suit, one in normal day clothes and a man from a SWAT team, bristling with weapons and in full gear.

The man in the suit walked to the window.

Ray started to play the video at normal speed.

Listening to the conversation, Ray discovered that they were talking about him. The man in the suit wanted to know where he was. They were looking for him after all!

Ray rewound the tape back to the part just before they all entered the lounge. He couldn't see them all clearly, because they were standing to the side of the camera in the hallway, but he could easily make out their voices and what they were saying.

Yep, they had come looking for Ray. Best had argued that he needed to go the Prime Minister urgently, but they had pressed in on him, even discussing the conversation Best had had with the Prime Minister!

Ray listened in disbelief as Best challenged them over it:

"You've been listening to my private communications. Communications between the Foreign Minister and the Prime Minister are top secret. You should know that."

"But we are the Security Service, and our job is to protect you. Our warrants enable us to listen to every word you speak. And you already know that."

Ray looked up. Security Service. That confirmed it!

He carried on listening, following the conversation through until they all appeared in the lounge.

He watched as they moved back into the room, until Best addressed the man in the suit by name.

Jacobson.

Ray made a mental note.

He carried on watching. The conversation went on.

Then suddenly, out of the blue a gun was pulled...no, it was a taser! Ray saw the taser fire, the wires jumping from the short barrel and embedding themselves in Best's chest.

He watched Best fall to the floor...he saw the whole scene play itself out, Ray holding his breath and not believing anything that he was seeing.

Best tried to stand, he was tasered again, then...suddenly the two other men in the room - their names were 'Giles' and 'Ferris' - they bent down, picked up and pushed Best towards the window.

Giles pushed him over the windowsill, Ferris lifted his feet,...and then...then...

"Bloody hell!" Ray exclaimed, his hands shaking and his heart pounding in his chest from what he had just witnessed. "The British Security Service just murdered Randolph Best, the Foreign Secretary!"

He pushed back in his seat.

His head was buzzing, his mind struggling to grasp what he had just seen.

For a few precious moments he just sat there, staring into space, not able to think properly.

Then, almost as if a little voice spoke to him, he suddenly realised the importance of what he had just seen, and why he was here.

"Shit...shit...I've got to get this. I've got to download this!"

Once more fully alert, his eyes darted back to the window on the laptop which showed the progress of the video downloads.

They were complete.

Ray pulled out the USB stick, and stuck it in his trouser pocket.

He quickly loaded another USB memory stick in the USB drive and grabbed the video he had just watched and started downloading it.

Looking in the file directory he then located the video recorded from the other CCTV camera in the lounge and queued that up to download next.

"Shit this is taking ages!" Ray swore to himself.

Nervously, he looked around himself, just checking that he was still alone in the lab.

As he waited for the video to download, he thought about the importance of what he had discovered.

With these videos he could prove to the Prime Minister that Best was innocent of Bayla's murder. Before this they only had Best's word for it...which at the time had been enough...but now that Ray's own video had been so publically aired to the world, Randolph Best's own video could and would prove categorically that he didn't do it!

And then, the other videos would prove that he didn't commit suicide and that he was assassinated by the British Security Service.

This stuff was dynamite!

If he could get it to the Prime Minister it would save his government, and save the Prime Minister's career!

It was also all the evidence they needed to bring Best's murderers to justice!

Ray looked at the download again. Still only 50% done.
"Hurry up, hurry up..." he wished aloud.

While he waited, he opened up the live CCTV video stream that was coming from Best's flat.
The forensic teams, all dressed in white and wearing white slippers, were still busy in the lounge, and a few of them have now moved through to one of the bedrooms.
Looking at the CCTV camera in the bedroom Bayla had been killed in, Ray once more saw the man who was going around the walls knocking on the walls and listening to the response.
He was definitely looking for something... but what?

Ray followed him for a while, one eye on the man, the other on the reading which told him what percentage of the new video had successfully been downloaded.

The man in the bedroom was now looking around the wall. His eyes seemed to rest on the lights near the camera, and then move slightly around the area, before coming to rest on what seemed to be the centre of the camera lens.
The man was now looking directly at the lens.
Then the man disappeared from view, but a few seconds later instantly popped up just in front of the camera, his face filling the whole screen, one eye now so large and front and centre that it was distorted.
The man's face pulled back again. He was obviously now standing on a chair and looking directly at the camera lens.
Ray stared straight back.
Now he was so close and his features were so clearly illuminated by the light, with a shock Ray realised that he recognised the man.
His name was Ferris.
And he was the one that had lifted Randolph Best's feet up and helped throw him out of the window!

00.55 a.m

Ferris stared at the tiny hole in the wall just beside the light.
The moment he saw it he froze.
"Fuck!" he swore to himself.

He stepped back off the chair and onto the ground.

"How many more cameras were there?" he immediately asked himself.

He hurried through to the hallway, carrying the chair with him.

Shit! There was another one in the hallway.

If it was live it would have recorded them all coming into the flat earlier that afternoon.

It would have recorded them talking to Randolph Best, who was supposed to have committed suicide before they got there.

'He'd jumped before we got into the lounge,' - was that not what Jacobson had told the police on the phone?

Grabbing the chair he stormed into the lounge, every one turning to look at him.

Ferris froze.

What should he do?

Fuck, he didn't care what they thought. He had to know the answer.

He put the chair underneath one of the wall lights in the lounge, stood up, and quickly confirmed his worst nightmare.

There was a camera in that room too.

Maybe there were even more.

And from the viewpoint of this one - it faced the window and would capture the whole lounge - Ferris knew that it would easily have seen himself picking up Best and throwing him out of the window.

If it had been recording.

Ferris quickly stepped down and darted back into the hallway before anyone could ask him any questions.

He needed some space.

He needed to think.

Seeing the doorway to the bathroom, Ferris hurried inside, closed the door, put the toilet lid down and sat down on it.

As if things weren't bad enough, it was then that Ferris looked up and saw the trapdoor to the attic.

"Shit!" Ferris shouted, this time not caring who heard him.

"Shit! Shit! *SHIT!*"

Castle Security Defence Offices in South West London

1.10 a.m.

Ray had followed the man through to the lounge, watching him move from one camera to the other on the video CCTV dashboard.

He saw him find the camera in the hallway, and then discover another of them in the lounge.

Ferris knew about the cameras.

And from the look of shock on Ferris's face when he saw the one in the lounge, Ray knew Ferris had realised what that potentially meant.

"I spy, I saw him die!" Ray said aloud to the image on the screen. "And I spy, I saw *YOU* kill him!"

He said it before realising what he had just said.

The moment the words had left his mouth, the irony of them hit him hard.

First he had used the cameras to watch Best kill the foreign spy sent to kill him, and now he had watched the British Security Service complete the job for her, by killing Best themselves!

It was even weirder to realise that he actually felt really bad about Best having been murdered.

Only this time last night he had thought the man was a murdering bastard, and now Best himself had been murdered and Ray knew the man was innocent. He even quite liked the guy.

Had quite liked him.

Ray looked at the download. 83% complete. This file was taking longer because it was much larger. He'd got a lot already, but he needed to get it all!

On the CCTV dashboard, he saw Ferris disappear into the bathroom.

One of the policemen came into the hall and called after him.

Ferris shouted something back, then the policeman left.

A few moments later Ferris emerged.

His face was red, almost as if he was mad with anger. Furious. Enraged.

He opened some cupboards in the hallway and stuck his head in.

He was looking for something new. Not in the walls.

Something more tangible.

86%.

Ferris walked through to the bedroom. He opened the bedroom door and walked in, saying something to the policemen in the room.

Ray saw him rushing round the room, looking for something.

What?

What was he looking for?

89%.

As Ray looked at the % increment, wishing it to go faster, it suddenly dawned on him what he was looking for.

The CCTV system.

And the server on which all the videos were stored.

90%

'Oh shit!' It was Ray's turn to swear.

Still 90%.

Ferris was going through the cupboards. Pulling stuff out, throwing it on the floor behind him.

One of the policemen shouted something at him. Ferris told him to fuck off.

The policeman came over and put his hand on Ferris's shoulder.

"Don't touch anything..."

92%.

Ferris stood up and faced the man. He pulled out something from his pocket...his credentials, and waved them at the man.

93% now downloaded.

Ferris shouted at the man and pointed at something in the cupboard. He'd obviously found something.

94%.

The policeman left the room, saying he would be straight back.

Ferris bent down and his shoulders disappeared back into the cupboard. Ray saw him pull at something.

95%.

Ferris pulled back, and stood up. It was a server.

Ray's heart jumped. He stared at his laptop screen again.

96%. The number was still incrementing. He'd got the wrong server.

Ferris moved back towards the cupboard.

Two police officers came into the room.

The new police officer walked straight over to Ferris and shouted at him.

"Leave that alone. Do not touch another thing. This is our turf. It's our case. Back off!"

97%.

Ferris looked at the man, and considered saying something. He turned back to the cupboard, and was just about to go back in again, when he turned to the new police officer, obviously the man in charge.

He faced him square on.

98%.

"Don't start with me, mister. You know who I work for. You know my authority. I have higher authority here, and you know it. And if you don't know it, I suggest you check. Immediately. And don't speak to me again until you know just how much you need to grovel in apology to me. Do it now...and I'll tell you this one more time, just as I told this other monkey here a minute ago. FUCK RIGHT OFF!"

99%.

The officer hesitated. Visibly flustered.

He turned and looked at the other officer. The forensic team in the room were standing around watching them.

99% still.

Ferris turned around, reached back into the cupboard.

100%.

100%!

"Yes!" Ray shouted, pumping the air with his fist.

It was only the first video, but the other one would start downloading immediately afterwards.

Ray grabbed the USB stick and yanked it out, pushing a new, fresh one into the USB port.

Back on the CCTV feed, Ferris knelt forward into the cupboard. Ray couldn't see his head, but he could tell from his actions he was just about to lift something.

Suddenly the screen went blank.

Ferris had disconnected the CCTV server.

His eyes and ears had just gone dark.

Ray sat back in his seat and breathed out.

He hadn't got the second video, but with any luck, the video he'd just downloaded would give him everything he needed.

Chapter 53

London

Monday

October 9th

Castle Security Defence Offices in South West London

01.35 a.m.

Looking down at his hands, Ray realised that he was actually shaking. That had been intense!

He picked up the memory stick and stared at it.

Wow... what was on this stick could save the British Government!

And the peace treaty that had been so important to Randolph Best.

Realising the importance of it, Ray knew that he should really make a copy of it. Back it up. Ensure that the future of a country wasn't lost through accidentally dropping the USB stick down a drain, or something.

Putting the flash stick back in the USB port, he copied it to the laptop, and then inserted a fresh USB stick and downloaded the complete video file back on to it, before deleting it from the CSD laptop.

He was still shaking.

His gut reaction now was to run.

To get as far away from CSD as possible, just in case someone somehow found him working there and he was arrested.

But Ray knew that he needed to be smart about this. In the lab he had access to all the tools he needed. Once he left, there would probably be no coming back.

He stood up, put his arms behind his back, and stretched.

Walking to the bathroom, he bent over the sink and washed his face in cold water, patting some on the back of his neck.

He dried his hands and dabbed the water off his face, leaving some moisture to evaporate and cool his face down, and refresh him even more.

What was his next step?

Now he had the video, what was he going to do with it?

He would have to watch it all the way through to see exactly what had happened, but he could do that later. What else did he need to do now, while he was still in the labs?

He knew that the government was vulnerable at this moment. That the future of the PM hung in the balance.

The PM knew the story about Ray. He was one of the last things that Randolph Best had discussed with him.

Admittedly, if the PM didn't believe that Best had committed suicide, then it could be that the PM may think that Ray was a suspect for his murder.

Ray wasn't too worried about that though, because he had the videos! They would prove him innocent, ...if the PM saw them.

Instinctively Ray knew that the future of the PM and his own life were inextricably linked. Ray's value to the PM was immediate. Whilst the PM was vulnerable, Ray would be important to him, and in return he would be able to help Ray.

Once the PM was ousted from power, Ray would be beyond help. No one would want to help him.

In other words, Ray had to contact the PM, and he had do it soon!

The only question was, *how*?

He left the bathroom and walked back to the bench in the lab.

Sitting down, he stared at the laptop.

How on earth was he going to get to speak to the Prime Minister of the United Kingdom?

Ray was a nobody.

It wasn't as if he could just call him up and say 'hi!'

And even if he were able to, knowing that the Security Service were the ones behind Randolph's death, he would have to make sure that conversations he had were not monitored. If he was intercepted and they heard him tell the PM what he would say, he would probably only last a few minutes before parachutists dropped out the sky and nabbed him, or he was hit by a drone strike!

Somehow he needed to find a way to contact the PM directly. If he went through someone else, they would filter him out: he would be just an unknown member of the public.

So how on earth could he talk to the PM directly?

It wasn't as if he had his personal mobile phone number!

Ray sat up straight in his stool, his mind suddenly wide awake, another large shot of adrenaline pumped straight into his veins.

In a moment of pure genius, Ray had just figured out how to do it!

Castle Security Defence Offices in South West London

01.55 a.m.

Turning back to the laptop and his internet connection, Ray was pleased to find that he was still logged in to Randolph Best's home network.

Scanning the network once more he soon had the list back up on the screen of all the IP connected devices on the network.

Including four VoIP phones.

VoIP phones - or Voice-over-IP phones - were essentially just computers that captured voice through a microphone, transformed sound into IP packets, and then transmitted it over the internet to a voice gateway. Once the IP packets hit the voice gateway, they would be converted into normal voice traffic and routed through the normal telephone voice network.

Making VoIP calls was dirt cheap, if not free, and the quality was now so high, that VoIP was already used by most businesses today, or by yuppie professionals who loved to use the latest technologies.

Randolph Best easily fell into the latter category.

The fact that VoIP phones were essentially computers, made them very interesting to Ray: he could hack into them, and then play with them.

He'd done it many times before. This time would be no different.

The big question was, which one was the one in the lounge?

It took him only two minutes to connect to the phones, hack into them, and then by looking at the internal records of all the IP calls that had been made that day, to locate the one that must be the one in the lounge.

It was the last one to be used, and according to the call records, the others had not been used at all that day.

Ray closed his eyes and tried to remember what time it was that Randolph Best had called the PM.

It must have been sometime just after 11.15 a.m.? Around that time.

Ray opened his eyes and scanned down the list of all the calls that had been made with that phone. He found the record he needed, and then, on impulse, he took a screen-dump of the entire list and saved it to the USB drive.

According to the record, the call was very short, which was true, because the Prime Minister had been on the phone to someone else and couldn't take the call.

Ray looked at the number: the last two digits were zeros.

The number was no good to him. It was a landline number and almost definitely the number of a reception desk. It wasn't a direct number.

If Ray called that number, he would be told to leave a message. There was no way the PM's secretary, or whoever else answered it, would just put him through to the PM.

Shit.

Ray thought again, immediately recalling that when Randolph had actually spoken to the PM, it was because the PM had called him back.

He did a mental calculation and decided it must have been around a quarter to twelve.

Checking the list for received calls Ray found one at 11.49 a.m.

Ray remembered that the call had lasted a long time, eventually forcing Ray to put his finger on the receiver and end the call: looking at the call duration, Ray saw it tallied.

It was then that he remembered one more important point.

When Best had picked the call up, he'd at first complained to the PM that he couldn't hear him. He'd asked him if he was on his mobile, and the PM had affirmed it.

Ray looked at the number.

It was a mobile number.

Bingo.

Ray had got the personal, direct mobile number of the Prime Minister of the United Kingdom.

He memorised the number, scribbled it down on two different pieces of paper just to be safe, and then wrapped the two USBs sticks with all the videos on them into one of the pieces of paper and stuck it in his shoe.

Five minutes later Ray was ready to leave.

He switched off the lights, walked to the back of the building and was just about to push open the fire escape door and leave, when a thought occurred to him.

Where was he going to go?

Outside it was raining.

Looking through a window into the dark, unfriendly world outside, he could see the water pelting down and bouncing off the car park tarmac, cold, and wet.

At this time of night, there were no more night buses or trains, and in this part of town, taxis would be few and far between.

He could walk into central London, but how long would that take him?

Ray was still a criminal, wanted, hunted and with no friends to hide him.

Without the burqa, it would only be a matter of hours or minutes before he walked past a CCTV camera, and his image triggered an alert on some Security Service agent's dashboard.

Standing at the window, looking at the world outside, Ray shivered.
He was so tired. And so alone. So *very* alone.
It was still him against the British establishment, and the might of the British Security Service.
Even though he had the video, and the telephone number of the PM, what chance did he really have?
Realistically?

Then he thought of Emma, and knew he couldn't give up.
With any luck, she would soon be free. Maybe even home in the UK.

Ray had made her a promise, and somehow he had to find a way to keep it.

Vauxhall

02.05 a.m.

Ferris sat at his station with the servers he had taken from Best's apartment connected to his workstation: he had just located the video files from the CCTV camera on one of the servers and was ten minutes into watching the first video.
He had already learned two things.
First, the CCTV cameras had recorded *everything*.
Best's wonderful, state-of-the-bloody-art cameras had captured in magnificent, incredible, bloody brilliant high-definition detail, full documentary evidence of how he, Giles and Jacobson had murdered Best.
Ferris stopped the video.
For now, he'd seen enough.
The main question was, could anyone else have seen this too?
He was sure the answer was probably no, but he had to be sure.

Changing tack completely, Ferris started to dig around in the routing records of Best's home network, looking at the traffic records that had been captured in the log files and stored in several records of activity kept on the servers.

Vauxhall

02.15 a.m.

'Shit! Fuck!'
Ferris swore aloud.
How? How was that possible?
For the first time since Ferris had begun the Unicorn operation, and for the first time since he was a young intelligence officer who had found himself isolated in the dark in Helmand Province in Afghanistan, surrounded by Taliban and certain he was going to be killed, Ferris felt fear.
Someone else had been accessing the CCTV files only several hours ago. At the same time he was in Best's flat.
And not only that, someone had downloaded them: taken copies and transferred them across the internet to some external hard drive.

But who? Who else knew about this? And who else would have the capability to do it?
The answer dawned on him before he had even finished asking himself the question.
Ray Luck.

Vauxhall

02.25 a.m.

Ferris picked up the phone.
"Andrews? Get up here now. Bring Simons, Davis, Peters and Jones. I need your help to track an SOI down..."
He couldn't be certain that Luck was behind this, but his instinct told him he was. Either way, it didn't matter, what Ferris had to do now was the same either way - he had to find out where that hard-drive was that the files had been downloaded to.
And he had to find it quick, before the person did anything with them.
The clock was ticking.

Chapter 54

London

Monday

October 9th

Castle Security Defence Offices in South West London

04.20 a.m.

Ray stood up and stretched.

His legs ached: he couldn't bear sitting down anymore, and the stench of damp in the small, musty cupboard was making him feel sick. The plus side of that however, was that the smell had kept him awake.

Ray had stood at the window beside the fire escape door for five minutes; he'd come close to stepping out and leaving the building, which would have been one of the biggest mistakes he'd made in his life.

Right now, time was of the essence. Leaving CSD and going somewhere else would have been stupid.

He had everything he needed right here. There was nowhere better.

Plus, it was the middle of the night, the building was empty and no one knew he was there.

Ray knew this place. As long as he left by 6 a.m. the likelihood of him being discovered was pretty close to nil.

That was over two hours ago.

Once he had realised that he had a window of opportunity to do what he needed to do, right here, along with all the resources he needed, he walked back to the basement lab, found a cupboard hidden somewhere in a corner and made himself comfortable on the floor.

Switching the lights off in the lab, and closing the door to the cupboard with the lock snibbed so he couldn't get locked in, he'd taken his notebook out, and started watching the videos he recorded on one of the laptops from the lab.

As he watched, he made notes.

Lots of notes.

Several times he had to stop and think about what he had just seen, trying to grasp the enormity of the evidence that he'd captured, and trying to understand the politics behind what was going on.

His videos were dynamite.

They had the power to save the PM and the government, but also to destroy the upper layers of the security services. They also posed serious questions about who actually ran the security services?

He watched all the videos from start to finish and then examined the phone call records he'd screen-captured from Best's VoIP phones.

After Best had been murdered, *assassinated*, Jacobson had made several very interesting phone calls.

Using Best's phone.

A stupid, stupid mistake.

Ray now had the telephone numbers of the people he had called, along with videos which captured what had been said in perfect HD audio.

Ray looked at his watch, shocked to see how much time had elapsed.

Taking off his headphones, switching the laptop off and putting the USB memory stick back in his pocket, he opened the door and listened to make sure everything was still quiet.

Apart from the sound of the building creaking and settling, Ray was sure he was still alone.

He stepped out of the cupboard, switched off the light and returned to the bathroom.

Once again he soaked his face with cold water, and tried to revive himself and freshen up.

Returning to the lab he made himself comfortable in his chair, and took a piece of paper from his pocket which had the telephone number of the Prime Minister scribbled on it.

The rest of his life would depend upon the phone call he was just about to make.

This was it.

There was no backup plan.

In one minute he was going to call the Prime Minister of the UK.

If the PM would listen to him, believe him and work with him, Ray's life would be saved.

But now, just as Ray picked up the phone to dial the number, two thoughts occurred to him.

First, what happened next if the Prime Minister never answered his call? It was almost four-thirty in the morning, - the dying time, the time when a human being was at his lowest ebb, and the Prime Minister would be fast asleep, his phone turned off.

What would he do if the call went to voice mail?

Secondly, what if...the Prime Minister was working with the Security Service and was on their side? Could it all be a conspiracy? Was the Prime

Minister in on it? That was something that Ray hadn't thought about before...

Was Ray about to hand himself in to the devil?

There was only one way to find out.
He started to dial the number.

Vauxhall

04.31 a.m.

Ferris nodded. Jones and Peters seemed to have finally cracked it.

Access to Best's network had been gained through a remote connection made via the electricity Smart Meter in Best's house.

Peters had found a few crumbs of traffic - practically nothing more than that - just a few little traces of data packets that had not yet flushed out of the buffers, probably because Ferris had ripped the server out of the network without giving them a chance to clear: the packets contained the information they needed in their IP headers, revealing the source and destinations of the network flow.

Jones had traced the traffic back to the local energy supplier, and from there they had been able to trace IP traffic which flowed from there to the National Grid.

The rest of the work was a joint effort between Simons and himself.

They had traced the source of the original traffic that attacked the National Grid.

It was a true team effort.

Something they should all be proud off: good work, conducted under pressure, where every second counted.

That part was the good news.

The bad news was that it confirmed that Luck was behind it all.

Firstly, getting into Best's network in the apartment via the electricity meter was exactly the same attack vector that someone had used to talk with Best the day before at his mansion.

That was Ray Luck, and this was Ray Luck now.

The bastard was everywhere!

Secondly, the source of the traffic that Simons and himself had located was the South London offices of Castle Security Defences.

Which was where Ray Luck used to work. Or still did.

And that was the big question. Was Ray Luck hacking into Best's network with the blessing of his company? If so, Ferris and the rest of his department were in deep trouble. CSD were a well known, trusted security company. If Ray was not operating independently, but on behalf or as part of a government contract provided to CSD, then what were they really looking at? Was there something going on here that Ferris and Jacobson did not know about?

Or, was Luck a maverick who was still on the run but had broken into the CSD offices to use their resources, figuring that no one would be able to track him down to there?

If it was the former, they were screwed. Royally.

If it was the latter, then Ferris had to capture Luck before he got any further. Before he told the police, the newspapers, ...before he put the videos online, and told the world the truth.

Could it really be that only one man had caused so much damage, had frustrated the efforts of several governments and agencies to stop the peace initiative progressing? Could one man be so good?

Or were they up against far more?

For the first time Ferris began to have his doubts.

Either way, there was no time to lose.
Now they knew where Luck was, they were going after him. Again.
Ferris picked up the phone, and ordered transport.
He looked at his watch.
It was just gone 4.30. The dying time. The time when Ray Luck had to die.

Castle Security Defence Offices South West London

04.41a.m.

Ray dialled the last digit that was written down on the piece of paper and listened as the electronic tones began to sound off in his earpiece.

Di.DI.Do.Di.Do.DO.Di.De.DE.DE.Du.

The phone began to ring at the other end.
This was the worst part.
Would someone answer?
Would the PM answer?
Ray just didn't know what to expect.
Incredibly, someone picked up after only four rings.
"Paul, here. Whoever you are, this better be good. It's the middle of the night, and this is NOT a good time!"

For a second, Ray froze.

Paul ? *Paul who?*

Shit, Paul *Benton*, the Prime Minister! It's him. It's bloody him!

"Prime Minister?" Ray whispered, almost stupidly. He'd never expected to get this far.

"Last time I checked. Yes. Who's this?"

Ray hesitated... this was it... the point of total commitment and no going back.

"Prime Minister, this is Ray Luck. I was with Randolph Best moments before he was murdered."

"Ray Luck? Murdered? What on earth are you talking about? *Bloody hell*, do you know what sort of trouble you've caused? The future of our country and the Middle East is balancing on a knife edge, and all because of you and your bloody video! Randolph Best was a good man, and I hold you personally responsible for his death. You've got some nerve..."

"I didn't murder him, Prime Minister. I wasn't even there. I'd escaped by that time. It was the Security Service that assassinated him. Not me. And I can prove it. I have it all on video!"

"What? The Security Service? And another bloody video? Are you serious?"

"Yes. Do you know a man called Rowlinson, or another man called Jacobson or Ferris? Or Giles? They all seem to go by last names."

There was a pause at the other end of the line, then the Prime Minister came back on, his tone very different. More serious. More business-like. More in control.

"Don't say another word. Is your line secure?"

"I don't know."

"Blast...If what you are saying is true, then...we don't know who is listening. Where are you?"

"I'm at the offices of Castle Security Defence. It's where I work...*used* to work. I've probably been fired by now."

"Where are you *exactly*?"

Ray hesitated.

"How can I trust you?"

"You can't. It seems no one can trust anyone in this game," the Prime Minister replied. "But all I can say, is that I've been up all night. Fire-fighting. Trying to figure a way out of all this mess. The whole world thinks that Randolph took the easy way out and left us all to fry. By lunchtime, the Peace Initiative will be a distant memory, and my government will be close to collapse, unless we work together to stop it."

"I'm in the basement. Right at the bottom of the building, at the back."

"So, what's on these videos?"

"Everything. CCTV images of everything that happened in the flat, filmed in High Definition. It quite clearly shows the Security Service throwing him out of the window..., and I've also got internal CCTV videos of Bayla Adelstein trying to murder Randolph Best. You can see that she tries to kill him, but he then defends himself. It's conclusive. All of it. Watching it leaves no doubts. Anyone who sees the videos will know the truth. The peace initiative will be safe, and so will you and your government."

"Good. Stay right where you are. Don't move. Don't go anywhere. And don't talk to anyone else. We'll be there in fifteen minutes!"

The Prime Minister hung up.

Ray crunched up the paper with the PMs number on it and tossed it into a bin, then slid off his chair and sat on the floor.

It was done.

He prayed he'd just done the *right* thing.

Either way, it was too late.

They were coming for him.

And this time he wasn't going to run.

Chapter 55

London

Monday

October 9th

Castle Security Defence Offices in South London

04.56 a.m.

Ray was exhausted.

The adrenaline was beginning to leave his system, and he was finding it difficult to keep awake.

While he waited for the Prime Minister to arrive, he thought of Emma.

Was she now free? Was she on an aeroplane on the way back to the UK?

Ray was sure she would be.

With any luck, the PM would be able to find out where she was. Maybe, if she was on an aeroplane right now, Ray would be able to go and meet her when she landed.

If the PM was to be trusted, all Ray had to do now was hand over the videos into his safe keeping, give him the notes he had made, and then let him take over.

If the Government was still in control, and the UK was still being led by the good guys, then from that point forward, good should once more start to conquer over bad.

Ray would get his life back.

And he would make certain that this time round, Emma became his wife.

"Ray Luck, I presume!" a deep, coarse voice caught him by surprise.

Ray turned to face the door to the lab, and jumped to his feet.

Two men had come into the room. Both of them had guns pointed straight at him.

Neither of them was the Prime Minister.

"Who are you?" Ray asked, wondering for a second if they were the PM's security guards, or agents that he had sent ahead of himself.

From what the PM had said to him, Ray had assumed that the PM himself was coming to meet him and collect the videos.

On the other hand, they could be security guards for Castle Security Defence, thinking they had just come across Ray Luck, one of the most wanted terrorists in Europe.

Ray looked at the guns again and quickly realised that his last thought was way off the mark: civilian security guards did not carry guns.

"You don't need to know." The man replied.

This time, as soon as he spoke, Ray recognised him.

It was the man from the video. The one who had been looking at him over the CCTV cameras, the man who had found the CCTV servers and ripped them out of the network.

It was the man who had murdered Randolph Best.

'Ferris'.

Ray took a step backward, and turned to look at the other door at the back of the lab, the one that went out to the bathroom and the fire-exit which he had so nearly walked out of earlier that night.

Just as he looked at it, the door opened and another man stepped through into the lab.

He was also carrying a gun, and it too was pointing straight at Ray.

"Well," Ferris said, stepping forwards and towards Ray. "At last we meet. You've led us all on a merry dance. You *shit*. But no, you didn't escape. We're here now. And you belong to us."

"What do you want?" Ray asked, feigning innocence.

Ray knew. He'd already figured it out. Ferris must have looked at the videos on the server. Somehow, Ray didn't yet know how, Ferris had then figured out that Ray had seen the videos, and had tracked him down to here.

Ferris had killed Randolph Best. Ray knew that. Ferris knew that Ray knew.

So, the obvious thing was that having killed Randolph, they would now kill him.

"You recognise me, don't you?" Ferris asked, taking another step closer, the other man following him a few feet behind. "You know who I am? And what *I did*? Did you spy me with your little eye? Did you see it all, you fucker?"

Ray stepped backwards, coming up hard against a metal rack full of cables, plugs and a plethora of other IT bits and bobs.

"I have two questions for you Ray, and you will answer them for me. Believe me, you will. Of that I have no doubt." Ferris said, nodding at the other man who was now behind Ray and only a few feet away.

Ray spun around just in time to see the man behind lurching towards him, a large, muscle-bound arm trying to encircle his neck.

Ray ducked and shoved hard against the metal rack, making it first rock, then fall backwards.

Ray jumped to the side, spun and vaulted over the fallen rack.

At first, for a brief second, he thought he would be able to dodge around the back of the fallen rack, and quickly dart for the back door, pull it open and get out before the muscle man could get to him.

It didn't work out that way.

As soon as Ray took his attention away from Ferris, the accomplice beside Ferris dived for Ray, a pair of powerful heavy hands wrapping themselves quickly around Ray's chest, gripping him tight like a vice and lifting him off the floor.

Ray kicked backwards at the man's shins with his free feet, hitting them hard. The man swore aloud and immediately dropped him.

A second later Ray's world dissolved around him. A wall of pain, the like of which he had never experienced before, coursed across his chest and throughout his body.

Instantly he lost control of all his muscles, and he fell to the ground, shaking violently.

The pain seemed to go on forever: on and on and on.

Then suddenly, just as soon as it had begun, ...it stopped.

Castle Security Defence Offices in South West London

04.59 a.m.

"Pick him up and strap him to the chair," Ferris instructed the man who was busy nursing his legs. "But leave the taser barbs in him. Make sure you don't knock them out..."

Ray felt himself being lifted, and just as soon thrust into a chair. His hands were pulled behind him, around the back of the seat, and then he felt something cut into his skin. Groggy, and disorientated, he tried to move his hands apart and realised that he couldn't.

"Don't worry," Ferris said. "I know it hurts - it's meant to - but with any luck we'll be out of here soon. Any 'luck', get it? See, we're not without humour, are we?"

Ferris bent towards Luck and whispered in his ear.

"Now... before you die...you do know that you're going to die, don't you? I mean, *'I spy, you saw Best die'* didn't you? So, it's only fair that we kill you too! Anyway, before you die... I have these two interesting questions that you are going to answer for me, the first of which is this: *'who have you told about what you saw this evening?'* Then the second one will be, *'are you thinking that you might somehow be able to escape from here too, maybe climb up and over the roof, just like you did again at Best's this morning?"*

Ferris stood back and looked down at him, his eyes sparkling. He saw the recognition in Luck's eyes. Yep, *that* was how he escaped from them this morning.

"Of course, I already know the answer to the second question. It's no. On account of the fact that you will be dead, and we will be carrying your body out the door with us, and dropping it in a meat-grinder later on this morning. Which will incidentally leave no trace that you ever existed - especially once the sausages have been delivered to the shops, sold and eaten."

Ferris smiled.

He was holding two weapons now, one was a gun, and the other was the taser with which he had shot Luck.

He slipped the gun back into the holster under his arm, and then took hold of the barbs left in Ray's chest and yanked them out.

"I've changed my mind about these. We can do without them." Ferris reached into his pocket and pulled something out. "Did you know, that the initial punch of a taser is up to about 50,000 volts. But by the time the current flows down the wires and enters the body of the person who has been tasered, the charge is much less....probably only around 1,800 volts. I read that on Wikipedia, you know. It's full of interesting stuff. When I read that, it made me think...what a waste of perfectly good voltage! Why bother with the cables? Which is when I discovered that you can get this adapter which fits on here like this..." Ferris said, making a show of sticking something on the front of the taser, and showing it to Ray. "...Which allows you to put the taser directly against the skin, and give someone the benefit of the full 50,000 volts!"

Ferris pressed the trigger on the gun and a large blue light arced across the gap between two metal points now protruding from the front of the taser.

"Apparently," Ferris said, "...and I say 'apparently' because I've obviously never tried it out on myself..., the pain is way off the scale. Especially if I stick the taser against your testicles, like this..."

Without any further warning, Ferris pushed out his hand and stuck the front of the taser into Ray's groin, pulling the trigger for a couple of seconds.

Ray screamed, pushing back into the chair and writhing from side to side in pure, unadulterated agony.

Heavy hands now wearing rubber gloves pushed down upon him, keeping him pressed against the tips of the taser.

Then once again, the pain ceased, just as fast as it had appeared.

Ray felt drained, devoid of strength and will.

Ferris laughed.

"See what I mean? It's amazing isn't it? The taser across the chest is nothing in comparison, is it, even though it felt pretty bad at the time."

He took a step backwards and crossed his arms, cradling the taser against his chest.

Ferris was surprised just how much he was enjoying this.

"Well?" Ferris asked. "Shall I do it again, or are you going to tell me who you told about what you saw? I'll give you five seconds to think about it, then I'll zap you once again, but this time for ten seconds instead of three."

Ferris looked at the man on the left of Ray.

"Search his pockets, and his jacket. He must have a memory card on him somewhere if he downloaded the video. And check the laptop."

Coming round to stand in front of Ray, the man stuck his hand very roughly into each of his pockets, easily finding the USB that was there. He held it out to Ferris who quickly took it from him.

"Aha...so... Is this it? Is the video on here?"

Again, Ferris saw the recognition in Ray's eyes that told him that it was.

"You've got two seconds left...one second left.."

"*No!*" Ray screamed, "Please, I'll tell you who I told, just wait!"

Ferris's eyes opened wide. He hadn't expected that... that Ray had managed to tell someone.

"Who? Who did you tell?" he asked, bending across the chair and putting his face only inches from Ray.

"The fucking Prime Minister. Who do you bloody think? I called the Prime Minister on his mobile and told him *EVERYTHING!*"

Ferris stared at him. Not knowing how to react. Was Luck serious? Was he telling the truth?

Then he got the joke. He pushed back and stood up.

Ferris laughed.

"Nice one. You almost had me there for a second. But just for a second. Even I can't get to speak to the Prime Minister and I bloody work for him! You? *No chance!*"

Holding the USB stick out in his hand, he made a show of dropping it to the floor. Bending down he placed the tip of the taser against the USB stick and zapped it with 50,000 volts. Then, lifting his foot, he smashed it to pieces with his heel.

Ray's jaw dropped, watching Ferris grind the memory chip inside into the ground, and breaking it into several pieces.

"Actually, I think we're almost done here boys. Obviously Luck never managed to speak to anyone. And now...well, there's no proof of anything, is there? So it's time to go. Perhaps there's just time for one last burst with the taser where it really counts, and then we'll put you to sleep, carry you out to the van, and take you to the sausage factory. And by the way, just in case you think I'm joking, I'm not! About the sausage factory, or this..."

Ferris leant forward and pulled the trigger, letting Ray experience a full five seconds of hell before the battery went dead. He slumped forward and passed out.

"Shit..." Ferris said, looking at the gun. "I guess I was a bit too enthusiastic. Anyway, time to go. Free his hands from the chair and use the chloroform. It's high time we got out of here."

Ray was just coming around when he felt a tug on his wrists behind his back, his hands immediately falling free.

Somewhere, someone in the distant world around him had just mentioned the word chloroform.

Ray sniffed. He couldn't smell anything yet, but knew he would any second now.

From the depths of his being, Ray's subconscious summoned all the power it could muster in Ray's wrecked body.

"Now!" it shouted inside his mind. "*NOW! **RUN**!*"

Just as a hand appeared in front of his face, Ray sprung up from the chair, knocking the hand aside clumsily.

His mind willed his body to break into a run, to escape, but his legs did not respond.

Instead, Ray tumbled forward, knocking into Ferris and pushing him backwards.

"Bastard!" Ferris reacted, forcing Luck downwards, onto the floor.

The man with the chloroform soaked rag went to bend down to cover Ray's face, but Ferris shouted at him.

"Forget it. We'll do it now. I'm not going to wait another minute."

Ferris reached into his pocket and whipped out a silencer, loosing his gun from its holster and screwing the silencer onto the barrel.

Flicking the safety catch off, Ferris knelt on the floor beside Ray's head, and rested the barrel on his skull.

Ray had no more fight left in him. He looked up into Ferris's eyes, and saw only coldness, hatred and certain death. Ray closed his eyes and waited to die.

"Adios, amigo." Ferris taunted him. "This is definitely not your lucky day, pal. *I spy, now I'm going to watch you die.*"

The sound of the gun in the room was deafening.

Three bullets in rapid succession flew through the air, hit their target, and splattered the contents of the owner's skull across the floor.

Chapter 56

London

Monday

October 9th

Castle Security Defence Offices in South West London

05.02 a.m.

Simultaneously, two bursts of automatic fire sprayed across the room, slicing one of Ferris's men in half, and throwing the other off his feet and propelling him against a workbench where he slumped to the floor in a pool of blood.

Both men died before they knew what had happened to them.

On the floor, Ferris slumped down and across Ray's body, the top of his skull missing.

At first, Ray was sure that he had been shot. Confused, still feeling strange and not fully recovered from the effects of the taser, he struggled to understand what had just happened. After waiting for a few seconds for a wall of pain to hit him, or darkness and eternity to swallow him up, he found himself still conscious, but with what felt like a heavy weight pressing down upon him from above.

He opened his eyes.

Ferris's empty eyes, and an empty head gaped down at him, blood and brain material dripping down from his shattered skull onto Ray's face.

Fighting the instant urge to vomit, Ray pushed violently at Ferris's inert body, and managed to roll out from underneath him.

Trying to make sense of what had just happened, he turned as he stood up and saw the bodies of the other men.

"Are you okay?" a voice said to him.

Ray spun slowly back towards the door, searching for the man who had just spoken.

Dimly, Ray recognised him.

There were three men standing at the door, two men in suits on either side of a man dressed in a jacket, shirt and jeans, who, Ray's befuddled brain thought, was not as tall in real life as he was on the television.

All the men were armed: the men in the suits with small machine guns, and the man in the jeans with a gun, still held in an outstretched hand pointing at the body of Ferris on the floor.

Ray felt suddenly dizzy, queasy, and fell to his knees, the world around him beginning to spin.

The man with the gun stepped forward to catch him as he fell.

"Thanks," Ray whispered, "You just won my vote in the next election..."

Then the world went black, and Ray passed out.

Chapter 57

London

Monday

October 9th

Whitehall

09.30 a.m.

Rowlinson had not expected a call from the Concierge at No.11. Especially not so early.

Quite frankly, Rowlinson had been a little short with the man. It wasn't a good time. The man's request didn't upset him, but the last thing he needed right now was for the Members to summon him to an urgent meeting at the Club.

Only thirty minutes before, Jacobson had been on the phone, explaining that everything had not gone as sweetly as they had first thought.

Ferris, who was currently nowhere to be found, had apparently sent Jacobson an email from his office near Vauxhall at around four thirty that morning, explaining that he was worried that there was a potential problem. Not a minor problem. A fucking massive problem: Ferris had reason to believe that Ray Luck had witnessed the murder of Randolph Best and might have documentary evidence to prove it.

"What does that mean? Documentary evidence?" Rowlinson had demanded, his stress levels immediately returning to the levels they were early yesterday morning, before he had later heard the good news about Best's final demise.

"I don't know, sir. Ferris has gone off the grid. I can't contact him. Or his men. As far as I can make out, he ordered transport just after he wrote me the email, and then disappeared off into London somewhere with a couple of men from his team. The last thing he said in his email, was that he knew where Luck was, and that he was going to go and sort it out, once and for all. He promised to contact me as soon as he got back. That was five hours ago."

"And there's still no word from him?"

"None."

"Blast," Rowlinson had replied, reaching for his glass of water, and one of the new tablets that Mrs Rowlinson had got for him from their private doctor. It would help to relax him, apparently. In the past few days, Rowlinson had really begun to feel his age. This whole affair had begun to get the better of him. Mrs Rowlinson had even mentioned it to him last night, in close association with the 'R' word: *'You look tired darling. Exhausted. These long nights are beginning to take more of a toll on you darling. Maybe you should think again about that discussion we had about you retiring soon? Or at least, scaling everything back a little?'*

Rowlinson had smiled at her, made a promise to think about it, and then ignored her. He'd been back at his desk by six a.m. the next morning.

But maybe Mrs Rowlinson had a point after all?

"Well...if no one else has heard anything, and there's nothing coming in across the news feeds or any negative intelligence which would imply otherwise, I suppose all we can do is wait?" Rowlinson had eventually said, sitting back in his seat, closing his eyes and wondering how long it would be before the tablet would take effect. "Just make sure you call me the moment you hear anything new, okay?"

"I will, sir. I promise," Jacobson had assured him.

After Jacobson had hung up, Rowlinson's mind began to wander off into dark corners that he normally stayed well away from.

Awkward, dangerous *'What if...?'* scenarios began to play out in his imagination, and his stress levels started to rise. Rowlinson really didn't like the feeling.

Thankfully, a few minutes later, a much welcome but almost strange feeling of calm began to descend upon him.

By the time the call came in from No.11, he was feeling a lot more relaxed about everything.

Why the Members wanted to see him, the Concierge had not said, only that the meeting was mandatory, and that his presence had been specifically requested: unless there was an exceptional reason why not, Rowlinson should attend.

Rowlinson looked at his watch.

The meeting at the Club was scheduled to begin in thirty minutes.

Hopefully it would not last too long.

He should be back before one o'clock for a late lunch, and by that time Ferris would almost certainly be back, and the whole damned affair with Best and Luck would be over.

As Rowlinson left his office and took his private lift down to his waiting car, he began to wonder if Mrs Rowlinson was perhaps wrong after all. Rowlinson felt much better. He felt fine now. Maybe he had several years left in him after all.

No 11.

10.59 a.m.

It occurred to Rowlinson that the underground car park at the Club was surprisingly empty for the time of day. Normally people would be arriving for lunch by now, or to take up their seats in the library or at the card table for a game of lunchtime Bridge.

"Good Morning, sir," the Concierge had welcomed him, as he had stepped out of the lift. "The Executive Committee is waiting for you in the Osprey Room. Please go right up."

Curious.

"The Executive Committee?"

"Oh yes, sir? As I said on the phone, they specifically requested your presence this morning."

"Yes, I recall, you did mention that..."

Rowlinson stepped into the Members' lift and pressed the button to close the door.

In spite of the tablet he had taken earlier, he noticed that he was beginning to feel a little stressed again.

Maybe he should have taken two tablets instead of one?

Quickly, he reached into his pocket, taking out the small silver tin. He opened it up, selected a tablet and dropped it in his mouth, washing it down with a quick swig of the good stuff from his hip flask.

He was sure he would be fine now.

Still, he would ask Mrs Rowlinson about the dosage later on, when he arrived home.

At the door to the Osprey Room, Rowlinson pulled out the pocket watch on the end of his gold chain, flipped open the hunter case and checked the time.

Blast, the conversation with the Concierge had made him a couple of minutes late.

Out of habit, he gave the watch a few winds, and then popped the watch back into the pocket of his waistcoat.

Knowing he was already tardy, he grabbed hold of the large door handle and attempted to slip into the meeting without being noticed.

Inside the room, there were three Members. No one else was yet present.

The three Members were all silent, their expressions rather serious, their eyes immediately upon him as the door opened and Rowlinson stepped inside.

"Please, come in, sit down..." the most senior of the Members present invited. "You may take a seat, just there, in front of you, where you came in."

Rowlinson stood beside the table, and coughed nervously.

The table was long, made of the most beautiful, polished mahogany. It was reputedly over four hundred years old.

Rowlinson looked quizzically at the other members seated directly opposite him, but when the senior member once again gestured with his hand for Rowlinson to sit down, he felt obliged to comply.

And slightly more relaxed.

As soon as Rowlinson had taken his seat, the other two members who had not yet said a word, slowly stood up and left the room via a back door.

"I'm sorry, I thought this was an Executive Meeting?" Rowlinson asked, gesturing at the two men who had just left,"...but there are only two of us? Where are the other Members?"

"I was asked to talk to you. I think it's best if we talk alone."

Rowlinson felt a slight twinge in his chest. A rather uncomfortable feeling that he hadn't experienced before. And which he didn't like.

"About what?" Rowlinson queried.

"It's a rather delicate matter. Something that we feel, well, we feel it's not ideal if the Club is associated with the situation that seems to be developing. And quite frankly, we feel that, given that it's your affair, perhaps you may wish to consider the honour of the Club. Along with your own honour?"

The senior member stood up. He clapped his hands, and the door behind Rowlinson opened up.

The Concierge walked in, carrying a large gold tray.

There were two items on the tray: an iPad, and a white cloth, which seemed to be covering something more bulky underneath.

Rowlinson stared at the tray, beginning to feel a little strange. The tension in his chest had got worse. A lot worse. He felt clammy, hot, a little nauseous. He was no longer feeling relaxed at all.

The senior member on the other side of the room spoke again.

"I'm going to step outside the room again. Once I leave, I would invite you to touch the 'play' button on the screen of the iPad. We have loaded a video onto it for you. It's a video that was shared with us by a fellow member earlier on this morning. It's interesting, but rather shocking. And, your name is mentioned in it."

Rowlinson took a handkerchief from his jacket pocket and wiped his forehead.

He looked at the iPad and saw the symbol on the screen, a large triangle, inviting him to touch it.

"After you have seen the video, please feel free to look underneath the handkerchief. I, along with the rest of the Executive Committee felt assured that you will understand what to do."

The Senior Member smiled at him, took a step backwards from the table, turned and then exited the room through the door through which the others had previously left.

Rowlinson heard the door close, then a sudden silence descended upon the Osprey Room.

An oppressive silence.

Rowlinson listened for a second. For the first time ever, No 11 seemed to be devoid of sound.

The building sounded as if it was empty.

The only sound he could hear was his own, laboured breathing.

For a good three minutes Rowlinson stared at the iPad and the triangular symbol, his heart beating faster and faster, in spite of the medication Mrs Rowlinson had so kindly arranged for him.

Lifting his hand, curiosity finally got the better of him, and he gently pulled on the edge of the handkerchief to see what was underneath.

No 11.

11.28 a.m.

Downstairs, the Concierge had much earlier locked the door to the Club, the first time the Club had been closed in over twenty years.

The Concierge looked at the Senior Member, who stood beside him. They both looked up at the Grand Clock which adorned the wall above the Reception.

Time seemed to tick slowly by, the passing of each second echoing around the inside of the reception area, the movement of the clock's hands never having been so audible or pronounced before.

Tick. Tock. Tick. Tock.

Each second hung mercilessly in the air, the expectation so thick it pressed down upon them both.

Tick.

At 11.36 a.m. precisely, there was a single loud retort, the sound of the gunshot almost deafening the Senior Member and the Concierge, even though they had been expecting it.

Chapter 58

London

Monday

October 9th

A private hospital in Whitehall

11.40 a.m.

The doctor took his stethoscope off Ray's chest and smiled.
"It's all good. I'm happy to say that I can find nothing physically wrong with you that a good sleep and a few days' rest won't fix. Given that you experienced several taser blasts - is that the right word? - in quick succession, I'm not surprised you fainted, and were confused and disorientated for a while. Especially since you also took the full brunt of forty to fifty thousand volts straight in the groin! If that had happened to me, I don't think I would have walked for a week!" The doctor smiled. "And don't worry...in answer to your other question, the taser blast in your nether regions won't have any lasting effect on your ability to have children. And that's it... you're free to go!"
Ray thanked the doctor, and started to sit up in his bed.
One of the security guards who had been with the Prime Minister earlier that morning entered the room.
"Mr Luck, apparently you've got the all clear?"
Ray nodded.
"Excellent. The Prime Minister has requested that I drive you to No.10. He just convened an emergency meeting of his Cabinet, and he would like you to attend. That is, if you have the time, and you don't have any other plans?"
Ray laughed.
"Actually, strangely, I don't," he replied.
Had he really just been invited to No. 10?
His mum would never believe it!

En route to No.10

11.55 a.m.

The trip to the Prime Minister's office from the private hospital near Whitehall didn't last long, but it was amazing.

His 'luck' had definitely returned.

It wasn't every day that you were given the opportunity to ride in the PM's official limousine.

As he rode down Whitehall from Trafalgar Square to Downing Street, Ray started to relax for the first time in weeks.

The threat was gone.

It was over.

The PM had already promised that by the end of the day, Ray would have his life back again.

And not only that, there was a strong possibility that Ray would be a national hero.

'How quickly someone can go from one end of the spectrum to the other!' Ray thought to himself.

"Excuse me, sir," Ray said politely, trying to get the driver's attention. "Does this phone work? Would it be okay if I gave my Mum a quick call?"

"Certainly, sir. Just pick it up and dial the number. I'll close this window so that you can have some privacy. Shall I drive around Parliament Square a couple of times until you're finished?"

"Please. If you could? I mean, so long as you don't get in trouble with the police or anything..."

"Don't worry about that, Mr Luck. This is the Prime Minister's vehicle. And in case you hadn't noticed, we do actually have a police guard already. From what I hear, you're a very special man just now!"

The first call Ray made was long overdue.

"Hi, Mum! It's me, Ray! You will never guess where I am..."

The second call went to voice mail.

"Emma, hi! It's Ray. Are you okay? Are you well? I've been so worried about you...I was wondering, hoping, that you would be back in the UK by now...but I've just been told that you are coming home tomorrow. Don't worry. Everything is fine here. It's all over, Emma. *It's over.* I survived. *We* survived. I just hope you will find it in yourself to truly forgive me."

Ray paused.

"You won't believe this, but I'm just on my way to No. 10 Downing Street. I'm in the PM's own personal limousine. I've got a question for you. At first I couldn't think of anywhere else in the world better than here to ask it, but now I can. It can wait till then. Until you are in my arms...Emma, I love you. Please come back to me. I can't wait to see you!"

No. 10
Downing Street
London

It was all rather like a dream. As they approached the barricade at the entrance to Downing Street, the barrier dissolved in front of them, and Ray's limousine was admitted straight in.

When the car drew up to No. 10, Ray went to open the door to climb out, but found that a policeman had rushed forward from the door and opened it for him.

"Good morning, Mr Luck. Well done! The Prime Minister is expecting you!"

As he walked towards the door with the most famous two digits in the world on it, No. '10', the door swept open in front of him and he was ushered inside.

"Good morning, Mr Luck. Please follow me," a man, the PM's personal secretary, invited him. "The Cabinet is awaiting you."

"The Cabinet?" Ray swallowed hard.

"Yes, sir. The Cabinet. And the Prime Minister as well, naturally."

The next hour was very surreal.

Ray Luck, anarchist, hacker, criminal and world-terrorist was ushered into the very heart of the British establishment and unanimously declared a national hero by every member of the British Cabinet who shook his hands.

The PM had shown him around the long, grand table around which the Cabinet sat, and introduced him to each one personally.

At the end, he was given a glass of port, and the Prime Minister led a toast in Ray's honour.

"This, Mr Ray Luck, is the British Cabinet. Today, thanks to you and your bravery, the Cabinet still exists. Thanks to your heroic actions the British Government exists. Thanks to you, from your confession to Randolph Best concerning your friend Andy Grentham, London, its inhabitants and the Bank of England have been saved and the future of the UK as a leading centre of financial excellence is assured. And thanks to your vindication of Randolph Best, his life's work - the Middle East Peace Initiative - will survive. There are so many thanks that we owe to you, Mr Ray Luck. And for all of it we are grateful. We thank you, kind Sir. We thank you!"

There followed a round of "Hear! Hear!" and Ray Luck blushed.

And realising he was actually blushing, he blushed again.

A double blush.

"And now, if you will excuse us Ladies and Gentlemen, Ray and I have some things to discuss..."

Ray followed the PM through to the other room.

It was hard not to be impressed by the man.

Not only was he good looking, and endowed with more than a fair share of charm, but this was the man that earlier on that morning had saved Ray Luck's life.

From this day forward, to the day he died, Ray Luck would be indebted to him.

He had Ray's vote.

"So," the PM said, waving to a beautiful leather armchair in an adjoining room. "We have a lot to discuss."

Ray was with the PM for a whole hour.

They started with idle chit chat but quickly moved on to more serious matters.

"First, Ray, may I call you Ray? Good...I would like to apologise to you on behalf of the British Government for all that has happened to you. Agencies that work for us wrongly described you as an International Terrorist, and for the past few weeks your life has been stolen from you. Also, we accept that unauthorised actions were taken against your girlfriend - Emma Purvis - by our colleagues in Canada. For that we also apologise. And please, rest assured, I can promise you that a significant level of compensation will be paid to you both. In return, we just ask that you will not discuss this matter further beyond the confines of this room. Today, my focus is all about rebuilding the trust in the Government, not in destabilising it further. If possible, I would like to have your assurance before we leave the room that this matter rests here?"

The PM reached into his pocket and passed Ray a slip of paper.

Ray took it in his hands and examined it.

A cheque.

For a lot of money.

A lot.

He whistled.

"To be quite honest," Ray replied. "I would be happy to agree to that, even without the compensation - although Emma will have to decide for herself obviously - if you can just guarantee to me in writing that this is all over. I did a silly thing, I know, and perhaps I got punished for it. I learned a lesson. I learned just how much I love Emma, my life, and living. Give me those back, and we have a deal."

"Ray, it's not that simple. You have those back anyway. And, although you don't know it yet, perhaps you were not such an innocent bystander as you might think. Perhaps you became involved, because there are people who wanted you to get involved. You saw what you did, because you were meant to see it."

"What do you mean?"

"I'm afraid, I can't really say. But I am just being honest with you, because you deserve it."

Ray was silent. He could tell from the PM's tone that he wouldn't get anything more out of him than that. However, the seed of doubt had been planted and already his mind was beginning to run in circles?

Was it an accident that he saw Randolph Best murder Bayla Adelstein, or was there more to it.

Was he *meant* to see it?

"You'll never know." The PM said.

"What?"

"I said, you will never know the answer to the question you are just asking yourself."

Ray stared at the PM. How did he know what he was thinking?

"And the answer to that question, is that in my job we are trained in the ability to make people think certain things, to ask certain questions. Questions which we can answer, instead of questions we can't. Although in this case, I won't. And I can't."

Ray lifted his eyebrows.

The PM leant forward.

"I also have a personal request of you, Ray. I would like you to promise me that you will never ever mention that you saw me with a gun this morning. I am authorised to have one and use one, but it's something that I am not proud of, and I don't want to be known for. Could you do that?"

"But you saved my life! You're a hero, too!"

"That doesn't matter. I did what was necessary. Only that. Do you agree not to mention it again?"

"Certainly, if that's what you want. But I will never forget what you did for me. Never."

The PM smiled.

A moment passed.

"So, who was behind it all? And what will happen to Giles and Rowlinson and Jacobson."

"We're trying to work all that out just now. We don't know all the answers yet. Just some. Later today we will be releasing selected sequences from the films you provided to me to the news agencies and the general public. There will be a press conference. We will put a slight spin on it. We won't tell the whole truth, but we will tell as much of it as we can. After that, we will let justice take its own course. However, I understand that Rowlinson will not be prosecuted. Rather than face the music, he took his own life earlier this morning. Strangely no one knows where Jacobson is just now. He seems to have disappeared. Personally, I don't expect we will ever see him again..."

A sudden vision of a meat grinder and sausages came into Ray's mind, and he shuddered. If that's what was going to happen to Jacobson, to make him disappear, perhaps he deserved it. Earlier on that morning, that was apparently the fate that had been chosen for him.

"...and Giles? Well, Giles is actually a good man. He was ordered to do what he did. And he did it. Such loyalty, even though it was misguided by his superiors, is exactly what we need in the Security Service. I suspect he may be promoted."

Ray coughed and spluttered.

"Are you serious?"

"Yes."

That was the first of several surprises that morning.

"Can I ask you about Andy Grentham, Prime Minister. What will happen to him?"

"He is missing. I'm afraid I genuinely can't tell you where he is. I understand that Rowlinson was in charge of the operation to bring him in. For now, that is an ongoing area of investigation. Where the Security Service is involved, sometimes these things take time."

"Will you find him?"

"If Rowlinson spirited him away somewhere for interrogation, to be truthful, I don't know. But I can only promise you that we will do our best."

"And the attacks that he was planning? You stopped them all?"

"As far as I know, yes, we have."

"What will happen to him, if you find him?"

"He's dying isn't he? And you asked Randolph to go easy on him, didn't you?"

"Yes...and he did agree to it..."

"Then I will honour that pledge. If we find him, we'll put him under house arrest somewhere, maybe even in his own home, and let him spend his last few days in peace. From what you say, that won't be long?"

"No."

"Then, so be it." The PM paused. "Ray..., don't worry about it. I've seen the videos. I know you were caught between a rock and a hard place: report a friend to the police, or keep quiet to protect him and then watch people die as a result. You made the right choice. You did the right thing, Ray. I can promise you. Not everyone would have, but *you* did!"

Ray nodded, feeling both sad and happy at the same time.

At the back of his mind, just for a second, Ray wished that Emma had been here to hear what the Prime Minister had just said.

Ray looked away for a moment, and out of the window. The PM gave him some space.

"Prime Minister. I need to ask *you* a favour, if I may. Now this is all over, I think I need to tell you about a small problem I may have...I want to start my new life with a clean slate, so as you prepare or negotiate my 'pardon', perhaps there is something else about me that you need to know... "

"Which is?"

"Well, one night, when I was drunk...and just after my world had begun to collapse, I think that I may have pulled off one of Britain's largest cyber bank robberies?"

"You stole money from a bank?"

"You could say that."

"How much?"

"Actually, I can't remember exactly. But it was a lot. To be truthful. I was rather drunk, and it was a mistake. I think I was a little bored..."

The PM stared at Ray, and then laughed.

"Ray Luck, you don't cease to amaze me. Please confess all, and then let's see what I can do..."

Chapter 59

London

Tuesday

October 10th

London Heathrow

11.40 a.m.

Ray watched, bleary eyed, but awake and incredibly - against all the odds - very much alive, as the passengers from Air Canada 854 from Vancouver began to stream out into the arrivals hall through Customs.

Poorly hidden behind his back and held in his left hand was the largest bouquet of red roses he was able to find in the airport florist. His other hand was free and ready to wrap Emma into the biggest cuddle in the world.

Where was she?

As the people swept past him, his eyes fervently scanned the crowds, searching for her but without any luck.

All around him people were shouting and waving, and wrapping their arms around the newly arrived, but Emma...she was nowhere to be seen.

Nowhere.

After a while, as the number of people coming through the doors began to thin out, Ray began to get scared.

Did the Prime Minister's secretary give him the wrong flight details?

Did she miss the flight?

Or worse still, once she got her freedom, did she have second thoughts about him? Did she decide to stay in Canada, and not come home?

Had she changed her mind about wanting to be with Ray?

Had he saved her life, but then lost her after all?

Was this the end of his 'lucky' streak?

Was the 'high' that he had been surfing on since yesterday morning just about to crash and drop him on the rocky shore of broken hearts?

Slowly, as every minute ticked by, the euphoria of the past twenty-four hours began to fade away.

Soon, the stream of people became a trickle, and then dried up.
Emma was not there.
She hadn't come home.
Hoping against hope, Ray stood there for another thirty minutes, watching arrivals from several other planes disgorge into the airport around him.
Maybe she was sick? Perhaps her luggage had got lost and she was trying to sort it out?
If he waited a little longer, maybe she would still come...

He tried calling her several times on her old telephone number. If she had come home, it made sense to think her number would still be active.
The phone rang, but each time it went to voicemail. There was no reply.

Eventually, at 1.30 p.m. Ray took a seat, sitting at the back of the Arrival's Hall, no longer scanning the electronic doors each time they opened, no longer hoping beyond all hope that she would still come.
It was obvious now.
She had made a decision, made her choice...and she had chosen Canada, and not Ray.
Perhaps she blamed it all on him, and now it was all over, she realised that there was no way, given everything that had happened, that she could be with him!

In a way, it was understandable.

Emma was a beautiful woman, she had so much to offer anyone she chose, so why would she want to be with him?
Really?
Why?

"Are you okay, mate?"
A man's voice.
A security guard, in a blue uniform. Crisp. Neat.
"You've been sitting there for a while, mate...I'm guessing your friend didn't turn up?"
Ray looked up at him.
"What time is it, please?"
"It's 4.00 p.m. Hey, I hope you don't mind me asking, but are you the guy that was in the news? The man who the government just apologised to and pardoned. The hero guy?"

"No." Ray replied, "I'm no hero. It won't have been me. Here, would you like some flowers for your Mrs? They're pretty. It would be a shame to throw them away, and I don't need them anymore."

The train back into London was full of happy, smiling people.
All people from a different planet.
As he sat there, he noticed several people looking at him. Watching him. Staring at him.
Did they all know that he had just been dumped? Was it that obvious?
Then one of them left their paper behind when they got out at Clapham Junction and he picked it up.
His picture was all over the front page: **"The Truth is Revealed! Meet the Hero!"**
Ray dropped the paper, and turned to look out the window.
He felt empty.
Emma.
Why....?

At Waterloo, he dropped into a chemist and bought a fresh toothbrush. He'd spent last night visiting his mum, and convincing her that life was back to normal. Telling her that everything was going to be fine.
Except now that was a lie, wasn't it?
The tube journey back to South Kensington took another twenty minutes.
He'd better get some milk. Some bread. Something to eat tonight.
What would the flat be like now? What state had the police left it in?

It would be weird walking up the steps and in through the front door. He'd honestly thought that he would never be back. That his life in St Cecilia's Square was over.
Perhaps it was. Maybe now he would sell it, and move somewhere else.

Letting himself in with his key at the main door, he checked for letters and bills in his mail box, and then walked slowly up the stairwell.
Strangely, there was no mail at all.
Not even junk-mail.
Maybe the police or the Security Service had put a divert on it, so that they could read all his letters and pry into his life. He'd have to call them - who would he call? - to get it changed back? Ray Luck was still alive. He was free. He was home.
At the top of the stairs, he stopped. Hesitating.
The neighbour's door was a different colour.

He looked at the name plate. That was new too.
Mr Grace?
What had happened to the old lady who lived there?
He rang the doorbell.
"Hi? I'm your neighbour. Ray Luck?....Oh...she died? In hospital? When?...Oh....Shit...I'm sorry..."
Fuck.
Poor Mrs Simons.

The neighbour's door closed and Ray stood by himself at the top of the stairs.
He lifted the key to open his door, but froze.
He couldn't do it.
He couldn't go in.
Perhaps it would be better if he just started a new life, here, now...leave the old one behind. Just walk away.

Suddenly, he noticed a smell in the stairwell.
The smell of curry.
Someone was cooking, and Ray realised with an involuntary flood of saliva in his mouth that he hadn't eaten since breakfast.
He was starving.
Knowing that there were biscuits in his kitchen, and maybe some pasta, he put the key in the door, and turned it.

He sensed the person inside his flat before he saw them.
It was an instinct.
A primordial skill that he'd finely tuned in the past few weeks.
Suddenly all the hairs on his arms and neck jumped to attention, and his heart skipped a beat.
For a second he thought about turning, running, escaping... while he still could.
But then an anger flared within him.
Who the hell's here? This is MY flat. I live here. I've been pardoned. I'm innocent.
And I've had enough.
No more running. No more living in fear.
It ends here. And now.
Whoever you are, I'm going to face up to you, stand my ground, and throw you out!

Ray pushed the door open wide and stepped inside.
In the next second his life changed. Forever.

Chapter 60

London

Tuesday 10th

St. Cecilia's Square.

7.15 p.m.

The woman inside the flat looked up at Ray.
She was kneeling on one knee.
Her eyes glistened.
There were tears pouring down her face, the bruises now fading.
Her hand was outstretched.
Palm up.
A small open box, sitting there, on her soft skin, its contents glistening in the light.
"Ray Luck," the woman said, "Will you marry me?"

Chapter 61

Epilogue

Friday 13th

St. Cecilia's Square.

11.55 a.m.

Ray lay in his bed and laughed.
He reached out with his fingers and caressed Emma's hair.
Soft, golden, beautiful.
As was the rest of Emma.
He turned towards her, cuddled up closer and whispered in her ear.
"I'm the luckiest man in the world."
She replied.
"And I'm going to be the luckiest woman in the world. Emma Luck. It sounds good!"

After the tears, the shock, the disbelief, the realisation that it was real, that Emma really, *truly*, was actually kneeling on the floor in his hallway, his engagement ring being proffered to him, Ray had collapsed to his knee, cradled her face in his hands and whispered one word: 'Yes!'

That was on Tuesday.
The past three days had been spent in the bedroom.
Crying. Cuddling. Eating. Drinking. Breathing. Sleeping.
Making love.
And then more crying. Cuddling. Eating. Drinking. Breathing. Sleeping.
And more making love.
A pattern had developed.
A lovely, beautiful pattern that Ray hoped would go on forever.
Well, perhaps, less of the crying, and more of the laughing would be good.

They had locked themselves away. Not answering the phone. Or the door.
Only twice did Ray make contact with the outside world.
Once to call his sister.
And once to call the Prime Minister's secretary: had there been any news of Andy?

There had.

The news was both good and bad.
The bad news, the somewhat sad news, was that Andy was dead.
He had been tracked down to a hospice in Chelsea.
A private room, with Level Two police security. No one was to know he was there.
He had died early on Wednesday morning.
Whether it was suicide or just a natural death it was difficult to tell.
Apparently the pain had become unbearable. He'd been allowed to self-administer the morphine by simply pressing on a button.
He'd pressed the button a lot.
Once too often.

The good news was that in the days after he was put in the room, he had started to cooperate fully with the people who had put him there.
In exchange for medication he had told them almost everything.
Almost.
Then on the Tuesday night, once he had all the medication he would ever need, he had asked for a laptop and he had shown them one more thing that they had never known about: Andy's plan to lower the Thames Tidal Barrier and destroy London.

It seemed that in the last few hours of his life, he had reconsidered it all.
There had been a message, a simple message for Ray.

"If he's alive, tell him that he was right. It's better to die a hero, than a fool."

12.10 p.m.

Emma screamed at Ray, "Quick, come through, you've got to see this!"
Ray jumped out of the bed, and followed Emma through to the lounge where she had gone to catch the news.

The news reporter was laughing, standing in front of a crowd of people in a street in the City of London.
"...apparently it's the same, all over London. Today, at around 12.00 noon on the dot, ATM machines all over the capital started spewing out £10, £20, and £50 notes onto the street. The machines are literally throwing money at people, and they continue until the machines are empty. No one can stop them. Apparently the banks can't switch them off.

People all over the Capital are helping themselves to whatever they can get. The authorities seem powerless to stop it."

The camera zoomed in on the faces of the people who were walking away from the cash machines.

They were laughing, happy, exuberant.

"It's like Christmas!" someone was shouting.

"Whoever RobinHood is, he's a bloody national hero!" another shouted.

The reporter came back on the screen.

"Nobody seems to know who RobinHood is, but his name is on the lips of everyone in the capital today. It seems that every ATM machine in London has a message posted on its screen. It's just a few sentences..."

"The message reads... *'On behalf of all the bankers in the world who stole your money, please accept this gift! And have a drink on me! RobinHood.'* "

It seemed that in the end Ray and Andy had both learned how to do the right thing.

Chapter 62

Friday 13th

St. Cecilia's Square.

7.15 p.m.

Jacobson sat patiently in the car on the opposite side of the road from the entrance to the building Ray Luck lived in.

He'd been waiting now for over seventy-two hours.

His intelligence was that Ray was in the building, with his girlfriend Emma.

They hadn't come out in days.

Jacobson knew that it would be soon.

Very soon.

Reaching into the pocket of his jacket, he fingered the edge of his new passport, subconsciously reaffirming to himself that it was actually there.

If Ray walked out the door in the next few hours, there would still be time to make it to Dover, and slip across the channel on the boat that was waiting for him.

Once in France, he'd catch the train, and make his way slowly to Munich. From there, he'd fly directly to Israel.

He was looking forward to finally seeing Tel Aviv again. After all these years.

And finally being able to use his real name, Avi Levy.

He'd served Mossad well over the past twenty years, and now it was time for Israel to welcome him home.

This was his last job.

Killing had never really meant anything to Jacobson. After the first person who he killed in hand-to-hand combat, taking another life had never bothered him again.

That said, he was beginning to think twice about what he was going to do next.

Ray Luck had served them all well.

Naively. Without realising it.

But, he had done a good job.

Sadly, the Peace Initiative looked as if it was going to survive, but Jacobson knew that Mossad had other plans that could still derail it yet.

But thankfully Randolph Best was gone.
And no one was bringing him back.

It would also be rather ironic.
Ray Luck.
Killed on Friday 13th.
Not so lucky today, then, huh?

Just then, the door to No. 23 opened.
Jacobson immediately tensed.
Two people were coming out.
A woman, and a man.
The man partially shielded by the woman.
Jacobson reached under the car seat, flicked a switch and caught the gun as it dropped from its hiding place.
He quickly checked the silencer to make sure it was still attached firmly, slipped off the safety catch, and lowered the electric window nearest to the targets.
It was dark now, and the street around was empty.
Jacobson raised the gun and pointed it at Luck, waiting for him to take a few steps more down the street, hopefully giving him a better shot, clear of the woman.
For a second, Jacobson thought of the woman.
Did she know she was pregnant?
Had the doctors who had examined her in Canada to make sure she was fit to leave told her the news before she had been set free?
Jacobson had seen the report two days ago, provided to him by one of his contacts from the Embassy where he had been lying low.

Ray Luck was going to be a father.
Did *he* know?
Had she told him?

Maybe neither of them knew.

The woman was pointing at something, and Ray had stopped to listen to her.

Ray was in front now, closer to Jacobson, between him and the woman.
It was a clear shot.

In total, Jacobson has killed sixty three people in his career to date.
Ray would be sixty four.

Jacobson's finger tensed, the pressure on the trigger increasing.
In less than a second, Ray Luck would be dead.

"My shoelace is undone?" Ray said, "You sound just like my mother!" Ray laughed, turning to Emma and bending down.

The bullet zipped past the top of Ray's head, flattening out on impact against the wall several metres behind.

For a second Jacobson stared in disbelief. He couldn't believe it.
It was almost like a scene from a comedy film.
Then Jacobson laughed, shaking his head.
He lowered his gun, and slid it under his jacket on the seat beside him.
Taking another look at Ray and Emma, he smiled to himself.
Sixty three was just as good a number as sixty four.

Turning the key in the ignition, he eased the car into the centre of the road and drove past Ray and Emma, and their unborn child.

Jacobson had just retired.

And today was Ray Luck's lucky day.

THE END

Have you enjoyed the book?

What should you do next?

May I suggest the following....

1: Go to Goodreads, Amazon or wherever you purchased the book from and write a review…tell people what you thought of the book, now, while it is still fresh in your mind!

2: If you have enjoyed this book, you may want to read another book by Ian C.P. Irvine. You can find details below of the omnibus editions of all my books, or you can 'Try-and-Buy' by going to www.free-ebooks.co.uk.

Why not download them all?

3: For those of you have been up all night reading, now it's time to get some sleep! Good night!

A Personal Note from the Author

"*Hi,*

Thanks for reading this novel. I am really flattered that you chose one of my books to read, from all of the millions of books on Amazon. I hope you enjoyed it. I would love to hear from you if you did! You can contact me on iancpirvine@hotmail.co.uk .
If you would like to be kept informed of any new books I will be publishing, may I invite you to sign up to my mailing list at http://eepurl.com/AnYs9. Details of my other books already available on Amazon can be found below. Good luck with your next choice of book!
For information on my other Free Ebooks, please visit www.free-ebook.co.uk.

Kind regards,
Ian C.P. Irvine."

Please look out for others books by IAN C.P.IRVINE:-

Haunted From Within

For some, death is not the end. Thanks to modern medicine, they are given a second chance. A second chance to live, and another chance to kill.

A fast paced contemporary medical thriller, based upon a true medical mystery that scientists and doctors do not yet understand.

Readers should be warned that the novel contains strong language and scenes of sex and violence.

The Story:
When Peter Nicolson, a reporter with the Edinburgh Evening News, is almost killed by a gang leader out to make his mark, the only way to save his life is through a double kidney transplant. One of the first people in the world to be treated with the new genetic wonder drug 'SP-X4', Peter makes a remarkable recovery. Yet as he recovers, his personality begins to change, and he discovers that he can see visions of unsolved killings committed by a murderer that no one has ever caught. Peter sets out to solve the murders, to track down the killer, and find out the truth behind the visions that he sees.

As time progresses, and as Peter uncovers a trail of death that stretches across the United Kingdom and Europe, the makers of 'SP-X4' watch his actions from afar, anxious that he will uncover the incredible truth behind their new drug treatment, and conspiring to make sure he does not succeed in revealing it to the world.

'Haunted From Within' is also the story of seven separate lives: readers will follow each character as the plot develops and their lives intersect, culminating in a surprise ending that few will predict.

Please beware: this book is based on fact: a medical phenomena that few understand and most are unaware of. At first, it may seem hard to believe. This is after all, just a story, a fast-paced thriller written to entertain you . . . but it will leave you wondering and talking about the definition of 'life' itself. Enjoy!

Haunted From Without

The Sequel to Haunted From Within, after you have read 'Haunted From Within (Book Two): Peter's Story"

Following the international success of Haunted From Within, Haunted From Without is the latest thought-provoking medical thriller from Ian C.P. Irvine.

Based upon a real life mystery, Haunted From Without will make you question the meaning of life itself. It will shock you, scare you and have you turning the pages until late into the night.

Haunted From Without is a unique combination of medical thriller, conspiracy thriller, mystery, detective fiction and ghost story.

With several stories that twist and turn together, culminating in an ending you will not predict, Haunted From Without will keep you riveted to your Kindle for hour after hour.

Who are 'the Others'? Why are an increasing number of people throughout the world developing the ability to see and speak with the dead?

Why have a farmers' guild from Iowa secretly enlisted the help of Scottish reporter Peter Nicolson? If they are correct, is the world stumbling blindly into a disaster that could threaten the survival of the human race? And what is contained within the missing 'GM File' that threatens to destroy some of the world's most powerful companies? To what lengths will these companies go to prevent Peter Nicolson uncovering the truth and publishing it to the world?

Who has kidnapped the Scottish teenager Debbie McCrae? Will she manage to escape, or will she be killed by her mysterious abductor?

What is the secret that Susie's dad tried to tell her as he died? And who is the mysterious Timothy?

Can Peter Nicolson help stop the biggest terrorist attack the world has ever seen and prevent the destruction of the city of London?

Will Peter Nicolson meet Maciek, his nemesis and erstwhile saviour? And if he does, who will survive?

To find the answers to all these question and more, download Haunted From Without today, find a comfortable seat, and forget about doing anything else for the next few days!

Happy Reading!
(But don't switch the light off... you don't know who might be watching you!)

The Orlando File : A page-turning Mystery & Detective Medical Thriller Available in Paperback or Ebook

The Orlando File is a fast paced thriller, based upon the latest state-of-the-art discoveries in genetics and stem-cell research. The result is a truly scientific adventure but with a thrilling twist.

When Kerrin Graham, a retired cop and now an investigative journalist with the Washington Post, receives a call in the middle of the night, his life is about to be turned upside down.

Six of the world's leading geneticists have all 'committed suicide' in the past seven days, his brother-in-law being the latest to die. Establishing that those who died were all employees of the Gen8tyx Company, a secretive research company based in Orlando, Kerrin sets out to discover the truth behind their deaths.

Discovering that those who died were killed to stop them unveiling the results of their revolutionary stem-cell research, a discovery that could usher in a new age of hope and health for all humanity, Kerrin vows to find who was responsible for their deaths and to uncover the powerful secret they were killed to protect.

On a trail that takes him around the world and back, Kerrin uncovers a sinister organisation that will stop at nothing to protect the secret behind the mysterious 'Orlando Treatment'.

When those around him start to die, and his wife disappears, it becomes a race against time to find the missing 'Orlando File', the only hope of saving his crippled wife and proving to an unsuspecting world, the truth behind the sinister Chymera Corporation of America.

And yet, when Kerrin eventually understands just what the Orlando File contains, he is faced with a choice no man should ever have to make, and everyone who reads this book must ask the same question:

"What would I do, if I were him?"

... and anyone who reads this book could learn a simple little known medical fact that could extend their life by 20 years.

The Sleeping Truth : A Romantic Medical Thriller

In 2005 London is the best and most exciting city in the world. But then the terrorist bombs of July 7th blow the city apart, and lives and worlds are shattered . . . For some, nothing will ever be the same again.

The Story:
In an attempt to escape from his past and start a new life, Andrew Jardine moves to London in July 2005 and moves in with his best friend Guy.

But when out one night in London, Andrew accidentally sees Guy's new girlfriend, Sal, intimately kissing another man. Knowing that Guy thinks Sal is 'the one', Andrew is now faced with a terrible dilemma: does he tell Guy what he has seen, or does he ignore what he saw?

But before Andrew can make up his mind what to do, the train Sal is commuting to work on is blown up by the terrorist bombs of the 7th July 2005. Suddenly everything changes. Sal is left in a coma on the edge of life, and in the aftermath of the explosions, Andrew is thrust into the centre of a complex web of relationships where the lives and happiness of those closest to him suddenly become dependent upon him making the right set of choices.

Who is the girl in the coma, really? What is the truth behind her illicit encounter with the stranger in a night club? Should he tell his best friend the truth? Or should he let nature and events take their own course?

While struggling with his conscience in an effort to decide what decisions he should make, Andrew meets a beautiful doctor from Slovakia, and he begins to fall in love.

But can he trust her? What is the truth behind her past, and her feelings for Andrew?

Then, just when events seem to be coming to a happy conclusion, Andrew discovers that everything in his life is based upon a set of lies, and his world falls apart.

What is the real truth behind Andrew's past? And where does his future lie?

Set against the backdrop of London in 2005, this is a tale of our time.

The Sleeping Truth starts slowly, builds steadily, and then speeds on to an unexpected and emotional conclusion!

TIME SHIP: A Time Travel Romantic Adventure

Image the combination of four amazing films - 'The Perfect Storm' meets 'The Philadelphia Experiment' meets ' Contagion' meets 'Pirates of the Caribbean', and you will have the plot for TIME SHIP.

During a daring raid on a secret Pirate stronghold in the Caribbean, Captain Rob McGregor of the Sea Dancer and his own pirate crew steal the infamous treasure belonging to Captain William Kidd. Rich beyond their wildest dreams, Captain McGregor and his band of pirates set out to sea, their ships' holds full of pirate booty.

When they are hit by the most intense electrical storm of the 17th Century, the Sea Dancer is transported through time to the year 2014. Bemused, hungry and thirsty, Captain McGregor and his crew sneak into a secluded bay in Puerto Rico, hoping to find food and water.

Instead they find a 'palace' : an exclusive five-star holiday resort for the rich and famous.

Scared, bewildered and desperate, they take over the resort, holding everyone hostage.

Quickly, the situation goes from bad to worse. Within hours of landing at the Blue Emerald Bay Resort, several of the crew fall sick. When one dies, the resort doctor identifies it as a unique and new strain of pneumonic plague, never before seen in the 21st Century, and an infection so deadly, that if it infects the residents of the Blue Emerald Bay and escapes the confines of the resort, could threaten to wipe out the human race...

Download, settle back in a comfortable chair, and enjoy!

<u>London 2012 : What If ?</u>
<u>Available in Paperback or Ebook</u>

'What If?' was written for the commuter, for anyone who sits for hours every day travelling to work, and wondering . . . 'is this the life I should be living? Have I made the right choices? ' . . . and then wished for something else . . .

The new alternative to The Time Traveler's Wife, this is a must read for everyone, regardless of what city you work in.

'What If?' raises many interesting questions that make great topics to be discussed in Book Clubs. This edition comes complete with guideline questions for your book club to debate and discuss.

The Story :
Contemplating having an affair, bored with work, and convinced there must be something more to it all, James Quinn is a man just about to enter a mid-life crisis. James leads a successful life. But is it the right life? Instead of a Product Manager in Telecoms, should he have been a plumber, an Olympic athlete, or an artist? Life, as they say, isn't a practice run. This is it.

Convinced the 'grass is greener' everywhere else, and worried that he may be missing out, James Quinn is a man full of doubts.

It's not that he hates his own life. Far from it. His 'life', as others may call it, is good. It's just that, nowadays he can't stop looking at other people and wondering if he is living the right one? What if James has got it wrong?

And then there's Jane, the first girl he kissed at school, and the one that got away. What would life have been like if he had married her instead of his wife? Unable to control his curiosity he tracks her down through Facebook and discovers that she is now a beautiful woman, living in London, and unhappy in her marriage: like a moth drawn to a flame James finds himself heading for infidelity and feels powerless to stop.

Then one day, during the normal underground commute to work in

London, he looks up from his book and doesn't recognise the station name on the Jubilee Line, …and in a split-second, everything changes.

Emerging onto a platform at "New Cross Gate North", a station that shouldn't exist, James finds that Canary Wharf has vanished. Gone. And so have Selfridges and mobile phones.

Instead, James finds himself in a parallel world, where the city he lived in has changed, and every moment is now a voyage of discovery into a new life: a new career in advertising, a new house, and a new wife: Jane-the object of all his fantasies.

In this new world, James discovers that he is a flamboyant, intelligent, charismatic, successful businessman. Yet, even though he now has everything he has always dreamt of, he finds that he longs for everything else that he used to have but has now lost: his two children, Keira and Nicole, and his wife Sarah. Sarah, the woman he loved but took for granted.

Convinced that both the past and present are real, he realises that somewhere Sarah must be as real in this world as she was in the last. Longing to hold her in his arms again, and with no apparent way back to his old world, he sets out to find Sarah in his new world. Wherever she is.

Using knowledge from their previous life together, he manages to track her down. But James realises that before he can truly be together with Sarah once again, he must first understand what went wrong between them in the other world to avoid it happening again.

What is the secret that his subconscious has hidden from his conscious mind, and which made him want to turn away from Sarah and into the arms of another woman? Will it be possible for Sarah to fall in love with him again in this new world? And is it too late to find a way back to the old world, and his old life?

Or will he be stuck forever in this other world, yearning for the green, green grass of home?

The Messiah Conspiracy - The race to clone Jesus Christ: The Controversial page-turning Medical Thriller

The Messiah Conspiracy is a fictional thriller which takes place in the field of genetics and human cloning.

Hugely controversial, you will either love this book or hate it. Some will feel challenged and uncomfortable by the topic it deals with, and others will be drawn into it and unable to put it down . . . the question is, what will you think?

A young student at Oxford University has an idea for his doctor's thesis (Ph.D.), which fulfils not only the criteria for 'originality', but goes far beyond it. For if Jason Dyke is right, his idea will soon change the world and shift the delicate balance of power from one nation to another.

Jason's idea is simple: In the genetics laboratory at Oxford University, he will clone Jesus Christ.

But when the CIA finds out about his plan, the President of America realises that if the UK succeeds, the balance of power will shift from the USA to Europe. And he realises that the only way to stop this happening is for America to create its very own clone of Jesus Christ.

The race is on . . .

Genetics is the future. In the coming years, or maybe even months, the single most important scientific development in the history of mankind will be the development of human cloning. This book is based upon a simple idea, which takes the inevitable science of human cloning, one step further.

What makes this book stand out from other novels that deal with a similar concept is the way the author makes the science seem plausible, by explaining simply what genetics is and how cloning works. By leading the reader through the latest advances in cloning techniques until even the impossible seems possible, the reader cannot help but get sucked into the story. Right to the very end the author successfully maintains the thrill of the ride, and manages to keep a surprise up his sleeve . . .

Whoever reads this book will never forget it. And they will ask . . . .one of two questions:-
1: Is it really possible?
2: When will it happen?

If you have any comments, please contact the author at :-
iancpirvine@hotmail.co.uk

To connect with Ian C.P.Irvine on Twitter, connect with Ian at @IanCPIrvine

With thanks to Isabel Luckett, Sue Alexander, Paula Gruber, Linda Huxley, Joe Howard, Robert Ralston, Martin and many others!!!

And a BIG BIG 'Thank you!' to Ray Luck.

ABOUT THE AUTHOR

Ian Irvine was brought up in Scotland, and studied Physics for far too many years, before travelling the world working for high-technology companies. Ian has spent a career helping build the internet and delivering its benefits to users throughout the world,...as well as helping to bring up a family. Ian enjoys writing, painting and composing music in his spare time. His particular joy is found in taking scientific fact and creating a thrilling story around it in such a way that readers learn science whilst enjoying the thrill of the ride. It is Ian's hope that everyone who reads an Ian C.P. Irvine novel will come away learning something interesting that they would never otherwise have found an interest in. Never Science fiction. Always science fact. With a twist.

Printed in Poland
by Amazon Fulfillment
Poland Sp. z o.o., Wrocław